CHAOS

WARRIOR SERIES

Also by Melanie P. Smith

CHAOS

Warrior Series
Book Five

---

by:
Melanie P. Smith

MPSmith Publishing

Dedication:

To my sister Cindy...

Our many adventures would never have been

As memorable without you.

Chapter One

Bastian Carrigan slowly walked down O'Connell Street. His thoughts continued to alternate between his current dilemma and memories of the past. At the moment, the past was winning. Dublin had definitely changed since the 1600's when he lived here as a child. How many times had he walked this very road with his mother, then later with his father? Too many to count. Of course back then it was Drogheda Street and about a third the size of the massive thoroughfare it was today. The last time he was here there were carriages, not cars, making their way through the city. He glanced at his watch and realized he'd been wandering aimlessly for over an hour. It was time to head toward the airport. He needed to find a decent hotel and get settled for the night. Roaming the streets aimlessly wasn't getting him anywhere. He was no closer to making a decision than he had been before he left New York.

His thoughts turned to home. The conflict with the vampires hadn't changed. Bastian knew, without a doubt, that situation was going to get worse before it got better. Then there was the new crisis they were dealing with out at the fort. Melissa, Patricia and Lawson Dillinger's last victim, was fighting for her life. He was actually surprised the girl was still alive. The crazy half-baked formula those two came up with to create a Paladin was ludicrous and absurd. There was no rhyme or reason to it whatsoever; which made using logic to create an antidote impossible. Seriously, was facing one megalomaniac at a time too much to ask for? Bastian sighed. Deep down, he was afraid Melissa's condition was irreversible. In all likelihood, the woman would end up being one more casualty in the Dillinger's quest for power. He hoped more than anything he was wrong, but time was running out and so were his ideas.

He continued to walk along the crowded sidewalk, slowly making his way toward his rental car, when an item in one of the display windows caught his attention. He didn't really think about it, he just entered the store, walked to the register and asked to purchase the large butterfly broach in the window. The clerk was obviously thrilled; it was probably the easiest sale she'd ever made. He stepped back outside and paused, wondering what in the world he was doing. He couldn't give something that expensive to Kylee. Their relationship hadn't progressed that far yet. He abruptly stopped that train of thought. Kylee was human and they didn't have a relationship, they couldn't have a relationship. They would never progress to the level of intimacy required to give a woman such an expensive present. He slipped the small box into his pocket as a slow grin spread across his face. He couldn't help it, the sparkling broach was so perfect for Kylee. It must have been special ordered for another doctor. The delicate wings of the butterfly were decorated with various sizes of diamonds and rubies. The body of the insect was made of platinum and depicted the Rod of Asclepius; the true symbol of medicine and health. He knew that in the United States the Caduceus was often used to symbolize medicine, but he preferred the original symbol. Instead of two snakes intertwined and topped with wings, the Rod of Asclepius was a single serpent entwined around a staff. If he ever got the chance to give the broach to Kylee, he knew she'd love it. He sighed, accepting the situation for what it was. Maybe he could never give her the gift, but he could keep it for himself. A physical reminder of Kylee that he would cherish once she was no longer a part of his life.

Bastian continued down the sidewalk once again headed toward the car he had abandoned earlier that afternoon. As he took in the scene before him, he realized he'd changed as much as Ireland had. He stared at the busy street and wondered how much his past had changed him. Had previous events altered his destiny? Who would he be today if his mother hadn't died prematurely? If his father hadn't gone into such a deep depression, then followed her in death a few years later. Bastian was certain his father's futile attempt to keep his mother alive forever was the catalyst that killed them both. Adrian Carrigan's death had been unexpected, but not a huge surprise. To this day, Bastian wondered if his father had died valiantly in battle like they told him, or if he'd allowed himself to be killed so he didn't have to deal with the sorrow and the guilt any longer. He would probably never know the answer to that particular question, but he suspected the latter.

Bastian exhaled in frustration before climbing into the compact rental. He mechanically started the engine and pulled into traffic. His mind was still a jumbled mess, alternating between his family history and the many dilemmas waiting for him back home. Before he knew it, he was turning onto the long drive that led to his old farmhouse. That was the second time today he'd mindlessly wandered somewhere he didn't really want to go. It bothered him a little, but at least this spontaneous action wasn't going to cost him as much as that butterfly had. Well, financially anyway. The emotional toll might be far more costly. He put the car in park and studied his surroundings. He was here now, he might as well make the most of it.

Bastian still owned the place, but he hadn't been here in over three hundred years. The ancient barn was now a heap of wood and the house was barely standing. His gaze shifted to the large field and his heart clenched at the memories that flooded his mind. He had always loved working the fields with his father. It was overrun by tall grass and weeds now but his parents had worked so hard to make this place a thriving success. If they saw it today, they'd be heartbroken. His childhood home had become a physical reminder of how acutely Bastian had failed them. He sighed deeply, knowing he fell drastically short of the man they had hoped he would become. He climbed out of the car and closed his eyes as he ran his palms over his face in sorrow. What was he doing here anyway? It was ridiculous to think he could find the answers to his future in the past. But for some reason he just couldn't pull himself away.

Bastian slowly walked to the rundown porch and studied his old home. After a moment's hesitation he lowered himself onto the sturdy cedar bench. Before he could stop them, memories began to flood his mind. His mother had spent so much time relaxing on this very bench. He remembered watching his father night after night as he lovingly constructed it. The comfortable bench had been a birthday gift for mom the day she turned forty five. Dad worked so hard every night, making sure it was perfect. Bastian knew, without a doubt, his father had loved his mother more than anything. She was his life, his anchor. They always seemed so happy together. Well, until that night just before his fourteenth birthday anyway. He knew that argument was the reason his father finally gave in and attempted the transition. He pushed the memory away out of habit. Why did dad have to try to turn his mother into a warrior anyway? The transition had gone terribly wrong. Probably because of his mother's age. By the time his father made the attempt, Charlotte

Carrigan was forty nine years old. Bastian didn't understand why his father had waited so long. If he was going to attempt the change, why hadn't he tried it when his mother was young and strong?

Bastian laid his head back against the ancient cabin wall. Since he was here, maybe it was time to face his unpleasant family history. He'd been avoiding it for centuries. Actually he'd gone to great lengths to block out all of his memories, good and bad, that pertained to his parents. It was easier not to think about it. Now, for the first time in over three hundred years, he allowed them to flow. Sitting here, on this farm, he couldn't fight them anyway. He smiled as he remembered his mother sitting here on a warm summer day as she watched him play kickball with the neighbor boys. The small clearing that separated the house from the field was their playground. She loved to watch as Bastian played with his friends. Mostly she loved to cheer him on and make a spectacle of herself. He was always so embarrassed when his friends saw her act like that. Well, if he was going to be honest, deep down he enjoyed it. It made him feel loved and cherished somehow.

Bastian's thoughts turned to his father. As much as he loved to play kickball, wasting time with his friends always made him feel a little guilty. He was playing and having fun while his father continued to work the fields… alone. Mother had insisted though. Charlotte Carrigan wanted a well-rounded son. One that could work hard but would still take time to enjoy life. His father hadn't argued, he agreed with his wife. Adrian wanted his son to enjoy being a kid for as long as he could. Probably because he knew firsthand what was in store for his son when he officially became a warrior. Bastian loved the life of a warrior, but sometimes it was difficult. So many things had become difficult lately. He used to enjoy the solitary life he had chosen for so long, but lately he was starting to feel lonely. He ran his fingers through his hair as he fought the overwhelming emotions. He missed his father. He missed having such a close,

Chaos

unfiltered relationship with someone he trusted completely. After his father died, Bastian swore he'd never let anyone get that close again; and he hadn't. Even after all that had happened, Bastian still loved and respected his father unconditionally. He cherished the long hours they'd spent together working the ground and talking about nothing. He knew, without a doubt, the lessons he had learned as a boy working that field, had made him a better man.

Adrian Carrigan was a good, honorable gentleman. Bastian knew that. He just didn't understand why his dad had risked his mother's life that way. Why did he finally give in to her? Why did he give in to his sorrow and leave Bastian all alone? Bastian's mind continued to wander, reliving the past. It was agonizing to remember the love and the happiness they had all shared, then the sorrow and the pain that came with the loss of his mother… then his father. As Bastian relived the past and tried to deal with the ancient emotions, he wondered if his parents would be proud of the man he had ultimately become. He rarely played or did anything just for fun these days. 'So much for well rounded,' he thought to himself. Had they known that would happen? Is that why they insisted he make friends and play when there was work to be done? Had he failed them as much as they had failed him? Glancing around at the wreck this place had become, he was afraid the answer was a resounding yes.

One particular memory kept forcing its way to the surface. Bastian closed his eyes and stopped trying to block it. Over the years he had worked so hard to forget that night, but he never really could. Sitting here at his childhood home, on his mother's bench, brought it all back in vivid detail. The evening had been pitch black with just a small sliver of moonlight shining through the trees. Bastian was just a kid then. He was lying in his bed trying to force himself to sleep. It was a hot summer night just two weeks before his fourteenth birthday. He was curious what his gift would be. His parents always surprised him with such wonderful presents. As he daydreamed about the possibilities, he could hear voices through his open window and knew his parents were out on the back porch talking. Bastian was certain they must be discussing his upcoming birthday and his present, so he quietly snuck downstairs to eavesdrop. That's when he realized his mother was upset. She was crying. His father sounded frustrated. Mom was begging dad to turn her. She wanted to be a warrior. She insisted fifty or so years with the man she loved was not enough. She wanted hundreds of years with her husband and her son. She told his father he was being unfair. Then, she accused him of not loving her. Bastian remembered his father pleading with her to let it be, the process was too dangerous. What if neither of them survived? Was she willing to leave their son alone, without parents for hundreds of years? But his mother wouldn't budge, she wanted to be turned. She maintained the decision should be hers to make and she thought her husband was being overly dramatic.

Dad tried to make her understand. He told her he couldn't do it. He loved her too much to risk her life that way. Bastian clearly remembered his mother sobbing and begging. Then she became angry. Again, she accused his father of not loving her. She deduced from his resistance that the only reason he wouldn't turn her was because he didn't want to be with her forever. She wondered aloud if her husband was looking forward to the day she would grow old and die so he could be rid of her and move on. Bastian lowered his head into his hands and closed his eyes tightly. He hated to recall the desperation in his mother's voice and the pain in his father's eyes. Had he blocked this out completely because it was easier to blame his father than to face the truth? The look on dad's face came back to him so clearly now. He could almost see the pain and sorrow his mother's words had inflicted. She had hurt Adrian deeply with her accusations. Dad had turned and stared into the distance for a long time before he faced Charlotte again. He didn't say a word, he

Chaos

just nodded once in surrender. Mom had jumped from the bench and leapt into his father's arms. She was so happy about the decision. But Bastian only saw worry and pain reflected in his father's eyes. Mostly he remembered the look of defeat. For the first time in years, Bastian realized his father hadn't been selfish. His mother had wanted to be changed so badly she was willing to say and do anything to get her way. Adrian simply surrendered. His father never could deny his mother anything. How long was she trying to convince him to turn her? Bastian would never know the answer to that question, either. But, knowing his mother… probably from the beginning.

Bastian ran his fingers through his thick hair then leaned back against the tattered wall of their old cabin, trying to work through the intense emotions he could no longer contain. He felt anger towards his mother and disappointment in his father for giving in, but mostly he felt sadness and a little self-pity over the loss of both his parents in such a short period of time. He sat there for hours, finally allowing himself to remember, and then wishing he hadn't remembered some things so clearly.

Before he knew it, darkness had fallen over the old rundown farmhouse. Bastian soberly pushed himself from the bench and headed for the car. The unplanned trip to his childhood home hadn't helped him resolve the Kylee situation. He hadn't really expected it to, but hope does run eternal. Once he got back to New York he would still have a difficult decision to make. But at least this impromptu trip had helped him understand his father a little better. Over the years, he'd harbored such resentment towards his dad over his mother's death. Coming here had forced him to remember and accept the reason behind the decision. His father wasn't being selfish, he had simply given in to the woman he loved. Bastian still couldn't excuse that, but it helped to remember his mother had played an integral part in her own demise. They were both to blame, not just his dad. Bastian was still deep in thought when he heard a slight noise. It sounded like a twig snapping close by. He froze and looked around, trying to find cover. If vampires were nearby, he'd need the element of surprise.

"Is that you, Bastian?" A male voice called in disbelief. Bryan saw the car in the drive and thought it was just another group of teenagers, troublemakers no doubt. He'd made his way through the woods planning to surprise the kids and scare them away. As he moved into the clearing, he saw one solitary man. The guy looked lonely and depressed, but not lost. It had to be Bastian Carrigan, who else could it be? The place was too isolated to attract tourists.

Bastian straightened. He couldn't see the man's features, only a silhouette, but the guy knew his name. It couldn't be a vampire but that didn't rule out danger. "That depends on who's asking," Bastian answered evasively.

"It's Bryan," the man called. "Bryan O'Malley. You're gonna crush me if you say you don't remember me." He let out a short laugh as he stood before Bastian, smirking.

Bastian grinned as new memories flooded his mind, happy memories of his cocky childhood friend and his heavy Irish accent. "I remember you," he admitted. "Who could forget such an obnoxious poor sport? I've never met a bigger showoff."

Bryan threw an arm around Bastian's shoulders. "Still vexed that I'm better at kickball than you, I see. It's not poor sportsmanship to win my friend. It's talent." He grinned a little wider then sobered. "It's good to see ya, Bastian. I wasn't sure you'd ever come back. The old place isn't exactly habitable these days." He glanced over his shoulder and exhaled. "But I still make sure the kids don't use it for target practice or cause too much damage."

9

Chaos

Bastian was surprised and touched by his old friend's diligence. "Thanks," he said sincerely. "I should probably burn the place down before I go. It's a hazard and there is no way I can repair it. If I ever decide to build here, I'll have to start from scratch anyway."

"I hate to see it go, but you're probably right. Can I have the old bench?" he asked eagerly.

"Sorry, I think I'm going to keep that. Dad carved it for mom himself. It's the only thing I still love about the place," Bastian confided.

"Well, it's too late for burning tonight. Come on over to the pub and have a Guinness. We can catch up on old times and you can tell me what finally brought you back to Dublin," Bryan requested.

"I don't know," Bastian said looking at his watch. "I still need to find a hotel. Otherwise I'll be sleeping on that old bench tonight."

"Bollocks, you'll stay with me. I won't take no for an answer," Bryan pressed.

"I don't know," Bastian continued to hesitate. "I don't want to impose. What will your wife say? Shouldn't you talk to her first?"

"Clever boy. No, I don't have a wife. I guess I'm married to the pub," Bryan admitted. "And she won't care. It's not much, but she's mine. Anyway, I live upstairs and I have a guest room that rarely gets used. Be a sport, we can have a Guinness and you can grab a bite to eat. I have the best food in town. It's been donkey's years, Bastian. We have a lot of catching up to do. Come on, I'm just around the corner."

Bastian only hesitated a minute. It would be good to catch up with Bryan. He hadn't seen him since he had left for America. After his father died, Bastian caught a ship for the new land and never looked back. "Okay," he finally said. "If you're sure."

"Positive," Bryan said enthusiastically. "I can't wait for you to see the place. Of course I'm not a multi-millionaire with a gazillion pharmaceutical companies, but I can't complain. And I'm sure I have more fun than you do," Bryan grinned. "But then again, I always did." He laughed at the look Bastian was giving him. "You know it's true old friend," he added in his thick Irish brogue.

The two men walked through the back door leading to the pub. Bryan immediately went upstairs and showed Bastian the guest room.

"Not bad," Bastian admitted with a smile. "I guess I can hang here for the night. As I recall you mentioned Guinness." He slapped his friend on the back and the two of them headed downstairs to the bar. Bryan immediately began piling food onto two plates. When nothing else would fit, he sauntered to an empty table and motioned for Bastian to join him.

"Dig in," Bryan grinned. "Like I said, it's the best food in town."

Bastian sat across from Bryan and the two men immediately fell into conversation. Bastian knew Bryan was avoiding the topic of his parents and he was grateful. He really didn't want to talk about their deaths tonight. He finished his meal and sat back, satisfied. Bryan was right, the food was good. "Thank you," he finally said. "For everything. Good food, good beer and a nice place to stay for the night. You're like a lighthouse in a storm," he said as he gave Bryan a half-hearted smile.

Chaos

"You never said if you have a lady back home," Bryan finally pushed, more direct this time. Bastian had conveniently avoided the question and changed the subject each time Bryan had brought up the topic of women. He was determined to get a straight answer from his old pal. It was probably the reason for his visit.

Bastian looked at Bryan and grimaced. The guy was persistent. "Not exactly," he finally told him.

"Should'o known it would be a female that sent you back here." Bryan nodded in understanding. "Do ya love her?"

Bastian laughed long and hard. Bryan always was observant. It had been a long time since he had felt this good, the beer was partially responsible for that. But, Bryan always could make him feel lighthearted and carefree. "I think I do," Bastian finally said. "But she's human. It's not something I can consider."

Bryan nodded, again understanding the dilemma his friend faced. "Then drink away the memories, old and new. It's on the house." He stood and headed to the bar. Moments later, Bryan returned with another tall Guinness. "I have a pub to run," he sighed. "Make yourself at home. I'll be here all night and we'll keep them coming as long as you like."

Bastian watched as Bryan slid behind the bar and began filling orders. He studied the large glass of beer momentarily then took another long hard drink. He'd forgotten how much he enjoyed a good Guinness. Maybe he would get a little drunk tonight. Considering the day he'd had, he deserved a break from reality. After consuming a couple more beers, Bastian longed for conversation and companionship. He glanced around then relocated to a stool at the bar. With each beer, his tongue loosened a little more. As the hours faded away, Bastian ended up telling Bryan all about Kylee and his dilemma back home.

Bryan felt for his childhood pal. When they were kids, Bryan had envied the relationship Bastian had with his parents. They were so close and always so happy. But that closeness had come with a high price for Bastian. Losing his mom like that had scarred him forever. Now, years later he was still suffering over the loss. Bryan hoped Bastian could overcome his fear and give the woman he loved a chance, but that was not a bet he'd ever take. His childhood pal was wounded. It was far more likely Bastian would walk away to avoid the risk. Bryan smiled as the warrior ordered another drink. At least his old friend was enjoying himself tonight.

* * * *

Kylee sat in the lab, debating. She needed Bastian's input, but she'd never called him before. It seemed too personal... too friendly. They worked well together in the lab and they'd been getting along in their free time as well, but were they friends? Was it appropriate for her to just call him and ask his opinion on the serum? That was about work though, right? She knew she could convince herself the call was legit, but was it appropriate? She was still a little intimidated by the man. "It's not like I'm just calling to chat," Kylee mumbled. She had a legitimate reason to phone him. She needed his input and guidance. Kylee rolled her eyes at herself. She did want his opinion, but she certainly didn't need it. She needed to hear his voice. He'd been gone longer than usual this trip and she missed him. There, she admitted it. So, she was a pathetic sap.

Kylee sighed and checked her watch, almost six o'clock. If she was going to call, she needed to do it now. Otherwise she would interrupt his dinner. She laughed a little and realized she felt like a teenager. This was silly. She would just call and ask his opinion on the serum. Then she'd know he was okay and she could get back to work. Maybe she would actually get some sleep tonight for a change. Familiar questions began to run through her mind. Was Bastian okay? He'd seemed different, off somehow, just before he left. That was another reason she couldn't get him off her mind. Another reason she needed to call him. She was concerned about his wellbeing. An image of Bastian popped into her head. In her mind his six foot two, tall dark and sexy frame was dressed in her favorite jeans and black t-shirt. The one that practically made her drool because it hugged his muscles so perfectly. She wanted to believe what she felt was just a silly crush, but she knew better. She was falling for the guy. She had been for a while. He was too handsome for his own good, but that wasn't what got to her. He was smart. No, he was brilliant. She'd met good looking men before, but they hadn't had this effect on her. With Bastian it was the whole package, his looks, his body, his kindness, but mostly his mind. She respected him. His intelligence had enabled him to form the most successful pharmaceutical company in the world. He was constantly developing new and amazing solutions to ancient problems. She felt challenged by him and she had to admit that was definitely a turn on.

She debated again for the slightest moment then pulled out her cellphone. Bastian had programmed the number in there himself. He told her to call anytime, but she never had. This would be a first. If he didn't want her to call he wouldn't have given her the number, she reasoned. Kylee paused, she wasn't sure he had actually meant it. What if he was just being polite? She took a deep breath and prayed for strength.

"Hello?" Bastian answered. He could barely hear, the noise from the pub was loud and jovial in the background. Bryan was trying to wind down and close up. It was almost one in the morning and closing time. As usual, the patrons were resisting. They were having too much fun and didn't want to leave.

"Oh! Sorry," Kylee hesitated. Was he at a party? "It's Kylee, but you sound busy. I'll figure it out on my own," she blurted.

"Kylee?" Bastian said, his voice slurring. "Beautiful, sexy Kylee." Bastian let out a sigh. "My brilliant, perfect angel."

Kylee froze, wide eyed. Did Bastian really think she was beautiful and sexy? Then it hit her, he was drunk. His voice was slurred and the noise in the background sounded like a bar or a club.

"I finally found the perfect woman," Bastian continued to slur his words. "But I'm a warrior and you're a human. It could never work." Then he fell off the chair with a thud.

Kylee heard the loud clattering and wondered what had happened. "Bastian?" she asked, no answer. "Bastian!" she yelled. Still no answer. What was going on here? And what did he mean by that? Why could it never work?

Bryan sighed and picked Bastian up off the floor. Poor clod. He was in no shape to talk to anyone, especially Kylee. He picked up the phone and hesitated, then he lifted it to his ear. "I'm sorry las, but Bastian's not in any condition to have a conversation at the moment. Forget everything he just said. The poor boy is drunk and doesn't know what he's saying." Bryan silently ended the call and slipped the phone back into his old friend's pocket.

"That was the girl of my dreams," Bastian mumbled then passed out.

Kylee stared at the phone for a long moment. Bastian wasn't okay. She frowned and considered her options. What options? She

Chaos

didn't even know where he was. When he left, he said he had pressing business and would be gone for a while. Was he in New York? She didn't think so. He sounded far away, and the stranger at the end of that call had sounded...Irish maybe. She needed answers before she could decide what to do. She glanced back at her serum, which ingredient to use? She only hesitated a second then poured in the powdered yucca root. She pushed in the cork, shook the glass tube back and forth, then quickly poured the contents into a petri dish and slapped on the cover. She'd have to wait until morning to see if she'd made any progress on that project, but she was sure she could get some answers about Bastian tonight.

Kylee walked purposefully into the large farmhouse and headed straight for the study. Ty and Sam were lounging on the oversized couch watching TV. Kylee marched over and stood in front of them, blocking their view.

"Hey," Ty said as Sam sat up. "What's the idea? You make a better door than a window you know?" He studied Kylee. She was upset about something. He grabbed the remote and switched off the television.

"What's wrong?" Sam asked immediately.

"Where is Bastian?" Kylee demanded.

Ty looked at Sam and then back at Kylee and shrugged. "New York I assume, why?" He asked furrowing his brow. Was something up with Bastian or did Kylee just need to talk to him?

"No... he's not," Kylee persisted then she hesitated. She really wasn't sure where he was, but she didn't think he was in New York. "Well, I don't think he is anyway," she corrected.

"Why not?" Sam asked curiously.

"Because I just called him and he was completely drunk. Then some stranger got on the phone and told me Bastian couldn't talk and I shouldn't listen to anything he said. Then he hung up on me. They sounded like they were in a bar or a club and the stranger sounded Irish," Kylee said realizing her explanation was weak.

"You do realize New York has Irish Pubs and some of the men that frequent them have Irish accents, don't you?" Ty asked, not convinced. However, he was surprised and concerned at the news that Bastian was drunk. He needed to call Dimitri.

"Of course," Kylee admitted. "I just don't think he's in New York. I can't explain why, not in a way that will convince anyone," she said defeated. "But I don't think he's okay. When he left, he seemed upset about something, now this. Bastian doesn't get drunk. Bastian is refined and sophisticated and always in control. I didn't even know you guys could get drunk," she paused as she thought about that. "Why doesn't the blood alter the effects of the alcohol? I would think warrior blood would clean the toxins before you got inebriated," she stated curiously.

"It does eventually," Ty said hesitantly. He was still a little uncomfortable sharing so many of their secrets with a human. "If Bastian is drunk, he consumed a large amount of alcohol in a short amount of time. His blood will clean out his system eventually as long as he doesn't keep drinking," Ty admitted.

"Look, I know I'm not very convincing but would you at least call Dimitri or Alex? They're in New York and maybe they know where Bastian is," Kylee almost begged.

Ty studied Kylee, she looked tired and defeated. Was it just the pressure of helping Melissa keeping her up, or was worrying about Bastian adding to her stress? He was pretty sure Kylee was losing just as much sleep over Bastian as she was Melissa. He

Chaos

needed to call Dimitri anyway. If he did it now, it might put Kylee at ease. Ty gave Sam a gentle push so he could sit up, then he pulled his phone from his pocket and dialed Dimitri.

"Hello Ty," Dimitri said casually. "What's up?"

"Uh, do you know where Bastian is?" he asked hesitantly.

"I do," Dimitri answered. "Well… in a roundabout general way I do," he sobered. He was pretty sure Dimitri was drunk. His warrior leader senses were a little off kilter when it came to Bastian tonight, but why was Ty asking about him. "Why?" he demanded.

"Well, Kylee just called him to discuss something about her lab work and apparently Bastian is drunk," Ty admitted. "The news is a little concerning to all of us and I just thought I'd call and see if you knew what was going on."

Dimitri hesitated. He was pretty sure Bastian's condition had something to do with Kylee. He wasn't sure how much he should share. Bastian was very closed off about his personal life. "Ty," Dimitri began. "Bastian is dealing with some personal ghosts right now. I'm not sure how much he would want me to tell you, but I assure you I already knew he was drunk. I also know he's not hurt. In fact, I think he finally passed out. He'll sleep this off and hopefully he'll be back tomorrow or the next day."

"So, he's not in New York then?" Ty accused.

"No. He's not," Dimitri admitted. "He went to Dublin. I think he was finally going back to his childhood home. A lot has happened over the past few months. First, Jake turned Marta. That was a hard blow to Bastian, he's become very close to Marta over the last few years. I'm not sure he's forgiven Jake for risking her life that way. Then… you and Sam. I know we need him here to help save Melissa, but I thought it was more important to give him a little time to deal with whatever's bothering him. I gave him a few days off and promised not to interrupt while he tries to deal with his past. For what it's worth, I'm concerned about Bastian but not worried about this. I don't think Bastian is in any danger at the moment, he's just struggling a bit. I'll let you know if he needs an intervention," Dimitri promised.

"Okay," Ty said soberly. He saw how Bastian had reacted to the news about Marta. It had completely escaped him that Sam's transition had caused Bastian stress. "I understand."

"Thanks," Dimitri said. He knew Ty had questions, but he was going to respect Bastian's privacy and he wouldn't pry. "How is Melissa anyway?" he asked as an afterthought.

"Okay," Ty assured him. "No improvement, but Kylee is keeping her as comfortable as she can. We're going to need Alex again in a few days," Ty added.

"As soon as Bastian gets back he and Alex will head out," Dimitri promised. "Until then, do what you can. This might be a losing battle, but we need to fight it anyway."

"I agree," Ty nodded. "Say 'hey' to Alex for me. I'll talk to you soon." Ty hung up and turned to Kylee. She was watching him intently, anxious for information. What should he tell her? The truth was always best. "You were right, Bastian is not in New York." He leaned back against the couch and pulled Sam onto his lap.

"Where is he?" Kylee demanded.

"Ireland," Ty admitted. "Just like you thought." He tightened his grip on Sam when he felt her try to pull away. He didn't want

Chaos

her to go anywhere. He enjoyed the closeness he felt with her in his arms.

"He's..." Kylee stared, dumbfounded. What was Bastian doing in Ireland?

"Kylee," Ty said softly. "Dimitri didn't tell me a lot. But I'll try to help you understand if I can. Bastian was originally from Ireland. He still has a few issues to deal with from his past, his childhood. It's been a long time, but apparently Bastian is finally willing to face them. He went back home for a couple days to work on his... baggage I guess you could say. If I had to guess, I'd say things were more difficult than he thought they were going to be. So, Bastian got drunk tonight to escape the pain or the sorrow or whatever. I agree that's unusual for him but not tragic, or anything to be concerned about. Let him deal with this his way. I know a little about his history and this is not going to be easy for him. Maybe you should give him a little space when he gets back." Ty turned toward Sam. "I think we all should."

"Okay," Sam agreed. She could sense Ty's emotions. He was concerned, but not extremely worried. He was being honest with Kylee. So, Bastian had some ghost to deal with. She understood what that was like. She liked and respected Bastian. Sam hoped he would get past this okay. She never had, not until she met Ty anyway. Maybe that's what was driving this. She'd noticed the way Bastian looked at Kylee. Maybe he was falling for her and had some things to deal with before he could act on his feelings.

"That's it?" Kylee asked in disbelief. "That's all I get? And you expect me to just go back to my work and act as if nothing is wrong? Well, that's not possible." She said angrily and stomped out of the room.

"So," Ty said softly, "she's in love with him, too."

Sam shifted so she could look her husband in the eyes. Then she smiled. "I think she is," she finally told him. "Is Bastian really going to be okay? You know I never dealt with my past until we got together. Well, to be honest I'm still dealing with it. Is Bastian's history as horrible as mine was?"

"Not exactly," Ty told her. "He did lose his parents at a fairly young age, though. It's not going to be easy for him to deal with this. More than any of us, you can understand that Bastian is going to need space. I don't think we should ask him a lot of personal questions when he gets back. Dimitri said he should return to New York in a day or two and then Bastian and Alex will head out to heal Melissa again. Please don't ask him anything. Bastian is a very private person and personal questions would be harder coming from us."

"Why?" Sam asked intrigued.

"Because his mother died while his father was trying to turn her. Watching what we went through during your transition was hard on him. I don't think he would talk to either of us about what's going on anyway. It's too painful for him, and we are both a reminder of what he lost," Ty said soberly.

"Oh," Sam said sadly. She liked Bastian, she didn't want to make him uncomfortable. Sam was quiet for several seconds; deep in thought. "That makes sense. But it also makes things worse. If his mother died while his father was trying to turn her, Bastian wouldn't have anyone to go after. I have Radek to blame. I focused all my hatred and vengeance on him for years. It helped me deal with the loss. That's why I focused on vampire hunting… it was therapeutic. The only person Bastian had to blame was his father." Sam sat up before Ty could stop her again. "He didn't blame his father, did he?"

Chaos

"Bastian doesn't talk about it much. However, I think on some level he has. Unfortunately, a few years later his father was killed in battle. Adrian, Jake, Luke and Dimitri's father Dylan were fighting together one night when Adrian was killed. From what I understand they were greatly outnumbered. Bastian was in his thirties when his father died, I think his mother died when he was around fourteen or fifteen. He's had a rough life and, as far as I know, this is the first time he's ever been back to Dublin since he moved to America. He has labs and businesses all around the world, but he's never built one in Ireland. He's avoided the place for centuries. Bastian going back now is huge. I'm not surprised he decided to get a little drunk tonight." Ty leaned forward and gently kissed Sam's forehead. "Are you still in the mood to finish the movie?" he questioned, picking up the remote.

"Not really," she admitted.

Ty smiled. "Good," he jumped up holding Sam securely in his arms. "I was hoping you'd say that." He laughed as he headed for their room. Sam struggled to get free for about a minute before she relaxed and enjoyed the feeling of love and anticipation emulating from her husband.

* * * *

Bastian woke early the next morning. His head was killing him and his mouth was dry. He needed coffee if he couldn't have blood, but first he needed a shower. He slid from the bed and quietly slipped into the bathroom. The cool water felt good, refreshing. Moments later he entered the kitchen in search of a coffee pot. When he couldn't find one anywhere, he decided to check downstairs. Maybe Bryan had one in the bar. Bastian walked into the kitchen and found what he was looking for. Once the coffee was made, he casually sat at the small table and savored the flavor. His head was feeling a little better now. What he really needed was blood, but he didn't have a supplier here. He supposed that was his consequence for avoiding Ireland most of his life. He'd be fine in a couple hours anyway. His blood would replenish itself and the headache would be gone completely.

Bastian turned as Bryan groggily walked down the stairs and spotted his friend at the table. "You make enough for two?" he asked.

"Plenty," Bastian assured him. "Why don't you sit and I'll take care of you this morning? I'm guessing I owe you that much after last night and I'm not completely sure you're awake," he paused. "How bad? Did I make a complete fool of myself?"

"No," Bryan said pulling out a chair and immediately falling into it. "You are actually a pretty decent drunk." He paused, what should he tell him about the call?

"What does that mean, exactly?" Bastian asked as he handed Bryan a steaming mug of coffee.

"It means you talk a lot, but you didn't get wild and crazy. You have nothing to worry about. It's too bad really. I was actually hoping for table dancing or maybe a little stripping… but nothing," Bryan grinned. "How is a guy supposed to blackmail a wealthy old friend when he's not even out of control when he gets drunk?" Bryan joked.

"I talked a lot, huh?" Bastian said worried about what he might have told Bryan. "Did I say anything I should worry about?"

"Your secrets are safe with me," Bryan said seriously. "You just told me about your girl. The beautiful, sexy, intelligent woman

Chaos

you are madly in love with, but you won't act on it because she's human. For what it's worth, I think you're making a mistake. If she's that wonderful, you should give her a chance."

Bastian closed his eyes. He did talk too much when he drank. "Sorry to dump all that on you," Bastian sighed. "I intended to keep it light after so many years away."

"Nonsense," Bryan took a sip of his coffee and studied his old friend. "That's what friends are for." He stood and walked to Bastian. "I know you've been gone a long time, but I'm still your friend. I'll always be here for you if you need me." Bryan paused, then decided to continue. "Bastian, I think that's the one thing you never understood. When we were kids I was so envious of you, we all were. You didn't need any of us guys, you had your parents. They were your best friends… your confidants. The rest of us needed each other. None of us could talk to our parents the way you talked to your dad. We talked to one another about our problems. We were there for each other when things got difficult. I realize you probably have friends in New York, but I'm always here for you," he smiled. "So, please tell me I'm not going to have to wait another three hundred years before I see you again."

Bastian smiled back at his old friend. It was a relief to finally talk to someone he knew he could trust about his feelings for Kylee. He hadn't felt comfortable discussing his feelings with anyone back home; not even the warriors. Still, Bryan didn't understand why Bastian wouldn't just act on his feelings. Well, he wasn't going to try to explain it. His friend would never understand. Nobody did, not really. "Actually, I think I can make that promise. It won't be that long before I return," Bastian told him taking another sip of his coffee. "I was wandering around yesterday, lost in the past, trying to work out the present, wondering about the future," Bastian paused. "You know, the usual stuff."

Bryan laughed. "Usual for you Bastian. You always did plan ahead."

"Anyway, I saw an abandoned factory just off O'Connell over by Mary Street. Do you have any idea who owns that?" Bastian asked curiously.

"Sure," Bryan said. "It was old man Ferguson, but he passed away a few years back. His kids own the property now. What did you have in mind?"

"Well if they are willing to sell, I'm considering opening a lab here. I think we could renovate that building to fit our needs," Bastian said enthusiastically. He was always more alive when he talked business.

"I'll tell you everything you need to know if you let me help," Bryan offered. "I have a bit of a grudge against the Ferguson boys. I'd love to see you pull one over on them." Bryan's eyes hardened. "Their dad was wealthy; richest man in town for years. Those two think that entitles them to anything they want," Bryan scowled. "They roughed up one of my patrons a few years back. The poor girl's never been the same after those two got their hands on her. If we play this right, I think you could practically steal the place away from them. They have no idea what a gold mine they're sitting on. Plus, the place has a few flaws. Flaws that won't matter for what you have in mind. If you play it up, they'll practically give you the place. They didn't exactly inherit their father's business sense. I'm not sure they have any sense at all."

"I see," Bastian mused. He was never opposed to payback. Especially when it involved men who abused women. "Keep this one under your belt, Bryan. I want my people to do a little research. I'll come back in a few weeks, a month tops, and we can work out a plan," he smiled. "I think I can help you with a little payback."

Chaos

Bryan smiled back. "Only if you agree to stay at my place again. The door is always open, you know."

"Thanks," Bastian told him. "I'll stay on my next visit, but we'll play it by ear after that. I'll have to come out pretty regularly once we get the renovation started. I wouldn't want to wear out my welcome." He smiled, then sobered. "Uh, I was wondering if you're busy this morning."

"No, why?" Bryan asked hesitantly.

"I was hoping you'd help me take care of the mess on the old farm. I think it's time to burn that heap down and start over," Bastian told him.

"Does that mean you will start over?" Bryan asked hopefully. "Are you going to build a new place out there?"

Bastian hadn't gotten that far last night. As he sat at the table drinking and watching the crowd, he'd decided it was time to destroy the old memories and start fresh. Burning the old wood from the collapsed barn and the dilapidated farmhouse seemed like a good start. He hadn't considered rebuilding though. He thought about it for another minute. If he was going to open a lab out here, maybe he should rebuild. It would give him a comfortable place to stay and Bryan wouldn't get his feelings hurt when Bastian refused to impose on him. He couldn't force his company on Bryan forever. "Maybe I will," he finally answered. "If I'm going to make a fresh start, I might as well go all the way."

"Good answer," Bryan put a hand on Bastian's shoulder. "Good answer."

"So, you game?" Bastian asked.

"Absolutely. Follow me to the old shed. I think I have enough hose to run from my place to yours. You don't have any water out there other than the old well. We don't want the fire to get out of control."

"Good idea," Bastian agreed, following Bryan out the back door. It felt good to know he was finally going to take a step toward putting his past behind him. Then he'd go back, face Kylee and decide what to do about her. A vague memory hit him. "Uh, Bryan?" Bastian asked.

"Yeah?" Bryan answered absently as he pulled hose from a shed.

"Did I talk to anyone on the phone last night? You know, while I was drunk," Bastian asked.

"I think so," Bryan admitted. "Not for long. The phone rang and you answered. I think you immediately fell off your stool though. I doubt you had enough time to say anything. I told them you were drunk and to call back later." He wasn't going to admit he knew Bastian had spoken to Kylee. The guy would find out soon enough and maybe that call would force Bastian to deal with his feelings.

Bastian immediately pulled out his phone to display his call log. He stared at the screen in disbelief. Kylee had actually called him. He'd programmed his number into her phone months ago. Every time he left the fort, he'd hoped for a call but never heard a word. Then the one night he got drunk and stupid, she called. What had he said to her? He had no idea. He couldn't even remember talking to her, not really. He just had a vague recollection. Great, one more thing to worry about. In his state he could have blabbed anything.

Chaos

"Stop fretting," Bryan scolded. "Whoever it was won't judge you for getting a little drunk."

"That's not what concerns me," Bastian sighed. But Bryan was right, there was no use worrying now. Whatever had happened, it couldn't be undone. "Let's get started on the burning. I think it might be therapeutic."

Bryan laughed and handed Bastian a large roll of hose.

* * * *

Late the following evening Bastian knocked softly on Dimitri's door and waited. He wondered if there would be questions. The bigger problem, how would he answer them? Before he could develop a plan, Alex swung the door open and gave him a genuine smile.

"I'm so glad you're back." She motioned for Bastian to enter. "Kylee called a few hours ago. She's worried about Melissa. Apparently she's getting worse. I need to head out tomorrow and was hoping you'd be recovered enough to fly me in the chopper."

"Sure," Bastian agreed, then frowned. "It concerns me that Melissa is getting worse though. So far I haven't been able to come up with anything to help her condition. Before I left, Kylee and I decided we'd try to break it into parts but that hasn't helped either."

Alex furrowed her brow, not understanding what he meant.

Bastian smiled at her. "Let me explain," he said, following her into the study. Alex sat in a large lounge chair and motioned for him to do the same. Bastian sat across from her and continued.

"When Kylee and I began this project we were trying to find a cure for the entire condition. Something that would counter the effects of whatever the Dillinger's gave her. The problem is, we have no idea what the Dillinger's really gave their victims or how many doses. They kidnapped Melissa and held her for at least four days before we found their hiding place. So, I think it's safe to assume she's had at least four injections of the toxin those maniacs developed. But that's the problem. We still can't figure out exactly what was in that concoction. Patricia started with her late husband's formula, but things have changed. Some of the ingredients are no longer available. Patricia and Lawson, I think mostly Patricia though, improvised. We know they added meth, but Patricia's notes were jumbled and most of them didn't make sense. At this point we are simply guessing, which isn't very scientific. It would be impossible to develop an antidote when you don't know what the poison is."

"That makes sense," Alex agreed.

"So Kylee and I thought maybe we could try taking things one step at a time. You know, work on the individual pieces to cure one symptom at a time. Then work on the bigger picture later if we can get the cells to stop breaking down. We believe that's the priority right now, to stop this thing from eating that woman from the inside out."

"Do you think that will work?" Alex asked. "Do you think you can find an antidote to part of the problem then move on to another part until she's cured?"

Bastian studied Alex soberly. "I hope so. But to be honest, I don't know if that girl will ever be cured completely. Patricia is like a mad scientist. I think she just kept changing things for the fun of it. I'm surprised that girl lived as long as she did considering the chemicals they injected into her system. We'll do the best we can, but you need to be prepared for the worst Alex. We may still lose her. Time is not on our side," Bastian warned.

Dimitri entered the room and sat next to Alex. He studied Bastian for a moment before he spoke. "Did you take care of your ghosts in Dublin?" he finally asked.

Alex stood. "I need to go pack an overnight bag," she said turning to Bastian. "What time do you think we could leave tomorrow? I'm busy until two, but I can go any time after that."

"Let's shoot for five," he told her. "That will give me time to check on some things at the lab and get to the airport."

"Five it is. I'll see you at the hanger." She gave him a quick smile. "Goodnight Bastian. I really am glad you're back. I know Melissa may not make it, but it's not going to be because we didn't give it our all." She silently turned and left the room.

"She's going to be heartbroken if that woman doesn't survive," Dimitri admitted. "I'm not saying that to put pressure on you. I know you and Kylee are doing everything you can, but Alex blames herself. She thinks she should have known the Dillinger's were up to something. She's convinced herself that if Marlena was alive and still our queen, she would have known somehow."

"That's ridiculous," Bastian countered. "There is no way Marlena could have done anything that Alex didn't do. I realize Marlena is Alex's mother, but she didn't have mind reading capabilities. She wasn't a shadow. How exactly would Marlena have known about the Dillinger's covert operations when nobody else did? Not even her own son."

"Alex doesn't know. She just thinks her mother would have done better. I can't talk any sense into her at this point so I've stopped trying. I've decided to hope for the best and deal with the worst if it happens," Dimitri told Bastian. "Anyway, back to my original question. Did you work through anything while you were in Dublin?"

"Maybe a little," Bastian admitted.

"Do you want to talk about it?" Dimitri asked.

"I don't know," Bastian said deflated. "You know I'm not one to share my personal problems with anyone."

"I'm not going to pressure you, Bastian. I just want you to know I'm here if you need me. I might be able to help. Sometimes just talking about a problem helps me to make peace with things," Dimitri offered.

"I was wondering something," Bastian said hesitantly.

"What's that?" Dimitri asked.

"It's about dad. Well, more specifically about his death," Bastian told him.

"What about it?" Dimitri asked, curious now.

"Well, Luke told me that dad died valiantly in battle. I was just wondering if that was really true?" he admitted.

Dimitri studied Bastian. What exactly was he asking? "I wasn't there, but if Luke said your father died in battle why would you doubt that? As far as I know Luke never lied about anything. Especially not something so important."

Chaos

Bastian studied Dimitri for a long moment then decided to confide in him. "I remembered something I had forgotten while in Dublin. More specifically while I was visiting my old home. I overheard a conversation between mom and dad just before I turned fourteen. Mom was begging dad to turn her. She wanted to be a warrior," Bastian paused.

"That makes sense. A warrior would never try to turn a human without their consent. I believe your mother would have been completely on board before your father attempted the transition. I knew your father. He was an honorable man Bastian," Dimitri provided. "He wouldn't have risked something so dangerous without your mother's knowledge and consent."

"I'm not sure dad was completely on board," Bastian said softly. "That night, mom was begging him to turn her but dad was refusing. He told her it was too dangerous. He didn't want to risk losing her." Bastian proceeded to relay the rest of the story as he remembered it. "I've always loved and respected dad. I agree he was an honorable man. But he was also depressed. Mom and dad attempted the transformation a few months after I turned fourteen. Mom died and everything changed. I know dad loved me, but he changed profoundly. He was always depressed and I believe he felt guilty and responsible for mom's death." Bastian closed his eyes and considered what he would say next.

Dimitri sat quietly allowing Bastian to work this out himself.

"Dad died eighteen years after mom. I was only thirty two at the time. Things had gotten a little better by then, but not a lot. I never saw dad truly happy after mom died. He tried, for me I think, but I know he never forgave himself for what happened. I think that's why it was so easy for me to resent him over mom. I assume that's why I blocked out what I knew. Mom was dead so it was easier to blame dad," Bastian said regretfully.

"So did your trip help you to forgive him?" Dimitri asked.

"Partially," Bastian admitted. "Except for one thing," he paused. "If dad died on purpose, I'm not sure I can ever forgive him for that. I lost mom and had to deal with the loss, but if dad allowed a vampire to kill him so he didn't have to go on living with the guilt and the sorrow, I'm not sure I can forgive him for that. I still needed him."

"I see," Dimitri said seriously. "So even though Luke told you that your father died valiantly, you prefer to believe he committed suicide by vampire?"

Bastian looked up at Dimitri. "I don't prefer to believe that. I just wonder if that was the case. I guess I won't ever know the truth. I worry that dad gave up on life and saw an easy way out."

"Bastian," Dimitri paused to make sure Bastian was listening. "Your father loved you very much. He was so proud of you. Sure, he was upset over the loss of your mother. Until you find your true mate, I'm not sure you can understand how profound that loss would have been for him. I have no doubt your father suffered every minute of every day for the entire eighteen years he lived after your mother's death. If I ever lost Alex, I think I'd go insane. But that doesn't mean he would willingly allow a vampire to kill him just to relieve his pain."

"What makes you so sure?" Bastian asked.

"Because he had you," Dimitri said simply. "I guess he might have considered such a thing if it wasn't for you, but your father loved you too much to put you through that kind of pain. Like I said, he was an honorable man. Committing suicide that way would have been selfish. Your father was not selfish," Dimitri assured him. "Even without you, I don't believe Adrian would have allowed himself to be killed that way. He just wasn't that kind of man."

"I'd like to believe you, but you weren't there. You already told me that," Bastian stated.

Dimitri studied Bastian. "You said you talked to Luke about your father's death. Did you talk to him about these concerns?"

"No," Bastian admitted. "Luke and dad were close. Luke was visibly upset when we talked. It was right after dad's death and we were both trying to deal with the loss," Bastian paused. "I guess I didn't want to mention it in case I was wrong."

"So at least you haven't convinced yourself that you're right," Dimitri asked. "You do have doubts?" he pressed.

"Sure I do," Bastian admitted. "I guess deep down I don't want to believe it, but as much as I don't want that to be the case, I just can't brush it aside. It's a possibility, I guess I feel like I have to face it no matter how unpleasant it is."

"I think you need to talk to Jake about this." Dimitri told him.

"Look," Bastian sighed. "I confided in you, but that doesn't mean I'm comfortable sharing this with everyone. It's too personal. I know Jake's a warrior but..."

"Because he was there," Dimitri interrupted. "Jake was in that battle with Luke and your father. My father was with them as well. Jake is the only surviving member of that group. He can answer your questions. If you really want to know the truth, talk to Jake."

"You're sure he was there?" Bastian asked. "He's never mentioned that to me."

"I am," Dimitri said soberly. "My father told me a little about the battle. It happened in Dublin after Radek had signed the treaty. Marlena and some of the fae had already moved to America. The rest of the group was planning on joining them, but things were still unsettled in Ireland. The warriors continued their regular patrols, in groups, to fight the vampires and protect the people. The four of them set out together and came across a large nest of vampires. They were seriously outnumbered. Dad said they were lucky. All of them should have been killed that night. It must have been really bad because dad wouldn't go into detail with me like he usually did. I know they all felt guilty that your father lost his life that night. Dad was paired with Luke, which was unusual. Typically Luke and Jake partnered up but this time dad hooked up with Luke for some reason. That left Jake and Adrian. Talk to Jake, Bastian. He'll tell you the truth and he's probably the only one that can clear this up once and for all."

"I'll think about it," he told Dimitri soberly. "So, it sounds like I'm heading to the fort tomorrow," he said lightly, changing the subject. "Do you need me back here in town or can I stay out there awhile? I'll have one of my pilot's take us out so he can bring Alex back. I'd like to hang out and help Kylee work on the antidote for as long as I can. I'm not getting anywhere by myself and it doesn't sound like she's doing much better. Maybe if we put our heads together, we can come up with something new."

"No, I'd prefer you to stay out there. Melissa's life is our first priority right now," Dimitri told him. "Oberon and the rest of the council are conducting meetings and sifting through evidence on the Dillinger's. Alex has to be here, so I would appreciate the use of one of your pilots. She has to sign off on the final decision once the

Chaos

council is ready for the sentencing hearing. Plus the DeLacy's are still our guests. They're helping us muddle through this mess and have had a few suggestions on punishment as well. They've dealt with criminal behavior more than anyone back in Dublin, so we're lucky to have them here. Anyway, Alex and I need to stay in New York but I think you're going to do us more good out at the fort. In fact, I'd appreciate it if you stayed as long as possible, or at least until there's a resolution to Melissa's situation."

"I'll stay as long as I can," Bastian promised. "I'll see you and Alex at the airport tomorrow at five. Don't get up. I'll let myself out." He stood and walked towards the door.

Chapter Two

Kylee Quintana sat in the sterile lab trying to concentrate on her new project but all she could think about was Bastian. She glanced back over her shoulder as the woman let out another painful scream. Kylee sighed. This couldn't go on much longer. A human body wasn't capable of taking that kind of pain for long. Pretty soon Melissa Tate was going to shut down completely. Kylee glanced at the clock. Where were they? Bastian and Alex should be here by now.

Kylee turned her attention back to the complicated formula she'd been working on all day. She carefully placed two drops of amphetamine into the liquid. Now she needed to wait and watch. Melissa let out another scream. Kylee slowly rose from her chair and walked to the bed. She was such a lovely young girl. Her whole life was supposed to be ahead of her. Instead, she was lying strapped to a hospital bed fighting for her life. The unknown substance was literally eating her cells from the inside out. It was such a waste.

Chaos

Kylee quickly turned when she heard a noise outside the lab. She watched in anticipation as the door slowly opened and Breena walked in.

"Sorry to disappoint you," Breena said with a slight smile. She too moved to the side of the bed. "How is she?"

Kylee sighed again out of frustration. "Bad," she admitted. "Where are they? She needs Alex."

"They should be here any minute," Breena assured her. She studied the young girl. Even when the woman wasn't screaming out in pain, the internal torment Melissa was experiencing was written all over her delicate features. Breena's eyes began to water and she blinked back tears. Being pregnant was torture on her emotions.

Kylee put a hand on Breena's shoulder. "Don't worry, that part passes too. Once the baby's born, you won't even remember all the sickness and the hormones."

"Fat chance," Breena told her. "I'm never going to forget the morning sickness and I don't think Orin will let me forget the hormones. He's so patient, but I know he's getting tired of the constant waterworks. I'm just glad the council is allowing him to view the court proceedings remotely. I don't think I could handle it if he had to go back to the city without me."

"Hang in there," Kylee smiled at her new friend. "You look a lot better today. How long has it been since you were sick?"

"Two weeks," Breena said triumphantly. "That new tea you developed feels like a miracle cure."

"You mean the tea you developed," Kylee corrected. "I just tweaked your invention a little. The real credit goes to you. You're amazing when it comes to turning herbs into medicine."

"Okay, the tea we developed." Breena became excited. "I think this is going to do wonders for our people. The Fae have such a hard time with pregnancy. Once we finally conceive many have miscarriages and those that don't, are sick almost the entire time. The tea won't do anything to help women get pregnant or stop the miscarriages but those that are able to carry the child will have a much easier time now. Thank you so much for your help and advice. Our people owe you a great debt, Dr. Kylee. You amaze me. Plus, you've accepted all the strange, unbelievable anomalies of our world so easily. We're lucky to have you."

Both women cringed as the young patient screamed out in pain again.

"I can't take this much longer," Kylee told her. "Alex can't come out here once a week forever. She has too much to do. Plus, Melissa's body can't withstand the continuous pain, it's too destructive on her system. Her mind is already shutting down. We don't have much time before the damage is irreversible. I've never been this motivated in my life, but I still can't find the solution."

Breena studied the doctor. "When was the last time you got a full night's rest?" she finally asked.

Kylee took Melissa's hand and sighed. She absently began rubbing her thumb over the back of the unconscious girl's hand, trying to sooth away the pain. "I don't know. I can't remember to be honest. I tried a few nights ago, but I just laid there wide awake worried about my patient. I felt guilty, like I was failing her. It just seemed selfish... like I was wasting time. Time is something Melissa doesn't have. I can sleep after this is over, one way or the other," she said soberly. "Until then, I've been catching an hour here and there." She shrugged at Breena's disapproving look.

Breena's head shot up. "That's them," she said, relieved when she heard the helicopter in the distance. The two women left the lab and rushed to the landing pad.

Alex jumped from the helicopter and rushed toward the waiting women. "How is she?" Alex asked as she continued toward the lab.

"Bad," Kylee told her. "What took you so long? Melissa is worse than she's ever been."

"I was afraid of that," Alex said soberly. "We had some problems at the airport. We couldn't get cleared for takeoff. I was stuck in that thing for almost an hour before Bastian got the go ahead." They reached the side of the bed just as Melissa let out another loud scream.

"She's been like that for the last hour," Kylee told her. "I think it's getting worse."

Alex gently took Melissa's hand and closed her eyes as she worked diligently to repair the damage the toxic formula had caused.

Kylee watched Alex silently heal Melissa. She was still amazed and flabbergasted after all this time. She'd worked in medicine for years. Something that typically took days, weeks and even months to heal, was taken care of by Alex in seconds. Kylee knew the instant Alex finished taking care of the problem. Melissa's body immediately relaxed and she appeared to be resting peacefully.

Alex straightened and faced Kylee and Breena, frowning. "You're right. It's getting worse." She took a deep breath. "I don't suppose you've had any luck with that antidote?" she asked hopefully.

Kylee glanced at the bench where she'd been working all day. "I don't know," she said honestly. "I had an idea this afternoon, but we won't know anything until tomorrow morning."

"I know you're doing all you can Kylee," Alex told her. "Thank you for that," she said sincerely. "I hate that Melissa is suffering like this because of my people." She glanced back at their helpless patient. "I feel responsible for her condition."

"That's nonsense," Kylee said immediately. "Just because two of your people used that girl to experiment like mad scientists doesn't mean you are responsible. That's like saying I'm responsible for all of Bundy's murders simply because we are both human, or Dr. Kevorkian's deaths because I'm a doctor too." She shook her head. "Sorry, I won't accept responsibility for that and you shouldn't take responsibility for this," she said motioning toward Melissa.

"That's different," Alex told her. "I'm the queen. I'm responsible for the actions of my people."

"You're talking about the same people that were experimenting with dangerous toxins. The people who wanted to kill all the warriors, including the man that you love?" she asked. "The people that were trying to dethrone you in any way they could. What if they had tried to kill you? Would you be responsible for your own death? I don't think so, Alex. Stop feeling guilty about her." She turned to Melissa. "I'm doing my best to figure this out. Bastian is also working on it and so is Breena. If there's a cure, we'll find it. I promise," Kylee assured her.

Chaos

Alex studied Kylee. She looked tired and worn out. "I'm worried about you Kylee," she finally said. "You're not getting enough sleep. I know this is important and you're working as hard as you can. Just take a little time for yourself. You're not at your best if you don't rest. You know that, you're a doctor."

"Maybe you could just heal my weariness and make me whole again. Then I'd have enough energy to work a few more hours tonight," Kylee said only half teasing.

"Sorry, it doesn't work that way. You know that. I can only heal injuries, otherwise I could just go in and take care of what's going on with Melissa. I can't heal her until the toxin does damage to her cells. Otherwise, I'm worthless. It's up to you doc," she paused. "I'm going to stay the night, then head back out in the morning. Go get a few hours' sleep, Kylee. That's an order."

"Can't," Kylee argued. "I need to work up a couple more tests." She smiled at Alex. "One now, another in about three hours. Typically I'd wait until the morning to prepare the second petri dish, but we don't have that kind of time. I'm going to mix my formula with Melissa's blood every few hours. That way we'll know conclusively by tomorrow night if it was a success."

"Okay. How about this," Alex conceded. They really didn't have much time left. "Breena will stay here with you while you prepare one more sample. Then you go to bed immediately."

Kylee began to shake her head.

"Not negotiable. Sorry," Alex cut in. "You sleep for four hours and then I will wake you up myself so you can prepare another sample. Then you go back to bed for at least three more hours."

"But..." Kylee began.

"Nope," Alex cut her off again. "You said you won't know if it worked until tomorrow anyway. There's nothing else you can do tonight. Either you get some sleep or you're returning to New York with me tomorrow and Bastian stays here, alone. Don't fight me on this. You know Thomas will back me, not you."

Kylee studied her boss, who had also become her friend. "Okay," she finally conceded. "One night then I get back to work."

Alex shrugged. "I'm leaving in the morning. What you do after I'm gone is up to you." She turned and walked out the door.

Bastian stood at the window watching the three women. He missed Kylee, but he needed space. He still didn't know what to do. Dublin had helped him to realize one thing, he was in love with Dr. Kylee Quintana. Totally and irrevocably in love. She was so beautiful and sexy. Not in a sleazy or flashy kind of way, but in a classy professional way. She was also brilliant and fun. He realized on his long flight home that all the stress and indecision he was feeling might be for nothing. Kylee was fun. She loved life. Bastian, not so much... in fact, he was boring. Who said she would even want him if he decided to try. He exhaled as the powerful feeling of emptiness and longing overcame him. Still, he couldn't take his eyes off her.

His stomach clenched involuntarily as he remembered how brave and competent she'd been on the battlefield. It had only been a few weeks, but somehow it seemed like ages ago. At first he tried to shield her from the vampires. He was terrified she'd get injured. But when one snuck through and Kylee took it out fearlessly, he backed off. It was impossible to shield her completely anyway and he knew if he let her hold her own, it would boost her confidence; which would make her stronger. Allowing her to fight had almost killed him. He had pretended like it was okay, like it didn't matter one way or the other... but it did. He was just thankful she only received minor wounds that day. Bastian frowned when he realized how tired she looked. When was the last time she'd gotten any sleep? He continued to study Kylee as she prepared another sample. Alex had left, but Breena was still by her side. Hopefully the two of them would leave soon. He wanted to work, but he wouldn't get anything done if Kylee stayed.

Bastian slowly slid into a sitting position, resting his weight against the wall. He'd know if they left. He'd be able to hear them, but from this location there was no way they could see him. He would just have to wait her out. She needed sleep, he didn't. Passing out drunk had at least given him a full nights rest. Something he hadn't had in weeks. He always had good intentions. Every night when he slipped into bed, he thought he'd catch at least a few hours. But it never failed, once his head hit the pillow all he could think about was Kylee. Then he'd lay there all night wishing they had never met. Life would be so much easier if he didn't know her.

Bastian remained in the shadows when he heard the large door slam shut. Good, they were leaving. He'd remain hidden for a little longer just to be sure. Once they reached the gate he'd know if both women had left, or just Breena. Moments later he saw them. He let out a sigh of relief. He would have the lab to himself tonight. Bastian casually walked into the vacant building and slipped through the door of the sterile room. He felt at home here. It was strange, but the instant he walked through that door he relaxed a little. His body, mind and soul knew this was where he belonged. He quickly moved to his work station and began working on an antidote for Melissa.

Kylee walked through the large doors of the farmhouse. She expected to see Bastian lounging in the study with Ty, but the room was empty. Maybe he was tired from all the traveling. Once she reached the top of the stairs she glanced back to wish Breena a goodnight, thinking her friend was a few steps behind her. But Breena was still standing at the bottom of the stairs. "Aren't you going to bed?" Kylee asked.

"Yes," Breena assured her. "Orin and I moved out to the apartments a couple days ago. If you took a break every once in a while you'd already know that. I called him while you were finishing up at the lab. He's headed over to walk me back. Go to bed, Kylee. I promised Alex I wouldn't leave until you were in your room."

Kylee rolled her eyes. "I'm not a teenager waiting for the right moment to bolt. I said I'd get some sleep. I'll try to get some sleep. Alex was right, there's nothing I can do for the next few hours. And, I'm beat so I'll try to rest until Alex wakes me to prepare another dish."

"Good," Breena smiled as Orin walked through the front door. "Goodnight then." The couple slipped back out the door and disappeared into the darkness.

Kylee closed her bedroom door and sank onto her bed. She was exhausted. She was also a little disappointed. She wanted to see Bastian. She knew he was here. Alex said if she didn't cooperate, Bastian would stay here without her. Kylee still didn't know what to think about his drunken confession. Did he really think she was beautiful and sexy? She climbed into bed and shut out the lamp. The idea that a man like Bastian might find her attractive felt nice. Okay, it felt amazing. But if he was interested in her, why hadn't he acted on it? He had plenty of chances. They'd been spending a lot of time together lately. Which brought her back to the part about it never working. Kylee sighed. How was she going to get any sleep tonight? She had too many questions.

Chaos

Tonight it was going to be Bastian, not Melissa that kept her awake. She stared out the window expecting to be up all night, but her eyes drooped closed and she drifted off to sleep almost immediately.

* * * *

Alex awoke to the quiet beeping of her cellphone. She groggily glanced at the display, it was only two o'clock in the morning. Why had she set her alarm for two in the morning? Oh yeah, she promised Kylee she would wake her up. Alex moaned as she slipped on her jeans and stepped outside her door. Which one was Kylee's room again? She stood motionless, staring down the hallway for another moment. Then she had an idea. She didn't know anything about science, but maybe she could just check the sample herself. If it was growing or something, then she'd wake Kylee. If nothing appeared to be happening, she'd be gone before Kylee woke anyway. The woman needed sleep.

Alex pulled on her shoes and headed out the door. As she approached the large building she realized the light in the lab was still on. That was strange. Alex cautiously entered the room and stopped just inside the doorway. She relaxed when she spotted a large man leaning over the workbench. Bastian was still up and he was diligently working on something, but he looked upset. Alex gently closed the door and slowly walked toward him.

Bastian heard the door shut and turned his attention to the opening. "Alex?" What was she doing here at this time of night?

"Bastian, would you mind helping me with something?" she asked, grateful to see him. He'd know what to look for in Kylee's serum.

"Sure, what do you need?" He stood and walked towards her. His latest attempt was a bust. He'd just thrown it in the garbage and was about to start over.

"Well, I promised Kylee I'd wake her so she could come down and check her latest formula. But she's so tired, I thought maybe I could see for myself if it was worth interrupting her sleep. If it's obviously not working, she might as well rest and start fresh in the morning," Alex told him. "The problem is, I don't know anything about science or chemistry. I was hoping since you're here, you might check and help me decide if I should wake her or not."

Bastian moved to Kylee's workspace. He carefully pulled out the petri dish and studied the contents. Then he placed the dish under a microscope and studied it closer. She hadn't solved their problem, but her idea was interesting. He stood up and looked at Alex soberly. "Sorry. It didn't work," he told her. "Let Kylee sleep. There's no use waking her up just to disappoint her. Like you said, she needs the rest."

Alex sighed, slumping her shoulders. "I was hoping maybe this time..." She didn't finish, she didn't know what to say.

"Don't give up on us just yet," Bastian told her. "We're all coming up with some good ideas. So far none of them have worked, but the odds are on our side. We're going to keep trying until we find a solution."

"I know." Alex gave him a weak smile. "I just feel bad for Melissa. I'm not stupid, I know her body won't take the pain forever. Eventually she's going to give up and shut down completely." Alex rubbed her eyes and started to turn, then stopped. "Why are you still up?" she demanded.

Chaos

Bastian smiled at her. "I was trying out an idea I had on the plane. Sorry, it didn't work either. I was just about to start a fresh approach when you walked in."

Alex folded her arms over her chest. "I think it's time we all got some sleep. That means you, too." She raised her eyebrow at him in challenge. "You have to be jet lagged from all that flying. Come to bed, it can wait until morning."

Bastian was about to protest, then decided to concede. He was tired and if he didn't get at least a little rest, he wouldn't make it through the day tomorrow. Well, technically today. He laughed as he shook his head to clear his mind, he was getting punchy. A couple hours would be enough, then he'd get started again.

"Something funny?" Alex scowled.

"No," he said, putting his hands on her shoulders and turning her toward the door. "I agree, let's both get some rest. You have an early flight and I want to get a jump start on a new serum first thing." The two of them walked silently toward the house.

"Bastian?" Alex finally spoke as they started up the drive.

"Yeah?" he said curiously.

"I know I'm new at all this queen stuff and it's too early for you guys to really trust me, but I'm so sorry for all this," she paused. "I'm sorry I didn't stop them before it got this far. I'm sorry you have to lose sleep over a problem I should have prevented."

Bastian stopped abruptly. "What?" he said angrily.

"Uh… I'm just saying I'm sorry," Alex said a little surprise at the anger she heard in his voice. "I know you've lost a lot of sleep over this and you've taken so much time out of your busy schedule to work on such a complicated problem. I just want you to know how much I appreciate all you're doing and to say I'm sorry," she finished lamely.

"Alex," Bastian said taking a deep breath. "Why do you think you have to take the weight of the world on your shoulders? Why do you always feel responsible for the bad things other people do? As I recall, you also felt guilty when Dahl died. Then, you decided it was your fault Thomas was going through his trouble with the police and the unknown killer. Why do you demand the impossible? You have unrealistic expectations for yourself. Nobody blames you for this. It was Patricia and Lawson's doing. I don't think either of those two would be happy if they learned you were trying to take responsibility for this. From what I hear, they're proud of their Frankenstein project."

Alex sighed. "You too?" she said defeated. "Why won't anyone allow me to take responsibility for my failures?"

"Oh, I will not only allow you to take responsibility for your failures, but I expect you to. If you don't, I'll lose the high regard I have for you as my queen… and my friend. But this was not your failure. Those two are insane. Their experiment was insane. Melissa is a victim of that insanity. There's nothing more to this. We have enough to worry about right now. Radek hasn't changed his mind about wanting you dead. He isn't any less determined to pursue his plan to take your kingdom by force. Focus on that. We need you to lead and prepare our people, not waste your energy feeling guilty about something that has absolutely nothing to do with you. You can be sorry I'm losing sleep over this, that Kylee and Breena are losing sleep over this, but you cannot be sorry because you blame yourself. Don't apologize for that again. It's annoying and just makes me angry," he smiled.

Chaos

Alex laughed. "Well, I'm sorry for that then, too." They had arrived at the house and stepped onto the front porch. Alex waited as Bastian opened the door and held it for her. When they reached the top of the stairs Alex paused again. "Thank you," she finally told him as she leaned in and gave him a friendly hug. "I guess I needed the scolding. I just feel responsible for my people and I want to be a good queen for them. With everything going on, I sometimes think you've picked the wrong person for the job."

"Alex, we are all very proud of our queen. Nobody could care more about their people than you do. Nobody would sacrifice more than you have for our wellbeing and the safety of our community. You're right, you haven't had the job long, but you've already proven how passionate you are about your people and your responsibilities. A burden that was forced on you because of your lineage not your choice, I might add. We're lucky to have you during such a terrible time. I hope the turmoil will be over soon but until it is, remember the warriors are behind you one hundred and ten percent. We all trust you and believe in you. There is no way we've picked the wrong person for the job. If you don't believe me, have a chat with Ty before you leave tomorrow. He's still amazed and extremely loyal. We all are." Once again he gently placed his hands on her shoulders and pushed her toward her room. "Goodnight, Alex."

"Goodnight Bastian," she said touched by his words. "And I hope you remember the feeling is mutual. Every one of you amaze me every day." She stepped into her room and gently closed the door behind her.

Bastian watched the door close then quietly slipped into his own room. He was tired. If he slept for two or three hours, he could get up with the sun and begin fresh. Kylee's failed formula gave him an idea. The reminder of Kylee made his insides churn. How was he going to work by her side day after day and fight the attraction he felt for her? They needed to find an antidote soon so he could escape. At least when he was in New York, he didn't have to see her every day. Sure, he thought about her all the time, but he didn't have the constant temptation; just the agony of missing her. He settled himself into bed and pulled a pillow over his face. What was he going to do? For the first time in his life he wished he'd been born human. Bastian bolted into a sitting position and stared out the window, wide eyed. Had he just come up with a plan? Why hadn't he considered this earlier? If he were human too, they wouldn't have a problem. Was it possible though? Could he actually come up with a way to turn a warrior into a human? He was already working on one impossible experiment, he might as well add another one.

He laid back down and pondered the possibilities. He'd made a haphazard attempt at this a few years ago. Back then he hadn't really taken it seriously. Nobody seemed interested even if he had succeeded. For the next thirty minutes Bastian concentrated on formulating a plan. He would spend most of his time working on an antidote for Melissa, but he'd be sure to spend at least an hour every day trying to find a way to make himself human. Before he did anything that permanent, he'd need to know how Kylee felt. He would never take such a drastic step if she didn't love him, too. If there was no hope, if she wasn't interested, he couldn't make that kind of sacrifice. But if she cared about him, he'd take the formula as soon as he developed it. He wanted as much time as possible with her. He wanted to start their short lives together right away. Bastian drifted off to sleep content for the first time in weeks.

Chaos

* * * *

Kylee woke to the sun shining brightly through her window. She smiled and lazily stretched to enjoy the warmth. Her eyes flew open and she shot into a sitting position. Alex didn't wake her up. She needed to get to the lab and see if her new formula had worked. She pulled on a sweatshirt and jeans then brushed her hair into a ponytail. That was going to have to be good enough. She flung open the door and darted down the stairs. Alex would be gone. She said she was leaving early this morning. Lucky for her. Kylee was angry and disappointed. She had trusted Alex. What if her formula had worked, they could have administered it to Melissa last night, well tonight anyway. This put her hours behind. Kylee stopped as she pulled open the door to the lab and stepped inside. Bastian was already there.

"Morning," Bastian said not looking up. He knew it was Kylee. He'd seen her through the window rushing through across the large expanse of the fort. She was definitely on the warpath. It was good Alex had left so early this morning.

"Morning," Kylee said cautiously. Now that she was standing in the same room as Bastian she didn't know what to say. She didn't know how to act. She was nervous after that phone conversation. Maybe if she just got to work, things would go back to normal. She hurried to her work station and froze. Someone had already studied her formula and discounted it. She jerked around and glared at Bastian's back. "Did you do this?" She asked trying not to sound angry but failing. But it was her work. He didn't have the right to beat her to the punch.

Bastian glanced Kylee's way and saw her fuming. He knew she would be, he was prepared for this. "I did," he answered casually. "I worked late last night. Around two o'clock, Alex rushed in and requested my help. She asked me to check your work and see if there was any indication you had been successful. If you had, she was going to wake you right away. Once we learned the formula didn't work, we decided to let you sleep the rest of the night. It seemed cruel to wake you up just to give you bad news." Bastian dropped some skullcap, St. John's Wort and oat straw into his glass tube. The cylinder also contained a fair amount of his own blood and some willow bark. He casually shook the container and waited, hoping Kylee was too angry and caught up in her own work to notice what he was doing.

Kylee walked over to stand before Bastian. She immediately put her hands on her hips and waited. Once Bastian looked her way, she lost it. "I'm glad you think this is funny. That formula was important to me. I worked on it all day. I've been adjusting and trying to perfect it all week. The only reason I agreed to go to bed was because Alex promised me she would wake me up in four hours. I should have been the one to check it. I should have been the one to determine if it worked or not. I should have been the one to..."

"Kylee," Bastian interrupted then smiled as Kylee narrowed her eyes at him. She was about to erupt. "We didn't do this to hurt you. We did it so you wouldn't be hurt. Tell me, if you were in my position, would you have woken me up just to give me bad news when you knew I hadn't slept for days?"

"That's different," Kylee growled.

"Why? I didn't realize there were different rules for you than there are for the rest of us," Bastian said a little annoyed himself.

Kylee slumped her shoulders in defeat. Bastian was right. Alex had been right. She needed the rest and it would have been

Chaos

stupid to wake her up just to tell her she'd failed, again. "Sorry," she said softly and turned to go back to her desk.

Bastian hated this. He wanted to pull her into his arms and comfort her. But he knew once he stepped over that line, he'd never go back. When he woke this morning he had decided to wait a little longer. He couldn't take a chance, couldn't let Kylee see how he felt, until he had experimented a little with his blood. He needed to know if his idea was even possible. He knew he could never get close to her then let her go. His only hope was to find a way to turn himself into a human. "Why yucca root?" he finally asked her.

"What?" she asked in surprise. Had he also studied her notes? She grew hot with anger then stopped herself. What was wrong with her? They were supposed to be working together to find a solution. Why was she so upset at him, they'd shared notes before.

"Yucca?" Bastian said again. "I was just wondering why you decided on yucca. What were you trying to accomplish with that?"

Kylee took a deep breath. "I don't know exactly. I just thought I would try. Some studies claim it prevents blood vessel damage. The toxin is damaging Melissa's blood vessels. It's also an anti-inflammatory. I was hoping it might help her with the pain. A recent study also came out declaring yucca helps prevent tumors and promotes colon health. I just thought it was worth a try since it has so many benefits," she said defensively.

"I see," Bastian said without emotion. Her theory wasn't bad, but yucca wasn't going to accomplish what she was after.

"What does that mean?" she asked angrily. "I realize I'm not as experienced as you are in this area, but I don't appreciate your condescending tone. I've worked hard to find a solution to our problem. I guess I could have taken a break to hang out in bars and get drunk too, but I thought saving that girls' life was a little more important."

Bastian swung his chair around so he could face Kylee. She was trying to make him feel guilty, but it wasn't going to work. He studied her intently without saying a word. He could wait, Kylee wasn't that patient. With a little time she'd tell him exactly what was on her mind.

Kylee didn't move. She didn't blink. She hadn't meant to say that, but he had made her so angry. Now what? He was waiting on her. What should she say? Where should she go from here? She wanted to ask him how he felt about her. She wanted him to hold her close and make her feel safe and loved. Without him here she felt so alone. Now, with him back, she was on edge. She didn't know how to deal with this. She took a deep breath and turned away from him. As she walked back to her desk she quickly blinked back tears. She was still tired, lonely and so confused, but she would not let Bastian see her cry.

Bastian stood and followed her to her desk. Once she sat down he crouched beside her and turned her chair around. He needed to see her. He still had no idea what he had said to her that night. Is that what this was about? "I'm not going to apologize for leaving. I had some difficult things that needed my immediate attention. But I am sorry if I offended you somehow. I'm also sorry if you thought I was being condescending. That was not my intent," he paused. She still looked tired and worn out. He wished she would take a break. "Actually, I found your formula intriguing," he confessed. "I was just trying to understand why you used a few of the ingredients you decided on."

Chaos

Kylee took a deep breath. She was still overreacting. "It sounds like you disagree with my use of yucca. What would you have chosen instead?"

Bastian studied her. Did she really want to know? If he told her, would she be offended again?

"Really. Please tell me," Kylee pressed.

"Well, for starters I would have used St. John's Wort and Lavender for the pain. And I probably would have thrown in a little rosemary. Angelica tincture is an anti-inflammatory which also builds the immune system. The steroids in bark of willow also strengthens the immune system and builds bone and hormonal balance. So, I would have used a combination of all of them instead of yucca. Typically using multiple ingredients instead of one, works more efficiently." He shrugged at the look on her face. Then he smiled at her. "Why are you looking at me that way?"

"Because you're so good at this," she said honestly. "I never would have thought of any of those. I'm terrible at lab work. If we come up with an antidote it will be because of you Bastian, not me. Sometimes I feel like I'm just as ignorant as Patricia and Lawson."

"That's not true," he said standing. He glanced around the room until he found a nearby chair. He set it next to Kylee and cautiously sat down. He wanted to talk to her about her formula, but he was afraid he'd offend her again.

"What's on your mind?" she asked. "I've locked paranoid, psycho Kylee away now. Tell me what you're thinking. There's something else wrong with my formula. What is it?"

"Well, it's missing an active ingredient," he finally told her.

"What do you mean?" she asked. She really didn't understand.

"The meat?" he pressed. "You have all the supporting details but where's the main ingredient? Where's the meat of the thing?" he asked again. "You're building an antidote that builds strength and suppresses the pain, but what's the real point? What are we trying to accomplish?"

Kylee studied Bastian. He was right. Her formula was missing substance. They needed something that would halt the progression of the toxin. They needed something that would stop the rapid destruction that was occurring inside Melissa's body. Even the amphetamine was fodder, not substance. They needed the active ingredient as he put it. Kylee stood in frustration. What could they use? What chemical or herb or substance of any kind would accomplish their goal; not just suppress the symptoms? She began to pace the room without thinking, it was a habit of hers. Something she always did when she was deep in thought.

"We'll work on it together," Bastian told her. "I haven't figured it out either. But I think you might be onto something with the rest," he told her honestly.

Kylee stopped pacing and studied him. "Do you really mean it?" she asked. "Or are you just trying to make me feel better?"

"I really mean it," Bastian confirmed. "Exchange the yucca for the ingredients I mentioned and I think we're off to a good start. We just need to find something that has actual healing power. We'll go to work trying different things and combine them with your formula to see what happens," he smiled at her. "I think you just came up with our first breakthrough. I'd say you're wrong. You are very good at this."

Chaos

"You're still better," she said then smiled at him. "Thanks, and I'm sorry. I don't know what got into me, but I'm sorry for what I said. It's none of my business what you do in your free time."

Bastian shrugged her comments off. He wasn't prepared to discuss this with her. "So are we friends again?" he asked hesitantly. He didn't want to be just friends.

They both looked up as Breena walked in. "Uh... I was wondering if I could talk to the two of you about something," she asked hesitantly.

"Sure, what's up?" Bastian asked.

"Well, I was thinking about the situation with Melissa," Breena began. "I don't know if Kylee knows about this but I know you do, Bastian." She paused as she glanced at Kylee then back to the warrior. "This may not work and it's okay if you think it's a bad idea, but I wondered if we could alter the medication I made to fight off the effects of the vampiric animal venom," she said a little hesitantly. "It worked to heal Victor and Ariel against that toxin. Maybe it would help Melissa fight this toxin as well."

Bastian raised an eyebrow. Would Breena's formula work as the base they were looking for? "Why do you have to alter it?" he asked.

"Oh," Breena smiled. "Well, because it has some ingredients that are harmful to humans," she admitted. "We'll have to take out the lead. That causes lead poisoning in humans but it speeds up the effectiveness in the supernatural."

"Are you serious?" Kylee asked intrigued. "There are so many things I still don't know about your people. Will I ever understand the differences?" she asked, overwhelmed by what she still didn't know.

Breena smiled. "Of course you will. But for now, leave that to me. Anyway, my original formula also has arsenic in it. Again, harmful to humans but not us. We can just leave the lead out, but I'll need to come up with an alternative to the arsenic. For us arsenic helps our system absorb the medicine. I'm going to have to do some research to see if there is anything that accomplishes the same thing in humans."

Kylee was thinking, what would work as a substitute? "Vitamin D helps humans absorb calcium. We could try that," she suggested. "There are also amino acids like Lysine that increases calcium absorption. Acai berry is also supposed to help your immune system. Maybe we could start with those, including calcium and go from there."

"I agree," Bastian told Breena. "We'll eliminate the arsenic and lead completely. Then we can start by adding vitamin D and see what happens. I also agree with the acai berry. Let's add them both for starters. If that doesn't work, we can add lysine with the acai berry." He looked at Kylee and grinned. "I think we just found our base. Breena, can you make us a large amount of the stuff with those minor changes? Kylee and I will do the rest. Kylee has come up with a formula that I think we could add to your serum. If nothing else, it's a good starting point. We'll need to take blood at regular intervals while we try to work this out." Bastian was finally hopeful. He was sure they were headed in the right direction.

Breena was relieved. She'd been so worried they would think she was nuts to suggest something that drastic. "Do you really think this is going to work?" she finally asked.

Chaos

"I think with a little tweaking we may have just found what we were looking for." Bastian said confidently. "Let's get started. We still have a lot of work ahead of us."

"I'll go make the tea, minus the hazardous ingredients," Breena said leaving the room.

* * * *

A couple nights later Kylee sat at her desk hoping for the best. Her formula was finally ready to dissect. She slipped the dish under the microscope and sighed. Failure again. Kylee threw the petri dish in the garbage in frustration. They had all been so excited over the new idea, but so far she didn't feel like they were any closer to finding a solution than they had been before. She plopped her head on the cold metal table and closed her eyes. She was so tired.

Bastian walked into the lab just in time to see Kylee throw her latest experiment in the trash. He didn't need to ask for the results. He quietly walked to her side and retrieved the dish from the can. Then he slipped the petri dish under the microscope. "You added too much ginger and not enough willow bark," he said placing the dish on the table. "Instead of using the Lysine go back to Vitamin D."

"Why?" Kylee asked talking into the table. She hadn't moved an inch.

"Any chance I can talk to you, instead of the back of your head?" Bastian asked.

Kylee slowly rolled her head to the side so she could look at Bastian. "When do we give up?"

"Never," he answered confidently. "I'm positive we're on the right track, we just need to tweak it a little until we find our solution."

"How can you be so sure?" she asked unconvinced.

"Because I do this for a living," he assured her. "Maybe you could trust me a little."

"Whatever," Kylee said depressed.

"Thanks a lot," he said as he shook his head. He was trying to keep it light, but her lack of confidence hurt. He'd been feeling like a failure lately anyway. He was no closer to figuring out his human/warrior problem. And, every moment he was with Kylee it became more difficult to keep his distance. How long could he stand this? Not much longer. He was going crazy.

Kylee straightened, prepared to leave for the night but decided to give it one more try. She implemented Bastian's suggestions then pushed away from the table and headed for the door.

"You leaving for good or just taking a break?" Bastian asked. He wanted to work on another idea but needed to keep his new project a secret. If he drew his own blood then started adding other ingredients Kylee would want an explanation.

"I think I'm done for tonight," she told him. She was losing her optimism for the project and she was beat. It had been days since she'd slept well. "I'm going to bed."

Bastian watched her stop to clean up her area. "I think that's a good idea. You need rest Kylee. You know how important sleep is for your stamina; mental and physical. We'll check your new formula in the morning." He watched her walk out the door and

Chaos

down the hall. Bastian turned back to his desk and pulled his notes from his pocket. He was going to bed early tonight, too. He just wanted to try this new idea first.

* * * *

Kylee entered the lab the following morning. She wasn't surprised to see Bastian at his desk but she was surprised he hadn't checked out her most recent test results. "You haven't touched it," she said amazed.

"No," he agreed. "I didn't want to get yelled at again." He teased, then laughed at the look on Kylee's face. "I was hoping we could do it together," he corrected. "Do you mind if I join you?"

"Not at all," she told him. "We've been working on this together. If this was successful, it's because of you." She smiled at him. "Let's do it." She was anxious to see if they'd made any progress.

Bastian walked to Kylee's side and waited as she pulled the small dish from the glass enclosure. The two of them studied the dish before placing it under the microscope. So far so good, Bastian thought. He was beginning to feel hopeful. Had they actually succeeded this time?

Kylee looked up at Bastian and smiled. "It passed the first test. Let's see how it holds up under the microscope." She was excited but reserved. She slid the dish under the small scope and was about to look in the eye piece then stopped. "You go first," she offered. "I'm too nervous."

"Nope," Bastian said pushing her toward the table. "You put this together, you get to view it first."

Kylee studied Bastian for a minute then pulled the microscope toward her and lowered her eyes to the glass piece. She didn't want to get her hopes up but she couldn't help it. She cautiously glanced at the scene before her. She was shocked. It looked like they'd done it. She focused in closer and studied the dish intently. Kylee stood and looked at Bastian. "Your turn," she said excited now. "I think it might have worked."

Bastian studied the dish for a very long time. He was looking for flaws. They would need to prepare another dish, but it looked like they had finally accomplished the first step in this problem. He stood and smiled at Kylee. "Congratulations," he said with a slight nod and a wink. "I think you just developed your first drug."

"Really?" Kylee asked. She couldn't believe they had actually found an antidote.

"Really," Bastian affirmed. "I can't see any problems or abnormalities in the blood. Of course we're going to have to prepare another sample to make sure we get the same results. Then we need to prepare another one. If we get the same results after three tries, I think we should give Melissa a small dose. Obviously we've fast tracked this but we don't need FDA approval and it's not a drug we're going to need again. Are you okay with that?"

Kylee grinned. She couldn't help it. She wanted to dance. "I agree." She nodded as her smile widened. She was trying to contain her excitement. But why? This was something to celebrate. She did a little jig then grabbed Bastian's hands and pulled him to her.

Bastian laughed at Kylee. She was so excited, but she was trying to maintain control. Then she lost it and began dancing in place. His heart swelled. She was the most wonderful woman in the world. The woman he'd always dreamed of. There was no denying it, he was completely in love with her. He'd never met anyone like her and he knew he never would again. He froze as Kylee grabbed his hands and pulled him toward her. Then, Kylee pressed her body against his. Did she know what she was doing to him?

Kylee threw her head back and laughed out loud. "Bastian we did it!" she exclaimed. "We really did it." She smiled at him again as she wrapped her arms around his neck. "Dance with me," she requested.

Bastian couldn't stop himself. The closeness was too much. He lowered his head and took her mouth with his as he gently placed one hand on the small of Kylee's back and the other at the base of her neck. Then he pulled her closer, waiting for a reaction.

Kylee froze. She couldn't believe this was happening. Was Bastian really kissing her? After all this time he was finally making a move on her? She was shocked and thrilled. What should she do? Make the most of it, stupid. She told herself as she shifted her mouth and deepened the kiss.

The couple stood in the middle of the room enjoying each other for several minutes. Then Bastian lifted Kylee off the floor and maneuvered her to the table. Kylee was having a hard time breathing. She'd dreamt of this moment for months now. She never would have imagined her dreams could become a reality. Bastian gently set Kylee on the table and stood back. He was just studying her, not saying anything, not touching her... nothing. "What's wrong?" she finally asked.

"Nothing," he said a little breathless himself. "You are so beautiful," he whispered as he brushed a strand of hair away from her face. She always wore it in a ponytail, but in her excitement a few strands had come free and clung to her slightly flushed cheek. He wanted to run his fingers through her hair. He wanted to make love to her.

Kylee swung her legs around and let them dangle off the table as she gently placed a hand on Bastian's chest. "Why didn't we do that sooner?" she asked with a smile.

Bastian didn't answer. He silently ran his hand over Kylee's hair and stopped where the elastic secured the ponytail. "Can I?" he asked hesitantly.

Kylee nodded once, never taking her eyes off Bastian's face. She closed her eyes trying desperately to slow her heart rate as he pulled the tie from her hair. She failed miserably when Bastian gently ran his fingers through the long strands that fell over her shoulders.

Bastian inhaled. He'd imagined doing that for so long. He knew he was making a mistake, but there was no going back now. He had finally kissed her and there was no way he could give that up again. Bastian slid his fingers through the front of her hair and ran it down the back of her head stopping when he reached the nape of her neck. He needed more, he'd waited too long for this moment. Bastian lowered his lips to Kylee's again and gently slid his hands down her back, stopping when he reached her waist.

Kylee didn't know what to think. She'd dreamt of this moment, longed for it every time they were in the lab together. But after all this time without a hint of interest, she'd given up hope. Once Bastian returned from Ireland, it only took Kylee a couple days to decide he'd made a mistake that night on the phone. Bastian was drunk and there was no way he thought she was beautiful. It was absurd to think Bastian would ever consider her sexy. Since

Chaos

she'd been at the fort she always put her hair in a ponytail for convenience. She hadn't done her makeup once and her attire was limited to t-shirts, sweatshirts and jeans. There was nothing sexy about that. Now, here she was kissing the most wonderful man in the world. How had this happened?

Bastian straightened. "I think I lost you somewhere back there." He rested his forehead against Kylee's and drew in a long, deep breath. He was feeling a little unsteady and slightly self-conscious. Her reaction didn't exactly scream mutual attraction. "Are you okay with this?"

"More than okay," Kylee said honestly. "You didn't exactly lose me. I'm just wondering how this happened and if it's a fluke. Are you really interested in me, Bastian? Or is this just a onetime event because of our accomplishment today?"

Bastian smiled at her. Kylee wasn't one to beat around the bush. He knew there was no turning back, so he might as well test the waters and see how she felt about him. "I have been interested in you for a very long time, Kylee." He reached up and hooked her hair behind her ear with his index finger. "I hope you feel the same."

Kylee studied Bastian, could he really be serious. She closed her eyes and gave a little nod. "I do," she finally told him. "I thought..." she stopped. Should she bring up their conversation?

"You thought what?" Bastian pressed.

"Um...well..." Kylee paused again.

Bastian leaned forward and pressed his lips to Kylee's once more. The kiss was soft and gentle this time. "Go ahead. I really want to know."

"Well, that night on the phone," she began.

Bastian sobered. What had he said that night on the phone? "Yes?" he asked.

"Well, you said I was beautiful and sexy but then when you got back it was like that call had never happened. I just thought you mistook me for someone else," she finally told him. "I thought you must have been talking about some woman at the bar."

"You know, I gave you that number months before I left but you never called. Then, the one night I got drunk and stupid, you decided to use it. I always did have terrible luck." He smiled at her. "You are beautiful and sexy, Kylee." He watched her intently. Had he said anything else that night? "I was definitely talking about you, not some random woman in a bar."

Kylee debated for the slightest moment then decided to get it all out there. "You also said things could never work between us. Do you still feel that way?"

He hoped that was it. That he hadn't had time to tell her anything else. "Not really," he said simply. If he accomplished the impossible, things would work out just fine. "Did I say anything else?" he asked. "I have to be honest, I was pretty drunk and I can't remember our conversation."

"No," she shook her head slightly. "I think you fell off your chair or something. I heard a noise then some guy got on the phone and told me you were drunk and couldn't talk. He said I should forget anything you said that night because you didn't know what you were saying."

Bastian smiled. "That was Bryan," he told her. "It was his pub. I knew Bryan when I was a kid. He used to come to the house and play kickball with me and a couple other guys from the area. I'm sorry," he added then furrowed his brow. "Why did you call me that night anyway?"

"A couple of reasons," she admitted. "First, because I was worried about you. You didn't seem like yourself before you left. Then, because I was working on my formula and I wasn't sure yucca root was the right way to go with it. I couldn't decide if it was going to accomplish what I was aiming for. I wanted your input," she paused. "I guess we both know the answer to that question now."

Bastian smiled at her. "You were worried about me?" he asked. Somehow knowing that made him feel...what? He wasn't sure, but he liked it.

"Yes, I was worried about you." Kylee smiled. "And it seems I had good reason. You never get drunk. After that call, I was even more concerned," she admitted.

"What did you do?" he asked.

"I confronted Ty and insisted he call Dimitri. I needed to know where you were," she said hesitantly. "Dimitri confirmed you were in Ireland but he wouldn't say anything else," she paused. "Well, I assume he didn't. I know the conversation was pretty short and then Ty wouldn't tell me anything else. The only thing he told me was that you were in Ireland dealing with your past and you were okay."

"I see," Bastian said absently. He wondered what Dimitri had told Ty. Neither Ty nor Sam had said anything since he got back. In fact, he was beginning to think they were avoiding him.

"Is that it?" she asked. "I understand if you don't want to talk about it, but someday I'd like to hear why you suddenly went to

Ireland. Maybe one day you'll trust me with the details so I'll understand what happened over there."

Bastian took Kylee's hand and pulled her toward the door. "Let's go for a walk," he told her casually.

The couple walked out the door and headed for the woods. Bastian didn't stop until they reached the beach. It was empty, he knew it would be. It was almost winter and humans avoided the beach when it was cold. Bastian sat on the soft sand and leaned against a rock pulling Kylee down in front of him. His mind had been racing the entire way there. He was debating with himself, trying to decide what he should tell her.

Kylee leaned back against Bastian and waited. She knew he was a private person. She'd learned that working side by side with him all this time. He'd have to do this at his own pace. Hopefully she'd get a few answers if she was patient. She knew he would only tell her as much as he was comfortable discussing.

Bastian wrapped his arms around Kylee's waist and relaxed a little. It was hard to believe this was really happening. He might regret it if he couldn't perfect his formula, but he'd suffer the consequences later. Right now he wanted to enjoy their closeness. "My parents died when I was young," he began. Kylee started to sit up but he wouldn't let her. He needed to get through this and he didn't want to face her while he did it. He couldn't stand the look of pity he knew he'd see on her face.

"Bastian," Kylee protested. "Let me up."

"I'd rather not," he told her honestly. But he loosened his grip a little so she could get free.

Kylee twisted and looked him in the eyes. "Why?" she asked.

Chaos

"Because I don't want you to feel sorry for me. I don't want pity from you," he told her.

"Too bad," she said taking his face between her hands. "My father died when I was an infant. I never knew him, but my mother and I were very close. I know what it's like to lose your parents. It's devastating. It's something you never get over. I believe the loss stays with you forever." She gently pushed on his shoulders but he didn't move. Kylee pushed herself up onto her knees and shoved him harder.

Bastian smiled. "You do know you're never going to be strong enough to push me around, don't you?"

"Yeah, but I thought maybe you'd be a gentleman about it and make me feel good," Kylee said coyly.

Bastian shifted then grabbed Kylee around the waist and pulled her on top of him as he laid flat on the soft sand. "I wouldn't want to disappoint you," he smiled. "Is that gentlemanly enough?"

Kylee leaned in and gently kissed Bastian's lips. "I'm not sure it was gentlemanly, but it did make me feel good." She shifted so she was lying next to him and rested her head on his shoulder. Then she rested her hand on his chest, hoping the contact would give him comfort. "Now I'm comfortable. You can continue your story," she prompted.

Bastian sighed, it felt nice to finally hold Kylee this way. He thought he could lay here forever. He was always surprised that Kylee could make him feel so alive. She made him feel playful somehow. It was easy to joke and tease with her, something he never did with anyone else. He leaned down and kissed the top of her head. "Mom died when I was fourteen," he finally continued. "Dad died in a battle with some vampires when I was thirty two."

"Were you close?" she asked softly.

"Very," Bastian admitted. "I think mom was my biggest fan. I only had her in my life for a short time, but she had a very profound impact on my life."

"And your father?" Kylee asked.

"He died when I was only thirty two, but I believe anything good and honorable about me is because of my father. He taught me a lot in a very short amount of time. I loved them both and was a little lost once they were gone. I guess that's why it took me so long to revisit my childhood home. I was there, trying to face my past when Bryan found me. He invited me back to his pub and I ended up getting drunk. You're right, I never drink and I certainly never get drunk." He shook his head. "I still can't believe you picked that night to call me."

Kylee was silent. Bastian wasn't sharing any details about his parents' deaths. Maybe he would feel more comfortable if she talked about her loss. "I'm glad I did," she admitted. "It was the first time you said you think I'm beautiful."

"Why do you say that like you don't believe me?" he asked curiously.

"Because I'm not," she said simply. "And because you have never seen me in anything but a ponytail and jeans. There's nothing beautiful or sexy about that."

"You're wrong," Bastian told her leaning up on one elbow so he could see her better. "You have such natural beauty, Kylee. I'm not talking about fake glamour. I'm talking about real beauty," Bastian paused. "You are beautiful on the outside, but more importantly you are gorgeous on the inside. You are so smart and fun, and you make me laugh. When I look at you all I see is beauty, I see the entire package and I don't think there's anyone in the world more stunning than you." He put his finger under her chin and lifted her face so he could look at her. "I mean that. You are gorgeous and sexy." He laughed at the expression on Kylee's face. "You're like the sexy librarian," he added. "Maybe you didn't know intelligence was sexy, but it is." He leaned down and kissed Kylee again. He didn't think he'd ever get enough of her.

"Bastian, I'm sorry you lost your parents," Kylee began as she pulled back to look at him. She needed to keep him on track or he might never talk to her. "Mom died five years ago. It's hardest for me when good, exciting things happen in my life. Things I know mom would enjoy hearing about. I can't count the number of times I've picked up the phone to call her, only to remember she's gone."

"I'm sorry," Bastian said soberly. He hadn't realized they had this in common, too.

"It was difficult, but by the time she died I guess I was ready for her to go. Mom had cancer. She suffered a great deal before she finally passed on. Sometimes I watch Alex healing and I wish I had known her while mom was still alive. I feel jipped somehow. I know it's wrong, but I would have asked Alex to heal mom without hesitation," Kylee admitted.

"I don't think that's wrong and neither would Alex," Bastian told her.

"Maybe," Kylee conceded. "But it doesn't really matter now, it's too late."

Bastian pulled Kylee close and held her to him. So many thoughts were running through his mind. He felt like he was holding a stick of dynamite that could explode at any minute. He was being reckless and he was never reckless. Now that the first phase of Melissa's treatment was resolved, maybe he could spend more time on his human potion. Coming up with a drug for that would be nothing less than a miracle.

Kylee was watching Bastian. He was definitely thinking about something. Why wouldn't he talk about his parents? Saying his father died in battle was extremely vague. "Was the battle bigger than the attack on us last month?"

"Huh?" Bastian asked. He was so lost in his own thoughts he was confused at Kylee's question.

"The battle that killed your father," she told him. "Was it bigger than the attack on us? Did a lot of warriors die?"

"No," Bastian answered. "To both. It wasn't bigger and only dad lost his life."

"Oh," Kylee said not really understanding. If it wasn't bigger, how come they couldn't handle the fight?

Bastian sat up and leaned against the rock again. He watched as Kylee followed suit. But, she didn't speak. She just sat there completely still, facing him, waiting for an explanation. "I wasn't there, so I don't know the details," he finally told her. "I only know what I was told. Thomas' father, Luke, was there. He and dad were friends. Luke said they came onto a group of vampires and were taken by surprise. They didn't expect that large of a group to be in one place. There was supposed to be a treaty." Bastian paused, how much should he tell her? "Anyway, it was a difficult battle and they said dad died valiantly protecting the others."

Kylee waited, there was more to the story that Bastian wasn't sharing. "But?" she finally asked.

73

Chaos

"But what?" Bastian asked.

"You've said twice now 'they say' or 'they said'. It sounds like you don't believe them. I'm just wondering why you feel that way," she asked casually.

"It's not that I don't believe them," Bastian corrected. "It's that I don't know if I believe them." He knew that didn't make any sense. He was splitting hairs.

"Will you tell me why?" she finally asked. "Why do you doubt the heroic actions of your father? I doubt he was a coward, but did he shy away from danger? That seems unlikely for a warrior."

Bastian looked up at Kylee in shock. There wasn't a cowardly bone in dad's body.

"I guess not," Kylee said at Bastian's reaction. "Then what's the sticking point? Why do you doubt the account that was given to you by your father's friend?"

Bastian sighed. "I'd appreciate it if you kept this particular conversation to yourself," he began. "I've only discussed my...concerns with Dimitri. I'd prefer nobody else knows about this."

"You can trust me, Bastian. I won't say a word to anyone," Kylee assured him.

Bastian wasn't sure why, but he did trust Kylee. He felt like he could tell her anything. "Dad was depressed going into that battle," he finally said. "He'd been depressed since mom died. They were very close. Dad loved her more than anything else in the world. Her loss was hard on him. He was never the same again.

Anyway, I know how depressed he was. How lonely and sad he was. I just wonder if he went into that battle and decided it was a good way to end it all. I don't know that to be the case. There's no proof, but I have my suspicions. I have doubts," he concluded.

"I see," Kylee said studying Bastian. He looked so sad and vulnerable right now. "Well, I guess I can see how you might think that." She finally told him. "I didn't know the man so I couldn't say for sure, but it seems unlikely to me."

"Why?" he asked honestly curious.

"Well, you told me that you loved your father very much and that all the good and honorable characteristics you have, you got from him," Kylee began.

"I did," Bastian agreed. "I truly believe that."

"Then your father was good and honorable?" she asked.

"More than any other man I've ever met," he confirmed.

"Well giving up, especially when you have a son that loves you and still needs you, is not honorable. If your father was really the man you say he was, the two don't fit. Either you have honor or you don't, Bastian. Suicide by vampire or any other means is never honorable, especially when you have a child that is counting on you. I know sometimes things happen and life seems unbearable but warriors are fighters, not quitters. I can't believe a warrior would take what he would see as the easy way out like that. Either you are holding on to an image you created in your mind of your father that is actually fabricated, or he died valiantly in battle like Luke said he did," Kylee concluded.

Chaos

"But you're a doctor, you know people do desperate things when they're depressed," Bastian argued. "Why couldn't the two fit under those circumstances?" Bastian asked.

"It sounds to me like you are trying to convince yourself your father gave up. Why is that? Why do you want to believe your father willingly left you? Why is it so hard to believe he was taken from you prematurely in battle?" Kylee asked.

Bastian inhaled sharply. Is that the way he was making it sound, like he wanted to believe his father gave up? Was that the truth? Did he want to believe that? "I don't know," Bastian finally admitted, defeated and weary of this conversation already.

Kylee sighed then moved in close to Bastian. She was getting cold and his warmth felt good. She snuggled against him and considered Bastian's situation. "I assume Luke is no longer around since I've never met him," she finally asked.

"No. He died almost a year ago," Bastian told her.

"Oh, that must have been Luke Deveraux. I heard about his death, it was all over the news. What about the others that were involved in that battle?" she asked. "Are they gone as well?"

"Uh..." Bastian stalled. "No, one of them is still around."

"Have you talked to him?" she asked.

"No," Bastian told her.

"Why not?" Kylee wondered.

"Because I don't want to cast doubt on my father unjustly. What if I'm wrong? What if dad died valiantly like Luke said and I'm the one blowing this out of proportion? Once I put it out there,

I can't take it back and dad isn't here to defend himself… to defend his reputation," Bastian told her. "I just haven't been willing to do that to him."

"So you don't trust this guy that's left to keep things confidential? If you talked to him, he would tell everyone you suspect your father may have died on purpose?" she asked.

"Well no," Bastian mused. "Jake would never tell anyone anything."

Kylee raised one eyebrow at Bastian. He really wasn't making sense. She thought he was just too afraid of the answer to actually ask the question.

"You think I should talk to Jake?" Bastian asked.

"If it were my problem, that's what I would do. But you know Jake, I don't. You know your father, I don't. It's hard for me to help you figure this out when I don't know any of the players," Kylee said honestly. The two sat in silence for a long while before Kylee finally changed the subject. "Speaking of vampire battles," she said softly. "Do you think we're going to be attacked again?"

"I'm sure we will at some point," Bastian said absently. "Why? You fought pretty well the last time. I was really proud of you," he smiled at her.

"Well, because I haven't been practicing lately. I've been so caught up in work I haven't taken time to use the droids. I'm afraid if we get attacked again I won't be as prepared. Maybe now that we figured out the first drug to help Melissa I should start working out again." She wasn't looking forward to fighting the droid again.

Chaos

"Maybe we could practice together," Bastian told her. "We could work out each morning before we hit the lab," he offered.

"Really? You would do that?" she asked enthusiastically.

"Sure," Bastian grinned. "I think I'd enjoy wrestling around on the mats with my sexy lab partner."

Kylee laughed then sobered. "We forgot to tell Breena the good news." She felt a little guilty. "Breena's tea was the base we needed for our formula. She needs to know it worked so well." She jumped up and took a step toward the fort then paused. "Well, are you coming?" she asked.

Bastian laughed and stood, brushing the sand from his jeans. "I'm coming," he said taking her hand in his and leading her toward the forest. He frowned as he realized Kylee's hands were freezing. "Your hands are ice cold," he scolded. "Why didn't you tell me it was too cold for you out here?" He took both hands in his and began rubbing them intently.

"Oh stop it," Kylee said brushing him off. "We can't walk while you rub my hands. I'm fine. I'll get a cup of coffee when we get back. That will warm me up."

Bastian didn't stop. He took her petite left hand between his two large ones and rubbed gently as they headed back to the lab. Once they stepped out of the forest, he shifted his position and took her right hand in his and continued the rubbing.

Kylee smiled. Bastian was such a gentleman. If he was anything like his father, there was no way that man died on purpose. She hoped Bastian would talk to this Jake guy, but she wasn't going to press him. It had been difficult enough to get him to talk to her. She wasn't going to nag or pry into his affairs this soon.

They reached the edge of the bunkers just as Breena was exiting the apartments. "Breena?" Kylee called and quickened her pace.

Breena smiled when she saw the two headed her way. She couldn't wait to hear how things had turned out. "So?" she said with anticipation. "Any news?"

Kylee pulled Breena into a huge hug. "I think we did it," she exclaimed. "The first sample was a success. We are just heading back to the lab to prepare another one. Then tonight I'll do a third. As long as all three show the same results we're going to give Melissa a small dose tomorrow afternoon!" She grinned at Breena. "Can you believe it?"

"That's wonderful!" Breena exclaimed. "Have you told the others?"

"Uh… well not yet," Kylee said. "We had some other business we needed to talk about. Plus, you had to be the first. We never could have done this without you."

"Well, let's go spread the good news." Breena slid her arm through Kylee's and headed for the farmhouse.

"I'm going to prepare the second sample," Bastian called to the two women. "Then I'll join you inside."

Kylee froze. "Oh, yeah. I almost forgot. I can help."

"No," Bastian shook his head. "You two go ahead, update the others. We could all use a little good news about now. I can take care of this sample and you can handle the one this evening." He paused to study Kylee and gave her a charming and maybe a little seductive smile before turning and heading for the lab.

Chaos

Kylee inhaled. He was so handsome when he smiled like that. She didn't want to leave him, but she also didn't want Breena or anyone else asking questions. Bastian would handle the sample then join them in the house with the others.

Chapter Three

Alex sat in the large chair and nervously glanced around her library, waiting for the other men to arrive. She was antsy. But it wasn't only because of the meeting she was about to conduct. She was anxiously awaiting a call from Bastian. He and Kylee were giving Melissa her first dose of the antidote tonight. The dose would be very low and then she'd be monitored closely for twenty four hours. If all went well, they would increase the dosage tomorrow. They planned to continue for at least a week until they were sure the antidote was working. Alex knew it was just as likely things would go terribly wrong as it was for success, but she was going to be optimistic and assume the best until she was told otherwise.

Alex smiled when she spotted Cane. The young dog bounced into the room and made a beeline straight for her. Just before he reached her chair, he took a flying leap and landed in her lap with a thud. The dog didn't hesitate, he immediately flipped onto his back raising his front paws slightly to reveal his belly. Alex laughed and began rubbing the dog's stomach. Cane moaned and begged for more, his back leg twitching happily in tempo with her rubbing. As soon as Alex stopped rubbing, Cane rolled over and sat on her lap. Then he placed his front paws on her shoulders and tried to give her a big, sloppy kiss. Alex was ready for him, she moved her head just in time and gently placed a hand on top of the dog's nose. "No slimy dog kisses. You know I don't allow that." She laughed and rubbed his nose lovingly. Cane moved in again, intent on giving his master affection. She dodged the large tongue and laughed at the game. Suddenly, Cane became alert. He pushed himself off her lap and ran for the front door. So, at least one visitor had arrived. The wait was almost over.

Alex glanced at Avery, then Oberon. The two men were clearly not friends. They tolerated each other because both were members of the council, but they would never be close. Avery was openly scowling at her. She glanced at Oberon and saw he was grinning. "They're great companions aren't they?" Oberon said softly.

"They are," she admitted then shrugged. "I know it's not proper behavior and all that but I just can't resist. The rascal thinks he's a lap dog and he gets so much pleasure from having his belly rubbed. Well, to be honest I get a lot of enjoyment out of it too. I always wanted a dog, but my parents would never let me have one. I never would have guessed that little monster would bring so much happiness into my life."

The doorbell rang and Alex jumped to her feet. She was on her way to the door when Victor and Atticus walked in, followed by Dimitri... Cane hot on his heels. "Look who I found at the front door," Dimitri announced. "Strange, I don't think Victor has ever politely rang the bell and waited to be invited in before. It was certainly a welcome surprise."

"Don't be silly," Alex said walking over to the new arrivals. "Victor doesn't have to ring the bell." She pulled him into a big hug then turned to Atticus. "I'm so glad you could make it. I thought you and Tala had already left for the fort."

"I decided to stay and see this thing through," he said without emotion.

"I'm grateful you did," she smiled warmly. "We're still waiting for Foster but he should be here any minute." Alex turned and held out a hand in invitation. "Please, make yourselves comfortable. I'll get some tea." She turned to leave when the doorbell rang again. "That must be Foster," she glanced at Dimitri. "I'll get the door, maybe you could grab the tea?" she asked.

"Of course," he said taking her hand and leading her out of the room. "Settle down," he whispered as he pressed his lips close to her ear. "Everything's going to be fine." Dimitri kissed Alex on the top of her head then quickly made his way to the kitchen, Cane following close behind.

Alex opened the door and studied Foster. He didn't look well. "Come in," she said softly. "Uh, are you okay Foster?" she finally asked.

"Yeah," he answered then cleared his throat. "I'm fine."

Alex patted the man's shoulder. "I know this is hard on you," she told him. "Hopefully it will all be over soon and you can move on with your life." They both entered the library and Alex settled back into her large chair. Oberon moved from the window and settled into the chair across from her, silently waiting for their meeting to begin. Within minutes, Dimitri returned with the tea and quickly distributed it. Once he was finished he sat next to Alex and took her hand in his, gently caressing it in an attempt to comfort her. Avery remained standing.

Cane re-entered the room, scanning the area for his next target. The instant he spotted Victor, he made a beeline for his favorite visitor. He was hopping around Victor's chair, hoping to find an opening that would allow him to climb into Victor's lap. The warrior was laughing but successfully blocking the rambunctious dog's attempts. Cane wasn't deterred. He continued to hop around, enjoying the attention Victor was giving him.

"Cane," Dimitri said sternly. The small dog ran to his master. "Platz" Dimitri told him. Cane obediently laid at Dimitri's feet. Alex knew he wouldn't move until Dimitri told him to go play. She smiled inwardly. She loved the little guy, but he was clearly Dimitri's dog. She knew that was only natural, they spent more time together. The bond they had developed was strong and mutual. She shifted her attention back to the room full of men. They were all waiting patiently, but it was obvious the group was anxious to learn the reason for the meeting.

"I guess you are wondering why I called you all here tonight," Alex began. "Let's just cut to the chase and get started shall we?"

"Before we do that," Oberon spoke up. "I think we need to get some formalities out of the way." Normally he would let Alex do things her way, but with Avery present it had to be more formal and precise.

"Yes," Avery agreed. "We need to establish whether this will be a formal or informal meeting," he began. "If it's formal, we will need a recording device."

"I don't think that's necessary Avery," Oberon supplied. "This is an informal meeting. You and I can testify if the council needs something official. We don't need to record anything." Oberon knew Avery couldn't help it. He always did everything by the book but that didn't make the man any less annoying. Oberon took a deep breath and silently reminded himself that Avery didn't want this meeting recorded any more than the rest of them did.

"Very well," Avery relaxed and leaned against the wall.

Alex was watching Oberon. This wasn't the way they typically did things. It must be Avery's presence that had Oberon acting so official. She assumed the council leader would give her some kind of signal when it was okay to move forward and begin the discussion.

Oberon pulled out a notebook and scribbled something onto the pad. "I'm just making note of who was present during this discussion," he told no one in particular. "My notes will be very generic," he continued. "The date, the time, who attended." He put down the pen and returned the pad to his pocket. "Nothing else will be recorded unless it is requested and agreed upon by the majority." Oberon looked to Avery, willing to give him additional time if he wanted it.

Avery shook his head once. Oberon nodded then turned to face Alex. "Queen Alexandria you now have the floor." He grinned at her, knowing that always made her uncomfortable.

"Thank you," Alex said deciding to ignore the formality. "We are here because some new information has come to light in the situation involving Patricia and Lawson Dillinger," she began.

Victor straightened. He had been watching Alex closely and knew something was up. They were about to get bad news, he was sure of it. He just didn't know how bad or how it was going to impact his family.

Chaos

Alex turned to Oberon. "Do you have a preference which item we discuss first?"

Oberon studied the room. Where to start? "Why don't you let me begin?" he finally decided. "After reviewing all the evidence and additional documentation provided on this case, the council still had a few questions. We weren't willing to make conclusions or render a verdict until those questions were answered," Oberon explained. "At that point we compelled Patricia to testify. We were pleasantly surprised that she actually cooperated. During this testimony, she admitted to something that we felt all of you should know." Oberon paused to turn toward Foster. "Your mother admitted to using her potion on your sister, Dannica." Oberon took another long, frustrated breath and released it. "I'm sorry. She was determined to create these paladins and clung to the idea that if Dannica was the first one, it would somehow give her additional power or standing in the community." Oberon glanced at the Keisser's, but Victor and his father remained perfectly still.

"I knew that," Foster said. "Remember, I told you that mom put that stuff in some cookies and made Lawson take them to her. That's when dad got so mad at mom and Danni got sick."

"She did it more than once," Avery said softly. "It was frequently and on a regular basis. Every time Atticus left town on a hunt, Lawson took cookies to Dannica. Your mother and Lawson were very careful to hide it from you and your father after that first incident. The doses were low, that's why Dannica never got sick again. Patricia thought extended exposure to the stuff would eventually change Dannica's chemistry." Avery paused and glanced at Atticus. "I suppose she was right about that."

"So mom was getting crazier because her mother and her brother were secretly poisoning her?" Victor asked in horror. "I had to endure years of torture and dad lost everything because those two maniacs thought it might be fun to see how far they could push their ridiculous experiments?" Victor was furious. His mother had ruined his life...and his father's life. Now, right when he was finally coming to grips with his past and actually putting it behind him, the tables turned again. His mother was actually a victim in all of this as well. "My mother was insane," Victor said softly. "But apparently simple, everyday insanity wasn't enough for good old Grandma Dillinger, she needed to enhance the craziness just for kicks. I feel so much better knowing I'm linked genetically to that nutcase!"

"Victor," Atticus said sternly watching Foster. "We can deal with this. We've dealt with much worse," he frowned. Could he have helped his wife if he had known about the poison? Could he have prevented this from getting so out of hand if he had just paid more attention to Dannica?

"Stop it dad," Victor barked. "I know you're trying to blame yourself for this. If I didn't know about the poison, you couldn't have known. So, how could you have prevented it?" he challenged.

"I don't know," Atticus admitted solemnly.

"I was the one being tortured," Victor continued. "I was the one that saw the crazy, irrational side of her. Not you. If anyone should have picked up on this, I should have. But I didn't. The transition was gradual," Victor said remembering how things had gotten worse and worse over the years. "We talked about this. There were two distinct turning points or triggers as I always thought of them, but it was all very gradual. There was nothing you or I could have done to help her."

"But I should have," Foster said resigned. "I should have known. I should have seen it." Foster turned to Victor and Atticus.

Chaos

"I want you to know I realize now that I was wrong," he paused, "I was so wrong about everything." He lowered his head in regret running his hands through his hair. "I wish I had it all to do over again. Sure, mom and dad pushed me to brainwash Dannica. I didn't think it was brainwashing at the time, but now I know it was. They hated the warriors, so they pushed us kids to hate you, too. When I saw what Danni was doing to Victor, I didn't believe it was wrong. I didn't look at it the same as I would have if she was harming a fae child. I honestly believed the warriors were monsters. I encouraged her to continue. I gave her ideas." Foster closed his eyes in agony. "I helped my sister torture a small child and never thought twice about it. How did I become that person? I know you will never forgive me, but I am so sorry for everything I did back then," Foster said looking directly at Victor.

Victor studied Foster. The man looked terrible. This was all having a profound effect on him. When this was over, Foster would never be the same. Victor and his father could just go on with their lives. Things would basically be the same for them as it was before. They had already dealt with most of this years ago. But, it was all new to Foster. "I understand," he finally said quietly. He didn't forgive him. Foster was the catalyst for the most severe torture techniques his mother experimented with when Victor was a child. He felt pity and compassion for this man who was technically his uncle, but he wouldn't exonerate him. Foster needed to accept responsibility for his actions.

"Once you are finished with my mother and my brother, I assume the council will have a hearing on my actions as well," Foster inquired.

"No. We won't," Avery answered sternly. "I think everyone in this room has suffered enough over the sadistic machinations of Patricia Dillinger."

"Avery is right," Oberon agreed. "Once we are finished with this conversation, I believe everyone will concur. This is over. The lies and deceit, the plots and scheming will stop. Each of you will have to take the new information, all of it, and carve out a new life for yourself. It's our hope you will all be able to put the past behind you and move forward."

"But I've committed a crime," Foster began.

"In part I agree," Oberon told him. "You should have stood up for a young boy in need. You should have gone to the authorities, but you didn't. You are going to have to live with that. You will have to figure out a way to make things right between you and the Keisser's, if that's even possible. But you will not be charged with a crime. You have enough to deal with Foster, let this go for now." Oberon turned to Atticus and Victor. "Do either of you wish to file a complaint against Foster for his crimes?"

"No," Atticus said at once.

"Victor?" Oberon asked.

Victor studied Foster. He was suffering enough, he didn't need to be punished for something he had done so many years ago. "No," he finally told the room. "I want the whole mess to be dropped. Like you said Foster has to live with what he did. That's enough for me."

"Then it's over," Obcron said locking eyes with Avery. Avery nodded in acceptance. Oberon turned to Alex. "Do either of you have any objections?"

"No," Alex and Dimitri said together.

Chaos

Oberon made a quick note on his pad and continued. "Atticus," Oberon said turning to face him. "I wonder if you could fill us in on the discovery of that box."

Atticus looked confused for a moment then understood. "Oh. Yes," he answered looking cautiously at Foster. "Well, as you know I was having a bit of trouble at my place in Pennsylvania. At first it started out harmless enough but then someone tried to kill my horses, and then they tried to kill me. I was lucky, Ty came by just in time. That's when I moved to the fort so Victor could keep an eye on me," he flashed a smile toward his son. "A short time later Tala joined our group. She assisted me in my efforts to track down the culprit." He paused, but continued when Oberon nodded his approval.

"Well anyway, after I left, my home was completely destroyed. I figured it was the Dillinger's. It was the only thing that made any sense to me. I assumed they didn't like my recent freedom. But Ty insisted all the bombs were made by the same person, including the ones that destroyed the shifter camps. Of course, I believed him. There's nobody better with bombs than Ty and he had dealt with all of them, but it still didn't make sense. I knew why they would be after me, but what did the Dillinger's have against the shifters? Tala wasn't convinced I was right no matter how adamant I was. She initially had everyone I knew on her suspect list and refused to limit the scope of her investigation to that family. It took time, but she finally caved and agreed to start her investigation by focusing on the Dillinger's. That's when the two of us headed out to the old farm to check things out. We were looking for evidence to prove Lawson's guilt… or to rule him out. If the Dillinger's were involved we knew we would have to find evidence that linked Lawson or his family to the harassment at my place and the bombs."

Foster was studying Atticus. He knew the council had evidence that Lawson was responsible for all the bombings, but he didn't know what it was or where it came from.

"And did you?" Oberon asked.

"We did," Atticus confirmed. "We found plenty, but we also found that box you're talking about. It was about the size of a woman's jewelry box but it had this strange lock on it. It was like no lock I'd ever seen before. I couldn't open it, neither could Tala. We ended up handing the thing over to the council. We had enough evidence to prove Lawson's guilt, so we didn't need to know what was inside the box, but we thought it might be important to you guys."

"I see," Oberon paused. "Where in the farmhouse did you find it?"

"Oh, sorry." Atticus took a deep breath. "It was down stairs, under George's workbench. It looked old, so we assumed it belonged to him. We knew Lawson had been using the space to build his explosives, but it didn't look like the box had been opened in a very long time. We both came to the same conclusion... it must have belonged to George."

"Thank you," Oberon told him then turned back to Avery. "You want to take it from here?"

Avery pushed himself away from the wall and slowly walked toward the couch to stand next to Foster. He quietly sat down and studied the man. "You doing okay, son?" he asked with compassion.

Foster nodded in the affirmative.

Chaos

"Foster, you know I was a close friend of your father's before his death," Avery began.

Foster nodded again.

"But there are some things that you don't know," he said never taking his eyes off Foster. "George was always uh..."

"Lazy," Oberon supplied.

Avery scowled. "Not exactly," he paused, "Well, yes. I suppose you could say he was lazy," Avery conceded. "George had grandiose ideas. He very strongly believed the monarchy should belong to him and his family. He never could forget that dream. I had no idea he was trying to create a special race to help him get the throne back, but to be honest I'm not that surprised. George's father, your grandfather, was also obsessed with the idea of reclaiming the monarchy. He was not a nice man. To be honest, Walter Dillinger was a tyrant. His life was spent on two things; complaining about the injustice his family had to endure, and belittling those around him. It was difficult to witness the abuse he inflicted on his wife and children, it was inexcusable." Avery paused clearly reliving some memory from the past. "George hated his father, but he still clung to the ridiculous notion he could somehow regain power. He thought it would make his father proud somehow. I'll never understand it." Avery shook his head in disbelief. "Anyway the obsession, the brainwashing, all of what you were exposed to Foster, was centuries in the making. Darren Dillinger really didn't care about the loss of the throne. In fact, I believe it was a huge relief to turn that responsibility over to someone else. It's ironic his lack of passion caused so much hate and discontent in his offspring.

I guess what I'm trying to explain is that your father did not grow up feeling loved. Not from anyone. There was no compassion in that home, only obsession. Walter was a tyrant and his wife was distant. They were all miserable. George didn't understand what a family was supposed to be like. All he knew was what he had lived… the reality he had grown up with. When George met Patricia he wasn't looking for love."

"You don't think dad loved my mother?" Foster asked offended.

"I know George didn't love Patricia," Avery said confidently. "Not really."

"Foster, Patricia was basically a meal ticket for your father. A means to an end," Oberon supplied.

Avery glared at Oberon. "That's not exactly true," he countered. "Sure, Patricia's family had money and George believed he could take advantage of that, but it wasn't the only reason he married Patricia. George did care about Patricia in the beginning, but it was a marriage of convenience I guess you could say. George wanted a wife, he wanted heirs. Patricia's family money was just an added bonus. George hoped he and Patricia would get a monthly allowance so he wouldn't have to work for a living, but he would have married Patricia even if she were poor. Patricia wanted a husband and she quickly became obsessed with George's goal of regaining the monarchy. They had a common goal. Patricia believed very strongly that one day she would be the Fae Queen. She was never in love with George just as George never loved Patricia. They met, they dated, they decided they were compatible and they married. I know that sounds callous, but it really is that simple."

"And the hits just keep on coming," Foster sighed. "I always knew mom and dad didn't have what you would call an affectionate relationship, but I thought they loved each other. I thought they were happy together, or at least content. Was everything I ever believed a complete lie?" Foster leaned back against the couch in defeat.

"I'm sorry, Foster but I think the answer to that question is yes," Avery said somberly. "This story gets worse before it gets better."

"I can hardly wait," Foster mumbled.

"Uh...Oberon?" Victor took advantage of the pause in their conversation to remind everyone he and Atticus were still there. "Should we leave now?" He could tell Foster was getting upset and they were starting to talk about private, family matters. Victor felt out of place. He was sure his father felt the same.

"No. Stay," Foster said without moving. "They're talking about your ancestor's too. I think you need to know this as much as I do. I sense a big reveal coming. You don't want to miss the real fun."

"Are you sure?" Atticus asked Foster.

"I am," Foster nodded slightly. "Go ahead Avery, continue."

Avery didn't speak. He wasn't sure where to go from here. How could he break the news to Foster? The room remained silent for several long, uncomfortable minutes. Finally Avery took a deep breath and spoke. "I don't know how to tell you the rest but I'll do my best." Avery sighed then glanced around the room. All eyes were on him. Alex, Dimitri and Oberon were looking at him in sympathy, the rest in anticipation. "Initially Patricia's family did give the couple a monthly stipend. But after a few years her parents grew frustrated with both Patricia and George. They didn't understand the unwavering obsession the two had with the monarchy and they were extremely disappointed in George's lack of ambition. Frankly, they had trouble reconciling the two. How did someone so lazy and unmotivated think he could be a king?" Avery paused to shift his weight.

"Eventually they cut off Patricia's funds completely. They told George he had to prove himself. If George wanted to start up some kind of business they would help out, but they insisted the couple needed to become self-sufficient. George took on odd jobs, just enough to get by. A short time later Patricia became pregnant with Lawson. I know George believed that once the child was born, Patricia's parents would reinstate their funds. They didn't. A few years later Patricia became pregnant with Dannica. George worked just enough over the years to buy the farm and keep it running. Then he began the chemistry experiments. I'm ashamed to say I had no idea what George was up to. I knew he'd become obsessed with his chemistry, but I honestly believed he was trying to perfect some concoction that would make him rich. That way he wouldn't have to work odd jobs or the farm. A short time later he inherited the hotel.

As you know, George came into that small hotel quite by accident. He unwittingly helped a woman in need and was rewarded a few years later when she passed away and left him the hotel in her will. George had no interest in running the business, but he soon discovered he could make money off the place with very little effort. That's the only reason he kept it at the time."

Hearing Avery talk about his father this way was embarrassing. Foster knew his dad was lazy and lacked ambition. He just hated it voiced in such a blunt manner in public. Avery was obviously leading up to something, Foster just hoped he would get to the point soon.

Chaos

"You have done wonders with the business Foster. Your parents would be so proud," he paused to let that sink in a little. When nobody commented Avery continued. "George just happened to be at the hotel one evening when a striking young woman arrived looking for a room. George was smitten immediately. It was love at first sight, which was amazing in and of itself. Prior to this George had never felt real love. The woman, Mary Jane Bowers, was just passing through. She had inherited a small cabin and some farm land from her uncle and wanted to see it before she listed it for sale. The land was a few miles out of town. George volunteered to escort her the following morning. The two became immediate friends. Mary Jane was enamored with George and decided to not only keep the cabin, but she moved there permanently. George couldn't stay away. He pampered her constantly. I have to admit, George was happier during that time in his life than I had ever seen him. Eventually the friendship turned into more. George confided in me early on in the relationship. He was truly in love with Mary Jane. He was a different person around her. Loving Mary Jane made George a better person, the person I believe he was meant to be. The two continued their relationship for several years. Finally George knew what he had to do. He decided to divorce Patricia."

"What?" Foster exclaimed. "Dad never divorced my mother."

"No, he didn't," Avery agreed. "Your father was never married to your mother."

Foster stared at Avery wide eyed. What exactly was he saying? That this Mary Jane woman was his mother? Impossible.

Both Victor and Atticus focused their attention on Avery. Was he saying what they thought he was saying? If that was true, it explained why Foster was the most normal sibling of the bunch. Maybe there was hope for the guy after all.

"I don't think George told anyone else about his decision to end his marriage," Avery continued. "I do think Patricia knew something was amiss. George had stopped the chemistry experiments completely. Once he began seeing Mary Jane, he spent more and more time at the hotel. The place was actually taking off, not just surviving but thriving. For the first time in George's life he had ambition. He wanted something more and he was willing to work for it."

"So what happened?" Atticus asked. He knew George. The guy had zero ambition and was unhappy and depressed most of the time.

"Mary Ann got pregnant," Avery answered. "With you, Foster."

Foster was shaking his head. This was not happening. This was impossible. There was no way some random woman he never met was his mother. He'd spent his entire life looking after Patricia...that was his mother. She had to be. Otherwise the burden he'd carried for so long was for nothing.

"I know it's hard to believe, but let me finish the story," Avery pled. "Once you hear it all, you'll understand."

"Fine," Foster said trying to act nonchalant but knowing he'd failed. "Go ahead." Foster gave a little wave of his hand to signal Avery to continue.

"Well, of course Patricia was livid. She wasn't about to share the throne with anyone. She'd married George because she was intent on becoming queen. She wouldn't tolerate his working at the hotel instead of perfecting his serum. Again, I had no idea what they were concocting out there but now it all makes more sense. At the time, I still believed he was trying to come up with some money making scam that would help with farming. George was always very careful when he talked about his chemistry experiments. He kept things vague and mysterious. I never gave it a second thought. That was just typical George.

To appease Patricia, George began working on the potion again. He spent less time at the hotel because all of his free time was spent visiting Mary Jane. He was so excited they were going to have a child together. It was the family and the life George had always wanted, but never knew to hope for. It was during this same period that I was appointed to the council. I didn't have as much free time anymore, so I rarely saw George. When I did see him, he looked haggard and worried. I ran into him one night and pulled him aside to find out what was going on. He told me Patricia was threatening him. She found out about Mary Jane and she wanted him to end the relationship. He still wanted a divorce but he hadn't figured out a plan yet. He also told me Mary Jane was seriously ill. He was extremely worried about her and didn't know if she could even survive the pregnancy. Many of our kind didn't back then. Things are still difficult, but not anywhere near the level it was centuries ago.

I tried to convince George to divorce Patricia anyway. Whatever the threat, she wouldn't win. And he didn't have to worry about her being taken care of. She could return to her parents. They had the finances to support her and I knew they would. George needed to move on and actually have a happy life with Mary Jane. We had a pretty lengthy discussion and by the end, I thought he was going to do the right thing. But for some reason he didn't take care of things right away.

A few months later, George was still married to Patricia and Mary Jane gave birth to you, Foster. Unfortunately, Mary Jane died in the process. George was devastated. Of course Patricia was thrilled. The threat had been removed and she could still become queen."

"Did anyone investigate that?" Victor asked sharply. "Are you sure she died naturally in child birth and wasn't conveniently murdered by that psychotic maniac at just the right moment?"

Avery jerked his head toward Oberon. "No," he told Victor. "That wasn't ever considered. It wasn't common knowledge that George was unfaithful to Patricia. She was never suspected of wrong doing. I, as did George, believed the pregnancy was just too hard on Mary Jane. She died while giving birth like so many others had."

"I think we have something else to discuss with Patricia tomorrow," Oberon said soberly. "I agree with Victor. Mary Jane may have been Patricia's first victim. She certainly had motive and from what I understand opportunity. With Mary Jane gone, Patricia's life went back to the way it had been before George got involved with another woman. It's all too convenient."

Avery sighed. How had he missed that? But George didn't see it either. He'd think about that later, right now he needed to finish the story. "So there George was, faced with trying to raise a child on his own without a mother. If that wasn't enough he still had to provide for his other two children. At the time he was also trying to deal with the loss of the only person he had ever loved, except his children of course. George knew Mary Jane was the only person that had ever truly loved him. As you can imagine, he was devastated. Mary Jane was laid to rest and George took you home to be raised by Patricia. At first she wasn't thrilled about it. She didn't want another woman's child growing up in her home. But she agreed, to appease George. She knew she had to if she wanted to remain his wife and, in her mind, the queen someday. Later, she saw the wisdom. Especially when you grew up and expanded the business, Foster. Patricia was grateful George had a third child. You are the only one that did anything to take care of Patricia. Dannica didn't have a chance. Patricia only has herself to blame for that one, but Lawson is worse than his father ever was. You Foster, you take after your mother. Thanks to you, Patricia was able to move into that penthouse and pamper herself day and night."

Foster wasn't moving. He was barely breathing. Was it possible Patricia had killed his mother? Was Avery's story true? It seemed like a work of fiction, like a made up story in a book or a magazine. He needed proof. He needed something tangible to convince him the story was actually real.

Oberon moved forward and handed the small box to Foster. "This was your father's," he told Foster softly. "Everything inside that box pertains to Mary Jane."

Foster reached out and took the box. He didn't know if he wanted to look inside. Seeing the contents would actually make this nightmare real.

"Foster, if you don't remember anything else I tell you today, please remember how much your father loved your mother. Mary Jane that is," Avery added. "I know you haven't met your mate yet. I think Patricia has been holding you back, but that's just my opinion. When you do, you will know just how much your father loved your mother. I hope you will hold out for that kind of love," he turned to Alex. "It's the kind of love Alex has for Dimitri. The kind of love Oberon shares with Mara. The love I was lucky enough to find in my Gracie. It's the kind of love that's worth waiting for.

I finally witnessed that same love in your father. Mary Jane meant more to George than life itself. When he lost her, he lost his desire to live. From that day forward George simply existed. I strongly believe that you are the only thing that got him through the pain, Foster. He couldn't trust Patricia with you if he were gone. The loss of a mate is a powerful thing. So, George gathered up all his memories of his dear love and saved them in that box. It also contains a journal that belonged to Mary Jane. I think if you read it as well as the letters your father wrote your mother, you will understand the passion those two had for each other." Avery sighed. "This whole mess is such a tragedy."

Foster wouldn't look in the box tonight. He needed time to digest this. Time to come to grips with his new reality. Everything he had believed was a lie. His entire life was a lie. Everyone had lied, including Avery. "Why did you hide this from me? You knew Patricia wasn't my mother, but you allowed me to care for her, to protect her, to sacrifice for her long after my father died. Why did you do that?"

Avery knew this was coming but he'd hoped Foster wouldn't bring it up tonight. "I made a promise to your father. George asked me to keep the secret at all cost. He said he'd caused Patricia enough pain. He didn't want anyone to know he'd betrayed her, especially not you. He was afraid you wouldn't love her if you knew she wasn't your mother. You know George set up a trust making sure Patricia never lost that farm. He felt responsible for her. He believed it was his fault she was so cynical and a little demented. Patricia is difficult to love, George knew nobody else would step in after his death and take care of her. He also realized you had the compassion and kindness of your mother, Mary Jane. He begged me until I swore to him I'd never tell."

Chaos

"Didn't you just break that promise?" Foster asked. "Another lie?"

"I guess I did," Avery admitted. "But now that the council knows about Mary Jane, I thought it would be better if you heard it from me, someone that had firsthand knowledge of the situation. I thought maybe I could help you understand. I also promised your father I would watch out for you. I told him I would always be there for you and I would do my best to protect you. I'm afraid I've failed you in most ways. I believe it's time you know the truth. That's how I can keep my promise now. I am here for you Foster. I always have been. Don't let all the secrets destroy your life. Your father was so proud of you. He loved you and your mother. That is real. You can deal with all the rest if you just remember those two things."

Atticus studied Foster. The man's life had just been turned upside down. Nothing was what it seemed anymore. He still disliked the man, but right now he also felt sorry for him.

"So, is there any other good news you want to share tonight?" Foster finally asked. "Because I think I've about reached my tolerance."

"No. There's nothing else," Avery told him.

"Foster?" Alex inquired. "There is one thing I need to talk to you about before you leave."

Foster sighed and turned toward Alex. "Yes, ma'am?" He tried to sound civil but was pretty sure he'd failed.

Alex smiled, at least he was trying. "The council will be holding the sentencing hearing on Patricia and Lawson in a week or so. We'd like you and the Keisser's to be there."

Foster studied Alex intently. Why did he have to be at the sentencing? "What if I can't make it?" he finally asked.

"Well," Alex began. "I'm making this a request because I'd like you there willingly, but it's important. If I have to, I will make it mandatory," she said gently.

"I see," Foster said in understanding. "Then I don't have a choice. I'll be there. I'll need to know when and where."

"Someone will let you know once the details are finalized," Alex assured him. She watched silently as Foster slowly stood and excused himself. Avery followed him out. Atticus and Victor stood with the intention of leaving as well but stopped when Alex called to them.

"There's one more thing I need to talk to you about Atticus," Alex said softly.

Atticus looked at Victor then the two of them sat back down. "Go ahead," he told her politely.

"It's about your future," she began. "Dimitri and I were wondering if you are still willing to stay on at the fort for a while. I realize things have changed a bit since the last time we talked, but if Tala's willing, we were hoping you would commit to the next year." She paused waiting for a reaction. She didn't get much of one.

"I think that's a good idea dad," Victor put in. "The farm in Lancaster is gone. It's going to take a while to rebuild. In the meantime your horses are already at the fort. Maybe you and Tala could stay there and help out."

Chaos

"What would I be doing at the fort?" Atticus asked. He wasn't a free loader and he wouldn't stay if Alex was offering charity. He and Tala could stay at the apartment in New York. He'd help out at the shelter to pay his way.

"Well, that's up to you," she admitted. "I'm in the market for a headmaster for the academy, though. I'd love it if you would accept the job." She smiled at him. "The kids have completed the bunkers. They're set up and ready for additional students. Orin and Breena have agreed to stay on for at least a year. That will give Breena time to have the baby. They've moved out of the farmhouse and into a two bedroom apartment on the fort. Tony and Megan won't commit to a full year, but they are willing to head back out once the DeLacy's leave for Dublin. Tony wants to spend time with his parents until they leave. I don't think Charles and Elizabeth are going to be here much longer though. Elizabeth said they have a few problems to deal with back home that can't be put off much longer."

"Morrigan is also staying on for a while," Dimitri added. "I'm grateful for that. He seems to enjoy it out there and he's good with the kids. I was worried about the shifter contingent. We don't know that much about them or how they fight. Morrigan is a lifesaver from our perspective."

"It sounds like you have everything taken care of," Atticus surmised. "Why do you need me?"

"Jake and Marta will be moving out to the fort in the next few days. Jake is bringing out a contractor so they can add on to the bakery. He wants to build a house onto the existing building so they are close to the business. They've agreed to stay for at least a year as well. If the bakery takes off the way we think it will, that arrangement will last a lot longer," she paused. "We don't just want the academy to be a fighting school. We want it to be a way for these kids to prepare for their future. The treaty is broken. Life is going to change for everyone, forever."

"What do you mean?" Victor asked.

"Orin has agreed to teach sword fighting, and he's also good with daggers. Breena is the best when it comes to using herbs for medicinal purposes. You already know I've asked Sam to come up with a 'how to' on archery. Then we have the droids for hand to hand and the Sims and the obstacle course. I think we're covered there, unless Atticus is willing to take on a couple courses in combat," she suggested.

"I might be," Atticus agreed.

"Jake can also help a little in that area. Since he married Marta, I don't think his heart is in hunting anymore," Alex thought out loud. "But I think he'll get a kick out of teaching the kids."

"His heart wasn't in it before that," Dimitri countered. "I don't think he's really wanted to participate since Luke died. He helps out here and there, but he really doesn't want anything to do with it anymore. I've been planning to talk to him about retiring, but we've needed him lately. I really think it's time for him to move on and the academy is a perfect solution for all of us. Now that he's married to Marta he's even less interested."

"I can understand that," Victor added. "Jake waited a long time before he allowed himself to accept his love for Marta and start a life together. Now that he has her, he doesn't want to do anything to risk that. He's more careful about his own safety these days." He paused. "I can relate. I'm a lot more careful now that I have Ariel. I don't take as many chances with the vamps as I used to."

Chaos

"Don't get any ideas," Dimitri warned. "You're not quitting yet. I can't afford to lose any more warriors."

Victor grinned. "I'm not asking to retire yet, gramps. Unlike you, I can hunt and still have a relationship."

Alex looked up, instantly studying Dimitri. He hadn't been going out hunting lately. Had he retired? But why? "Dimitri?" she called.

Dimitri scowled at Victor then turned to Alex. "Yes?"

"When is it your turn to hunt again?" She tried to sound innocent but she was annoyed.

"I'm the leader, I hunt when I decide to hunt," he said evasively.

"And when will that be exactly? This week? Next week? I realize you still can't use Thomas because the tabloids have seen him with Abby. It's difficult for him to go out and not be followed. Nick and Dante have been doing great, but Victor's here in town now. Why aren't the two of you giving Nick and Dante a break?"

Dimitri narrowed his eyes at Victor. "We will discuss this later," he hissed then he turned back to Alex. "We'll talk about it alone. Maybe I will go out in the next couple weeks."

Now Alex was pissed. "Why are you staying home? You love hunting. You're amazing at it. I want an explanation. And I want it now," she demanded.

"Later," Dimitri told her. "Right now we have business to discuss with Atticus and Victor."

Alex glared at the man she loved. He was so infuriating, but he was right. She needed to deal with Victor and Atticus then she'd deal with Dimitri. "Fine," she said giving Dimitri an icy stare. "Jake has agreed to teach a course on trusts," Alex continued, not taking her eyes off Dimitri. "Our people live a long time." She finally turned to focus on Atticus again. "Sure, everyone figures things out eventually, but why not include a course at the academy to help them diversify their money and juggle their property when they have to change identities. I also thought Tala could teach a basic investigation course if she's willing. Orin's great with finances. He's agreed to teach a budgeting class. But I still need someone to oversee it all. I'm offering that position to you, Atticus. You don't have to answer now. Talk to Tala and let me know. I can give you a little time, but not much. The rooms are ready for the kids, Sam and Ty have completed the Sims and Sam says the last order of droids should arrive any day. Ty and Sam are still working on the goggles for the obstacle course, but everything should be ready in a week or so. Dimitri and I have already started reviewing applications and choosing the first group. All I need is a head master." She grinned at Atticus, "I'd love that to be you."

"Wow," Atticus said surprised. "You've accomplished a lot in our absence."

"I can't take credit," Alex admitted. "Ty and Sam have done most of it, so have those kids. Morrigan's a lifesaver. Everyone came together so well and the plan is ready to be implemented."

"It's a huge weight off our shoulders," Dimitri admitted. "There are so many other things going on. Alex and I can't leave the city for long until the ordeal with the Dillinger's is over. We also want to stick around and make sure Kahn gets what's coming to him. The human justice system is a little slower than ours though. Thomas and Abby will remain here in New York, too. They can't

Chaos

really leave the city and they certainly can't visit the fort. We don't want reporters snooping around out there. We've put a lot of pressure on Bastian and Kylee. They're going to stay at the fort until they can figure out the Melissa situation. Unfortunately, that means they won't be much help to you. Ty said he and Sam can stay another week or so but then Ty has to head out to California, something to do with his new game. Morrigan is willing to stay as long as we need him. I think you'll have plenty of help out there with Jake and Marta joining you in a few days. If you agree to take this on we were thinking of starting with about a hundred kids then going from there. We're going to need additional instructors as we add more kids. But I thought that would be a good number to start with."

"That's a lot of kids," Victor said looking at his father. "Do you think you can handle that many?"

"I haven't taken the job yet," Atticus smiled. "But with Jake, Marta, Breena, Orin, Morrigan, Bastian and Kylee all there I think we'll manage. I'll also have Tala to help me and later we might be able to put Tony and Megan to work. Plus, Ty and Sam will be a big help until they have to leave for California. I don't see a problem."

"Ariel and I will be able to help off and on," Victor added. "But I need a little time. Up until last week we've spent all our time at the fort. I need a few days to take care of things here in the city. After that we're available again, unless Dimitri or Alex need us here that is."

"We'll play that by ear," Dimitri told Victor. "So far Nick and Dante have been able to handle the streets and the few remaining vamps. I'm worried about the long absence, though. That might mean Radek is building a massive army. Nick and Dante haven't had any real trouble for weeks, just small groups here and there. We may want to explore the possibility of taking the offensive again before we find ourselves out numbered facing hundreds, maybe thousands of vampires."

"I agree," Victor said soberly. "We're preparing for battle, but so is Radek. I'm sure of it. We may need to meet in the near future and develop a strategy."

Victor and Atticus stood to leave. "We'll see you at the hearing," Victor told them as the two men strolled out the door.

* * * *

Atticus and Victor stepped onto the front porch and paused. Both men silently gazing into the darkness, thoughts running rapidly through their minds. Victor was the first to spot Foster. He turned to address the man but stopped when Foster addressed him first.

"I was wondering if I could have a word before you go," Foster said hesitantly.

"Sure," Victor said trying to sound casual.

"Avery told me they want us at the sentencing hearing because the council plans to order restitution," Foster paused.

"I don't want anything from those maniacs," Victor said angrily.

"Good. I don't either," Foster smiled. "I was thinking... we're not the only victims here. The human families involved in this actually do need the money. It's entirely up to you, but I plan to give my restitution to the humans."

Chaos

"What did you have in mind?" Atticus asked, intrigued.

"I don't know. I didn't really have a plan. I wanted to talk to the two of you first," Foster paused. "I needed to know how you felt and if you were willing to give up your share. Uh, I've kind of already looked into the personal lives of the women Patricia and Lawson killed."

"And what did you find?" Victor asked. He'd been planning to do the same thing but hadn't had a chance yet.

"They're all struggling," he said soberly. "The first victim, Regina, was helping her grandmother out at the food stand because Ethel has a medical condition; bad heart. The long days are hard on her which is making her condition worse. She's gone back to manning the stand herself but if she keeps up the long days, she's not going to live much longer. Her heart can't handle it."

"And Tina?" Victor asked soberly.

"Tina was a single mother. She made enough as an aerobics instructor to make ends meet, but she didn't have anything extra. Her son, Bobby, is four. Tina's sister, Kathy immediately took custody of Bobby. She was struggling to juggle the added responsibility when Bobby got sick. She had to stay home with him for over a week and eventually got fired, for unrelated issues of course. Her employer knows they couldn't let her go legally over the sick leave so they conjured up another excuse. Now, Kathy and Bobby are about to get evicted from their apartment. Kathy still hasn't been able to find another job. Nothing pays well enough to cover living expenses and daycare and most employers won't allow children in the workplace.

You know about Melissa. What you might not know is that she had a boyfriend. A really nice, down-to-earth guy that has pretty much shut down since the incident. He too lost his job and for now he doesn't care. The apartment manager is cutting him a little slack on the rent, but that won't last much longer. The guy's a wreck. I tried to talk to him, but he rarely leaves the apartment. He rarely does anything including eat. He's making himself sick, but he doesn't seem to care."

"So you want to give whatever restitution the council orders to these three to help them deal with their troubles?" Atticus asked.

"Sort of," Foster admitted. "I haven't worked it all out yet. I was hoping you could help me with that. Dad gave mom the farm in a trust so she had a place to stay forever. Mom hates the farm anyway and I certainly don't want it. I thought I would start by trying to undo that trust. I'm going to ask the council to take the farm away based on mom's criminal actions, but I don't know if that's possible. If I can free up the property, I thought I'd offer it to Kathy. With a little work it would be a great place for Bobby to grow up. I also have a hotel out that way, Kathy has book keeping skills from her previous job. I could use her at the hotel keeping the books and scheduling rooms. There's a small cubby just off the reception area she could turn into a playroom for Bobby until he starts school. That way she doesn't have to worry about daycare."

Victor and Atticus stared at Foster. This was certainly a side of him they had never seen before. Maybe he did take after his mother after all.

Foster shrugged a little embarrassed. "It's just an idea," he finally told them.

"It's a great idea," Victor assured him. "She'll need funds to fix up the farm but it shouldn't take much to get her back on her feet. Jake can probably help break the trust if the council can't take care of it. What did you have in mind for Regina's grandmother?"

Chaos

"I don't know. I didn't really get past Kathy. I don't know how to help Regina's grandmother or Melissa's boyfriend. Well, there's the obvious, pay the guys rent for a while until we see what happens with the girl. But that doesn't seem like helping. I know there's a chance his girlfriend might not make it. If we pay his rent that's kind of enabling him to become a recluse and just shut down. I also don't know how to help Ethel. Money would help with medical bills and rent, but she seems to love the food business. I don't think she's ready to retire. I honestly don't know how to help her, either."

Victor was thinking. There had to be a way to help all of these people. Foster was right, paying the guys rent would give him a place to live, but it wouldn't help him long term. They needed another solution. "Let me talk to the boyfriend, what was his name?"

"John Sinclair," Foster said immediately.

"Do you know what he did before he got fired?" Victor pressed.

"Sure, well kind of. He worked for some computer company. I think he's an IT guy or something," Foster supplied.

"Well, everyone can use an IT guy. If he's good, I don't think he'll have any problem landing another job," Victor said confidently. "Especially with a little help."

"You have to get him to leave the apartment first. He won't go willingly," Foster warned.

"I think I can help with that," Atticus said soberly. "I have a little experience with trying to shut out the world."

Foster cringed. "I really am sorry about that," he began.

"Let's not go there right now," Atticus insisted. "I think we've spent enough time discussing the past tonight. No more old memories."

"Ethel is a difficult one," Victor mused. "Sure we could pay her medical bills no problem, but how do we help her work at the food stand part time and not lose the business? Let's think about the situation for a few days and meet up before the sentencing. I agree with you Foster, I don't want any money from those two maniacs. I'm more than willing to have them pay restitution to their victims but that could take a long time. Those people don't have time." Victor glanced at his father. "I'm willing to foot the bill in the meantime or we can pool our money and help these guys out now. Then the restitution can continue to help them in the future."

"I agree," Atticus nodded. "Let's take care of this ourselves and the council can worry about making Patricia and Foster pay for their bad deeds as they see fit."

The three men went their separate ways, each of them considering the situation. They all wanted to help the Dillinger's victims. The question was, how should they help?

* * * *

Radek stood in the opening of his large cave. Well, to be accurate, it was more like a cave city than a simple cave. When he originally moved to America, the place had been much smaller. Over the years he had ordered his vampires to carve out additional caverns making it a large maze of rooms and hallways that encompassed most of the enormous mountain that housed it. The construction and massive remodeling projects took centuries to build, but they were finally completed decades ago. So many things had changed since he first arrived in America, both good and bad.

Radek gazed at the setting sun and sighed. He always hated this time of night. Before, when he used to hunt for himself, he thought of it as a time of torture. It was twilight. The sun was still too high for vampires to leave their protective cover, but dark enough to tempt them. It was like Mother Nature was teasing his species, daring them to accept the challenge and pay the price for their impatience. As a young vampire, night after night, year after year, he stood in his father's cave waiting for the sun to finally sink below the horizon, yearning for the darkness to swallow the expanse so the hunting could begin. He never was a patient man. The years hadn't changed that. Radek scowled. Now, instead of waiting minutes to begin the thrill of the hunt, he had waited months without reward. He didn't think he could stand it much longer. He wanted his kingdom. He wanted to conquer this area, create an heir and move on to punish the four kings that were aligning themselves against him.

Radek had learned quite by accident the previous evening that DeMarco, the Canadian King, had joined up with Maedoc, Typhon and Ammit. Apparently DeMarco was angry that Radek had sent a team of vampires into Canada to build his army. The four kings were now allies. If Radek didn't watch his step, he'd find himself at war with all of them. He was so enraged by that knowledge he wanted to scream. How dare they threaten him? They thought they could control him but they were wrong, not forever. He was at war. This was his kingdom. He could run it any way he saw fit. But right now he couldn't. He didn't have a large enough army to wage war against the vampires as well as the fae. He took a deep breath to settle himself. In time, he promised himself. It was just a matter of time. Soon the war with the fae would be over and he would have countless shifters begging him to take them as his lover. Once he impregnated one of them, he would have his heir. A vampire like no other, an idol among his species. His son would be ruthless and unstoppable, Radek would make sure of that. Then in a few years, he would begin taking out the Canadians, the Egyptians, the Irish and the Amazonians… beginning with their kings. He would have the largest kingdom in the world. When he was finished, no one would dare threaten him again.

Radek turned when he sensed movement behind him. Sammael stepped from the shadows and stood by Radek's side. "Do you miss it?" Sammael asked curiously. "Do you ever miss going out yourself and hunting the humans?"

"No!" Radek barked, then softened. His bad mood wasn't Sammael's fault. "I've become accustomed to eating in," he said as he turned to head back toward his chambers. "What about you? Do you miss the thrill of the hunt?"

"No," Sammael said honestly. "I guess I too have become accustomed to eating in." The two vampires stopped when they heard someone running toward them. Sammael immediately grew alert and positioned himself between the potential threat and his king. "Stop," Sammael demanded.

Radek smiled, pleased. Sammael was the one vampire he never doubted. The man would be loyal 'til his dying day.

"I need to speak with King Radek," the young vampire demanded urgently. "I have a message from Tico."

Radek stepped forward. "I am King Radek," he said sternly. "What is your message?"

Chaos

"Tico said to come as fast as I could. He wanted to let you know that at the time of my departure there were two hundred and sixty four vampires in his company. I left a couple of weeks ago. He was going to remain in Kansas a few additional days to ensure the group was well fed, then they would begin the long journey back to New York. He said to tell you he plans to continue his assignment along the way. His goal is to have at least three hundred vampires in his company when he arrives home," the young vampire said earnestly.

Radek waited for more but the stranger remained silent for several long minutes. Clearly that was the extent of the message he was sent to relay. "Very good," Radek finally responded. "Help yourself to some dinner. Sammael will show you to the cages. You have brought me good news tonight." Radek turned and glided toward his room.

Sammael cleared his throat. "Master?" he called.

"Yes, Sammael?" Radek answered as he casually continued down the hallway.

"Are you ready for your dinner as well? Shall I bring you one of the captives while I'm selecting one for this man?"

Radek paused and turned to face Sammael. "Yes, I think I will have my dinner early this evening." He stopped to consider. "I'm in the mood for Chinese I think," he paused. "And send someone for Lilith. I have an assignment for her. I need her to head out right away." Radek turned and once again headed for his room.

Lilith knocked softly on Radek's door. She was curious. What assignment did he have for her? She was growing restless. Hopefully he would send her away tonight. She was beyond bored with Radek and his conservative intimacy. She needed a lover that was inventive and exciting, not boring and monogamous. If Kahn hadn't gotten caught and thrown into prison, she would be enjoying a little adventure with the human by now. She couldn't risk having sex with another vampire. Radek was already suspicious. That rat Sammael had seen too much between her and Hector. She was sure the guy had snitched to prove his loyalty to the king. Lilith grunted. She wasn't so sure Sammael was loyal. There was something about the twit that made her suspicious.

"Come in," Radek barked.

Lilith rolled her eyes as she pushed open the door and stepped into the enormous room. Radek was sitting in his lounge chair beside the fire. Lilith forced a smile and approached the powerful vampire she pretended to love. "You called for me?" she asked innocently.

Radek studied Lilith. He'd been angry with her ever since the human, Kahn, she'd enlisted from Columbia had failed. He had initially objected to using a human but he had to admit that in the beginning, the plan had worked perfectly. Kahn killed the women, then framed Thomas Deveraux for the murders. The human police were so easy to manipulate. While the warriors and that pesky fae queen focused on the killings and keeping Thomas out of trouble, Radek had moved forward with his goal to create an army. But Kahn was supposed to make sure Thomas was killed or imprisoned forever. He needed the warrior out of the way. Instead, Kahn was captured and Thomas went free. How was Radek and his minions supposed to get close to Alexandria if he couldn't eliminate the warriors protecting her?

Just thinking about the debacle still infuriated him. Radek's anger was starting to get out of hand again. He had to put the failure behind him and move forward. Dwelling on the past, allowing his anger to consume him, would seriously impede his ability to move forward. He needed a clear head if he wanted to succeed; and he would succeed. Anyway, he had received good news today. He would just dwell on that for now. If he added the vampires traveling with Tico, he now had over two thousand vampires headed his way. It was a good start. If he included the others, the possibilities were limitless. Close to a third of the vampire groups he had initially sent out hadn't checked in yet. Optimistically he believed there were at least three thousand vampires, maybe more on their way to New York. Once they arrived, the battle would begin. He planned to focus on the warriors and the queen as well as the council members first. Once they were killed, the rest of the fae would fall into place. He was sure of it. Then he could go after the shifters. He was so close to his goal he could almost taste the victory. Radek realized Lilith was standing patiently before him, waiting to learn what her new assignment was going to be.

He stood and began pacing the room. "Each time we develop a plan, it is thwarted by the warriors. We need a way to keep them occupied while the army gathers," he began.

Lilith stood motionless, silently listening for a clue. She had no idea where Radek was going with this.

"Each time a plan has failed, we've discarded it and moved in a different direction," Radek continued. "I now believe that was a mistake. The warriors expect something new. They won't expect us to go back and retry something that failed." He turned to Lilith. "Do you agree?"

"I suppose," she said hesitantly. "Exactly what did you have in mind?"

"I know you are the one that created the vampiric animals that Typhon complained about," Radek told her. "Don't try to deny it.

I saw the guilt written all over your face. I don't know how word got to the Amazon when it didn't reach me here in New York, but I've been thinking that creating more of those creatures might be a good diversion."

"Uh..." Lilith paused. Was he nuts? If they created vampiric animals, the other kings would obliterate them instantly. "I'm not sure that's such a good idea," she began. "What if they attack a human? New York is extremely populated. The humans will go nuts. It will be in every newspaper across the world," she carefully argued.

"That's why I need you to create the animals yourself. You have to control them. You have to prevent a human attack and make sure they only injure the warriors and the shifters," Radek said calmly.

"Radek, you know you can't control those things. I know firsthand you can't control those things. This won't work. And what am I supposed to turn anyway? A stray dog? There are very few animals that can run through the streets of New York and not cause panic or draw too much attention," she begged.

"Not in New York," Radek said annoyed with her lack of enthusiasm for his new plan. "I want you to go out to that fort again. The one where you killed the human. I thought you said there was a forest next to the base. Turn some animals in there. If they're using that obstacle course you discovered, they'll be easy targets for the animals," Radek surmised.

"The fort?" Lilith shrieked. She couldn't help herself. "You want me to create vampiric creatures and turn them loose next to a military base where human police, coast guard and military personnel still work. Are you nuts?" Lilith paused, she was going to overstep her bounds if she wasn't careful. "Don't you remember

Chaos

what Maedoc, Ammit and Typhon said? If we do this, the humans will get bit for sure. What if they are able to miraculously kill one of them? You know they'll dissect it and then our secret will be exposed. The other vampire kings won't allow that. They'll attack us without a word. You heard their threats," she argued. "We won't even see them coming."

"That's why I'm sending you," Radek bellowed. "I don't care if the things bite and kill a human. If they do, the human's body must disappear. If the humans discover the animals and somehow miraculously kill one, the animal must disappear before they can dissect it. You're a vampire, Lilith. You should be able to handle a human." He was taunting her, knowing he'd struck a nerve. "If you're not up to the challenge I'll find someone else. Maybe Sammael would like to go." Radek knew that final blow would shut down any further resistance. Lilith's competitive nature would never let Sammael assist in a task that would garner him attention and approval from the king.

Lilith studied Radek. The man was an idiot. He was going to do this with or without her help. Sammael couldn't handle the vampiric animals. The guy may have fooled Radek, but Lilith wasn't as gullible as the king. Sammael was a weasel, but he was also a wimp. He'd never be able to control this, and somehow that would end up being her fault too. She only had two choices, take on this assignment, or flee for her life. She wasn't ready to flee, yet. She was still hoping Radek would be killed in this risky war he was raging. Then she could step in and take over as queen. "Okay," she finally conceded. "I'll do it."

Radek smiled. He knew she would. It wasn't always easy, but he could usually manipulate Lilith into giving him anything he wanted. Unfortunately, he also knew she was just as successful at manipulating him.

"When do you want me to leave?" she asked hoping it was right away. She needed to get away from the nutcase. Tolerating him was becoming more and more difficult.

"Now," he said casually. "Travel tonight and begin to turn the animals tomorrow. Not one or two, I want dozens of them. I want those warriors, fae and shifters at the fort to have their hands full. They can't plan for an attack if they're busy fighting for their lives," he explained. "I think you're wrong about what's going on out there. If it was just an academy for humans there wouldn't be so many supernatural beings living at the place."

"What about the warriors here in town," Lilith asked. "They're killing off the vampires as soon as they arrive."

"I realize that," he barked, annoyed she still had enough confidence to comment on a weakness. It didn't do him any good to build an army if the warriors took them out in small groups as soon as they returned. "I have a solution for that as well," he lied. "Now go. You need to reach cover before morning."

Lilith slowly left the room. She didn't believe Radek. He had no idea how to deal with the warriors still in New York. The new vampires needed to hide out and stay away from the city. Otherwise they would never have enough left to take on the fae. Well, at least that wasn't her problem any longer. She'd just made sure of that. Radek didn't have a solution, but declaring he did got her off the hook. He couldn't blame her now, his failure would be his own fault in the end. Radek had always underestimated his enemy. That fact gave her hope. There was still a chance he would be killed soon, leaving his kingdom ripe for the taking. For now, she'd just play the dutiful servant. Radek wanted her at the fort, she'd go to the fort. Once she turned the animals, she'd remain in the area just in case. But if it looked like things were going to get ugly, she'd bolt.

Chaos

She was so close to ruling her own kingdom, but she wasn't willing to sacrifice her life for Radek's cause. Clearly the vampire didn't know what he was up against. Maedoc alone was more than they could handle. She wasn't going to stick around if his wrath came down on Radek. Lilith packed a few things and disappeared into the night.

Radek grinned as Lilith slid into the darkness. She was right, the plan was risky. But Radek's life wasn't the one at risk, Lilith's was. If anything went wrong, Radek knew Lilith would run. She was terrified of Maedoc. He was counting on that. Worse case, the kings would pay another visit and Radek would explain how Lilith had gotten out of control. He'd tell them he ordered her to stop but instead she'd rushed off to the fort to take matters into her own hands. Radek of course sent a few of his most trusted vampires after her but they were too late. Lilith had set the vampiric animals loose, then escaped. She was now a fugitive. Then he'd ask for their help. Any assistance the men could give him regarding her capture and punishment would be greatly appreciated. He would do it himself of course, but he couldn't leave in the middle of his war. He smiled an evil grin as he slowly made his way back to his chambers. The kings would believe him.

This plan would turn that one mistake to his advantage. He'd realized what he'd done immediately. When the nosy king had mentioned the vampiric animals, Radek had shown his confusion. Maedoc and Typhon had caught it for sure, he didn't know about Ammit. Radek had been chastising himself ever since that visit for letting them see one of his vampires was acting without his knowledge. Now that mistake was going to fit nicely into his plan. He'd use it to get himself out of trouble and take care of Lilith once and for all.

He knew he couldn't trust her. Lately, the sex wasn't even that great. He still regretted what had to be done, but Lilith needed to be punished. This way, he wouldn't have to do it himself. He wouldn't dwell on the loss. It was time to move on. With each passing day he was growing more and more excited about the droves of shifter women that would soon be vying for his attention. The growing anticipation was going to make the search for the right carrier for his child even more enjoyable. Radek salivated with excitement. His time was coming, he could feel it. Soon everything he ever wanted would be his.

* * * *

Bastian and Kylee walked up the large staircase of the farmhouse. Kylee was so exhausted. She'd been up all night and all day watching Melissa for a sign...any sign. Something that would tell them if the antidote was working. Nothing had changed. On the surface that seemed bad, but Kylee realized after taking Melissa's vitals that nothing at all had changed. Not for the good, but not for the bad either. Melissa should have been worse. The toxin inside her should have continued eating away at her cells. It wasn't and it hadn't been for almost a week. If she wasn't so tired she'd be excited by the discovery. They'd stopped the progression, now they just needed to find a cure.

Bastian walked Kylee to her door and paused. Then he leaned down and kissed her gently. "If I didn't know better, I'd swear you are already asleep sweetheart. Go to bed. She's not in danger anymore. We're not rushing against the clock now. We can afford to catch up on our rest."

"Okay," Kylee agreed. "I think if things are still the same in the morning we can confidently declare this one a success. We still have a long way to go, but this looks promising." She leaned against Bastian and raised her head pressing her lips against his again. "Goodnight. I'll see you first thing in the morning. Are we still on for training?"

Bastian smiled. He was enjoying their early morning matches. Wrestling around on the mat with a beautiful woman every morning was a great way to wake up. Unfortunately, it was also a frustrating way to begin his day. Kylee would only let him get so close. Kissing and wrestling a little was okay, but as soon as he tried to go further she pushed him away. He was trying to be patient, but the frustration was getting to him. What exactly was she waiting for? He had finally found the woman he wanted to be with forever, but what if the feeling wasn't mutual. Was this just a casual affair for Kylee? It didn't seem that way when they were together, but what if he was wrong about her feelings for him?

Kylee moved back and opened her door. "I'll take that as a yes. Tomorrow then," she said as she slipped into her room and closed the door. Once alone, Kylee leaned against the wall and sighed. What was she doing? She was frustrating both of them, that's what. Why couldn't she just give in to her desires? She knew Bastian wanted her as much as she wanted him. But she couldn't. She would not have sex with anyone until she was positive she was going to marry him. Thanks a lot mom. You drilled values into me from such a young age I can't bring myself to deviate no matter how much I want to. She pushed herself away from the wall and prepared for bed. As soon as her head hit the pillow she slipped into a deep, dreamless sleep.

Bastian woke early and headed to the lab. He wanted to check on Melissa. He was confident she was fine, but he still had to check. The antidote seemed to be working so far. They might need to increase the dosage, but after all this time things were finally looking up. However, checking on Melissa was only part of the reason he wanted to get to the lab. He had tossed and turned all night but sometime around two in the morning an extraordinary idea had struck him. He knew it was a long shot, but he was anxious to get to the lab and try it. So far his goal of turning a warrior into a human was looking impossible. The warrior blood was just too strong. It was all consuming. No matter what he mixed with the stuff, it just disbursed and altered it. That was good news for the warriors. So far he hadn't found anything that his blood couldn't overcome and alter. Great when dealing with injuries, but not so good for his current project. His biggest problem was the short life span of the blood. Warrior blood couldn't be stored. Once it hit oxygen it coagulated almost immediately.

An hour later, Bastian sat at the desk working on his formula. Melissa was stable but still the same. She hadn't improved overnight. At least she wasn't getting any worse. Bastian's attention returned to the vile as he shook the small glass tube and watched, waiting for a reaction. The blood consumed his ingredients almost instantly. He continued to watch as the plasma coagulated before his eyes. Bastian flung the tube into the small trash can, frustrated. He wasn't making any progress. Every day he spent with Kylee, he loved her more and more. He couldn't stand to be away from her. He knew she cared about him too, he could feel it. They spent so much time together now, her affection for him was obvious. In fact, they spent most of the day, every day, together now. Sometimes they would take long walks on the beach or play cards in the study. Even when they worked late on an idea in the lab, it was together. Plus they always had their early morning workouts in the gym. He especially enjoyed the afternoon they had borrowed the horses and went riding. What was he going to do if he never succeeded? What if he couldn't change into a human? It was too late to turn back now. Bastian couldn't leave her. He couldn't live without her. After everything that happened with his

Chaos

parents, he had somehow found himself in the exact same jam his father had been in. He was such an idiot. He should have avoided her from the beginning. He thought of the beautiful broach sitting in his dresser drawer. He still hadn't found the right moment to give it to Kylee. He wasn't sure how she would react to such an expensive gift. Especially if she wasn't as committed to this relationship as he was.

Bastian glanced at the clock and jumped to his feet. He was late. Kylee was going to wonder where he was. He rushed upstairs and through the double doors leading to the mat room. Kylee was on her back, stretching her legs. She looked up and smiled. "I know you didn't sleep in. You were gone before I was," she said pushing herself to her feet and approaching him.

Bastian inhaled. No, there was no way he could just walk away from this woman. He was trapped. He just hoped somehow he could find his way through this one. So far Kylee hadn't actually asked him to change her, but he knew it was coming. She'd been hinting more and more frequently. Bastian gave Kylee a friendly smile then casually lowered himself to the mat.

"How is Melissa?" Kylee finally asked, sitting down next to him. "I know you had to be in the lab this morning."

"I was," Bastian admitted, removing his shoes. "No change. I think we should increase the dosage by a few milligrams and see what happens. Maybe we didn't give her enough." He leaned against the mat with his elbows and began to stretch. "I don't want to give her too much though, so let's gradually increase the dosage and monitor her condition as we do. I think maybe we should take shifts for a while."

Kylee didn't like that idea at all. They wouldn't see each other if they were working and sleeping on opposite shifts. "For how long?" she asked.

Bastian could see the disappointment in Kylee's eyes. She didn't like his idea any more than he did, but they didn't have a choice. Melissa had to be their first priority. Bastian slowly rose and held out his hands to Kylee. She immediately took them and let him pull her to her feet. However, once she was standing Bastian tugged unexpectedly and Kylee stumbled forward colliding with his masculine body. Bastian grinned and wrapped his arms around her waist. Then he leaned down and gently kissed her lips. "We'll take it day by day, but I don't think it's going to take long to determine the correct dosage," he paused, "I'd like to work out a schedule so we can continue our morning training sessions, though."

Kylee smiled. "I'd like that too," she said a little relieved at the suggestion. At least they'd see each other for an hour each morning. That would have to suffice for now. Kylee sobered, "Are you worried about another attack?"

"There's nothing pointing to one, but eventually I think it's inevitable." Bastian said rubbing Kylee's back. "Radek's not going to give up. He wants to take over the fae kingdom as well as the shifters. He's crazy and unorganized but he's going to attack again somewhere. The question is where. We don't know if this time it will be in New York, or here at the fort again. We need to be prepared for anything." He released Kylee and gently pushed her a few inches away so he could look her in the eyes. "Don't worry. You handled yourself the first time, you'll be fine again. No, better than fine. Your skills are more advanced now. I'm surprised at how far you've come in such a short amount of time."

"Do you really think so?" she glowed.

Chaos

"I do," he assured her. "You're doing great, but you still need practice. Is there anything specific you want to work on this morning?"

The couple became serious as they focused on their training. Kylee didn't have any special requests, so Bastian skillfully taught her a few new tricks of his trade. After centuries of battling with the vampires, he knew quite a few moves that were easy to learn but effective.

Just over an hour later Kylee grabbed her water bottle and declared she'd had enough for the day. "I'm going to hit the shower. Do you want to meet me in the lab?" she asked Bastian.

Bastian was about to agree when Dusty stepped through the door. "Bastian?" the shifter called. "There's a guy at the door with a package for you. He says he needs a signature and will only accept yours. I tried to sign for you, but he wouldn't let me."

Bastian raised an eyebrow. That was unusual. "Okay," he said casually to Dusty then turned back to Kylee. "I'll meet you in the lab after I get this and grab a quick shower." He turned and strolled out the door.

Kylee entered the lab and immediately went to Melissa. There was still no change. It was like Melissa had gone into a coma. At least she wasn't getting any worse. Kylee pulled out her bag and began a thorough examination. Melissa's vitals were normal. She appeared to be a healthy young girl other than being comatose. Kylee decided to take a small vile of blood to test as well. As she placed the used syringe in the small garbage next to Bastian's desk she noticed a large flask of blood in the can.

Kylee reached in and retrieved the glass tube. She curiously studied the contents and knew without a doubt the blood was warrior blood. Was it Bastian's blood? Why was he studying his own blood? She probed the thick gel with a small stick. As she studied the tube, she realized Bastian had mixed other ingredients with the blood. There was some kind of powder residue on the outside of the glass. Why? Kylee worried. What was Bastian doing? More importantly, why was he keeping it such a secret? Was he sick? Could warriors even get sick? She hated her ignorance. She supposed it wasn't entirely out of the question that a warrior could have a birth defect or a serious illness. Kylee slumped into Bastian's large chair. What was she going to do? How could she find out what he was up to? She'd have to find a way to talk to him about it. Maybe he'd be honest with her if he knew she'd discovered the experiment. Had she finally found the man of her dreams only to lose him to disease like she had her mother? She glanced around her workspace looking for a spot to hide the discarded vile. She wanted to study it closer when she had time.

Bastian strolled to the door of the farmhouse and signed for the parcel. There was a large tube as well as a small package about the size of a notebook. He headed for the kitchen to use the table but stopped mid-stride. The door was open and he could hear voices. He could only see part of the table, but Marta and Jake were obviously having breakfast together. He wasn't ready to talk to them, yet. He felt conflicted every time he saw Jake these days. It always brought back his conversation with Dimitri and somehow made him feel like a coward. But on the other hand it felt like a betrayal to his father to discuss his fears with anyone else.

Bastian slowly backed down the hall and slipped out the front door. He'd go back to the gym to shower then take his package to the lab and study its contents at his desk.

Chapter Four

Marta watched out the window and sighed. Bastian was strolling down the long drive on his way back to the fort. "Do you think he'll ever forgive us?" she asked her husband. "I miss him terribly. We used to be so close."

"I'm sorry honey," Jake answered sorrowfully. "I don't think he's really upset with you. His anger is directed at me, but we're always together. When he avoids me, he also avoids you."

"I don't know. I think he's still upset with both of us," she said quietly. "I'm not sure that's all there is, though. I'm getting the feeling there's something else."

"We'll find a way to talk to him soon," Jake promised. "He can't avoid us forever."

Bastian quickly showered then grabbed the package and walked to the lab. Kylee was combining ingredients and barely acknowledged him when he walked in. He went straight to his desk and opened the small package then studied it. It looked like more of George's notes. There were three notebooks, all of them in the same writing. He set them aside and went to work on the large round tube. Ray must have sent the blueprints.

Kylee knew the moment Bastian stepped through the door. She could just sense his presence somehow. It had been like that since she'd met him. She added the last ingredient to her new formula then walked to Bastian's desk. He was looking at a book or notepad of some kind. Bastian casually set it aside and picked up the other package. "What is it?" she asked.

Bastian was surprised to see Kylee standing beside him. "Huh?" he asked. "Oh, it looks like more of George's notebooks," he shrugged. "I haven't found anything useful in the others, so I doubt those are going to help us." He removed the end of the tube and pulled a large set of plans from the package. Bastian picked up the discarded books and handed them to Kylee then flattened the rolled paper until it covered his entire desk. He was anxious to see what his architect had come up with. The day after he'd returned from Ireland, Bastian had tried to describe the house he wanted in detail. Something he had done time and time again as he opened new facilities around the world. He never knew if Ray understood his vision until he actually saw the completed plans.

Kylee absently took the books and set them on the counter. She wanted to know what the large plans were for. Once Bastian had them spread across his desk, Kylee realized they were architectural plans for a house. "Are you building a new home?" she asked, still looking at the large layout in amazement.

"Uh-huh," Bastian said absently. His mind was completely focused on the plans. So far it looked like Ray was in sync with

Chaos

what he wanted. This house had to be perfect. He was building it in his parents honor. Bastian turned the page and studied the picture of the front of the home. The bench was right where he wanted it.

"It's beautiful," Kylee said sincerely. She studied the front porch. She loved the bench but if it were her, she'd incorporate the intricate designs on the bench into the railing that ran along the wrap around porch. She couldn't help herself, she absently reached down and ran her fingers over the detailed picture in appreciation.

Bastian looked up at Kylee. He'd almost forgotten she was there. "You like it?" he asked.

Kylee smiled. "Uh-huh." She pulled her gaze away from the picture and looked at Bastian. "Where are you building it?"

"Ireland," he said casually.

Kylee froze. Was Bastian moving to Ireland? What did that mean for them? She furrowed her brow and frowned. "You're moving?" she asked, unable to keep the concern out of her voice.

Bastian pulled Kylee onto his lap. "No," he said as he wrapped his arms around her waist. "Not permanently. I've decided to open a lab in Dublin," he began. "I have labs in Paris, Sydney, Sacramento, Canada, and Mexico," he smiled at her confused look. "I also have a place to stay in each of those areas. They're not all homes, but I don't like staying in hotels, especially for extended periods. So, I have a home or a condo in each city where I have a large lab."

"Are you serious?" she asked surprised. "I knew you had to be rich, but I didn't realize you were that rich. It has to cost a fortune to pay for their upkeep alone," she said feeling a little overwhelmed by the news. Once again he seemed so out of her league.

"So… give me your honest opinion," he said centering the plans so Kylee could get a good look.

"I already told you the house is beautiful," she answered, continuing to study the drawings.

Bastian searched Kylee's face, trying to find a clue that would reveal her true feelings. "There's something you think I should change," he decided. "What?"

"I can't tell you how to build your house Bastian," she said feeling uncomfortable.

Bastian sat quietly waiting, Kylee would eventually tell him what was on her mind.

After a moment, Kylee sighed and began her explanation. "The intricate design on that bench is phenomenal. I was just thinking if it were me, I'd use similar wood for the large railing that runs along the porch and continue that design in the posts," she said hesitantly.

Bastian studied the picture. He originally thought it would make the bench stand out if he kept the rest of the porch bland, but Kylee was right. Using that design would bring out the beauty in the bench. He nodded in agreement and turned the page. This one showed the overview of the first floor. Bastian again asked Kylee for her input. He was having fun now. Bastian made a mental note of each suggestion Kylee made. Once he was alone again, he would jot them all down and send the corrected plans back to Ray. He liked the idea of creating this house with Kylee. With any luck one day it would be their home away from home. They sat for hours going over plans and talking about changes.

Chaos

Kylee was having fun. She'd never designed a house before. She secretly fantasized about it being their home. What would it be like to share a house with Bastian? To share a life with Bastian? To be with him forever? It was time to bring the subject up casually, lightly. "Bastian?" she began.

"Yeah?" he answered absently, still focused on the plans.

"Will you tell me how old you are?" She thought that might be a good way to slide into the conversation.

Bastian froze. He wasn't sure she was ready for the answer to that question. "Uh… very old," he finally said vaguely.

"You don't want to tell me?" she asked a little hurt. "Why not?"

"I'm not sure how you will react to the answer," he said honestly. "It might upset you."

"I know you guys live a long time. Are you over a hundred?" she guessed.

Bastian smiled. "Yes," he said simply.

"Come on, just tell me. I'm not going to get upset," she promised.

"Three hundred and ninety six," he said soberly watching for her reaction.

"Wow!" she said pausing to consider that. It was older than she'd expected. "I'm attracted to an older man," she finally said. "Hmm, I never saw that coming."

"Are you?" he asked. He was still trying to figure out where this was leading. He loved Kylee and he wanted desperately to make love to her. But, she seemed to have other ideas. He was beginning to wonder if she was even attracted to him at all.

"Of course," she laughed then studied him. "You're serious?" she observed, surprised. "It's a little weird to be involved with someone three hundred and ninety six years old. No wonder you're good at your job. You've had a lot of practice," she observed. "But I'm not going to freak out about it. It might take a little time to get used to, but you're still the same guy I fell for in the first place. You're just a little older than I would have guessed." Maybe this was a good time to broach the subject.

Bastian leaned in and kissed Kylee gently. "I never know how you're going to take new things. I guess I'm waiting for it all to become too much for you. Each time something strange or unusual comes up I expect you to go running out the door and back to New York."

"I have seen a lot of strange things. I can't explain why, but none of it seems frightening or upsetting to me," she tried to explain. "I feel like I should have been a part of this world all my life. I know that sounds weird, but that's how I really feel," she admitted.

"I'm glad you feel that way," he said honestly. "You've already done so much to help our people. The tea you and Breena developed is going to be a big hit once the fae learn of it. You've seen firsthand how difficult having a child is for the fae. It seems to be that way for all of them. Your tea is going to allow those women to enjoy a better quality of life while pregnant. Thank you," he said humbly. Nobody else could have accomplished what Kylee and Breena did in such a short amount of time.

Chaos

"So much has happened while I've been here at the fort." Kylee got a little lost in the memories. "I followed Sam here thinking I could save her and then I almost lost her anyway. If Ty hadn't changed her, Sam would be gone. It's terrifying to think about," she said broaching the subject just a little.

"Sam and Ty are lucky to be alive," Bastian said a little annoyed. "It was reckless for Ty to risk his life that way," he mumbled.

"If he hadn't, Sam wouldn't be alive today," Kylee argued.

"True," Bastian agreed. "But if it wasn't for Victor's idea, Ty wouldn't be alive today. We came very close to losing him. Then Sam almost lost her life again trying to save Ty. Turning a human into a warrior is nothing more than a recipe for disaster. There's no excuse for it."

Kylee's stomach clenched. Was Bastian saying he wouldn't even consider turning her? Of letting her join their world permanently? "You would never turn a human into a warrior?" she asked hoping she sounded uninterested in the answer.

Bastian stared out the window. He thought of his mother, of Marta, of Sam and Ty. "No," he said with finality. "It's reckless and selfish. Life is too precious. No warrior has the right to play with something so precious and fragile that way."

Kylee could barely breathe. Bastian was so unmoving. There was no doubt in her mind, he was serious. He would never turn her into a warrior. They would never be together forever. They could never be together period. How could she dedicate her life to Bastian and live day after day growing older while he remained the same. He might be attracted to her now, but he wouldn't be in thirty or forty years when she was old and gray. She slowly slid off Bastian's lap and walked to her desk. "Uh, I'm finished with this for the day. I think I'm going to go take a nap. I'm beat. Maybe with a little rest I'll have another epiphany." She hoped she sounded as casual as she was trying to sound. She couldn't breathe. It was a chore to force air through her nose. The tears were so close to falling. She needed to get out of here.

Bastian glanced at Kylee. "Good idea," he told her. "When you get up we'll increase Melissa's dosage by half a milligram and see what happens." He watched Kylee leave the room and anxiously pulled out the ingredients he needed to try his new formula. He was running out of ideas. He was starting to get discouraged and desperate. How could he get the warrior blood to stop consuming the human blood? Was it impossible? They used human blood for a reason, it was weak. They'd tried using fae blood, but the change was difficult. Not with human blood, the transition seemed to be quick and easy. So how was he going to stop the process?

Bastian pushed the needle into his arm and extracted enough blood to fill the tube. He quickly dumped in the dry ingredients then pressed on the lid and shook the tube vigorously. As usual, the antibodies in the warrior blood began to consume and destroy the foreign substance then coagulate. Bastian threw the flask across the room in frustration. What was he going to do? He pressed his face into his hands as sorrow consumed him. Was the whole thing hopeless? Was he destined to live the life his father had lived? Losing Kylee after only a few years together was going to destroy him. For the first time, he understood the all-consuming depression that had altered his father so profoundly. Bastian was shocked to realize he finally understood.

Kylee was thankful she'd made it to her room without running into anyone. In the state she was in, she couldn't handle casual conversation. She slipped through the door and closed it tightly behind her. After a moment's hesitation she flipped the lock then collapsed onto her bed. She was heartbroken. All the hopes and dreams she'd been building the last few weeks were shattered in a matter of seconds. There was no future for her and Bastian. She'd fallen completely in love with a man that was off-limits. Maybe some humans could spend their life getting older while their spouse stayed the same, but she couldn't. If Bastian wasn't willing to budge, a future together was impossible. Kylee didn't move, she remained huddled on the bed feeling sorry for herself and grieving over lost possibilities.

* * * *

Juan Martinez was getting tired. He was deep in the Amazon Rainforest, following the Amazon River, but hadn't come across a single vampire. Zaphrey made it sound like there were hundreds of them in this area, but Martinez couldn't find a single one. He paused, wondering what he should do now. He thought following the river was his best bet once he reached the plush tropical area, but maybe that had been a mistake. He glanced left, then right. Nothing. Where exactly would a vampire live in this vast region? Martinez had no idea.

He was about to continue along the river when he heard a soft noise. It almost sounded like a muffled moan. Martinez carefully moved into the trees and cautiously surveyed the area. So far the coast was clear. He pushed his way through a stand of thick brush and paused as a colorful snake slid over the ground before him. As he took another step forward, he saw them. There were two men, one was lying on the ground the other was leaning over him. Martinez smiled. Finally, another vampire. He took another cautious step forward then froze when the vampire raised its head in challenge.

Martinez slowly held up his hands in surrender. "I'm not here to take your meal," he said softly. "I need to know if you can tell me how to find your king." He casually sat on a large tree stump and waited. The vampire studied the intruder momentarily then dismissed the interruption and returned to his meal. Martinez sat patiently, waiting, hoping he could talk his way out of this one. The last thing he wanted was a fight.

Once the vampire finished he rose and approached Martinez. "What business do you have with the king?" he asked.

Martinez stood. "I'm new to the area. I would like to introduce myself and ask his permission to stay awhile," Martinez answered trying to exude an air of confidence he did not have.

The vampire continued to study Martinez. "Follow me," he finally said slipping deeper into the forest.

Martinez followed, staying as close on the man's heals as he dared. The last thing he wanted to do was to make his guide uncomfortable. Martinez and the vampire wandered through the forest for several minutes before they finally entered a small clearing. He could tell this was the vampire base. Several other vampires were milling around. They all looked very relaxed. Martinez slowly studied his surroundings. How would he know who was in charge? He turned back to ask his vampire guide but couldn't find him anywhere. The guy had vanished. So, Martinez thought, I'm on my own.

He began to make his way to the large cave prominently positioned in the center of the clearing. He thought chances were pretty good the king lived in there. It didn't take long before another

Chaos

vampire stopped him, then a second joined them immediately. Martinez was now flanked, one vampire on each side.

"Walk," one of the large vampires ordered. He motioned forward and began to walk.

Martinez obeyed. What had he got himself into? He really hoped he hadn't traveled all this way to be killed on his first day. Zaphrey had talked about the Amazon vampires like they were a hidden race. He claimed they were fierce, but friendly. Martinez had laughed at that, but Zaphrey explained his people were friendly unless they were crossed, then they were fierce and very unforgiving.

The small group entered the cave and continued walking through the elaborate tunnels. The small walkway opened into a large expanse. A man was sitting in a chair that looked like it belonged in a castle or a palace, not a cave. Martinez assumed this was the Amazon king. He wore very little, but his entire body was adorned with tattoos, jewelry and piercings.

"What is your name?" the king immediately demanded.

"Martinez," he said clearly.

"Just Martinez?" the king inquired.

"Juan Martinez," he corrected.

"Well, Juan Martinez," Typhon paused. "What brings you to my kingdom? I'm told you came here specifically wishing to speak to me."

"Well, I was hoping I would be allowed to stay here for a while," Martinez said humbly. "I was told your people are friendly and easygoing. It sounded like a place I would like to live," he said not sure how to explain why he was here.

"I suppose we can be," Typhon agreed. "Who told you about our people?" He didn't want word to get out about his leadership style. It could put his people in danger. "You are young," Typhon observed. "Who could you possibly know that is familiar with my people?"

"I am young," Martinez admitted. "But I think I'm different than the others," he said a little confused by his situation.

"Oh, and how's that?" Typhon asked. The boy amused him.

"I was turned with a friend of mine in Mexico. We were rounded up and forced to stay with a large group of vampires. The others seemed... I don't know, lost," he finally decided on.

"And you are not?" Typhon asked with a slight smile, the man had wandered into the Amazon after all.

"Not in the way I mean. The other vampires didn't seem to know who or what they were. They didn't seem to remember their lives. I can't seem to forget mine," Martinez said honestly.

"I see," Typhon studied the man closer. "I guess that is a little unusual. Do you know who turned you?"

"I do," Martinez affirmed. "His name was Felix. He was the leader of our group. I was told we belonged to a vampire king by the name of Radek. Apparently he wanted us for his army."

"Radek?" Typhon said sobering. This was no longer funny.

Chaos

"I can see you dislike that king," Martinez hurried on. "I hope you won't get the wrong idea. I've never met him, I guess you could say I deserted his army."

"Funny. You don't seem cowardly to me," Typhon said studying the man a little closer now.

"I didn't leave out of fear," Martinez said immediately. "I left because those morons were going to attack a military base and I didn't want any part of it. The things in that base were out of control. I refused to engage in a suicide mission for a king I've never met. The guy expected allegiance and unwavering loyalty from new vampires that didn't even know him. I think that's a lot to ask. It was for me anyway," Martinez admitted. "I was told you were different. That you aren't a dictator like Radek. That you let your people live the way they want for the most part, but you expect loyalty in return."

"Who exactly was it that told you about me and my people?" Typhon asked.

"A vampire named Zaphrey," Martinez said soberly.

Typhon relaxed a little. If Zaphrey had discussed this place with the new vamp, he had trusted him. "How is Zaphrey these days?" he asked jovially. He was anxious to hear from his old friend. They hadn't spoken in weeks.

"I'm sorry sir, but he was killed in a large battle," Martinez said hanging his head in sorrow.

Typhon narrowed his eyes, Zaphrey dead? The words cut through him like a knife. Zaphrey was like a son to him. Could he really be dead? "Are you certain?"

"I am," Martinez assured him. "He was killed with my brother, Gomez." Martinez took a deep breath, just saying the name was painful. The loss rushed back and almost overwhelmed him.

Typhon never took his eyes off the man. This Martinez was clearly distraught over the loss of Gomez, but was he responsible for Zaphrey's death as well? "You will tell me what happened," he finally decided.

Martinez kept his head hung, this wasn't something he wanted to relive. "We were ambushed by El Torro's men. We were greatly outnumbered and they seemed to know we were coming."

"I'm not familiar with this El Torro," Typhon said impatiently. "Is he a new ruler in Mexico?"

Martinez raised an eyebrow at Typhon. He'd never known anyone who didn't know who El Torro was. Apparently the human tyrants weren't as notorious in the vampire world. "El Torro is a very brutal man who is in charge of the Mexican drug cartel," he said simply.

"You were ambushed by humans?" Typhon said amazed. How had humans killed Zaphrey, he was better than that? "Impossible."

"They're not just humans. They are an organized gang. They're also brutal and ruthless. Plus, I believe Gomez and Zaphrey were targeted. So was Felix. Those three were killed almost instantly before any of the rest of us knew exactly what was happening."

"Why do you think Zaphrey was targeted?" Typhon asked.

Chaos

"The night before the attack Felix had a visitor. It upset Zaphrey. He was really pissed, saying he was going to kill the traitor immediately. Gomez and I stopped him. We knew if he barged into our leader's camp with murder in his eyes he would be killed for sure. We calmed him down the best we could but he wasn't making sense. I think the man was someone he knew, although he never said his name. He just called him a ratfink traitor and rambled on about hidden passages and karma. Oh, and something about a key. I honestly didn't understand most of what Zaphrey was talking about. I left to find him something to eat, thinking the distraction might take his mind off whatever had upset him. Before I made it back to the small fire pit where Zaphrey and Gomez were resting, the man exited Felix's cave. I saw him much better this time. He was definitely a vampire but before he was turned, he was a member of El Torro's army. He had the tattoo and the loyalty additions. Anyway the man spotted Zaphrey and Gomez then froze. He looked worried for about a second then masked his emotions and left camp. The following evening we were ambushed and the three of them were killed instantly.

Like I said, it seemed they were targeted. Several men were on them at once and they just kept focusing on those three until they were gone. It happened so fast I couldn't even help. Sure, other vampires got killed, but the fight was different after the three of them died."

"Then what happened?" Typhon asked angrily. Who had betrayed Zaphrey? If the man was telling the truth, it was one of his own.

"Tyrone took over as leader and ushered us to an abandoned air strip. Once he got us loaded onto the large cargo plane we left Mexico. After a few hours we landed in an old airfield that was no longer in use near Rochester, New York. The whole thing was pretty strange and the more I think about it, the more I believe Tyrone must be in cahoots with El Torro too. El Torro is the only person that could fly such a large group of us out of the country at night like that without a hitch. And who else would know about a large enough airstrip in New York where hundreds of vampires could offload without notice? The Mexican drug cartel of course."

"Then when did you leave?" Typhon asked.

"Tyrone kept marching us across the country at night. All along the way he was distributing this photo and calling the guy Thomas. He said this Thomas guy was our first target. We needed to kill him immediately if we came in contact with him. I wasn't going to kill the guy, I didn't even know him. I tried to ask Tyrone why we should kill him. I needed to know what he did that got him sentenced to death. Tyrone said because Radek wants him dead and that should be enough for me. It wasn't. Several nights later Tyrone was marching us across New York near the great lakes and we came across a military base. Tyrone ordered us to attack. Most of the vampires followed his order. I did not. There were also a couple others that left. Whatever was housed on that base was wicked. There were men, huge men that could fight off ten vampires at a time. One woman could throw fire from her fingertips. Then came the animals, humans that could change into lions and gorillas. I didn't want any part of that suicide mission. I took off for the peaceful Amazon Zaphrey always talked about, hoping I could find a new home and a new leader," Martinez said trying to keep his eagerness hidden. He wanted to be welcomed here but was afraid to hope.

Typhon studied the vampire for several minutes. What should he do? Zaphrey would never have told this man about his world if he didn't trust him, but was he the one that killed Zaphrey? Had Radek sent this vampire to spy and collect information or to find a weakness that could be exploited? It was hard to tell. In spite of himself, Typhon liked the guy. He knew it would be smarter to send Martinez packing but he was going to let him stay. If Martinez was an enemy, Typhon would learn more by keeping him close. Plus if the guy was living among them, his men could keep a closer eye on him. "Now you are here because you want to live in the Amazon with my people?" he asked.

"Yes," Martinez said.

"Kenta was killed a few months ago. You may stay in his cave for now. Keep in mind, this is temporary. Consider it a kind of probation if you will. For the next few months we will test each other out, see if it's a good fit. I will warn you, if you cannot live here with my people in peace, you will be forced to leave. I do not give second chances. Are we understood?" Typhon asked sternly.

"Absolutely," Martinez said relieved. "Will someone show me to my cave?" he asked.

Typhon nodded to one of the men that had accompanied Martinez into the cave. "Show him where he will be staying Trumak," Typhon said in dismissal.

The two men disappeared down the dark corridor and headed into the forest.

"Athtar?" Typhon said quietly.

"Yes, sir?" Athtar answered immediately.

"Keep an eye on him. Enlist Trumak. I want to know if he can be trusted or if he is asking questions and trying to find weaknesses. I do not trust Radek," Typhon explained. "I need to know if this man is acting on his behalf."

"Yes sir," Athtar promised. "I'll talk to Trumak immediately."

* * * *

Kylee rose from the bed. She couldn't hide in here all night. She was going to have to face Bastian sometime. She walked into the bathroom, rinsed her face then stared at her reflection. Her eyes were puffy and red. How was she going to face Bastian looking like this? She took a deep breath then decided to take a shower. Maybe that would help her look normal. She laughed humorlessly, she'd never be normal again. Not without Bastian in her life.

An hour later Kylee was walking across the large expanse of the fort headed to the lab. She wanted to increase Melissa's medication tonight. If the girl recovered soon, Kylee wouldn't have to spend so much time around Bastian. As much as she wanted to escape right now, she wouldn't. She had a job to do. Things might be over between her and Bastian, but Melissa still needed her. She'd always been able to lose herself in her work, she just hoped she could do it again. Work had gotten her through the loss of her mother and it helped her cope night after night with the loneliness. Could it get her through heartbreak too? Only time would tell. She took a deep breath then pulled open the large door leading into the building.

Bastian was studying a new sample of Melissa's blood when Kylee walked in. He glanced her way and knew immediately something was wrong. He'd been afraid of that. It hit him about an hour after Kylee left this morning. He hadn't meant to break the news to her that way, but he'd been preoccupied and didn't realize what he was saying until it was too late. He watched as she walked to her desk and began measuring the antidote.

Chaos

"Are you still okay with an extra half milligram?" Kylee said not looking Bastian's way.

Bastian turned his chair so he was facing Kylee. He silently studied her, but she continued to ignore him. "Are we going to talk about this?" he finally asked.

"About what?" she asked, trying to pretend like she didn't know what he was talking about.

"Kylee," Bastian pressed. "I know you're upset with me. I think we need to talk."

Kylee finally looked up at Bastian. "I don't think there's anything to discuss," she paused. "I'd say you made things pretty clear this morning. It's fine. I understand." She glanced at Melissa. "Are we going to do this or what?" She continued to focus on their patient, it was too painful to look Bastian in the eye. It was too painful being in the same room as him. Finally, she held up the syringe. "You okay with this?" she glanced back at Bastian waiting for an answer.

Bastian sighed. He wasn't going to let this go. They needed to talk about it. But as usual, Melissa had to come first. "Yeah, I'm okay with it." The two moved to Melissa's side. They were standing so close that their arms briefly touched before Kylee jerked away. Bastian cleaned Melissa's arm with an alcohol wipe and waited for Kylee to inject the antidote. Once the new formula had been administered, they both stood quietly… waiting… watching.

Everything seemed to happen at once. Melissa gasp then started to jerk. Her body raised up, and she started kicking violently. Kylee couldn't get out of the way quick enough. Melissa's leg kicked out and struck her square in the stomach. Kylee flew backwards, losing her balance and falling against Bastian's garbage can. The can immediately tipped over depositing its contents across the floor. Kylee hit the round can then bounced to the floor landing on her back on top of the debris.

Bastian grabbed onto Melissa, holding her to the table. He glanced at Kylee sprawled on the floor. "You okay?" he asked, concerned.

"I'm fine," Kylee said standing up. She glanced around her, studying the contents of the large garbage can scattered across the floor. Her back was killing her. She saw the shattered remnants of a glass flask and knew a piece had sliced her back. But it could wait. Melissa needed her help. She moved once again to Melissa's side. The girl was gasping for air. Kylee pressed her fingers against Melissa's neck, searching for a pulse. She instantly felt the swelling and knew Melissa's life was in danger. Kylee frantically searched for some kind of tube. If she didn't get the airway open, Melissa wouldn't make it. That's when she spotted her bag. She grabbed it and in one fluid motion moved back to the bed. Moments later Melissa's body relaxed and her vitals returned to normal.

Bastian glanced at Kylee and realized she'd been injured. "You have a cut on your arm," he said grabbing a towel and pressing it to her arm as he wiped away the blood.

Kylee looked down and took a deep breath. "I'm fine," she said pushing Bastian's hand away. "I'll take care of it." She glanced back at Melissa. "I'll be right back." She rushed to the bathroom and closed the door behind her. Kylee quickly pulled her shirt up and looked at her wound. A large piece of glass was protruding from her back. No wonder she was in pain. She gritted her teeth and gripped the jagged edge then yanked as hard as she could. The glass seemed to come out in one piece. At least that was something. Kylee pressed a wet wash cloth against the wound waiting for the

Chaos

bleeding to stop. To her surprise it didn't take long. Not nearly as long as it should have.

Kylee cleaned the blood off her arm then surveyed the rest of her body, looking for additional cuts and contusions. Thank goodness there weren't any. She took a deep breath and opened the door.

Bastian was standing just outside the room looking concerned. As soon as she took a step through the door he grabbed her arm and studied the cut. After a moment he sighed in relief. "It's not deep and it's already stopped bleeding," he said, "But we need to clean it out so you don't get an infection." He pulled her arm toward the bench and immediately began cleaning the wound with a fresh alcohol wipe.

Kylee glanced around the room and saw Bastian had already cleaned up the mess. He had even removed the tube from Melissa's windpipe. She seemed to be resting comfortably now. "What went wrong?" Kylee finally asked. "Why did her airway close up like that?" she said concerned. "Do we need to stop the antidote completely? Do you think her body's had too much and it's overloaded?"

"No," Bastian said simply. "I don't."

"You don't to which one?" Kylee asked irritated. "You don't think we need to stop or you don't think her body's overloaded?"

"Both," Bastian said. "I tested her blood before you arrived and I just finished testing it again," he said seriously. "Her levels are up a little, but not dangerously high. For some reason the extra medication sent her body into shock."

"It was more like an allergic reaction," Kylee argued.

Bastian shook his head. "It may have seemed that way, but the tests aren't indicating that. For some reason, the extra antidote was too much. She's fine now. I've put her on oxygen as a precaution but she's fine. She's breathing on her own and everything is returning to normal," he assured her. "I'm just glad we decided to go with half a milligram instead of a full milligram. I'm not sure we could have saved her if she had more."

Kylee didn't feel well. She took a step backwards and sunk into her chair. Her back felt like it was on fire. "We almost lost her," Kylee said defeated. "After all the work we've done week after week, we almost lost her in a matter of seconds."

"But we didn't," Bastian said firmly. He pulled out his chair and settled in next to her. "Kylee, I'm sorry about what I said this morning," he began.

"Bastian stop," she closed her eyes. She wasn't up for this right now. "I get it. We don't need to dwell on it."

Bastian studied her for a minute. She was still upset. Was it over Melissa or him? He slid closer and took her hands in his. "Kylee, transforming someone into a warrior is dangerous. You saw that with Sam and Ty. The only reason Ty even considered it was because Sam was dying," he told her. "Doing it for any other reason is inexcusable. I know I wasn't very sensitive earlier, but my mind was on other things. I'm sorry. We should have discussed it differently. But I can't change you. I won't risk your life that way."

"Forget it," she said pulling her hands away. "I said I get it," she took a deep breath. "I misunderstood the situation, but it's clear now."

"What do you mean by that?" he asked cautiously.

Chaos

"I mean I thought I meant something to you. Now I know you were just trying to get me into bed. You were never serious about us. It was just a misunderstanding and now I get it. My saying no to you created a challenge. I'm sorry, but the challenge is over. I'm too tired for games. You made it clear where we stand. You don't want me, not really. Not permanently. So I'm afraid this is over," she said with finality.

"I won't change you so you're no longer interested in me? Or were you ever?" he asked quietly.

"What does that mean?" she asked angrily.

"I think you know," Bastian said defeated. "It seems you were more interested in the transformation than the man," he stood and slowly moved to the window. Had Kylee been using him? Was she only pretending to be interested because she wanted to live forever? Clearly she didn't understand the kind of bond two people shared after the transition. "It seems I misjudged you. I misjudged us, what we had together. The pure innocent act works well for you," he said angrily. "I thought you were honest and sweet. I trusted you. It seems I was wrong. I really didn't see that coming," Bastian was hurt. He was so in love with her and she was only using him. How was he going to get over this?

"Oh, you want to talk about honesty? That's rich," she said furious at his accusations. How could he not know how much she loved him? "That really is comical coming from the man who has a little secret project on the side. You want to tell me why you're testing your own blood? Why you keep mixing flasks of strange chemicals and warrior blood then discarding it?"

So, she knew about his project. Good. "I was trying to find a way to turn myself into a human," he said flatly, not looking at her. He continued to stare out the window. "Changing you isn't an option. I thought we might have a chance if I could change myself into a human."

"You what?" Kylee asked, dumbfounded. "Are you completely nuts?"

"Apparently I was," he said softly. "I planned to give up everything for you. For us," he turned to face her. "I'm glad I found out now, before it was too late. There never was an us." He closed his eyes, the pain was unbearable. "There are a lot of warriors out there, Kylee. Maybe you can find one that feels differently. You are part of our world now. If it means that much to you, I hope you find what you're looking for," he brushed past her and left the room, crushed. How had he been so wrong? How was he fooled so completely?

Kylee sat stunned. Bastian was trying to turn himself into a human? The thought touched and enraged her all at once. He was such an idiot. He'd never be happy as a human. He loved fighting vampires. He loved being a warrior. He couldn't be happy as anything else. The very idea was ridiculous. How could he not realize what he was trying to do? If he changed himself for her, he'd resent her. They might be happy for a while but it would always be there, a huge gulf between them. How long could they last that way? Not long, she was sure of it.

Kylee stood and almost screamed out in pain. She grabbed the bench to support her weight. What was in that flask? Her back was on fire. Whatever Bastian mixed with his blood was not agreeing with her system. She took a deep breath and stood. After a couple seconds she decided she could make it back to her room. She just needed rest and she would be fine.

Kylee stepped through the door and glanced around. So far so good. She slowly made her way up the stairs and slipped into her

Chaos

room. Once Bastian cooled off she'd try to talk to him. She had time. The way they ended things, he wasn't about to try to turn himself into anything for her. Plus, it didn't sound like he'd figured it out anyway. Once in her room she slid onto the bed and curled into a ball. If she could just get some sleep, she'd be fine. As she slowly drifted into a deep sleep, she wondered if she was right or if she just kept telling herself that because she knew she was wrong.

Bastian packed his bag and headed for the helicopter. He needed to get away from here. He needed to get away from Kylee. He slid into the pilot's seat and started his check off. He thought about calling Dimitri, but decided against it. Dimitri couldn't order him to stay if he didn't know he was leaving. Once he reached New York he'd call Dimitri and let his friend know he was going to Ireland. They would just have to manage without him for a while.

Kylee woke and could barely swallow. Her throat was dry and she felt dehydrated. She glanced at the clock and saw it was almost eleven. Everyone would be in bed by now. She slowly stood and immediately grabbed the night stand. Whew, head rush. She was definitely dehydrated. Hopefully there was something in the fridge to help. She didn't want to use an IV, but she would if necessary. Kylee took a deep breath and straightened. She carefully exited the room, walked down the stairs and entered the kitchen. As soon as she opened the fridge, she knew what she wanted. She was never a big fan of Gatorade, but right now it was exactly what she was craving. She pulled out a large bottle and guzzled it down. Once it was gone she opened a second bottle and drank half of that one as well. She only hesitated a moment then grabbed a third. By the time she reached her room the second bottle was gone and she had to admit she felt a little better. She opened the third bottle and tried to force herself to drink that one too. She could only get half of it down. She felt full, a little sloshy and completely wiped out. The trip to the kitchen had been exhausting. Kylee twisted on the lid and placed the remaining bottle on the night stand. Then she climbed back into bed and immediately fell into a deep sleep.

* * * *

Foster sat on the bench outside the council building waiting for Victor and Atticus to arrive. He still hadn't come up with a solution to help the families of the other human victims and they needed to have a plan before the hearing. A car pulled into the lot and Foster stood. He watched as Victor, Ariel, Tala and Atticus walked casually toward him.

"Foster," Atticus said in greeting as the group approached the building.

"Morning," Foster said in return.

Victor turned to Ariel and gave her a quick kiss. "Babe, would you and Tala mind giving us a minute? We have some things we need to talk to Foster about before the hearing."

"Of course," Ariel said turning to Tala. "Shall we?" The two women headed into the building.

Victor didn't take his eyes off Ariel until she disappeared through the large double doors. He was still surprised that such an amazing woman loved him the way she did. He was the luckiest man in the world and just hoped he could always make her as happy as she made him. Victor absently reached into his pocket and twisted the small ring between his fingers as he turned toward Foster and cleared his throat. "Things have been resolved with Melissa's boyfriend John and Regina's grandmother Ethel," he announced calmly.

Chaos

"Oh?" Foster said surprised. He'd been worried all this time for nothing.

Atticus put a hand on Foster's shoulder. "Yes," he said softly. "Everything just seemed to fall into place with very little help on our part." He smiled at Victor silently turning the conversation back over to his son.

"We didn't mean to leave you out of this, Foster. Like dad said, it all just fell into place. He went to talk to John and I met up with Ethel." Victor smiled at the memory. "She's a delightful woman. I began by explaining the trust to her and made sure she knew how to access the funds. Then I filled her in on who she would be sharing that trust with. She was immediately concerned about the boy, Bobby. I assured her they would be taken care of and explained the authorities were in the process of seizing the farm so she would have a place to live. That placated her, but only temporarily. She then wanted to know all about John," Victor paused. "That woman has a heart of gold. I didn't even get finished with my explanation before she was up on her feet and pulling on her coat. She demanded I take her to him at once. I started to argue, but decided it might be a good idea. We met up with dad, who had just finished explaining the situation to John. The four of us sat in John's apartment discussing the situation. Ethel and John hit it off right away. They both believe they are helping the other through this rough time. In a way I guess they are. John is going to work for Ethel a few nights a week. It's a win for everyone. John gets out of the house and Ethel gets a break. I don't know how long the arrangement will last, but for now it seemed perfect. Dad and I left the two comfortably making arrangements and finalizing schedules," Victor said triumphantly.

Atticus had to smile. "I was actually surprised at how quickly they bonded," he told Foster. "I think it has a lot to do with Ethel.

156

She really is a delightful woman and Victor's right, she truly has a heart of gold. She took that boy in like he was her own grandson. He really had no hope of resisting. Her open and honest demeanor is hard to resist. One thing you may not know is why John left his job. He was planning to propose to Melissa the night she was kidnapped. He said work had been extremely busy for weeks so it was hard to get time off. He'd made arrangements with his boss and worked late for several days prior to that fateful night to ensure he wouldn't be interrupted. He had the whole thing planned out. A romantic dinner, a candle light proposal then a day relaxing and enjoying each other. He was twenty minutes late for their dinner appointment because some urgent problem came up on his way out the door. After the abduction, John went to work every day positive the job had cost him the woman he loved. Pretty soon he just couldn't stand it. He walked out and never went back."

"It took a lot of work but dad and I finally convinced him it wouldn't have mattered if he was on time," Victor added. "We said Kahn confessed to everything, that he told the police he grabbed Melissa as soon as she left work that night. We told him Kahn was lying in wait, watching for Melissa to leave, knowing she would be alone. We told him she had been targeted because Kahn had eaten there the previous week and thought she was strong and independent. It was basically the truth, that's what Lawson did. I just changed the name to fit our needs," Victor confessed. "I immediately called McBride and he's on board. He said he'd inform Monroe so the little white lie won't be a problem. I could see how relieved John was at the news. The poor guy had convinced himself Melissa was grabbed because she was sitting in the restaurant alone waiting for him."

"But he's okay now?" Foster asked.

"I think he will be," Victor assured him.

Chaos

Foster finally let out a breath. "That was easy. I've been losing sleep for weeks, trying to develop a solution and they worked it all out themselves. Maybe I'm meddling too much," he said a little ashamed.

"Nonsense," Atticus brushed off his concerns. "We got lucky and things are working out perfectly. Now it's up to you to go get that farm for Kathy and Bobby." He turned and reached for the door.

Victor and Atticus entered the large council chamber and searched for their women. They were easy to find. Tala and Ariel were sitting in the back of the room deep in discussion. They were so preoccupied they didn't even notice when the men entered the room. Victor slid in beside Ariel while Atticus settled next to Tala. The room was empty besides their small group and Foster so Victor decided talking wouldn't be a problem. He leaned forward so he could see past Ariel to question Tala. "I've been meaning to ask you, what happened to Cornelia? Did she head back to Utah to spend some more time with her mother?"

"No," Tala said with a smile. "Actually Rand McBride hired her. She's going to be in New York for a while it seems."

"McBride? Why?" Victor asked curiously.

"He hired her to track down his biological parents." Tala confided. "But first she's doing some research on his current parents. McBride wanted ammunition, so to speak. He thought it might help when he confronts his parents about his origins. Cornelia is investigating them, then she'll see what she can find on his real family history."

Tighe stepped into the large room. "We're almost ready to start. Once we begin we'll need complete silence until the hearing is concluded."

"We understand," Atticus assured him then watched as the elderly councilman exited the room. Atticus subconsciously began to rub Tala's knee.

Victor smiled. He was happy for his father. Atticus had been so alone and isolated for centuries. It was nice to see him trust again... to be able to function in the open, not hiding on the farm. He had to admit Tala was good for his dad. At first, he had his doubts. After the rocky start they'd gotten off to, Victor was worried Tala would eventually drive a wedge between him and his father. He couldn't bare it if that happened. He loved his father more than anything and could never live without him.

The last few months seemed like a miracle. Victor had spent more time with Atticus than they had in the previous decade. He didn't know what he'd do if he lost his father now. But his concerns had been for nothing. Once he got to know Tala, he liked her. She needed to lighten up a bit, but his father was making progress on that front too. Victor smiled at Ariel. Things had changed so drastically so quickly. He silently compared where he and his father had been just last year to where they both were now. Life had a way of working things out. He sobered when the door opened and several members of the council stepped into the room.

* * * *

Alex paced the small room, waiting for one of the councilmen to signal it was time to start the hearing. She really wished this thing

Chaos

was over already. She walked to the window and stared vacantly outside.

Elizabeth DeLacy moved to her side. "Relax dear, this will be over soon." She slipped her strong arm through Alex's tiny one in comfort. "I know it's difficult. The first one always is."

Alex turned to look at her new friend and forced a feeble smile. "Thank you for being here. I'd never get through this without you."

"Of course you would," Elizabeth disagreed. "I remember my first trial. I was just as tense as you are now. We had to punish a couple for theft and embezzlement. Not as clear cut as this one, but almost as difficult. The couple was very well liked throughout the community. I felt so guilty afterwards. I knew we'd done the right thing, but it was still very difficult. I kept track of the children for years. I had to make sure I hadn't ruined the entire family forever."

"And?" Alex asked. "Did the kids turn out okay?"

Elizabeth grinned. "They turned out fine," she assured Alex. "And I finally realized it didn't matter. If the family had been ruined, it wouldn't have been because I agreed with our council's ruling. It would have been because the children made poor choices just as their parents had. You know what the council is going to rule in there. It's a fair punishment for the Dillinger's crimes. None of this is your fault or your responsibility. Your only choice in there is whether you pardon those people for their heinous crimes or you agree with the council and send them to the island. And in truth, do you really have a choice?" Elizabeth asked. "Pardoning those killers would endanger your community. It's your job, your responsibility, to protect your people at all cost. You think you have a difficult choice to make, but in reality there is no choice to be made at all."

Alex didn't say a word. She was considering what Queen Elizabeth was saying. She had to agree, Elizabeth was right. There was no choice to be made. The Dillinger's could not be set free. They would just pick up where they left off and more people would die. "The Island of Mautzkan just sounds so harsh," she told Elizabeth. "Patricia will have a harder time with it than Lawson. She's always been pampered. Having to work a full time job to pay her own way is going to be a shock."

"The custodians of the island have dealt with worse," Elizabeth assured her. "That's why we hire shadows for the job. They have the tools they need to handle anything. Anyway, they only take a portion of each charges income for expenses and restitution. Those two will still have money to burn, they'll just have to work for it now. Considering their crimes they should be thankful for the punishment. Everyone on that island is a criminal, except for the custodians. This way we don't have to worry about the two of them resuming their experiments. Their neighbors can take care of themselves. Now enough about the island, walk into that room tonight with confidence. Put aside your emotions and go in there and represent your people." They both turned when the door opened and Dimitri announced they were ready.

"Charles is already on his way, he'll be waiting inside for you to join him," he told Elizabeth. Then he lowered his voice to whisper in her ear. "Thank you so much for being here. She needs you tonight. You have no idea how much your approval and support means to her."

Elizabeth nodded and stepped into the room, pausing momentarily to locate her husband. Alex and Dimitri took a step forward when Dimitri's phone rang. He glanced at the display then whispered to Alex, "I need to take this. Go ahead, I'll join you in a minute." Alex continued into the room. Dimitri flipped open the phone then pressed it abruptly to his ear. "Bastian, is this important? We're about to begin the hearing."

"I only need a moment. I'm in New York and I need to get to Dublin tonight. Can I catch a ride with you or should I make my own arrangements," Bastian asked. There obviously wasn't time for casual conversation.

"We have room," Dimitri said a little hesitantly. "But what about Melissa? You know she's our first priority."

"Melissa is stable. I'm still working on that problem, but I have pressing business in Dublin. I don't want to keep you, I know you need to get into the hearing. I just need to know if I can catch a ride with you, or if I need to charter my own jet," he asked again.

"No, no." Dimitri sighed glancing into the large room and seeing the hearing was about to begin. "I need to go. Be ready. I'll call you when we're finished and you can meet us at the airport." He snapped the phone shut and silently slipped into the room taking his seat beside Alex.

Hours later Bastian sat in the small waiting room just outside the hanger. He watched as Ty's pilot, Lillie he thought, conducted her walk through. She was thorough. Bastian had watched the routine a million times before. It was easy to discern between the conscientious pilots and the lackadaisical ones. He immediately stood when the large black limo pulled up and stopped just outside.

Lillie looked up. Ty had told her she would be flying to Dublin and that she would be taking some important friends of his. She froze when she saw Alex Deveraux step from the limo. She exhaled a long, deep breath and finished her inspection. She shouldn't be surprised. It had only taken about five minutes working for Ty to realize he knew every important, influential person in the city. But Alex Deveraux? She was probably the richest, most successful woman in the world. He wasn't kidding when he said this flight was important. She caught a glimpse of another couple exiting the limo. She knew those faces, too. Who were they? She couldn't put a finger on it, but she knew they were also influential people and she was pretty sure they were here from out of town. Of course, they were from Ireland. What were their names? The DeLacy's or the Delaney's something like that. She couldn't remember, but she was determined to make this a perfect flight for them all. She wanted Ty to look good, he'd given her so much this was her chance to give something back. Lillie was determined to make this the best flight ever. The last thing she'd ever do was let Ty down.

Another couple exited the limo. She didn't recognize these two. They followed the DeLacy's, that's right it was the DeLacy's, to the plane. It looked like they were close personal friends and they were saying goodbye. Apparently the last couple wouldn't be passengers. She immediately looked away to give them privacy. Watching them made her feel like a voyeur or something. Another couple stepped from the limo, closed the door then casually leaned against the back door. The man looked familiar. She paused trying to remember who he was. She was sure he was someone's father, one of Ty's friends. Oh yeah, it was Victor's dad. The man that had been injured back in Pennsylvania. A second car pulled down the drive and stopped directly beside the limo. Two large, buff men stepped out and immediately pulled a man and a woman from the car. The passengers looked angry, or annoyed maybe. Victor's father and the woman with him approached the new arrivals and had a brief conversation with the two large men. Then they flanked the... what? The new arrivals didn't seem like a couple. Lillie watched as Victor's father and his partner escorted the man and woman from the second car to the plane. That seemed strange to her. The new arrivals seemed out of place in the original crowd. She would have

Chaos

pegged them as prisoners but they weren't in handcuffs. The friends of the DeLacy's returned to the limo and waited. Lillie spotted the man who had been sitting in the lounge. He exited the building and made his way to the plane. That should be it. All of her passengers were accounted for. The young couple and the two men must be staying in New York.

She glanced again at the two guys standing beside the car. Why was it that Ty only had hot, sexy friends? She never saw him with a wimpy looking guy or a nerd. She thought that was unusual since he was in the computer business. Okay, it was gaming but still. Most of Ty's friends were big and buff and hot. How was that possible? If she didn't know better she'd think Ty was shallow, but he wasn't. He was the kindest, most easy going man she'd ever met. With him what you saw, was what you got. Too bad he'd come back from that last trip with a ring on his finger. Lillie smiled. Had she pegged that one or what? She knew once Ty had a wife, he'd have a ring. There were too many single, seductive women in the city to take a chance. Lillie thought of Samantha and her smile widened. She liked Ty's wife. Sam was no nonsense and down to earth. They made a good couple and it only took seconds around them to see how in love they were. She was happy for her boss. He deserved happiness. Heaven knew he always did his best to make everyone around him happy.

Lillie turned to head for the open door and froze. The hotties were watching her. Well, she wasn't interested. She'd learned her lesson with hot men. Her husband had been dashing and sophisticated and a dirty, rotten, cheating pig. No thank you. It was the single life for her from now on. If she ever did fall in love again, which was unlikely, the guy would have to be normal and average and drab. Hot, sexy, exciting men got bored with monogamy. The good just didn't outweigh the bad on that scale. The last thing she needed was another heartbreak. She gave the men a nod. Then

Lillie quickly slipped through the door and headed for the cockpit. It was time to get this show on the road. They had a long flight ahead of them.

Dante and Nick watched as the pilot gave them a quick nod then climbed the stairs and closed the door firmly behind her. Nick let out a long sigh as he turned to Dante then froze. "What?"

"Oh, no you don't!" Dante demanded. "You will not abandon me, man. I need you," he practically begged. "We're the only sane, single ones left." He gently hit the palm of his hand on Nick's forehead. "Snap out of it," he said briskly. "We already lost Thomas. Warriors are dropping like flies. It's an epidemic," he whined. "You're all I have left. Forget that woman and avoid her like the plague. You promised we would stick together. Now, keep your word and let's go hunt." Dante studied Nick for a reaction.

Nick smiled. "You know she's hot," he countered. "I saw you checking her out. Don't jump all over me when you were thinking the same thing I was. I'm not going anywhere, but I'm not dead. She's an attractive woman and I was simply admiring the scenery." He slipped behind the wheel and started the car. "Where do you want to go first?"

Dante let out a long breath in relief then smiled. "Let's head to the park. They seem to be flocking that way lately for some reason. I'm in the mood to kick a little vampire butt tonight. How 'bout you my man?"

Nick smiled then took off for the park. He glanced in the rearview mirror just in time to see Megan and Tony climb back into the limo. "You distracted me," he told Dante. "We left Tony and Megan back there without a single word."

Chaos

Dante flipped around and looked through the rear window. "Oops," he said feeling a little ashamed. "Well... too late now," he turned back around to look straight ahead. "We'll apologize next time we see them."

* * * *

Dimitri studied the occupants of the plane. Alex was seated next to Elizabeth, who was sitting next to her husband Charles DeLacy. Patricia and Lawson were on the other side of the row, Atticus and Tala were seated slightly behind them just in case Tala needed to do her thing and control them. Bastian had distanced himself from everyone. He was at the back of the plane silently staring out the window. Dimitri leaned in closer to Alex then whispered in her ear. "Do you mind staying here with the DeLacy's? I need a little time with Bastian alone."

Alex turned her head and kissed Dimitri gently on the lips. "I'll be fine," she assured him. "Go see what's bothering him. I'm sure it has to do with Kylee," she frowned. "I hope everything is okay." She patted Dimitri's leg then turned her attention back to Elizabeth and Charles.

"I can't believe you're leaving," Dimitri heard Alex say mournfully. "I'm going to miss you so much."

"Me too dear," Elizabeth said sincerely. "But you promised me you would keep in touch. I'm going to hold you to that."

"Absolutely," Alex said with enthusiasm.

"I do regret we didn't have time to stop off at the Jackson's store," Elizabeth sobered. "Promise me you won't let the cat out of the bag. Charles and I want a little payback for the way they treated our boy." Her eyes went cold and dark. "In addition to the Jackson's I have an ax to grind with the Sanders. Nobody treats my kids that way. They will pay for their behavior," she promised. Her mood lightened when she saw the amused look on Alex's face.

Alex was grinning from ear to ear. "I promise. I can't wait to see how you handle them. There's no way I'd spoil the surprise. Tony and Megan plan on returning to the fort now that you guys are leaving so Megan can spend some time with Tala. Only a few people know they're in town and none of them know they have a connection to you and your family. I'll do my best to keep it that way," Alex smiled mischievously. "Secrets are hard to keep, though. You might want to return soon just to be safe."

"You are a little imp aren't you?" Elizabeth said amused.

Dimitri blocked them out. He needed to find out what was going on with Bastian. He studied his friend momentarily then sank into a chair. "So, you going to tell me what this is all about?" he asked keeping his voice flat.

"Huh?" Bastian said pulling his attention away from the window. "Uh, nothing really. I just need to get to Dublin to finalize the purchase of that factory. I want it for a lab and if I wait too long, someone else is going to realize what a steal it is."

"And?" Dimitri said casually.

Bastian furrowed his brow. "And what?" he asked.

"That's my question." Dimitri said never taking his eyes off Bastian's face. "There's more. I suspect it has to do with Kylee. Oh sure, I understand the need to get the ball rolling on the factory, but that's not what has you urgently rushing out of New York. Tell me what's going on."

Bastian hesitated. He really didn't want to talk about this. "I won't concede that it has anything to do with this trip, but you're right. Kylee and I are no longer involved. We've decided it's not in either of our best interest to continue a relationship."

Dimitri raised his eyebrows. "Oh?" he asked. "Why's that?"

Bastian sighed. He wasn't going to get any privacy until he explained the situation to Dimitri, so he might as well bite the bullet and bare his soul. "I realized she's not in love with me. She's in love with the idea of becoming a warrior and living forever. I'm not willing to give her that. So it's over," he answered calmly. The realization still made him feel like a sharp knife was stabbing him directly through the heart. He loved Kylee, but she loved the idea of living forever. How had he been so blind?

"I don't believe that," Dimitri told him. "Sure, Kylee has grabbed onto our world with both hands. I can see that." He said when Bastian looked at him skeptically and a little exasperated. "But she is risking her life to be a part of it. She's completely devoted to saving Melissa. Her passion and dedication doesn't have strings attached and neither does her love for you," he said confidently.

"I guess we'll just have to disagree on this one," Bastian said soberly.

"So whose idea was it to end the relationship?" Dimitri asked curiously.

"Hers," Bastian said. "Well, actually ours. It was a mutual decision. I told her I would never turn her. So, she decided not to waste her time with me any longer. I wished her well and told her there are a lot of warriors in the community. Maybe she'll find someone else that feels differently about the transition."

"How does that make things better?" Dimitri asked. "It's going to be just as dangerous for someone else to attempt the change. If the transition is too much for her to take, she'll still be dead." Dimitri knew he was being harsh, but he wanted to shock Bastian into fighting for the woman he loved. It was ridiculous for Bastian to believe Kylee was using him. She was obviously in love with Bastian. She might not admit it, but she was hooked. Neither one of them would be able to move on. Dimitri didn't know the solution to this problem. He knew Bastian would never attempt the transition. The loss of his mother was too painful. And after all this time it was still too fresh. Kylee was human. Dimitri couldn't imagine what it would be like to find Alex then lose her after a few short years because she was human and her life span was so short. He feared Bastian's resistance to risk a transition might alter his life forever. He just hoped the impact wasn't too profound.

Bastian didn't know how to answer that. He'd thought of it, of course. But he was trying to avoid that reality. The thought of Kylee attempting the transition with someone else was just too painful. Knowing how close she would be to the man that changed her almost killed him. He also knew the risk was just as great with another man as it would be with him. Each time his mind went there, he shut it down. Thinking about Kylee's death made him physically ill. His heart beat quickened and he started to breathe faster. He needed to shut this down. "Thanks for the reminder," he said angrily. "You think I haven't thought of that? You think it doesn't kill me every time I consider what might happen to her? But it's not my choice is it? If Kylee wants to be changed, I can't stop her from finding someone that will risk her that way. The only control I have is over what I do." He looked up at Dimitri. "I won't risk her life. The rest is up to her." Bastian shifted his gaze back to the window. He sat there, empty and depressed. He'd tried so hard not to fall in love with Kylee. He knew it was reckless and stupid, but he just couldn't help it. He had fallen for her totally and completely and now she was gone. Almost as quickly as she had entered his life, she left it and there was nothing he could do about it.

Dimitri studied Bastian and knew the conversation was over. Bastian needed a distraction. "How is the fort coming along?" he asked. "Are we ready to start sending out the kids?"

Bastian knew Dimitri was trying to change the subject to get his mind off Kylee. He considered ignoring his old friend, but decided the distraction might be nice. "I think it is close enough. Ty and Sam have the droids ready. The only thing still in the works are the goggles for the obstacle course. We can start the kids on the course without the goggles then introduce them to the scenarios once Ty and Sam work out the bugs." He glanced at Alex and the DeLacy's then moved his gaze to the Dillinger's. "How'd the hearing go?" he asked soberly. "I realize their presence here means they've been sent to the island, but did everything go smooth in there today?"

Dimitri laughed. "Not in the least," he said with a smile. "This case keeps taking turn after turn. Just when you think you have it all figured out another surprise slaps you in the face."

Bastian studied Dimitri. "Can you tell me anything about it?" he asked curiously.

"A little," Dimitri said hesitantly. He could share most of the details with Bastian and the rest of the warriors. Maybe this was just the thing to get Bastian's mind off Kylee for a while. "The council started off by outlining the crimes each member committed.

After our conversation the other night with Foster and the Keisser's, we questioned Patricia again. She admitted to killing Mary Jane Bowers. She did it because George was going to divorce her and marry the woman he loved. Patricia wouldn't allow that. Victor was right, Patricia killed Foster's mother because she was obsessed with the idea of becoming queen. If George divorced her, the dream would be lost."

"That had to be hard on Foster," Bastian surmised. "To find out you're real mother was murdered by the woman you've believed for centuries was your mother. Is he doing okay?"

"I don't know," Dimitri admitted. "He seems to be taking it all in stride, but I think he's going to have a break down in the near future. Avery has vowed to keep an eye on him and help him through this. He'll do it. Avery is feeling guilty right now. He thinks he failed George and is very protective of Foster. I'm not an Avery fan, but I think he's the perfect one for the job in this instance."

"I agree," Bastian said watching Dimitri. There had to be more, they already knew about Patricia before going into the hearing this morning.

"So, the council gets finished outlining the crimes when Foster throws in the first unexpected twist," Dimitri continued. "He demanded to know why Patricia killed his father. Of course everyone was shocked by the accusation. The council asked him why he believed Patricia was responsible. It was Atticus that answered. He simply said, location."

Bastian sat silent, curious about the new twist.

"Patricia gleefully admitted to killing George. She believes it makes her clever. She said she rigged the machine to blow once

Chaos

George assembled it. It was in the garage because she was still living in the house and didn't want to deal with the inconvenience of the mess. Apparently George was going to leave her. He had confronted her about Dannica's death and Patricia finally admitted she'd been drugging their daughter. George couldn't forgive that particular transgression. He had many faults, but he truly loved his kids. Patricia didn't know George had already drawn up the trust giving everything to Foster. She believed by killing him, she'd inherit everything. She planned to distance herself from Foster immediately but once she found out Foster controlled her future, she still needed him. So, she continued to keep the secret about his real mother and let him believe the lie."

Bastian let out a long breath. "Wow," he finally said. "That's got to be a blow. The woman he's been taking care of all these years, thinking she was his loving mother, is actually the woman that murdered both his parents. I've never been a Foster fan, but I have to admit I feel sorry for the guy."

"I think we all do," Dimitri said. "So, the council added the charge to Patricia's long list of crimes and began to move on to the sentencing portion of the hearing. That's when Victor interrupted. He made a formal request to charge Lawson and Patricia with Manslaughter for their responsibility in his mother's death. The council denied the request. They said they would only consider the motion if there was a witness that was willing to testify. If a witness had new information regarding the night Dannica died, they could reopen the case. Atticus wasn't happy about it, but Victor told the council the entire story. He outlined everything that happened that night, not sparing the gory details."

"What happened?" Bastian pressed. "Wait, that had to be hard on Victor and Atticus. Are they okay?" His gaze immediately shifted to Atticus and Tala. He seemed alright now.

172

"Yes," Dimitri said proudly. "Victor stood there and told the whole story, never faltering. Once he was finished, he not only made a formal request for the Dillinger's to be charged, but he also requested the council revisit their original verdict on Atticus. He insisted Atticus acted in self-defense and that his father saved his life that night. He made a pretty good case against the Dillinger's in the process. Then he pointed out that if they hadn't been feeding Dannica that toxic potion for years, she wouldn't have gone crazy and tried to kill him and his father."

"Did the council agree?" Bastian asked. There was no doubt in his mind Atticus should be officially acquitted and the Dillinger's should be charged, but the council didn't always see things the way the warriors did.

"I have to admit I was surprised, but they did," Dimitri told him. "They acquitted Atticus of all charges and apologized to him for the banishment. The council decisions are supposed to be kept confidential but we all know the results will spread throughout the community within a matter of days. Soon our people will know they have mistreated Atticus for centuries. They will also learn of the heinous crimes the Dillinger's committed. We still haven't found the leak, but in this case I'm glad we have one. I realize people like the Sanders and the Jackson's won't change their mind about the Keisser's, but the rest of the community will. I'm sure Tala could take it, but now she doesn't have to be ostracized for something Atticus was forced to do so long ago."

"So how long?" Bastian asked. "How many years did those two get on the island?"

"Life," Dimitri said immediately. "Actually they both got life sentences for killing Tina and Regina as well as attempting to kill Melissa. Patricia also got life sentences for killing George Dillinger and Mary Jane Bowers. Lawson was given a life sentence for his treasonous actions in selling bombs to vampires and his attempt to murder Atticus. They'll never leave that island. I'm sure they'll try to escape, but people far more clever than those two have tried and failed. Nobody can get off that island unless they're supposed to," Dimitri said confidently.

"Good," Bastian said relieved. "It's nice to know they can never come back. But what if someone down the road decides to revisit this? The same as the council just did with Atticus. The Keisser's have dealt with the harassment and threats for too long. They need closure and somehow it needs to be permanent."

Dimitri smiled. "Elizabeth and Charles took care of that," he said smugly. "They argued that letting Patricia or Lawson go free would endanger all fae communities, not just ours. They insisted a clause be written into the official record requiring a committee of council members from at least five regions to review this case before any change can be made. They argued that if the Dillinger's were set free, chances were slim they'd return to America. It was far more likely they'd take up residency in another community and pick up where they left off. The experiments and the deaths would continue. For the safety of the entire fae species, the decision on their status could not be left to one community. Of course Alex immediately backed her on that. She also wanted to make sure those two could never go free. The council agreed unanimously. The stipulation is part of the official record. Those two will never leave that island. The Keisser's have their closure as does Foster. I'm not sure he understands what a blessing that is yet, but eventually he will. He'll be just as grateful as we are that the council added that clause and the connection is over."

"I've never heard of that before," Bastian admitted. "Was it something they just made up and convinced the council to go along with?"

"Not exactly," Dimitri told him. "Charles and Elizabeth are smart. In their free time here, they researched previous convictions and punishments. They found a case over a thousand years ago where the council put a similar clause in the record. We're lucky to have them on our side."

"I'm glad it's over. Now we just need to wait out the human trial on Kahn and this whole thing can be put behind us. Well, once we figure out the solution to Melissa's condition that is," Bastian added as an afterthought. Once again he turned to the window and casually stared into the darkness.

Dimitri knew his conversation was over. He glanced at Alex and smiled. Just the short distance between them was too much. He needed to feel her by his side. They had become so close in such a short amount of time. He grinned as he casually strolled down the aisle. In a few more months they would be married. Alex would be his forever. He knew she already was, but somehow the ceremony had become important to him. He took the promises made in that simple ritual very seriously. He just hoped this thing with Radek would be over by then. He didn't want a huge black cloud hanging over them when they went on their honeymoon.

Chaos

Chapter Five

Kylee couldn't sleep. She pushed herself into a sitting position and glanced around the room. It was still dark so it must be early. She focused on the window and realized she'd risen before the sun. After closing her eyes for several seconds she blinked a few times, trying to adjust to the darkness. She still felt a little weak and she was so thirsty. Wait! There was half a bottle of Gatorade left. She fumbled around for several seconds before her hand brushed against the soft plastic. She guzzled it down then considered. No way could she go back to sleep. She needed a shower then she'd grab something else to drink and head to the lab for an antibiotic. Over the next few days she'd be sure to watch her liquid intake. How many times had she counseled ER patients to double their water consumption following an injury? Most people don't drink nearly enough liquid during the day and she'd fallen into the same trap. It couldn't be coincidental that she felt weak and dehydrated following her injury. She reached back and rubbed the wound on her back then winced. It was getting worse. A shower would do her good. It would give her a chance to thoroughly clean the wounds.

She pushed herself out of bed and slowly made her way to the bathroom. Kylee studied herself in the large mirror. She looked awful and she felt like an old woman. She took a deep breath, gritted her teeth and pulled the large shirt over her head. She was shocked at how much that simple act took out of her. She braced her hands on the counter and tried to pull herself together. While she stood there, she glanced down at the wound on her arm. It was getting worse. The skin was inflamed and puffy. She pushed gently on the cut and winced. It was definitely infected. Why was it getting infected? Bastian had cleaned it thoroughly then bandaged it immediately. It should be fine. The injury on her back worried her. She hadn't cleaned it properly and if her arm was infected she was sure her back was too. She straightened and turned to study the damage in the mirror.

Kylee's eyes widened. It was even worse than she'd feared. Her back was inflamed and puss was hardening around the incision. She needed to douse it with alcohol then saturate her system with a strong antibiotic. But first, she needed a shower. After scrubbing herself down she dressed in loose clothes and headed for the kitchen. Why was her mouth like cotton already? Her stomach growled and she realized she was hungry. When was the last time she'd eaten anyway? Kylee opened the fridge and grabbed another Gatorade. She rummaged around and found a package of ham. That sounded good. She pulled out the package and cut off a few pieces. Maybe she'd throw in an egg or two. She pulled out a pan to begin the chore of making breakfast.

Chaos

Lilith hid behind a large tree and watched the white deer enter the enormous base. She felt jittery with anticipation, this had to work. She was starting to get a little worried. Radek was going to be angry. He'd been very clear. He wanted dozens of vampiric animals running around and she'd only created two so far. She cringed as she remembered the beaver. The instant she spotted it, she knew it would be perfect. But once she'd turned the thing, there was no way to control its movements. It ran the wrong way and almost attacked a couple of military guys taking a break from their flight training. She was able to create a distraction and lure it back into the forest but the damage was done. The guys got a good look at the beaver and knew something was amiss. She had to fix it before the humans panicked. Radek clearly didn't understand he was playing with fire. But as usual, he didn't care because he wasn't the one in danger of getting burned.

She'd been thinking about Radek's plan since she arrived. He sent her out here and ordered her to wreak havoc knowing she couldn't control it. It didn't take her long to realize he was sacrificing her for his cause. The knowledge made her beyond pissed. So much so, she had almost left without going through with it. If he wanted vampiric animals, he could bring his butt out here and create them himself. But she changed her mind by the end of that first day. Radek thought he was clever, but he underestimated Maedoc and the others. She realized Radek was counting on another meeting with the three kings. A meeting where he could somehow turn this around and blame her. She smiled. Radek would never get another meeting. The kings had threatened to act swiftly and without mercy. Their strike would be fast and furious. She'd be gone by then of course. She didn't like it, but her time here was finished. She glanced back at the deer, disappointed that she couldn't wait to see what happened. But it was getting late. Lilith sighed and took a long, deep breath. It would be light soon. If she didn't hurry, she wouldn't make it back to the cave in time. With any luck the deer would do its job and at least one of the people at the fort would be killed today. Lilith turned and disappeared into the darkness.

* * * *

Jordan wandered into the large field. Feeding the white deer had become routine. She'd heard somewhere that they weren't albino, they had a special gene that made them wintery white and so beautiful. It was surprising how friendly they had become once they got used to her. She felt privileged to have the chance to interact with this rare herd of deer. For once, the military's obsession with security had resulted in something positive. Erecting the fence around the fort had isolated the small herd and probably saved their lives. She glanced around, funny they were usually out and about by now. Maybe she'd missed them. She'd slept in this morning and had gotten a later start than usual. Then, once she was up, she decided to work out with the droid. She hoped they wouldn't have another battle out here but it was always a possibility and she needed to be prepared. It was after ten now, but not one deer was in sight. Jordan paused in the middle of the field and took a seat on the grass. If she remained perfectly still, maybe they'd smell her and move this way. She laid the bag on the ground and slowly lowered herself onto her back. She'd hear the deer coming and could adjust slowly as they approached. Right now, she wanted to enjoy the sunshine. She knew it would be winter soon and once the snow started falling she wouldn't be able to enjoy nature for a while.

A single deer moved from the shadows and headed her way. Jordan got excited. No matter how many times she fed them, she still got a little thrill. Her stomach always did that little somersault when she saw one. These were wild animals. She knew that. She was very cautious around them. If they got spooked the most likely response would be flight, but wild animals were unpredictable. She reached into the bag and pulled out the oats. She'd found them in the barn with the horses a few days ago and discovered the deer loved them. She remained perfectly still as the small deer slowly walked across the clearing headed her way.

* * * *

Kylee entered the lab and immediately went to Melissa. Within minutes she'd finished checking and recording her vitals. Everything seemed the same. Melissa wasn't getting any better, but luckily she wasn't getting any worse either. Kylee checked the chart and noticed Melissa had missed a dose of medication last night. Why hadn't Bastian taken care of that? He didn't have any notes cancelling her treatment. Maybe he retired early like her. Or he could have assumed Kylee would come back to take care of it. Just as she had assumed he would. After a slight hesitation Kylee measured out the exact dose and moved to Melissa's side. She gently prepared the vein for the injection and pressed the needle into the woman's limp arm. Melissa didn't react. Thank goodness. Kylee half expected another violent episode. Bastian must have been right. She wasn't developing an allergic reaction, the larger amount was just too much for her system. If they kept the dosage the same Melissa would remain stable. They would still need to find a cure, but at least they had bought themselves some time.

Kylee walked to the bench and started to sit on her stool then paused. She felt a little better after eating breakfast but her back was still killing her and she knew she had developed an infection.

Her body ached and she was burning up, the lab was so hot but her hands felt clammy. Maybe the infection was causing a fever. Kylee slowly walked to the side of the room and settled onto the small daybed. She'd just rest for a minute then she could get started on another formula.

Kylee woke with a start. Had she fallen asleep? She sat up and winced. Her back was going to be a problem if she didn't get some antibiotics into her system immediately. She stood, intending to make her way to the medicine cabinet but hesitated. It was so hot in here, she needed air. Kylee walked to the small window and opened it as wide as possible. She stood there, taking in the cool morning breeze then froze. What was that smell? It was potent and a little disgusting. Kylee moved closer to the window to study her surroundings and the smell got stronger. She looked around but couldn't see anything obvious. She glanced down and studied the ground directly outside the window. Was there something dead out there? She really wasn't sure.

Kylee exited the building just in time to see a small white deer approaching the young shifter. What was her name again? Oh yeah, Jordan. Jordan was a little shy, but she seemed to be picking things up pretty quickly. The training routine Morrigan set up for the shifters was brilliant. The kids were advancing rapidly. All the students here were talented and had a lot of potential. Kylee still felt blessed that Alex and the others had let her stay. Things were bad with Bastian right now, but that didn't change her excitement for this project. Kylee slowly made her way toward Jordan. As she got closer, the smell got stronger. Could it be the deer that smelled so awful? Maybe he'd rolled around in something dead in the forest.

Everything happened at once. Jordan stood motionless, waiting for the deer to gently take the oats from her hand. She spoke softly, trying to sooth the majestic animal. As she looked into his once beautiful face, she froze. There was something wrong with this deer. It seemed to be foaming from the mouth and its expression looked evil somehow. Jordan panicked and turned to run, at that exact moment the deer lunged forward and sunk its sharp teeth into her upper arm. Jordan squealed out in pain. She tried to pull away, but the deer had her in a death grip. She frantically tried to get away but couldn't, no matter how hard she twisted and pulled. Finally, she stopped fighting and started to scream.

* * * *

Dusty and Nebi woke early and headed for the beach. It wasn't often they had a morning free. Things were going so well in their relationship and they wanted to enjoy it. Neither teen had been in love before, which made them a little nervous about the situation. They reacted to the uncertainty by taking things slow and enjoying the moment. Their lives and the world they had grown up in was changing drastically. They were two of a kind and that knowledge brought comfort. Each shifter understood the other's need to fight and defend their community. Initially that's what had brought them together. They were both talented, driven and strived to be the best in their class. Which is why they found themselves constantly competing with one another.

The young couple believed if it was meant to be, everything would work out. But their future was so uncertain. Rough times were coming and people would lose their lives. They had sat on the beach all morning talking about their future. Both of them knew another fight was inevitable, they just hoped everyone would be ready when it arrived. Eventually serious talk turned to playful expression and they were able to relax in each other's arms and enjoyed the peace and tranquility of the morning. It was nearly noon when they finally decided to head back to the fort.

The couple was just coming into the clearing when they spotted the white deer. At first they were enchanted by it. Neither one had seen a white deer before they moved to the fort. No matter how many times they spotted them, it still felt unreal and special. Nebi turned to Dusty and commented on Jordan's dedication. Every day she was out in the clearing patiently waiting for the unique herd to arrive. The rest of the group seemed to be solely focused on their studies and their training, but Jordan was different. She took her studies seriously, but always took time out for herself as well. More often than not that time was spent admiring the wildlife that was so abundant here at the fort. Everything appeared to be quiet and peaceful then instantly it changed to chaos. Something had frightened Jordan, but when she turned to move away, the deer attacked. Dusty and Nebi didn't think, they both rushed to Jordan's defense.

The deer must have sensed the two shifters approaching. It immediately turned, flinging Jordan around in the process. The girl had gone limp and was no longer fighting. Dusty reacted. He lunged forward and was able to position himself to the side of the large beast. Then he wrapped his strong arms around the vicious animal's neck, locking his hands together as he tried to choke the deer enough to force it to drop Jordan. What was wrong with this thing?

Jordan fell to the ground but didn't move. Dusty was still wrapped around the deer's neck holding on with all his might. Now what? He needed to somehow manipulate the deer's position so when he let go it would run back into the forest not towards the fort. He anchored his feet and tried to forcibly turn the animal in the other direction. The deer wouldn't have it, it immediately began thrashing

Chaos

around clearly trying to throw Dusty from its back. Dusty knew he was running out of time. He needed a plan. He was losing his grip and once he let go, the deer would come after him; or worse Nebi. He took a deep breath and released the animal then jumped back quickly.

Nebi realized what Dusty was doing. It wouldn't work. She was sure of it. The deer was too quick and there was something wrong with it. Did it have rabies or something? She rushed forward in an attempt to distract the animal and give Dusty time to escape. The deer tried to clamp down on Dusty's arm, but he was too quick and the animal couldn't get a good grip. His large snout slid across Dusty's bare arm leaving saliva in its wake. The liquid immediately began to burn and felt like acid eating away at his skin. Dusty dropped to the ground, the pain was excruciating. He slid his forearm back and forth as he tried to wipe the toxin off with the tall grass.

Nebi saw Dusty was in trouble and reacted. She started yelling at the deer, jumping around and waving her hands. Bad idea. The deer charged her. Nebi pulled the large knife from a sheath on her belt and held her ground. She'd only have one shot at this. The moment the deer got within striking distance, Nebi pivoted then lunged; slicing through the animal's large shoulder. The deer immediately whipped around, splashing blood across Nebi's leg. The red liquid instantly ate through the thin material of her sweats. The toxic acid began to burn, eating away the soft flesh as it sizzled and spread. Nebi tried not to scream but her calf was on fire. What was going on here? Dusty was back on his feet in an instant. He needed to save Nebi. The two kids continued to fight off the deer, each one worried about the other. Dusty and Nebi continued to fight as they tried to ignore their burning limbs, both of them knowing their lives depended on their endurance.

Morrigan heard the commotion and ran into the yard. As soon as he saw the deer he knew what it was. Vampires had bitten another animal and the kids were in danger. If he didn't resolve this fast they might not survive. He broke into a run, pulling his dagger from his belt as he shot across the clearing.

Samantha and Ty were working on the obstacle course when they heard the screaming. They immediately rushed to the field and took in the scene. "Sam, go get Jake. We need help out there. I could use Orin, too." He took off in the opposite direction.

Sam started for the apartments then changed her mind. There was a bow and arrow in the warehouse. If she could get up on the roof, she could easily take that thing out. Sam rushed through the building grabbing the weapon on the move. She climbed the ladder that led to the roof and rushed to the edge of the building. Sam crouched down, steadied her bow and shot the arrow directly into the deer's heart. The animal jerked then dropped to the ground. Morrigan and Ty were immediately on it. They both slammed their daggers directly into its heart then stepped back to check on the kids.

By this time Kylee had reached the group. Her wounds and her fever had slowed her down significantly, but she eventually made it. She dropped to the ground and studied Jordan. Her wound was serious. Her arm was a mangled mess and the teen was in shock. Kylee didn't want to move her patient but they didn't have a choice. They needed to get Jordan to the house where they could clean the wounds and bandage her immediately. The young girl's arm looked as if someone had splashed her with some kind of acid and it was still eating through her skin. Kylee moved to Dusty and Nebi. The two were frantically trying to survey the other's wounds.

Moments later, Sam joined the group. Once she was sure her arrow had hit its mark, she'd immediately climbed back down off

Chaos

the roof and ran to the apartments. She alerted Jake and Orin then rushed back to the scene. "What do you need?" she demanded.

Morrigan took charge. He turned to Dusty and Nebi. "Get to the lab. You need medical attention right away." He turned back, planning to give Kylee instructions when he saw Orin. "We need Breena," he barked. "She needs to get to work on that cream stuff she made for Ariel."

Orin stopped and looked at Jake. The senior warrior was the one to respond. "More vampiric animals?" he asked.

"Yes," Morrigan confirmed. "We need to carry Jordan to the lab. Her injuries are severe. I hope Breena can save her arm," Morrigan said concerned. "Ty can you help me carry her?"

Sam stepped forward. "What are you going to do with that thing?" She was worried someone else could come in contact with it before they had time to destroy it.

Morrigan paused. "We need to get the kids to safety, then we'll come back and burn it. And we need to do it very carefully. Contact with that liquid is lethal."

Sam looked at Kylee. "Can you help me carry Jordan to the lab?" she asked. "If we can get Jordan, the men can burn the deer and make sure nobody else gets hurt."

"Okay," Kylee said reluctantly. Could she help carry Jordan? She could barely walk herself.

Dusty stepped forward and lifted Jordan into his arms. "I got her," he called over his shoulder as he began walking toward the building.

Nebi moved up next to Dusty and kept pace with him as they strolled to the large building. Dusty's arm was clearly still hurting him and carrying Jordan was making things worse. Nebi could barely walk. They looked like seasoned fighters, wounded and sore, leaving the battlefield as they carried their injured comrade to safety. At that moment Kylee's heart swelled. Those kids were special. She vowed to do whatever it took to ensure a full recovery for all three of them.

Kylee took a deep breath. She didn't feel well at all. She took a step forward then faltered. How was she going to get to the lab?

Sam saw Kylee stumble and moved in next to her. She immediately took Kylee's arm and pulled her toward the lab. "Where did it hit you?" she asked silently.

"It didn't," Kylee assured her.

"Don't try to be heroic," Sam warned. "That was a vampiric animal. Ty told me about them. Their blood, their saliva, any liquid that comes from that animal is toxic. It won't get better on its own. The only way to cure the wound is by using Breena's medicine. So, I'm going to ask you again… where did it get you?"

Kylee was having a hard time walking. She felt weak and her body was on fire. "It's not the animal. I do have a wound, but it's not from that deer. I'm working on it. I just need some Tylenol and an antibiotic. That should break my fever. Once Breena finishes with the kids she can help me clean the wound on my back."

Sam studied Kylee, she was watching for any sign of deception. She didn't see one. "What happened to your back?" she asked.

Chaos

"Bastian was working on something in the lab and discarded the flask in his garbage can. When we gave too much antidote to Melissa yesterday she kicked me in the stomach and I flew backwards, falling on top of that garbage can. The flask broke and sliced my back as well as my arm." Kylee pulled her shirt sleeve up to show Sam the wound. "Bastian cleaned my arm with alcohol and then bandaged it, but it still looks infected. My back is worse," she admitted. "I tried to take care of it this morning but I'd like Breena to look at it for me once the kids are settled."

Sam studied Kylee's arm. It did look infected. If Kylee's back was worse this could be bad. She wasn't an expert but the infection looked severe. They needed Alex, but she was on her way to Ireland. Sam just hoped Breena would know what to do.

Kylee realized Bastian was conspicuously absent. Where was he? Bastian wouldn't ignore this kind of trouble, he'd be right in the middle of it. "Where is Bastian?" She was trying to sound casual but she had a sick feeling in her stomach. "If he can just tell me what was in that flask I should be able to fix my own wounds."

"Uh..." Sam paused. "Well, he's not here."

Kylee's head shot up. She was staring at Sam in disbelief. "Where is he?" she finally asked.

"He left yesterday, he initially went to New York but right now he's on a plane headed for Ireland," Sam admitted. She wouldn't lie to Kylee. The woman deserved to know the man she loved had deserted her.

"I see," Kylee said resigned. She hadn't seen that one coming. She mistakenly believed she had plenty of time to talk to Bastian about his experiment and their situation. Instead, her lack of response had sent him traveling to the other side of the world. Kylee refocused on her current dilemma. She was extremely dizzy but stubbornly fought the blackness that was trying to take over. She succeeded, but barely. And, she didn't need a thermometer to know she had a severe fever. She'd been neglectful and reckless since last night. First by not cleaning her wounds properly, then when she didn't take a strong antibiotic first thing this morning. She might pay dearly for allowing herself to be distracted.

Ty sensed Sam's discomfort and studied the back of the two woman. Something was wrong with Kylee. "Can you three handle things here?" he asked abruptly. "You're not going to try to move it, right? You're just going to douse it with gasoline and set it on fire?"

"Right," Morrigan said concentrating on the task. He wanted to get rid of the thing before anyone noticed. The fire would alert the coast guard in the tower, but that couldn't be helped.

"Good. I'll be back as soon as I can," Ty said as he turned and darted toward Samantha.

Sam was supporting Kylee's weight as well as she could, but it wasn't working. If Kylee passed out, Sam knew she wouldn't be able to prevent the doctor from falling to the ground. Maybe she should just pick her up and carry her to the building.

Ty slid in next to Sam and immediately lifted Kylee into his arms. His timing couldn't have been better. Once Kylee was situated, she lost consciousness. "Did she get bit or just come in contact with some of the saliva or blood from that thing?" he asked concerned.

"Neither," Sam told him. "She cut herself on a tainted flask in the lab yesterday. The injury looks infected to me." Sam pulled Kylee's sleeve up and showed the wound to Ty. "She said her back is worse than her arm. I'm really worried. It looks bad and Alex is in Ireland by now."

"We'll see what Breena can do," Ty said grimly. He too was worried, but he wasn't about to call Dimitri or Alex. They needed a break but their trip wasn't merely for pleasure. They had a lot to learn while they were in Dublin. They needed time to study and dissect. If they were forced to come back so soon just to heal Kylee, they'd miss out on some valuable information. Information their community needed right now.

Ty placed Kylee on the soft mat next to Jordan. Then he turned to Dusty and Nebi. Dusty was crouched in front of Nebi working on her leg. He ripped the tangled material away from her calf and was trying to wipe the deer blood off with the palm of his hand. Nebi was wincing and squirming with pain.

"Sit still," Dusty said impatiently. "I need to clean this blood off. The longer it remains on your skin, the worse your wound is going to be."

Ty walked to his side and put a hand on Dusty's shoulder. "You're going to make your wounds worse," he said softly. "You two go in the bathroom and rinse the saliva and the blood off immediately." He looked at Dusty's hands and noticed blood on his fingers. "Now you have a second wound. You're hands are going to be sore for at least a week. You can't fight that way." He jerked his head toward the open door. "Go, rinse off and then come back. Breena should be here by then. We need to get her cream on the wounds and some medication into you right away."

The two kids did as they were told. Within seconds Ty heard the water come on and the couple began to argue about who should be treated first. Ty smiled and moved back to Sam. "I'd like you to stay with her until Breena gets here," he said studying Kylee with a frown. "I'm going to call Victor. Nick and Dante can take care of things in New York until Alex and Dimitri return. Other than Morrigan, those two are the only ones that have experience with those animals. I wish I believed that was the only one out there, but I don't. I suspect one or more vampires spent the night creating those things to cause us problems," Ty stopped abruptly.

Sam could see the panic in Ty's eyes and wondered what had put it there. Then it hit her, they hadn't checked on the dogs yet. They considered taking Ace and Bo with them onto the course this morning, but decided against it. They needed a clear view and the dogs would just get in the way. "Go! Check on them," she said urgently. Her stomach clenched. She couldn't bare it if a vampire had bitten Bo or Ace. What if they'd both been attacked? She was so attached to them already. They were like her kids.

Ty took off at a dead run. He made it to the barn in record time. When he flung open the door the two dogs rushed to him, tails wagging, ready to play. Ty could finally breathe. There was no sign the barn had been tampered with. He crouched down and hugged the dogs in relief. It would have killed him if he had to put them down. He wasn't sure how long it took for an animal to turn completely but as he ran his hands over the dogs he knew they hadn't been bitten. Ty straightened and entered the barn. He wanted to check the horses. This reeked of Lilith. If he was right, she'd think she was clever if she could get into the barn and sacrifice one of their pets.

Ty took his time, gently running his hands over the horse's bodies. Once he was positive they hadn't been harmed, he shifted his attention to the barn. He would have to make sure the building was safe and to do that, he needed supplies from the city. It was time to call Victor.

Chaos

Once Ty disconnected the call, he studied the weaknesses in the barn. Victor would be here later tonight but he didn't want to wait that long. From now on the dogs would be spending their nights in the house, but they couldn't risk the horses. He glanced up when he heard Sam approach. He knew it was her, he could feel her presence and her stress.

Ace and Bo darted toward Sam. Ace reared up on his hind legs and began jumping in front of her. Bo kept both feet on the ground but circled Sam, silently begging her for attention. Sam laughed then knelt on the ground and began rubbing both dogs' stomachs enthusiastically. "I was so scared Ty," she said softly. "They feel like our kids and I was so terrified we might lose one or both of them. Realistically I knew it would be both. They are very protective of each other. If a vampire attacked one, the other would immediately jump in to defend his friend." She stood and walked to where Ty was carefully studying a small window.

Ty instinctively put an arm around Sam when she moved in beside him. "I know," he said soberly. "I realized the same thing. That panicked run from the fort took a few years off my life." He looked at Sam then gently kissed her forehead. "We're going to have to be more careful from now on. I'm bringing the dogs in at night. They'll sleep in our room," he told her. "They're quiet for the most part. They shouldn't bother anyone else in the house."

Sam smiled. "Nobody will mind having them inside at night," she assured him. "They all love the little monsters and everyone staying at the fort will want them safe. What do we need to do to the barn to protect the horses?" She glanced back at the window. "I saw you studying that," she raised a hand to point at the small opening. "How do we vampire proof it?"

"I don't like to do it, but I think for tonight we need to cover it. I'll find enough wood to nail it up. If we secure it from the inside, it will be far more difficult to get in." Ty released Sam and began walking the length of the barn looking for wood planks.

Sam walked to the back of the barn and slowly pushed the heavy door open. She propped a brick in front of it to prevent it from swinging shut and immediately began filling her arms with wooden planks. "I was cleaning up," she said when she noticed the surprised look on Ty's face. "I thought just outside would be a good place to store them. It gets them out of the way, but the roof hangs over enough it should give them some protection from the elements. I was also planning on covering them with that large tarp over there, but hadn't gotten that far yet."

Ty took the planks from Sam and walked to the far wall. He dropped the boards on the ground then turned back to her. "That should be good for now. We just need to get them through the night. I called Victor. He and Ariel are heading right out. Victor is going to bring some electronic and alarm equipment so we can set this up right but they won't get here until after dark. We'll fortify the barn first thing in the morning."

"Will it be enough?" Sam asked walking to the small tack room and returning with a can of nails. She set the container on the ground then headed for the tall ladder leaning against an empty stall.

"You can count on it." He grinned for the first time since Sam had arrived. "Atticus loves these horses. I asked Victor to bring a few items out to set things up, but Victor will go overboard. The barn will be just as secure as the house once we're finished. Actually, I planned it that way. If anyone gets cornered for any reason I want plenty of places they can go for safety. We're responsible for those kids. When I ran out of the forest and saw that deer attacking three of them I couldn't breathe. I never want to force Dimitri or Alex to visit one of those kids' homes to notify their parents their child is gone because we didn't protect them."

Sam placed her head against Ty's chest. "I was thinking the exact same thing. We've been relaxed here. We haven't really taken the threat as seriously as we should. I'm going to place boxes strategically around the place if that's okay. I found a bunch of padlocks you can open with a combination. I'll come up with something easy to remember and let you know what I decide on," she looked up at him. "I'm going to place a couple of bows and a stash of arrows in each box. I don't know if an arrow will kill one of those things, but we learned today it will take one down. That gave you and Morrigan time to move in for the kill."

"About that," Ty said placing a finger under Sam's chin and lifting her head so he could look her in the eye. "I was proud of you today." He leaned down and gave her a gentle, but passionate kiss. "I keep forgetting how skilled you are with a bow. The deer was jumping around, lunging at us, trying to attack the kids, then Morrigan, then me. Your aim is amazing, Sam. You saved all of us from getting wounded again. I'm confident Morrigan and I could have taken it eventually. But I'm almost as confident one or both of us would have been injured the same as Dusty and Nebi were."

"I agree," Sam said pleased. "It's just instinctual for me. I'm still learning to fight up close and personal with the vamps. It takes focus and concentration. But grabbing an arrow and shooting it at my attacker is second nature to me. I've been doing it for a long time. There are a couple kids that are also really good with a bow and arrow." Sam was considering the situation. "Gerty is still struggling, I've been watching her. Ever since the vampire attack she's lost her confidence. If nobody objects, I'd like to work with her a little more frequently with the bow and arrow. She has natural talent and I think it might help her regain the confidence she's going to need if we get attacked again."

"I'll talk to Morrigan. He's been frustrated with her for weeks now. In fact, he's asked me to send her home. I won't. Sending her back to her pack disgraced, isn't the answer. That's not what this academy is for. Plan on spending an hour with her on Monday, Wednesday and Friday. She'll meet with you instead of attending the combat class Morrigan's been teaching," he paused. "Is there anyone else we should move over to your class?" He grinned as he slid his body closer to hers. "You'll be the hottest teacher at the fort. All the guys will be begging to get in. I can just see it now, an immediate interest in learning bow and arrow skills."

Sam laughed and pushed Ty away. "Very funny." She kissed him playfully. "Let's get this window boarded up. I want to check on Kylee. I realize I'm no doctor, but I've cared for plenty of wounds over the years. Her back looks so awful. I've never seen an infection that bad before. Do you think Breena can save her?"

Ty sobered. "I hope so," he let out an exasperated sigh. "Kylee's a doctor. She knows better. What was she thinking?" he sounded annoyed.

"I know," Sam said in agreement. The two focused on the window for a moment in silence. "Uh, can we go back to your question for a minute? I'd also like to work with Vivian. She's doing okay in hand to hand, but her hearts not in it and she too has natural archery skills," she paused. "You said we're going to have to leave soon for California. I want to get in a few lessons with those two before we leave. If you're right and vampires are out there turning the wild life into vampiric mutations I want to know those two can handle things while I'm gone."

"Are they good enough to handle that?" Ty asked curiously.

Chaos

Sam smiled, "They are," she assured him. "Give me a week or two and I'll sleep a lot easier leaving everyone here alone when we go."

"You've got it," Ty said lifting the first board to the window. Sam immediately stepped forward and held it in place while Ty secured it to the building. The two worked on the barn for the next couple hours to ensure the safety of the horses until a more sophisticated system could be put in place.

* * * *

The large group quietly sat in the living area of Breena and Orin's apartment. Dusty, Nebi and Jordan were all doing much better. Jordan's injuries were the worst. Breena had ordered her to mix two tablespoons of that powdered substance with chocolate milk every four hours until she went to bed. She'd need to drink two doses as soon as she woke in the morning. Large amounts of the medicated cream had been lathered over the raw wound. Breena also bandaged Jordan's arm and placed it in a sling. She assured everyone the injury would be significantly better in the morning. Dusty and Nebi's injuries were far less severe. The two had drank the chocolate milk and slathered the cream over their wounds then proceeded out the door and onto the field to practice their fighting. The casual observer would never know the two had been injured at all.

Kylee was a different story. She was once again unconscious and had been for several hours. Her fever was still extremely high and when she did wake, she was confused and at times appeared to be hallucinating. No matter what Breena did, the fever would not dissipate. Kylee's body was fighting a massive infection and everyone was afraid it was losing. Even the heavy antibiotic solution being administered through the IV didn't seem to be helping. Breena refused to give up. She thoroughly cleaned the wounds at regular intervals. Clearing away the puss that continued to seep from the swollen, red gashes then dried to form a crusty barrier around the wounds. More than anything, Breena wished Alex was available. Nothing she tried seemed to be helping.

Jake spoke first. "What are we going to do about Kylee?" he asked no one in particular. "She's not getting better, she's getting worse. The longer she has that infection, the more likely the chance she'll have permanent damage. That's if she survives at all."

Victor stood and paced the room. "We need to develop a plan of attack," he said taking charge. He wasn't sure he was still responsible for what happened at the fort especially with Jake here, but nobody else seemed to want the job so he took the lead. He glanced at Samantha, studying her intently. "Every molecule in my body is telling me Lilith is responsible for the animals," he began.

"I agree," Sam said casually. "I've been battling her for a while now. I know her as well as anyone can. She's reckless and ruthless, but she's also curious. I think she'd enjoy experimenting with different animals to see how they react to her transformations. I also feel, very strongly, that she's not finished. We killed two of her animals today but I'm confident there are more. If not, there will be soon," Sam finished glumly. The very idea terrified her. Those things were hell to deal with.

The room fell quiet again. Everyone was exhausted after the long, stressful day. Once the initial threat was removed and the injured were turned over to Breena, the rest of the group went to work on securing the others. Every kid at the fort was warned about the potential danger. New rules were developed. There was to be no one outside after sunset and no one was allowed to leave their

Chaos

bunkers before eight o'clock each morning. The kids were also instructed to survey their own quarters. If there was even the slightest flaw in the bunker, they would be moved to a new room. Nobody wanted to take any chances with the children's lives.

Ty and Sam finished securing the barn then joined the others in the forest. Everyone methodically searched the area for additional animals. The only one they found was a beaver residing near a pond at the far south end of the forest. The group had immediately become concerned. What if the beaver had been spotted by the humans? If they were lucky that's all that had happened. What if that beaver had bitten or come in contact with a human? They didn't need that kind of human trouble, they had enough of the supernatural kind.

"I agree with Sam, which is why I believe it's urgent to develop a plan of attack tonight," Victor said again. "We've done the best we can to secure the fort and the farmhouse. Ty has the animals taken care of for tonight. Thank you Ty and Sam for that," Victor softened. "Dad loves those horses. He'd be devastated if he lost even one of them to this."

"We understand," Ty said. "I feel the same about my animals." He subconsciously laid a hand on Bo's head then let it travel lovingly down his back.

"I don't want to alarm Dimitri or Alex but I think we need to inform them," Victor finally told the group. "I'll call them. I'm going to down play things. I haven't decided what to tell them about Kylee yet. But I will tell them three of the kids came in contact with the animal. I'll be brief about their injuries and assure them Breena has it under control. They'll be worried, but not alarmed."

"I agree," Jake said in support. "Alex needs to stay in Ireland for now. The DeLacy's have taught her a great deal during their visit, but our world is going to change. Alex needs to learn about the Dublin contingent and bring back a plan we can implement and live by. If she's denied this opportunity, our entire community will suffer. We need to avoid that if possible."

"Okay, so do we all agree with the plan so far?" Victor asked. Everyone either nodded or verbally gave their support. "Good. I'll call them early tomorrow morning." He paused then shifted gears a little. "Thomas is already aware of the situation out here. I thought he needed to be in the loop because it's going to be up to him and Abby to jump in and assist if Nick and Dante get in over their heads."

"Can they manage that?" Sam asked concerned. "I mean every time they leave the house they're followed by reporters."

"If Thomas needs to go out, he'll find a way. I'm not worried about Abby. She goes out all the time without being detected." Victor shot a look at Morrigan. "It seems pretty unfair to me, but I guess being a shifter has its benefits."

Morrigan grinned. He knew nothing would stop his sister from doing exactly what she wanted to. She was stubborn and independent and smart. She definitely had a will, so she would find a way. "Jealous?" he joked and raised an eyebrow.

"Not in the least," Victor grinned back. "My point is that New York is covered. There aren't many vampires left there so Nick and Dante should be fine handling the streets alone for a while. The lack of vampire activity has us all concerned, but I think it can wait for now."

"I think it might have pertinence," Jake disagreed. "I've been thinking about this for a while. I believe these animals are just part of a bigger plan. Radek has been building an army. He needs us preoccupied so we don't attack until he's ready for us. The proof is that nonsense with Thomas, now the animals. I think he's throwing obstacles at us to keep us busy until his army arrives. We can put it aside for now, but I think we need to take a serious look at our options as soon as Alex and Dimitri return from Ireland."

Everyone agreed. They had all been thinking along the same lines but nobody really knew what the solution was. Victor took advantage of the silence to proceed. "Alex and Dimitri are planning on staying in Dublin for about two weeks. Dad and Tala are going to remain as well. As Jake pointed out, this trip is important. Let's give them all the time they need if we can. I don't want to call them back here unless it absolutely cannot be avoided."

"I agree," Ty said in support. "While we're making plans and discussing safety I want to fill you in on a slight adjustment I decided to make on two of the students schedules."

Morrigan became interested in this. He wondered if it had to do with Dusty or Nebi. He was getting frustrated with Dusty. He had tremendous talent and potential, but no matter the threat, Dusty always turned into a tiger. They couldn't send him out to scout or participate in a battle if he couldn't overcome that flaw. A tiger was too conspicuous in America.

"This morning when Sam saw the threat the animal was posing, she immediately rushed to the roof and shot it with an arrow. I'm not sure it killed the deer, but it did take the large animal down so Morrigan and I could finish the job," Ty began.

"Thanks for your quick actions Sam," Morrigan smiled at her. "And your accuracy," he added. "It was a big help and a great idea."

"Sam wants to work with Gerty and Vivian over the next couple weeks. They are both extremely talented in archery and neither is exceptionally adept in hand to hand," Ty continued.

"You can say that again," Morrigan said sarcastically. It was a good idea. He'd been impatient and disappointed in Gerty ever since the battle over a month ago. She wasn't improving, in fact he thought she had taken a huge step backwards. "Gerty doesn't have any self-confidence," he warned Sam. "You might be taking on more than you bargained for with her."

Sam smiled at Morrigan. "I know exactly what I'm taking on. Vivian does okay in a fight, but they are both more adept with an arrow. I think it might be good for Gerty. She's lost her nerve and the idea of another battle terrifies her. I think I can get a little of her confidence back and give the bunch of you an added layer of protection once Ty and I have to leave. Trust me, this is going to work." She assured the group, but she was mainly focusing her attention toward Morrigan. "I've placed several boxes around the fort and up on all the roofs today. They are loaded with a couple bows and plenty of arrows. The padlock is a combo lock and all the combos are the same. I used 4321 to keep it simple. I wish I could just leave them open, but I'm worried the vampires might find them and use them against us. This is better even though it's a little more time consuming."

"Good idea," Breena told Sam. "I can't fight, but I'm not bad at archery. I feel better knowing I have an option if things go bad. With Kylee down, I'm the only one here with any medical knowledge. Orin and I have to stay this time. Anyway, I don't think I'm up to a long ride again and flying is out of the question. Would you mind if I joined you while you work with the girls?"

"No," Sam told her. "I think that's a great idea."

Chaos

Ty continued where he left off. "Security is excellent during the night which is our biggest threat. The house, the fort, the bakery, the warehouse they all have top of the line systems installed. Any one of them will protect us in the event of a problem. After tomorrow the barn will fall into the same category. Victor brought a few things I asked for and knowing him a few I didn't. The horses will be safe from harm and the barn will serve as another shelter if anyone gets into trouble and needs somewhere safe to go. I hope nobody objects, but I plan to keep the dogs in my room until this threat has passed. When Sam and I leave I'll take them with me and have Lillie fly them back out to the ranch. It's not safe for them here any longer and they'll be happier where they don't have to be locked up all the time." Ty said a little depressed at the idea. He missed his dogs when they weren't around.

"That covers safety," Victor began. "Ty and I will get up early and take care of the barn. Now we need to talk about the other issues. I think the first thing we need to determine is if the humans have been injured. If not, did they encounter the beaver or the deer before we destroyed them? If Lilith keeps turning animals eventually the humans are going to find out. We need to come up with a plan to deal with that threat. I think the kids understand the gravity of the situation now and none of them will risk going into the woods alone. Our second problem is Kylee. She's not getting better, in fact she's getting worse. Breena has done all she can, but I'm not sure it's going to be enough. I'd like to have a discussion on how you guys think we should handle that."

"I don't know what to do about Kylee," Megan began. She'd been very quiet up until now but she had an idea. "But I was wondering if Marta was ready to open the bakery yet." She looked at the woman curiously.

"I hadn't planned on opening for a few more days. The crew is almost finished with the add-on, so I planned to hold off until they left. What did you have in mind?" Marta asked.

"Well, if you could open earlier I have an idea," Megan began. "We need to find out what the humans know about the animals. If you were to open tomorrow, the humans would come. They're all anxious to check out your shop. I was thinking I might join you. I could already be in place when you opened in the morning. If I set up at a table with a cup of coffee and a muffin or something, I'd blend in and nobody would really notice me. Then I could sift through their minds looking for information on the animals. I'm confident within a very short amount of time we'd know what they know about the situation. We'll also know what their reaction is and we could come up with a plan to deal with it."

"I like it," Victor said immediately. "That way we don't have to question them, we'll know what they know and we can use it to develop a plan. Marta, can you open in the morning?"

"Yes," she said confidently. "Like I said I can work in the bakery, I just thought I'd wait out of convenience. I like the plan. I think it will work and give us what we need. We're lucky to have you on our side Megan." Marta smiled at her compassionately.

"That's the truth," Victor told her. "I might kick your no good husband out of here, but I think we'll keep you. I'm beginning to rely on your talents as a matter of routine."

"You love me and you know it," Tony countered. "If I go, my wife goes. You just remember that when you're trying to determine my fate."

Victor laughed. "So tomorrow we'll find out what the humans know. Now, what about Kylee?" He didn't know what to do. The only two choices he could think of was to call Alex back or take her to a hospital.

Jake stood and walked to the window. "I think our best bet is to bring Bastian back," he finally said softly. He turned to address the group. "Bastian knows what was in the flask that injured her. He's amazing at developing antidotes. If anyone can save Kylee, I think it's him. We can't interrupt Alex, but we can try to appeal to Bastian. I know something happened between those two, but Bastian will take care of this. He's too compassionate not to. If you agree I'll go. I can leave tonight and head to New York then I'll take my jet out first thing in the morning. I can be in Ireland by early afternoon our time; which will be evening in Ireland. If I can swing it, I'd like to head back immediately. Kylee is getting worse. Bastian's going to have to act fast. I can't think of another solution to this. I'm open to suggestions but if nobody else has an idea I'll go pack and leave immediately."

The room was silent for a long time.

"Then we'll go with my plan," Jake decided. "Marta, I'm sorry. I need to do this. Can you handle opening the shop without me?"

"I can, but I'd rather not stay in the new wing alone. Can I stay in one of the apartments or a room in the farmhouse?" she asked softly.

"Of course," Sam said moving in to pat Marta's hand. "Don't feel bad about the request. I'd want to do the same if Ty had to leave without me. We're going back to the farm tonight. We need to be close to the barn in case there's an attack. Everyone else will be staying here at the apartments. You choose. Kylee is going to stay in the apartment across the hall, but the one next door is open."

"Actually, I think I'd rather take the spare bed in the apartment where Kylee is. It would make me feel better if someone was watching over her tonight," Marta said soberly.

"Come on babe," Jake said holding his hand out to Marta. "I need to pack a small bag before I head out. If you come with me now, I can walk you back myself. I'll feel better if you are settled here in the apartments before I leave.

* * * *

Bastian sat at a corner table in Bryan's pub. Business had gone well today. In fact, he was able to get the building for a fraction of the cost he'd expected to pay. Bryan was looking pretty smug. He'd practically danced out of the room when he heard the price the two moron's had settled for. Bastian planned to donate a portion of his savings to their victim. He could ask Bryan for help with that, his friend knew the woman the two men had roughed up a few years ago. If she was struggling as much as Bryan suggested, she'd need the boost. Maybe a little windfall from an unknown relative would help her take control of her life again.

He looked up as a man casually stepped through the front door. The intruder paused, obviously looking for someone in the crowd. Bastian practically growled out loud in frustration. The room had gone eerily quiet and every woman in the pub had their eyes focused on Jake. What was he doing here anyway? Bastian continued to silently watch the warrior. If he wasn't so annoyed by the intrusion, he would have found the patron's reaction to the old man entertaining. Bastian knew the instant Jake spotted him. He waited silently as Jake strolled confidently toward Bastian's table and took a seat. The waitress was hovering immediately, drooling

Chaos

over the hansom new arrival. Jake ordered a beer then studied Bastian intently.

"Why are you here?" Bastian asked coldly.

"It's really good to see you too," Jake said unoffended. He smiled casually at the charming waitress as she set a glass of beer in front of him. He slipped her a generous tip, then dismissed her immediately. He had important things to talk to Bastian about.

The woman frowned, paused, and then hesitantly walked away. "Do you even notice the affect you have on women, Jake?" Bastian asked.

"Huh?" Jake asked thrown for a minute.

Bastian glanced toward the attractive waitress that had just walked away. "Women? They fall all over you but you don't seem to notice. Aren't you even a little flattered by their attention?"

Jake glanced in the direction Bastian was looking and was honestly surprised to see the admiring look on the girl's face. He redirected his attention back to Bastian. "I guess I didn't notice," he admitted. "Look, I need to talk to you Bastian. It's important."

Bastian couldn't help it. Watching Jake's discomfort amused him. "So talk," he said casually.

"Is there somewhere we could go?" Jake asked. "What I need to talk to you about is too sensitive to discuss in a crowded pub."

Bryan approached the table and greeted Jake. "It's been a long time," Bryan said cheerfully. "How have you been Jake Wilder? The legal business treating you well?"

Jake grinned. He always liked Bryan, the kid was a lot like his mother. "I can't complain," he finally said. "How's your sweet mother these days?"

"Mom's great. She's decided to volunteer at the local shelter. The work is hard sometimes but she really gets a sense of satisfaction out of helping those women and children." Bryan shook his head in disgust. "It's hard to believe a society that claims to be civilized has so many monsters hidden among them."

Jake nodded in understanding. "Unfortunately they are everywhere, dear boy. How's your scoundrel of a father these days?" Jake said, smiling when he thought of Abraham O'Malley.

"Dad's great," Bryan said smiling back at Jake. "You should stop by the house. Dad would love to see you again."

Jake sobered. "I wish I had time to do that. Maybe next trip. I actually have some pressing issues at home. I plan to head back out tonight. Please give my best to your parents though. Maybe I can catch them next time around."

Bryan also sobered. It must be pretty important for Jake to fly to and from Ireland in one day. He glanced back at the bar. "Well, I'm glad I got to see you then. I'll tell my parents you said hello. But now I've got to get back to work. I hope you have a safe return."

"Thank you," Jake said watching Bryan retreat behind the bar. "Is there somewhere we could go to have a little privacy?" He asked turning his attention back to Bastian.

Bastian sighed. "Let's go to the apartment upstairs, Bryan's place. I'm staying with him. He won't mind if we use it for a private chat." Bastian stood, grabbing his glass of Guinness as an

Chaos

afterthought before he strolled reluctantly up the stairs that led to Bryan's apartment. Jake followed close behind.

Bastian closed the door behind Jake then went to the sitting area and fell into a large chair. He studied the man standing before him. He was curious about the visit, but also a little nervous. An unexpected visit from Jake couldn't be good. Bastian took another long drink of the Guinness and waited.

Jake slowly walked to the window and stared into the distance. The sun was beginning to lower. He didn't know where to start. "Before I go into the main reason for being here, I have a question for you Bastian." He turned to face the son of Adrian Carrigan. Every time he looked at the boy, he felt guilty.

"Okay," Bastian said immediately. "Go ahead."

"I know you're angry with me for turning Marta. I understand, I really do, but your anger is hurting her. She misses you terribly. She thinks of you as one of her adopted kids. Will you try to forgive her? Will you please try to get past your anger and let her into your life again?" he asked sincerely. "It is so hard for her to see you every day and not be able to talk to you. The two of you used to be so close. If you need to, be angry with me forever, but please try to find it in your heart to forgive my dear Marta."

Bastian scowled. "I'm not angry with either one of you, Jake." He cleared his throat when Jake looked at him skeptically. "I'm not. I used to be. I was furious. I was angry and disappointed in you at first, but not anymore." He shrugged. "I understand Jake, I really do. And to be honest, I'm happy for you. I'm happy for Marta. I know the two of you will have a long, happy life together. You both deserve that."

"Then why?" Jake asked moving back to the sitting area and settling into the large couch. "Why are you avoiding us?"

"Actually, I've been avoiding you," Bastian said honestly. Maybe it was time to have the conversation he'd been avoiding. "It doesn't have anything to do with your marriage or the transition of Marta. It has to do with dad." Bastian lowered his head and stared at his hands. He was fidgeting. He never fidgeted.

Jake stared at Bastian in shock. What did the boy know? Did he know it was his fault Adrian died that day? No wonder the man hated him. Jake was the one responsible for the lonely life Bastian was forced to live. The man was an orphan, and it was all Jake's fault.

"I guess it's time to face the past regardless of the outcome," Bastian began. "When dad died, Luke paid me a visit. He's the one that broke the news to me. I know dad and Luke were close. Luke struggled that day. He was more upset than I'd ever seen him. It was a difficult task, but he got through it." Bastian paused to take a deep breath. "I had some questions, but I knew my questions could wait. It was a time for sorrow, not doubts. Afterwards, even years later, I never could bring myself to talk to Luke about my concerns." He looked at Jake. The man looked upset, maybe even worried. So he was right, dad had died on purpose. "Jake?" Bastian closed his eyes, trying to prepare himself to hear the truth. "Dimitri told me you were there that day. The day dad died. I never knew that. You never said anything. Luke never could talk about the details of that day. Will you?" He looked at Jake in anticipation. He needed to hear it. He needed the truth.

Jake watched Bastian. The man was asking him to relive the worst moment of his life. Nothing he'd ever done before or since was burned into his memory as permanently as that day. Bastian would hate him, Adrian was dead because of his mistake. "What do you want to know, Bastian?" he asked as he felt his throat closing up.

Bastian took a deep breath. "I need to know how dad really died. He was depressed and lonely. I've always wondered if he allowed himself to be killed in battle so he wouldn't have to face life without mom any longer. Luke said he died valiantly but I've always had doubts about that. It would have been the perfect way out. I need to know if..."

"You think your dad...?" Jake sat motionless, horrified. How had this happened? "Bastian, your father did die valiantly just like Luke told you he did. Adrian was lonely, he missed your mother everyday but he was not depressed, not like you think. He was valiant and honorable and most of all he was a good man and a good father. Men like Adrian do not allow themselves to be killed. Especially not by a vampire."

"Then how did he die?" Bastian said, not convinced. There was something Jake was hiding. "Why are you so nervous and hesitant to talk about this?"

Jake looked at Bastian and knew he had to confess. "Because it's all my fault your dad is dead," he said ashamed. "He died saving my life. I was preoccupied and reckless. Your dad was killed because I wasn't paying attention. I was thinking about something else and before I knew it I was surrounded by vampires, wounded and fighting for my life. Not well either, I was losing the fight. Adrian was my partner, he saw the trouble I was in and he jumped in without hesitation. He was injured immediately but he kept on fighting, determined to save my life. I was down, barely hanging on so I couldn't help much. Luke and Dylan were across the clearing battling a large group of their own. Adrian was fierce and determined. He always was, but this time was different. He was so accomplished and formidable as a warrior. He took out most of them before he succumbed to his injuries. I am so sorry Bastian. It should have been me. I should have been the one that died that night. It took me a long time before I could face you, Adrian was all you had left. You had already lost your mother, but at least you still had your father. Because of me, you lost him too."

Bastian was watching Jake. He could tell the man still felt guilty about his father's death. "Jake, it's not your fault dad died. He died because he was a warrior. I'm sorry, but you don't get to take that away from him. You have nothing to be ashamed of. I'm the only one that needs to feel ashamed over this. For over three centuries I've doubted my father. I've cheated him out of the honor he deserves."

"I wish I knew you were struggling with that. I should have done so many things differently. Starting with the afternoon of that fateful night," Jake said quietly. "Well, it's time to fix things. I think you need to know the entire story, are you up for it?" Jake asked hesitantly.

"I'm not sure I need to know," Bastian said honestly. "I believe you."

Jake studied Bastian. "Why?" he finally asked. "Why do you believe me now, but you didn't believe Luke when he originally told you all those years ago?"

Bastian thought about that. "It's hard to explain." Bastian began. "I knew there was something Luke wasn't telling me when he broke the news of dad's death. I knew dad was lonely and depressed. I knew he felt guilty and he regretted trying to turn mom. I guess I just immediately assumed the worst. I'm older now, wiser I guess. I've had a lot of time to think about this and I never could reconcile the man I believed dad to be with the actions I worried he took. Does that make sense?" he asked Jake doubtfully.

"Actually it does," Jake told him. "You grew up with your father and knew he was a good, strong, honorable man. That image didn't mesh with the act you believed he took to end his life." Jake shook his head. "But that's why you need to know the truth, Bastian. You need to know how heroic your father really was."

"I'll leave that up to you. I think I can go on just fine with what I know. With the explanation you already gave," Bastian assured the man.

Jake smiled. "I won't let you spare me this," he told Bastian. "It's kind of you and so much like your father, but you need to know everything. It was a difficult time. Marlena and her parents had already left for the new world. They'd been gone for years. We had the treaty, but nobody really enforced it. Radek was still roaming the countryside with his vampire army. The groups were small, but they could be dangerous. Those of us that hadn't moved to America still patrolled each night. It was our turn that night. Luke, Dylan and your father and I met up to patrol the southern region. It was rumored a group of vampires had been focusing on that area for some time."

"But I'm getting ahead of myself. The day actually began much earlier." Jake stood and walked to the window. He needed a little space to get this out. "Luke and I were best friends. We'd known each other since we were children." Jake smiled remembering the man who had given him companionship for so many years. "We were inseparable and a little wild at times. I thought life was great. Luke wanted a new adventure. That afternoon we argued. Luke was tired of my refusal to leave Ireland. He wanted to go to America. He wanted to start a new life and take advantage of the promised land of opportunity. I wanted to remain where we were. It was comfortable to me. It was..." Jake shrugged. "I don't know... easy I guess."

"That's understandable. Ireland was the only home you had ever known. I imagine the thought of leaving for a new, unproven country was a little daunting," Bastian guessed.

Jake smiled. "You know, I've felt so guilty about that day that I've avoided you most of your life. I've always had a hard time facing you. I'm beginning to realize that decision has prevented me from getting to know a wonderful man. I'm sorry, Bastian. You are so much like your father. I don't know if you are aware of this, but your father and I were also very good friends."

Bastian was surprised at that. "Dad talked about the warriors a lot. He said he had some very good, loyal friends in that group. He never mentioned your name. I remember every man he ever mentioned. A few of them even came by the house. Luke was one of them. He visited dad sometimes, more frequently after mom's death but he always came alone."

"Another of my many faults," Jake confessed. "Back then I was antisocial and reserved. The only people I ever talked to were the warriors and the women I planned to bed. It's actually pretty sad and a little pathetic."

Bastian laughed. "I have a hard time believing that," Bastian told him. "You are so smooth and comfortable in a crowd."

"I am now," Jake conceded. "It's a learned behavior. I guess out of necessity." Jake shrugged it off. "You don't remember me because I went by a different name back then. I used my middle name, my parents started it. Dad was a Jacob, too. Mom started calling me Andy before I could walk. When I moved to America I wanted a clean start. It was then that I started going by Jake, which is my real name," he explained.

"You are Amorous Andy!" Bastian laughed. "I always wondered what happened to him and why I never met him. Dad loved you. I hope you know that. Of all the guys he talked about, you and Luke were his favorites. I think the two of you were instrumental in getting him through those tough times after mom died. I'm sorry I didn't know that before."

"It's my fault, Bastian. I should have been there for you after your dad died. I wasn't. It was too hard to face you," he paused. "Anyway back to my story, Luke talked to me the day of the battle. He told me he was leaving for America with or without me. He wanted it to be with me, but he had decided to go regardless of my decision. I was angry and I felt betrayed by my best friend. I felt like he was giving me an ultimatum. We had a huge argument. I told him I couldn't leave, I'd met a woman. I'd always met a woman and Luke knew it was just an excuse. He asked me flat out if she was important or just another fling. I lied. I told him I was sure she was the one. Luke laughed at me. He didn't believe it for a minute. That infuriated me even more. We both said some pretty harsh things that day. Then we left angry and frustrated with each other and ourselves. We still weren't speaking when the four of us met up that night. That's why I was partnered with Adrian. Typically Luke and I would have been a team and Dylan and your father would have hooked up. If Luke seemed to be hiding something the night he told you about your father's death, it was his guilt. We both felt awful, about everything. Luke told me he was just as distracted as I was. We were both thinking about our fight and the fact that we may never see each other again. It wasn't fair to Dylan or your father. Adrian paid the ultimate price for our mistakes."

"I think it's time for you to forgive yourself Jake," Bastian said sympathetically. "I know dad didn't blame you for his death and I don't either. Every one of us have gone into a fight less than focused. I can't count the number of times I've done that myself. Dad's death was not your fault. It was the vampires who attacked your small group's fault. It was Radek's fault. I know every time I go out to fight that something bad might happen. Dad knew that too. He used to talk to me about how to prepare for the time I'd take on that responsibility. He loved what he did, the warrior part and the farming. I was lucky to be raised by such a wonderful man. I'll remember that from now on. I think you should too. You should remember dad for the man he was, and not what you think you took away from me, or him."

Jake had mixed emotions about everything. He had been lucky to know Adrian Carrigan. Maybe it was time to put the guilt behind him. If nothing else, he felt relieved that Bastian finally knew the truth. He wished they could talk about this further but Kylee was in trouble. "I don't want you to think I'm minimizing the past but there are some other things I need to talk to you about. Do you have any other questions about your father before we discuss what actually brought me here tonight?"

"No," Bastian said. He was glad he'd finally had this conversation, but now that it was over he could feel the tension coming from Jake. Something bad was coming and he wasn't sure he was prepared for it. "So, I guess that brings me back to my original question. Why are you here, Jake?"

"Two reasons," Jake said soberly. "First, the vampires have been making more of the vampiric animals that attacked Ariel and Morrigan last summer. So far we've only found two. A white deer that attacked some of the kids and a beaver that was still hiding in the forest."

Chaos

"How are the kids?" Bastian asked immediately.

"They're okay," Jake assured him. "Sam got the deer with an arrow and then Ty and Morrigan killed and disposed of it. We were lucky Breena was at the fort. She quickly made up some of her cream and the powder stuff she developed. Jordan was injured more seriously than the others, but I think all of them will be okay. Dusty and Nebi's injuries were less severe. They're almost back to normal."

"Good," Bastian said relieved. "So what do you need from me?"

"We need you to come back to the fort," Jake said honestly. "Marta's going to open the bakery in the morning and Megan will hang out, scanning the humans to see what they know. We will need to develop a plan immediately. We won't know what needs to be done until Megan finishes gathering information. The beaver was close to the airstrip. We're worried the humans may have come in contact with it. Alex and Dimitri have to stay here as planned, but we need you. I'm not sure the rest of us have the contacts that will be necessary to take care of this without you. If I can get you to come back home, between you and Thomas, I think we can handle anything."

"I see," Bastian considered. He didn't want to return yet. He wasn't sure he could handle being so close to Kylee. How was he going to see her every day knowing she didn't want him?

"There's something else Bastian," Jake said soberly.

"What?" Bastian said sounding impatient. He hadn't meant to sound that harsh, but if Jake kept piling up problems, he knew he'd give in. His father had always taught him the community and responsibility came first. Dad believed very strongly that a warrior always sacrificed his personal well-being for the good of the people.

Jake took a deep breath knowing the news would be a blow. "Kylee is very ill," he said soberly. "Breena's doing what she can, but her wounds have become infected. She's getting worse not better," he paused. "We believe her life is in danger. We need your help."

"What wounds?" Bastian asked. "Did Kylee come in contact with the animals?"

"No," Jake said immediately. "She said the cuts came from a flask in the garbage can."

Bastian furrowed his brow. He'd cleaned that wound himself. It wasn't even deep. How had it become infected? "Wait, you said wounds. There was only one, and I cleaned it immediately. I don't understand."

"There are two wounds. The one on her arm that you cleaned. Then there is a deeper, more serious wound on her back. They are both infected and it doesn't make sense to any of us. Kylee has a severe fever. She's fighting for her life. When I left she was unconscious. Every once in a while she does wake up, but she's hallucinating and incoherent. Breena's had her hooked to an IV since we discovered the injuries but it's not helping. Kylee's infection is getting worse even with the high antibiotic solution. We're all stumped and we need your help."

Bastian stood. "Give me five minutes to pack and tell Bryan I'm leaving, then we'll go," Bastian couldn't breathe. None of this made any sense. "You should have told me about Kylee first. We could have discussed the rest on the way home," he said impatiently.

Chaos

"Maybe," Jake admitted. "But none of us know what went on with you two. I wasn't really sure how you would take the news or what you would do about it. I needed you to know there was more than that. I was counting on your father's sense of responsibility to get you back."

Bastian threw his bag over his shoulder and headed for the door. "Well, congratulations. It worked. Helping our community would have been enough to get me back. We'll deal with the problem together. But my first priority right now is to figure out what's going on with Kylee. No matter what you learn about the animals tomorrow, I won't leave until I know she's okay." Bastian strolled out the door and down the stairs. He had a brief conversation with Bryan then walked out the back door.

"None of what you are telling me about Kylee makes sense," Bastian told Jake. They were in the air, headed back to New York. "The injury occurred a couple days ago. I cleaned her arm myself, immediately. The wound should not be infected, especially not severely. Something else has to be going on with her." He couldn't imagine what though. "She should have told me about her back," Bastian said angrily. He stood and began pacing back and forth. Bastian was wracking his brain, trying to figure out the mystery. There was nothing in that flask that would cause the reaction Jake had described. Unless she was allergic to one of the ingredients. He needed to see her for himself. But that didn't make sense either, because his blood had consumed and neutralized the ingredients before it coagulated. What if she didn't make it? What if his stupid escape to Ireland cost Kylee her life. He turned to Jake in challenge. "Why did you wait so long before telling me? You should have called immediately."

"Bastian, sit down. There's nothing you can do for her until we get back to the fort. It's not like we waited days. We only waited hours. Breena was sure the IV would clear up the infection, which would lower her fever. We didn't think your help was needed. Okay, I admit we underestimated you. All of us honestly believed we needed to do this in person. I thought it would take more to convince you to come home. You're right. If we had called, you'd be there already. There's nothing that can be done about that now. We'll be there soon and you will take care of her. It's not too late, Bastian. I have faith in you and in Kylee's determination. She won't give up. That girl is strong."

Bastian sank back into his seat. This was going to be the longest flight of his life.

Jake hesitated, but decided Bastian needed to hear what he had to say. "I'm not trying to pry and you don't need to say anything in response, but there's something I want to tell you," he began.

Bastian looked at Jake exasperated. Of course the man was going to pry.

"I know you and Kylee have been spending a lot of time together lately. I can also see how much you care for that girl. Likewise, I understand the dilemma you face. It was hard losing your mother that way and I realize you would reject any suggestion to consider the same for Kylee." He rushed on before Bastian could interrupt. "No, just hear me out. I'm not going to tell you that's the wrong decision. I don't know what the two of you can work out, or even if there is a solution to your problem. I know you're the chemist here, and I'm sure you've thought of it already."

"What are you getting at Jake?" Bastian asked impatiently.

"You know there are warriors in our society that aren't willing to risk the change. They find a human mate and keep her human.

Chaos

It's difficult, but they decide for one reason or another that a short time with someone they love is enough," Jake began.

"Yes. I know," Bastian pressed.

"Well, most of them insure their mate's health and longevity so to speak," Jake said, pondering the best way to explain this. "I assume you know what I'm talking about?"

Bastian was confused for a minute then it hit him. "You're talking about the warriors that inject a small dose of warrior blood into their mates?" he considered.

"I am," Jake said, relieved Bastian was familiar with the practice. "Have you assisted in any of those procedures?"

"No," Bastian admitted. "Not personally, but I've heard of it being done."

"I see," Jake considered. "Our people have been doing this for centuries. It was fairly easy to determine the right amount to give a human to increase their immune system, but not enough to completely take them over. It actually takes very little. Giving a human some of your blood will prevent illness and extend their life span slightly. Most of the humans that have undergone this procedure live to be at least a hundred, some a little longer. I've never heard of one of these mates suffering from the normal human ailments that inflict them with old age. No dementia, no Alzheimer's."

"Jake, I appreciate what you're trying to do but that won't work for me and Kylee." Bastian interrupted. "We've decided not to see each other any longer. She's made it perfectly clear that if I won't turn her into a warrior, she doesn't want to have anything to

220

do with me," Bastian confided. "I just have to accept that and find a way to live without her."

"Oh," Jake said disappointed. He'd watched Kylee and Bastian together. He could see the difference in Bastian. He knew the man was in love with the doctor. He had mistakenly believed the feeling was mutual. If Kylee refused to see Bastian unless he turned her, did she really love Bastian or did she just see him as a convenient way to enter their world permanently? "I'm sorry, Bastian. I was really hoping you had found your mate."

"It's fine." Bastian said staring out the window. "It just wasn't meant to be."

Chapter Six

Bastian entered the small apartment and went straight to the bedroom. He swung open the door and froze. He had expected Kylee to look bad, but actually seeing her in this condition took his breath away. He felt like he'd been sucker punched. She was ghostly white and she looked gaunt. He rushed to the bed and pulled down the sheet. He needed to inspect the wound on her back. Jake said that was the worst one. He pulled up her shirt and studied the injury carefully. Something wasn't right here. He glanced around the room looking for a chair.

Breena stepped forward and set up a folding chair next to the bed. Bastian immediately sat down and slid his forefinger over the injury. "The IV has the strongest dose of antibiotic that I dare give her," Breena told him. "She was a little dehydrated so I've included a saline solution but nothing is helping. I've tried everything I can think of. The wound is sealed off, but the infection is causing the puss to accumulate around the edges. I've been cleaning it every hour without success. I thought if I knew what was in that flask maybe I'd know what to do. She's getting worse, not better."

"There wasn't anything in there that would cause this." He continued to study Kylee's back. "Would you do me a favor and get me a needle and a tube? I need to take a blood sample." He asked Breena never taking his eyes off Kylee. Bastian was confused. The wound was definitely infected. It was red and pussy and the area immediately near the wound was hard. But the cut itself was intriguing. It was sealed off like Breena said. It shouldn't be. It was like the injury had healed instantly. Warrior blood would do that. That's how it worked and the flask had warrior blood in it. But if she had warrior blood in her system she shouldn't have an infection. Unless...

Breena returned with a needle attached to a tube. Bastian abruptly stood once he had his sample and started for the door then stopped. "Uh, Breena?" he called.

"Yeah?" she asked. She was relieved Bastian was here. He wasn't a doctor, but he could be. He'd chosen chemistry instead. If anyone could help Kylee, Bastian could. If there was a cure, Bastian's company had developed it. Breena knew Kylee was now in the best hands possible.

"Would you mind getting Morrigan for me?" he tried to sound casual. If he was right, they would need to act fast.

"Okay," Breena said confused. "It might take a minute, I think he's staying in the bunkers so he can be close to the kids. I'll need to get Orin to help me. It's getting dark and I don't want to be out alone."

Chaos

"Of course," Bastian agreed. "Have him come to the lab. I need to analyze this blood." He disappeared out the door without another word.

Morrigan walked into the lab and paused. Bastian was sitting on a chair, staring into space. He wasn't moving, he looked like he was in shock. "Hey, what's up? You asked Breena to find me," Morrigan said approaching Bastian. He came to an abrupt stop in front of the chair. "What's going on?" he asked again.

Bastian blinked, twice. This didn't make any sense. He absently shook his head, trying to clear his mind then stood. "Could you please call your mother, Morrigan?"

Morrigan furrowed his brow. "Okay," he said hesitantly. "What am I supposed to tell her?"

Bastian began pacing the room. "Just tell her I need to talk to her." He stopped and locked eyes with the shifter. "It's important."

Morrigan pulled out his phone and dialed the number. "Hey mom," he said a moment later. "Things are okay here. Uh, maybe we could catch up later. Bastian needs to talk to you about something important." He held out the phone and Bastian immediately took it.

"Hello Jackie," he said as he regained his composure. "I'm sorry for interrupting your evening. I know it's late."

"No problem dear," Jackie Cooper said pleasantly. "I'm always available to help. What's up?"

"I need some information," Bastian began. "I don't have a lot of experience with shifters, until recently our species didn't really interact. However, I do remember hearing, several years ago, that warrior blood is toxic for your kind. Is that true, or was it just a rumor?"

"It's true," Jackie confirmed. "Well, let me qualify that. If a shifter has casual contact with a warriors blood, that's not a problem. For instance, if I'm treating a warrior for something and some of his blood gets on me, it won't have an adverse effect. It's only dangerous if warrior blood is somehow injected into a shifter. We are very careful about receiving blood from anyone. Nobody knows why, but it's not just warrior blood that harms us. It's anything supernatural. We couldn't receive fae blood either. We're even careful about human blood. Our bodies can tolerate it blood, but there are side effects. We only use it in an emergency. Why are you asking?"

"Because a shifter came in contact with warrior blood through an open wound," Bastian told her. "Now the wound is extremely infected. Well, actually the wound is healed over, but the infection is trapped inside. It appears to be spreading slowly. Her fever is sky high and..."

"I've heard enough," Jackie cut him off abruptly. "You need to act fast. Let me talk to Morrigan. He knows how to make what you need. While he works on a special drink, I need you to mix up an IV solution. Two parts saline one part sodium," she ordered. "Keep the IV constant. Even if she appears to improve she needs the constant drip for the next four days. Now let me talk to my son."

Bastian held out the phone and went to work gathering up the saline and the sodium he needed. "I'll meet you in Kylee's room," he said then rushed out the door.

Morrigan listened to his mother's instructions. He knew how to make the lime drink by heart. He and Abby loved the stuff. They drank it regularly in the heat of the summer. "Mom, you never told us that drink was actually medicinal."

"I was so thrilled you two liked it I didn't want to spoil anything. It's great for preventing multiple threats," she told him. "Now, tell me who's in trouble? Which shifter came in contact with warrior blood?" she asked. "I know it's not you because if the injury is that bad, the victim is probably unconscious. Is it one of the children?" Jackie was concerned. The injuries Bastian described were life threatening.

"Well… I'm a little confused about that," Morrigan admitted. "Mom, Kylee must be a shifter. How is that possible? If it's true, that's two shifters in a matter of months that fooled us. Two of them masked their scent. None of us had even the slightest suspicion Kylee was one of us. Not even dad. How is that possible? We've all believed for months that Kylee is human."

Jackie was floored. She'd met Kylee Quintana. She'd worked with her in the ER. The girl didn't even have a trace of shifter scent, how could she be one of them? "I don't know, Morrigan. I've worked with the doctor before. I never suspected a thing. I'm going to talk to your father about this. Go make that drink. She needs it right away. If she's unconscious use a feeding tube. If Kylee's wound is even half as bad as Bastian described, her life is in danger. I'll call you back later." Jackie hung up the phone still a little stunned. She slowly made her way through the house until she found Mason. They needed to talk about this. They needed to figure out what was going on.

* * * *

Megan sat at the small table in the corner of Marta's bakery. She knew the place would be a hit. From the moment Marta opened, the crowd had been steady. There were a lot of humans in and around the fort. Word spread fast among them. So far Megan hadn't discovered anything useful, but there seemed to be an underlying nervousness. A couple times she'd heard thoughts of concern for jobs and health. But nobody was giving her anything specific, nothing they could use. The one thing she had caught was an overwhelming concern the fort was going to be shut down completely. She wondered what was fueling the rumors, but nobody seemed to know the reason.

Megan approached the counter, she needed a refill. She was standing in line, focusing on the minds of those around her when two men walked into the room. They were both in uniform, flyboys for sure. Megan tried to act casual as she slipped into the mind of one of the men. Moments later she slipped back out. *Interesting*, she thought to herself. Let's see what the good captain knows about the situation. Megan reached the front of the line and winked at Marta. "I'll have another coffee," she said casually. "And make that to go please," she added with a huge smile. She'd gotten what they needed and couldn't wait to tell Victor and Tony.

The group sat in the large study of the farmhouse. Victor had contacted Thomas and they all agreed to meet later that night to discuss the situation. Abby, Dante and Nick sat with Thomas in front of the large screen. Everyone was in attendance at the fort other than the kids.

Victor stood and took control of the meeting. "Megan, we're here to discuss the information you were able to glean for us today.

Chaos

Before you begin, I would like to thank you for everything you've done for us not only today, but also over the past few months. You were very clear from the beginning that you dislike using your gift to intrude on the minds of others. It seems we keep calling on you to do just that. I for one appreciate your willingness to help us."

"Ditto," Thomas said immediately. "Things have been a little hectic here, but I too need to thank you for everything you've done for me and our community. If there's ever anything I can do for you, I hope you won't hesitate to ask."

Megan was surprised. True, she didn't usually like using her gift but she'd never felt uncomfortable helping her new friends. It seemed natural somehow. Since she'd arrived in New York Megan had felt more comfortable with who she was than she ever had before. "I'm happy to help," she said a little embarrassed something so simple was getting so much attention.

Victor sensed Megan's discomfort and immediately continued. "Let's move on to the real reason we are here today," he began. "As everyone knows, Marta opened her bakery this morning with the sole purpose of gathering information. Once again Megan came through for us." Victor turned to Marta grinning, "Before I turn the time over to Megan, I have to tell you Marta, you are never allowed to close your doors." He walked over and gave her a peck on the cheek. "I'm in love," he said dreamily. "Will you marry me?"

Ariel threw a decorative pillow at Victor.

Marta shook her head. "Sorry hon, I'm taken." She linked fingers with Jake as she continued to grin at Victor.

Jake turned and kissed his wife softly. "I'm so proud of you honey. I think we're going to be happy here for a very long time.

From now on, I'll be there to help you. I felt terrible about leaving you to deal with everything alone on opening day."

Megan cleared her throat. "Uh, I thought we were here so I could explain the situation and the group could develop a plan of attack," she smiled at Marta. "By the way, I'll conduct a stakeout at Marta's place any time you want. It's a tough job, but I'm willing to take one for the team and do my part. As long as Marta's willing to supply her delicious coffee and muffins."

Tony draped an arm around Megan and motioned for Victor to get things moving.

"We *are* here to discuss the information," Victor said. "Go ahead Megan, tell us what you learned."

"Well, at first all I was getting was concern. Most of the people that visited this morning had thoughts of being stressed. I wasn't getting specifics until the flyboys stepped into the room. Both men, Lt. Colonel Anthony Beck and Captain Ethan Malloy, had a very clear vision of your beaver in their mind. They were practicing maneuvers and took a break. They wanted it to be darker before they began the night training. It was a fairly nice evening, so they wandered over near Sampson State Park. That's when they saw the beaver. At first they thought it was just a normal animal. They were both intrigued and thought it would be fun to watch wildlife in its natural environment since they were each born and raised in big cities. But once they got close, they realized something was wrong. They stayed very still and initially thought it was going to come closer. Their hope was to catch it so the military could analyze it, but for some reason it turned and ran in the other direction. It was late, so they didn't try to follow. Captain Malloy immediately notified his superior back at West Point. He spoke to a Colonel Broderick," Megan said. She was surprised she'd remembered the names. Once she left the bakery she'd rushed home and written everything down.

"That's good news," Thomas told the group a little excited.

Jake looked at Thomas like he was nuts. "How exactly is this good news?"

"Jake," Thomas scolded. "You know Colonel Broderick. In fact, you know him better than I do. Dad conducted a lot of business with Evan over the years. I know you've met him. He asked me about you last time we talked."

Jake brightened. This was good news. "You're right. Megan please continue."

"The military thinks they have a leak. They're very concerned, almost to the point of panic. Apparently they still have radioactive material in those bunkers at the far end of the fort. They're the ones they refused to include in Luke's lease. Well, they refused because they have a lot of top secret chemicals and very volatile material stored out there. It's left over from the Manhattan project. They very strongly believe the bunkers have started leaking. They think the chemicals have seeped into the water supply and that beaver was some kind of mutation. They haven't decided what to do about it, but they are leaning towards closing everything down. The bigwigs are debating over the fallout. It's one thing to have a beaver mutate from toxic waste. It's another if the leak impacts a human."

Thomas stood and began pacing the room. "We can use this," he said confidently. "We need to be very careful but we can use this to our advantage."

"How?" Ty asked.

"Give me a minute to work this out," Thomas said still pacing. "You said you burned the deer, right?" he asked still deep in thought.

"We did," Morrigan answered. "What are you thinking Thomas? Tell us your plan and let us help formulate it."

"Jake and I know Colonel Broderick," he began. "Jake, do you mind coming back to New York? I think we need to pay a visit to our good friend out at West Point as soon as possible."

"I can leave tomorrow morning," Jake told him immediately.

"We've been dealing with the State Department for the most part, but the lease is actually with the Department of Defense," Thomas explained. "That too works to our advantage. The two organizations don't talk, in fact they compete. DOD will never know what we are doing at the fort. We can hint that it has something to do with national security. That falls under the State Department so nobody will check up on it. Did anyone see you burn the deer?" Thomas asked studying Morrigan.

"I wasn't really paying attention, but it was during the day and the Coast Guard would have been on duty. They had to see the fire. I knew it was risky, but I didn't feel like we had a choice. I thought if they challenged us on it, we'd make something up."

"Good," Thomas said smiling. "We're going to use that. Jake we're going to tell Colonel Evan Broderick about the deer attack. Then we're going to hint that we suspect they have something hazardous in those bunkers. In fact, I think we should ask him straight out if he has some kind of biological weapon or nuclear material stored out there. I'm going to demand he explains the situation immediately, I'll insist we can help if he's straight with us. They're going to know about the academy and that is going to make

Chaos

this worse. Once they know kids are living out there, I'm confident they'll cooperate. Romulus has been extremely active lately. The military has to know that. They always know everything that is going on around their installations, even the vacant ones. Dad already hinted to them when he made the agreement that the academy is a front. It's a way for Romulus to work on top secret projects without suspicion. If we play this right, they'll believe they have a lot to lose if they don't let us in."

"How does that help us?" Tony asked.

"Because then we offer them a solution," Thomas said calmly. "We offer to clean it up for them. If you're game Bastian, we offer you up on the science side. They're more likely to agree if they know you will be overseeing the project personally. As will I," Thomas told them.

"But you are in New York," Victor pointed out. "We can't have the media out here, Thomas. You know that."

"Abby and I need a break from the spotlight," Thomas told them. "I'm going to use this to get one. Do you honestly think the military can't get me out of the city without detection? You have very little faith in your government Victor," Thomas smiled. "Once I get them to agree with my plan, I'll voice my concerns about the media. You can't walk to the corner shop without seeing me and Abby on the cover of a magazine. The military will ensure nobody can get within miles of the fort. If I play this right, the media won't even know Abby and I are out there. Trust me, the government will not want a camera anywhere near that place when I'm finished."

The group spent the next several hours discussing their options and developing a plan of attack. There was no way to know how many additional animals were out there. Thomas had the perfect plan to address that problem. If they were the only ones allowed at the fort, they'd have no problem finding the rest and taking them out. If Thomas could get the military to shut things down, this would be a lot easier. It wouldn't matter how many animals were in the forest because they'd have free rein of the area and could hunt them without detection. The group continued to work well into the night, strategizing. Thomas and Jake needed an answer for anything the military threw at them.

* * * *

Kylee slowly opened her eyes. Where was she? She didn't recognize the place. What was the last thing she remembered? Melissa? She was checking her vitals and administering the medication. No, the smell. She remembered that awful smell and the attack. She shot up in bed. She needed to make sure those kids were okay.

Bastian rose from his chair and moved to the bed. He was towering over Kylee. "You can't get up," he said flatly. "You're not well. Drink this." He held out a large glass of liquid.

Kylee narrowed her eyes. Bastian shouldn't be here. She vaguely remembered someone telling her Bastian was in Ireland. "Why are you here?" she asked as she obediently took the liquid and began to drink.

Well, that was all he needed to know, wasn't it? Kylee still didn't want him around. Well, too bad. He had to be here now. Once Thomas made arrangements with the military, he was stuck at the fort until the problem was resolved. "I realize you work for the Deveraux's and they've hired you to work at the fort, but that doesn't make it your domain. I'm a warrior. I go where I'm needed.

Chaos

At the moment I'm needed at the fort. There are problems here that need my expertise. Don't worry, I won't get in your way."

"Where am I?" Kylee asked.

"You are in one of the apartments," he told her.

"Why?" she asked still a little confused.

"You passed out. This was the closest place to bring you. It was also more convenient. Breena's apartment is across the hall and she was the one caring for you." Bastian turned and headed for the door. "I'll get Morrigan. He needs to talk to you. He can explain all of this." Bastian pulled open the door and left without another word.

Kylee sat, stunned. Bastian was still angry with her. She'd definitely made a mistake. She never should have let him believe he was right. But really, after all the time they'd spent together how could he believe she'd just been using him to become a warrior. Sure, she wanted to be a warrior but that's not why she loved Bastian. She did love him, but it seemed he despised her. Could they ever get past this? No. She immediately shook her head. Nothing had changed. She was still human and would die in a few short years. Bastian was a warrior and would basically live forever. She took another drink of the liquid Bastian had given her. It was good. It was fruity, well actually it was a citrus drink with lime and something else she couldn't identify.

Kylee jumped at the knock on her door. "Uh… come in," she said hesitantly.

Morrigan slipped into Kylee's room and studied her closely. "You look better," he decided. "How do you feel?"

Kylee laughed a little. "I thought I was the doctor here," she said setting the drink on the night stand.

"No," Morrigan said picking up the small glass and handing it back to her. "You need to drink all of that. I'll bring you another one with lunch if you feel up to eating."

Kylee narrowed her eyes at the drink. It didn't taste like medication, but maybe they'd put something in it. "Why?" she finally asked.

"Just take it," he pressed. "Kylee, we've been taking care of you. Do you honestly think we'd give you something harmful?" he asked a little offended.

"Well...no," she conceded taking the glass. She drank down the remaining liquid a little defiantly. "Happy?" she asked.

Morrigan smiled. "I am." He glanced around the room and spotted a folding chair leaning against the far wall. As he sat down, he tried to decide on an approach. "I have something serious to discuss with you," he finally told her. He had to take this carefully. If she was here to spy on them for some reason, he didn't want to tip their hand completely.

Kylee instantly realized she wasn't in pain any longer. She casually pulled the sleeve of her shirt upward and stared at the wound. It was still a little red and tender, but nothing like it had been before. She could only assume her back was the same. She glanced down again and realized the actual wound looked healed. How was that possible? Was it because the flask had warrior blood? As a human she never should have healed that quickly. Wait. Her head shot up and she focused on Morrigan. "How long was I out?" she asked anxiously.

Chaos

"About forty eight hours. Well, a little less actually," he said noticing the IV bag needed to be changed. He stood and removed the bag, carefully prepared the sodium solution then secured the new bag on the IV stand.

"What is in that?" she asked curiously. "And why have I had such a quick recovery?"

"It's a sodium and saline solution," he said casually. "The rest I need to discuss with you." He took a deep breath. "Make yourself comfortable, this is going to take a while."

Kylee sat up and leaned against the wall for support. "Morrigan, whatever it is, tell me. If I didn't feel so much better, I'd assume you were here to tell me I was dying. What's going on?"

"Kylee?" Morrigan asked. "Are you human?" He was watching her closely. He may not be able to smell her shifter, but he thought he'd be able to smell out a lie. He hoped so.

Kylee furrowed her brow. "Of course I'm human. What is this about?"

Morrigan couldn't detect a thing. Kylee was telling the truth, well she thought she was anyway. He was going to trust his instincts and proceed.

"I needed to see if you were lying to us," Morrigan told her. "If you had come here to our community in disguise to make it easier to spy and gather information on our traditions and uh... defenses I guess."

"What are you talking about?" Kylee said offended. "I'm not a spy. I thought I'd proven that already. Why are you doubting my motives now? Because I got sick? Well, that wasn't exactly my fault. Bastian is the one that was experimenting. Then Melissa had a reaction to the antidote. I don't understand what is going on here."

"We are leery of your motives because you're really not human, Kylee." There it was, genuine shock. She really didn't know. Either that, or she was good.

"You're crazy," Kylee said immediately. "Of course I'm a human."

"No. You're not," Morrigan insisted. "You are a shifter. That's why your injury became so infected. That's why you had the reaction to Bastian's blood that your body had. That's why the only thing that saved your life is a remedy mom gave us that only works on shifters that have come into contact with the blood of a supernatural being," he said calmly. "Now, I'd like to talk to you about your history," Morrigan told her.

"I'm not a shifter," Kylee practically screamed. "I think I'd know if I were. Look at Rand. He knew he was a shifter since he was four. He fought it, but he knew. I have never shifted in my life nor have I had the desire to shift. It's simply not possible."

"Get up," he told her, standing and moving toward the door. "We're going to the lab. You'll need to bring the IV bag with you. The solution is helping, but you need to continue the treatment for the next three days."

"You want me to stay hooked to an IV for three days?" Kylee said, irritated. "I can't work this way. No way. I won't do it."

Morrigan ignored her complaints. They all knew she'd resist and they'd all agreed to do whatever necessary to make sure she followed the treatment his mother had ordered. "You will if you want to live," he said casually holding open the large door that led outside.

"I think you're being a little melodramatic. I guess I need to remind you again that I'm the doctor here. I can care for myself," Kylee countered.

Morrigan laughed. "Yeah, we all saw how well you've been handling that." They reached the door to the lab. Once again Morrigan held it open and waited for Kylee to walk past him, then quietly followed behind her.

The first thing Kylee noticed was Bastian. He was monitoring Melissa. She was sure he knew they were there, but he ignored them and remained focused on his current task.

Morrigan handed Kylee a glass microscope slide then immediately pricked his finger and let the blood run onto the flat glass. He motioned to the microscope. "Go ahead, study it."

Kylee moved to the microscope and lowered her head to the eyepiece. She couldn't help herself. She'd never analyzed shifter blood before. It was interesting. There was no mistaking it for human blood. The components were entirely different. She raised her head and looked at Morrigan. "Okay, now what?"

Morrigan took her finger and gave it a quick prick before she knew what he was doing. He caught the blood with another glass plate then handed it to her. "Go ahead," he told her, waiting patiently.

Kylee sighed then once again lowered her head to the microscope. She was shocked. Her head jerked up and she looked at Morrigan clearly confused, but something else. She almost looked scared or worried about the new discovery.

Morrigan watched as Kylee slowly sank into a chair. He felt sorry for the woman, but he couldn't give her time to adjust. They needed to know everything they could about her history. "Kylee, we need to figure out what's going on here."

"I just don't understand," she said again. "How could I be a shifter but not know it? It seems impossible. I'm sorry, but I'm a little freaked out here."

Morrigan took a seat beside her. "You had to know there was something different about your blood," he began. "I thought medical students studied their own blood all the time. How did you account for the oddities?"

"I never tested my blood. Mom told me I had a rare blood disease. She had a document from a doctor saying under no circumstance should we use my blood in any of my studies. A copy of the document was given to the university and the hospitals where I interned. I was never asked to give blood and I never did."

"That didn't seem odd to you?" Morrigan asked. "It didn't seem strange and mysterious, or a little off?"

"No," Kylee said honestly. "Like I said, she told me I had a rare blood disease. She said it wasn't terminal and shouldn't cause me any problems but that I could never give blood or share my blood or let anyone study my blood. She told me my disease was very, very rare. She didn't want me to become an experiment. I didn't want that either, so I took all the precautions she suggested."

Bastian couldn't stand being in the same room as Kylee. There were several reasons for that. The most pressing one right now was the fact that Kylee was struggling. She was having a hard time grasping her new reality. All he wanted to do was sit down next to her and pull her into his arms. He wanted to comfort her and assure her they would figure this out. He couldn't. She didn't want him here. Which was another reason he had to escape. It was killing him, loving someone this way and knowing she didn't love him back. The pain was too much to take. He had to get out of the room. Bastian stepped behind Morrigan and silently slid out the door. Once outside he decided to head to the beach. He needed to think.

Morrigan continued to press Kylee. He forced her to talk about her past, her family, especially her mother. It wasn't easy for her, but they needed all the information they could get if they were going to figure this out. Morrigan wasn't convinced Kylee was incapable of shifting. He'd heard of the gift lying dormant for years, especially in mixed races. If Kylee had a lot of human ancestors, her shifter might have a harder time surfacing. Especially without help or guidance.

"Let's take a break for now," Morrigan told her. "Before we go, would you mind if we took some more of your blood?" he tried to sound casual.

"Why?" Kylee asked, immediately suspicious.

"We want to run some DNA tests and try to figure out if you are connected to any of the local packs. If not, we need to try to determine where you came from. Having some of your blood will help with that."

Kylee only hesitated a moment. "Okay, go ahead." She held out her arm for Morrigan to take a generous amount of blood. "You need to put it in that fridge over there," Kylee told him. "I'm a little tired. Can I go back to the farmhouse or do I need to stay in the apartment?"

"Would you mind staying in the apartment where Breena or I can keep an eye on you until you're done with the IV? Once that's finished, you can move back into your old room."

"That's fine," Kylee said. Her mind was running a million miles a minute. She needed to be alone. She needed time to think. This was all so surreal. Was that why she had accepted all of this immediately? Until she came to the fort she'd never felt like she belonged, she always felt strange and out of place. Now she knew why. She was strange and out of place. She left the building and hurried back to the apartment, closing the door firmly behind her.

* * * *

Lilith paced the small cave trying to decide what to do now. She'd searched the forest. The deer was gone, so was the beaver. Maybe that was good news. But she'd also noticed the absence of activity at the fort. There were typically kids roaming the grounds until around ten each night. Last night, nothing. The entire place was eerily quiet. Okay, she thought to herself. Maybe the deer had done what she intended. It had attacked someone, so they'd shut down the place. That would be a natural reaction. Once they disposed of the deer, they would have searched the area for additional animals. That's probably when they found the beaver.

So what should she do now? She could follow Radek's orders and spend the night turning as many animals as she could capture, or she could just take off and leave this risky game to the king himself. What would Radek do if she took off? He would have someone track her down and kill her, that's what. She wasn't ready to go into hiding just yet. So, she'd spend the night turning animals. She couldn't control them during the day, but she could hide in the forest and see what happened all night. With an inward sigh, she exited the cave and got to work.

* * * *

Abby glanced up when Thomas walked into the room. "I see you had a successful day," she smiled as Thomas leaned in to kiss her gently. "I saw the press release. It looks like everything is falling into place." She swung her legs off the couch to give him room to sit down.

Thomas smiled as settled next to her. "Better than I could have hoped," he admitted. "The plan worked perfectly. Colonel Broderick was actually relieved to turn the whole mess over to us. Knowing Deveraux Industries and AC Pharmaceuticals would handle the problem together, put the man at ease."

"They made it look like they were just taking precautions," Abby said. "Mustard Gas?" she asked still amused.

Thomas pulled Abby in close. "The military came up with a pretty good plan. They announced they had mustard gas stored in the old bunkers. It's a lot less threatening than admitting they are storing atomic waste. You heard the press release, they're going to evacuate the area. Everyone within a five mile radius will be forced to relocate as a precaution. They haven't admitted to an actual leak, just a concern that the containers aren't stable which could lead to a leak. It's splitting hairs, but they're walking a fine line. DOD has agreed to pay for all relocation costs. That means there's going to be a lot of pressure on us to resolve this quickly." He leaned back his head. "I know everyone wants to give Alex and Dimitri time, but I really think we need to contact them."

"I've been thinking about that too," Abby admitted. "I think they need to know. Can't you advise one of them but convince them it's not something that requires their personal attention. Make it sound like you are just keeping them in the loop," she suggested. "I know how angry dad would be if any of us kept something this big from him just because he was out of town. Plus, the base closure is going to be big news. It might hit the international press and then they will panic. Somebody's got to tell them."

"I'm going to call Dimitri," he decided. "You need to pack. Uh, can you try to pack light?" He asked. "There is something else we need to talk about."

Abby studied Thomas, "What's wrong?"

"Nothing we can't overcome," he said confidently. "The military is willing to sneak me out of the house and get me to Ty's plane tonight. They've provided me with fake ID. Ty's pilot will have a fake name on the passenger list. But they wouldn't do the same for you. They are adamant that nobody can know about this other than those of us working on the project. You don't work for me or for Bastian, so they wouldn't budge. I gave in, or so they think. I told them Alex is out of town and I'm watching her dog and one of Ty's. I convinced them I had to take the two dogs with me and turn them over to Ty."

"I see, so I'm traveling as a dog?" she said trying to sound annoyed.

"As a cute, lovable, sweet Border collie. It's not that bad. I'll rub behind your ears," he pulled her in for a kiss. "I'm sorry. I tried, but once I realized they wouldn't budge I thought we'd go with plan B. I didn't want to draw too much attention to us."

Chaos

"It's fine," she told him. "I don't think there will be anyone around that knows Ty's dogs. As long as I'm close we should be able to pull this off. I'll go pack. When are we leaving?"

"Tonight in about an hour," he said pulling out his phone. "You pack, I'll call Dimitri. By then the car should be here."

"Okay, I need to call dad and fill him in. He's intrigued and a little worried about the new Kylee development. Morrigan's on top of things, but I think a woman's touch might help her cope with her new life." She rushed up the stairs to pack.

"Ready?" Thomas asked when Abby reached the bottom of the stair case.

"I am," she moved next to Thomas and wrapped her arms around him. "This wasn't exactly what I had in mind for a relaxing trip to the fort."

"Sorry," Thomas said leaning down to kiss her. "It's the best I could do."

"I talked to dad. He said Rand is going to fly out to the fort in a couple days. He's worried about Kylee. I guess they've been friends for a long time. He thought maybe he could help her deal with everything. He might be right. He's basically in the same boat as she is. Everything is pretty new to him, too. Don't worry, he'll find his own way out there and sneak in through the forest. I guess warriors drool and shifters rule!" Abby added with a laugh.

"That doesn't even make sense." Thomas said, trying to hide his grin. "Warriors drool? Do I need to remind you which one of us is going to be a dog for the next hour or so?"

They both looked out the window when they heard a car pull up to the house.

"I guess that's my cue," Abby said handing her bag to Thomas. Within seconds Abby stood on all fours, a well behaved Border collie at his side.

Thomas didn't wait for the bell. He casually picked up his luggage and strolled to the door. "Here we go," he said to Abby as he pulled the front door open and stepped outside.

A man in uniform was making his way up the stairs but paused when he saw Thomas. "Let me get those bags for you, sir," he said immediately. He glanced at Abby, then the smaller dog. "Maybe you could take care of them."

Thomas leaned down and gathered Cane into his arms. "Come," he said to Abby then tried to hide his grin. Abby was not going to like following commands. The only reason he didn't take advantage of the situation was because he knew he'd pay dearly for it later if he did. He climbed into the back seat and waited for Abby to bounce inside before pulling the door gently shut.

Lillie had just finished her inspection when the official looking car pulled up. She wondered who she was flying tonight. Working for Ty was always an adventure. She never knew who would be on the passenger list before she took off. Well, that wasn't always the case. She knew once she reached the fort she'd be picking up Ty and Sam. They needed to be in California by the following afternoon. She closed the steel door and locked it then turned to face the new arrivals. Thomas Deveraux stepped out of the car with a small dog in his arms, another dog trailing at his side. Whew, Lillie let out a long breath. For some reason Thomas and his sister Alex always made her nervous. She'd never felt so jittery with any other client. They were just people, she told herself.

Chaos

People with money, that's all. They're no different than anybody else.

Thomas walked to the plane and handed the pilot the paperwork. It was ridiculous to think the woman would be fooled by the fake name. He watched as she glanced at the paperwork, did a double take, readjusted her facial expression to that of a professional and handed them back.

"Right this way Mr. Abercrombey," Lillie said trying to act as if she believed the lie. She didn't know why Thomas Deveraux was pretending to be someone else, but it didn't matter. She'd been hired by Ty to fly to the fort, so she'd fly to the fort. "Are they friendly?" she asked glancing at the dogs.

"Yes, very." Thomas said with a smile following the pilot into the passenger section of the luxurious jet.

"Sir, I just need you to sign this paperwork. It's for the transportation of the animals. We understand neither dog is actually your property but as I transported you here, the Colonel required it." Thomas jumped a little, he hadn't realized the sergeant had followed them into the plane.

"Oh, yes." Thomas took the pen then hesitated. He was so used to signing paperwork he'd almost signed his own name. He caught himself just in time and signed the form Phillip Abercrombey, then handed the paperwork back to the sergeant.

"Thank you," the soldier said as he turned and left the plane. Thomas and Lillie watched as he slid into the vehicle and pulled away.

"If they're not your dogs, who do they belong to?" Lillie asked casually.

"Huh?" Thomas said, "Oh, the dogs. Well, this little rascal belongs to my sister and her fiancé. That one belongs to Ty," he said looking at Abby.

Lillie narrowed her eyes. She knew Ty's dogs and that was not one of them. Maybe Ty had three dogs. "Girl or boy?" she asked trying to sound casual.

"Boys, both of them," he said settling into a seat and laughing when Abby leapt onto his lap. Cane was happy to wander around the plane sniffing everything in sight.

"What are their names?" Lillie asked, holding her breath.

Thomas was getting uncomfortable with the pilot's questioning. Was it just casual conversation or was she trying to gather information for the tabloids? "That one over there is Cane and this one is Ace." he said watching her carefully. He saw something in her eyes, a slight twitch. She didn't believe him. He needed to end this right now. "Ms...I'm sorry I forgot your name already," he said turning the conversation around to her.

"Sorry, my name is Lillie and I will be your pilot today." She held out her hand, praying it wasn't shaking. Why was Thomas flying under a fake name and trying to pass this dog off as Ty's dog, Ace? It wasn't Ace. She knew that. Ace had the cutest heart shaped black spot just behind his ear. This dog did not. If she didn't know Ty was involved in this, it would worry her. But Ty was involved. Ty had arranged for the flight and told her she would be bringing a passenger. She'd just fly Thomas to the fort and decide later if she'd bring it up to her boss.

"Well, Lillie. I really hate to sound impatient but is there any chance we could get moving? It's late and it's going to be a long night." He gave her his most charming smile and waited.

Chaos

"Of course," Lillie said. No wonder the papers hounded the guy so much. He was hot and charming and women loved him. Now she knew why, she'd witnessed his flamboyance first hand. She recalled hearing he was taken, some new girlfriend that was practically living with him or something. Lillie shrugged, probably wouldn't last long. Thomas was young and rich and oh so handsome. Tying himself to one woman at such a young age was pretty unlikely. She glanced again at the dog Thomas claimed was Ace. "Do they need a potty break before takeoff?"

"No. I think they'll be fine," Thomas assured her. "They're used to traveling and I took care of that before we arrived at the airport."

"Well then, make yourself at home. It will only take me a minute to get cleared for takeoff." She made her way to the cockpit still curious about the lies. But that was none of her business. She was here to do a job and that was it.

Ty and Sam were waiting at the runway when Thomas arrived. He exited the plane and immediately pulled Ty off to the side. "She knows who I am," he whispered. "Are you sure she can be trusted? Are you absolutely positive she won't sell the story to the papers? Nobody can know I'm here."

"Relax," Ty assured him. "I didn't think the fake name would fool anyone. Lillie's not stupid, but she's loyal. She won't sell anything to the papers. If anything, she'll ask me or Sam about it. We can trust her. If she acts funny about this I'll explain the need to get you to the fort without anyone knowing where you went. She'll understand and she'll keep the secret, I'm sure of it."

"Uh... there's something else," Thomas sighed. "The military guy made a comment about the dogs not being mine and insisted I sign some form accepting responsibility. Your pilot quizzed me about them. I stuck to my original story but I could tell she didn't believe me. You should have warned me Lillie knew your dogs. Abby must have missed something that gave her away."

"Stop worrying. I'll think of something." He glanced at Abby. She'd gotten it pretty close, but Ty would have known it wasn't Ace and Lillie was perceptive. He didn't know what gave it away, but he'd come up with an explanation before he and Sam left in the morning just in case. "Come on, I'm sure Abby's tired of being a dog. Let's get you two settled. Sam and I have a long trip ahead of us in the morning. I also need to get Lillie settled for the night."

The two men returned to the women, Thomas excused himself and Cane and Abby followed. He paused momentarily. "Uh, Ty?" he called back. "Where do you want to keep the dogs?"

"Oh, they're staying in the house." Ty told him. "My room. Go ahead and put Cane in there, too. Sam and I will be leaving early in the morning. All three dogs will join us. Lillie's going to take them out to the ranch when she returns to New York. Pete's going to be thrilled to have the boy's back." he smiled. "And Cane will be a whole new dog once Pete gets finished with him. Goodnight, Thomas."

Lillie narrowed her eyes at Ty. "It was nice of Mr. Abercrombey to take care of Ace for you. Wasn't that hard on Bo to be alone without his buddy?"

Ty grinned at Lillie's sarcasm. She'd put him on the spot and he hadn't come up with a story yet.

Sam spoke up. "Lillie?" she said softly.

"Yes," Lillie said seriously.

Chaos

"That ruse wasn't for your benefit, it's for everybody else," she paused. "Thomas is not only rich, but he's also a very important man. A man that the government calls on frequently to assist them in highly confidential matters. I know that flight seemed strange, but I need to ask you to keep it to yourself." Sam didn't move, she didn't blink. She needed to know Lillie wasn't going to get nervous and talk about what was going on out here.

Lillie straightened her back and returned Sam's stare. "Of course," she assured them. "I can understand how difficult it would be for Thomas Deveraux to get out of town undetected. I was more curious about the dog. We both know that was not Ace that flew here with me tonight."

"Thomas needed to bring that dog with him," Ty answered. "The only way the government would allow it is if they thought it was one of my dogs. They needed to believe it would be leaving with us in the morning. Again that wasn't for you, it was for everyone else." He studied Lillie. "I hope you remember when I hired you, I told you I needed a pilot that could leave at a moment's notice and fly myself and my colleagues around the world. I also warned you there might be times when things seemed strange or out of place. You told me you would trust me and not divulge our activities to anyone. Are you still willing to do that, Lillie?" he asked.

"Look," Lillie began. "What you guys do is none of my business. If Thomas needs to fly out of New York and use an assumed name, a name that is listed on my passenger list, it's nothing to me. I do trust you, Ty. I have no intention of divulging any of this to anyone. The only thing I ask is what I've always asked. Don't expect me to do anything illegal or anything that will make me lose my pilot's license." She glanced over her shoulder at Thomas who was barely visible now. "You covered me on that tonight. That man's ID matched the name on my list. So, for now we're good. That last trip is behind me and forgotten. Are we still leaving at six?" she asked wearily.

Sam smiled. She really did like Lillie. Ty had been lucky to find her. "We are," she answered with a nod. "So, let's get you settled for the night. We all have an early morning and I don't like to be out after dark."

* * * *

Kylee rose and walked into the kitchen. It was pretty good sized for an apartment. She opened the fridge and saw more of the citrus drink Morrigan had given her earlier. Once she poured herself a glass, she walked to the living room and sat on the comfortable couch. Just that small amount of activity had worn her out. She wished she was back to normal, but she had to admit she was going to need a day or two of rest to shake this. She glanced up as the door opened and Breena walked in.

"Hey. You're up," Breena said cheerfully. "I came to change the IV."

"Breena?" Kylee asked. "Could I get you to do me a favor? Or maybe Orin could."

"Sure, what do you need?" Breena asked as she slipped the new bag onto the stand.

Kylee was getting tired of dragging that thing around with her, but she knew it was important to follow instructions. She was out of her element here and she was still extremely weak. "A few days ago Dimitri mailed some of George's notepads to Bastian. They're in the lab, near my work station. The top one is blue I think. I can see I'm going to be stuck here for a few days, so I thought maybe I could use my down time to study those books. We're kind of at a dead end on Melissa right now. Maybe I can find something useful," she smiled in anticipation.

"Sure," Breena told her. "I'll get Orin to take care of it. He'll need to find Victor, it's already dark and we all agreed nobody goes out alone anymore." She released the bag and stepped back. "There you go, all refreshed."

"What is in that bag?" Kylee asked.

"It's just a saline solution and sodium." Breena told her. "Apparently the salt helps kill the infection. Jackie was surprised it hadn't spread more than it did considering the amount of time that had gone by since the injury."

"Sodium?" Kylee asked absently. "Maybe the Gatorade helped," she surmised. "Why did the infection get so bad, so fast?"

Breena narrowed her eyes at Kylee. "I thought Morrigan was going to talk to you about this."

"Morrigan and I talked about the fact that I'm a shifter. I didn't believe him so he had to prove it to me. We talked a little, but not specifics. Then I got tired and came back for a nap," Kylee explained.

"I see," Breena said in understanding. "Okay, let me send Orin for the books and while we wait I'll see if I can answer some of your questions."

As soon as Breena returned Kylee asked again. "Why did my wound get infected?"

"Apparently shifter blood is very sensitive and can't be mixed with anything other than shifter blood. Jackie said they have to be very careful. A small amount can be fatal," Breena sobered.

"I see." Kylee inhaled deeply. "I don't know if Morrigan told you, but mom was adamant I never allow anyone to take or give me blood. She always stuck to the story that I had a rare disease and my blood could never be mixed with anyone else's. Not for any reason."

"Kylee is it possible that your mother was a shifter?" Breena asked.

"No," Kylee said. She was positive. She'd analyzed her mother's blood before. It was nothing like Kylee's. It did have an abnormality, but it was definitely human blood.

"Okay, then your father must have been the shifter." she concluded. They both looked up when Orin walked in with an arm load of note books.

"Breena said three, but this whole stack was together so I just brought them all. In the mood for a little easy reading, huh?" Orin joked.

Kylee smiled back, "Yeah. I'm dying to get my hands on a good mystery," she joked back.

"Well, you're in luck." He said placing the stack of books on the couch next to her. "A mystery it is."

Breena slid her hand into Orin's. "Honey, I'm getting tired. I'm going to head back to the apartment and lie down."

Chaos

"Sorry Kylee, duty calls." He wrapped an arm around his wife and led her out the door.

Kylee took a deep breath then picked up the top book and began to read.

* * * *

Bastian sat in the lab trying to concentrate on Melissa. With the threat of vampiric animals, they needed to get her healed and out of here immediately. He was studying her charts and realized there had been slight changes since her arrival. Nothing drastic. But he needed the chart from the day Melissa arrived.

Bastian walked over to Kylee's work space and searched for the documentation he needed. He began pulling sheet after sheet from the small divider, nothing. He started on the workbooks. He opened the first one and realized he'd already read through it earlier. It was Kylee's notes on her progress in developing the antidote. He glanced around and spotted another book. He immediately flipped it open and froze. What was Kylee doing? She had obviously talked Sam and Ty into giving her some of their blood. Kylee had analyzed it and made quite a few notes. There was also information on Atticus. He flipped the page and scowled. How had Kylee obtained his blood samples? She had half a page of information on him.

He heard a noise and returned to his desk. Orin walked in. "Kylee wanted the notebooks Dimitri sent over. The ones that belonged to George. Do you mind if I take them to her?"

"No, that's a good idea. It will keep her busy and maybe she'll find something useful." Bastian answered trying to sound casual. Once Orin left, Bastian pulled the notebook back out and flipped to the next page. He began thumbing through, page after page was filled with notes. Bastian dropped into her chair and began to read.

* * * *

Alex stood on the elegant porch of Clontarf Castle enjoying the view. It was so beautiful and peaceful here. She wrapped her coat tightly around her and inhaled a long, cold breath. It was snowing lightly. The delicate flakes made everything seem magical somehow. She turned her head when she heard the door open and smiled at Dimitri.

He silently closed the door then walked to her side handing her a cup of coffee.

Alex took it, lifted the cup to her lips and sipped cautiously. "It's wonderful," she said leaning against Dimitri as she continued to watch the white flecks slowly drift to the ground. It was warm enough to instantly dissolve the tiny flakes as soon as they hit the surface.

Dimitri wrapped his arms around her waist and pulled Alex against his chest as he kissed the top of her head. "What's on your mind?" he asked casually. "You seem deep in thought."

"I was just relaxing really. Taking in the beauty that is all around us here. I love New York, but it's always so busy. It has its own beauty I guess, but here on the castle grounds everything just seems so tranquil and right somehow. Will we ever have that Dimitri? Will things ever settle down enough that we can just sit out on our porch with a cup of coffee and watch the world go by?"

Chaos

"Of course it will," Dimitri assured her. "We're just in a rough patch right now. Once the threat is over, things will return to normal." He set his cup on the top of the railing that encircled the winding porch then brushed Alex's hair to the side and kissed her neck."

Alex smiled. Dimitri always could relax her. "Hum," she said softly. "I love it when you do that."

Dimitri moved his lips to her ear and whispered softly, "I love you."

Alex shifted a little so she could see Dimitri. "Me too," she said quietly. Then she turned around slowly and wrapped her arms around his neck. "Do you love me enough to take the horses out for a ride?" she grinned at him in anticipation.

"It's gonna be cold," Dimitri warned. "Are you sure you're up to it?"

"I'm sure," she said wistfully. "Ever since I had that talk with Sam about my family I keep getting little bits and pieces of memory back. I was sitting out here this morning admiring the view when a memory hit me unexpectedly," she admitted.

"I see," Dimitri said with understanding. So that's what she was thinking about when he arrived.

"It was a morning similar to this one. Me, dad, Sam and Michael had gone for a ride. Dad wouldn't let me ride my own horse because of the weather so I was riding in front of him. We were running and laughing and having a blast in the snow. We all seemed so carefree and happy." She stopped and looked up at Dimitri, moisture gathering in her eyes. "I just thought it would be nice to experience a little of that again today."

Dimitri reached up and wiped a tear away. It broke his heart when Alex cried. "Then let's see what we can do to make that happen." He leaned down to gently kiss her lips. "I'll go let Charles know. I'm sure he'll need to call down to the stables so they can prepare a couple of horses." He studied her. "Will you do me a favor and put on another layer? If you didn't bring a warmer shirt, I have a sweat shirt you can use. It's on the chair near the window."

Alex hadn't brought any warmer clothes with her. She didn't realize it would be this cold. She liked wearing Dimitri's clothes. At least one of them had planned ahead.

Alex and Dimitri crested a hill and stopped their horses immediately. The scene before them was spectacular. They could see the city sparkling below them. Dimitri tied the horses to a tree and took Alex by the hand. He lifted it to his lips and kissed her fingers softly. Alex shivered at the contact, Dimitri's touch always did that to her even after all this time. Dimitri immediately pulled her into his arms and began to rub her back trying to warm her.

"Dimitri?" Alex asked softly.

"Yeah," he answered, enjoying the morning.

"We need to talk about something," she said seriously. "Please don't get mad at me. It's such a perfect morning. I don't want to fight with you."

"Then it can wait," Dimitri said casually. He also needed to talk to her about the conversation he'd had with Thomas, but he didn't want to spoil the moment.

Alex pulled away so she could look him in the eye. "I need you to start fighting again," she told him without emotion.

Chaos

"Alex," Dimitri warned. "I'm not going to argue with you about this. I will fight when I need to, but other than that, I'm not leaving you alone at night."

"So this is about my safety?" she surmised. "You don't trust our security system so you won't go out and fight with the other warriors? That's bull and you know it. You installed the security Dimitri, you know I'm safe when I'm in the house."

"I won't leave you alone," he told her again. He did trust the security system, but he also knew it was possible someone could get in if they were determined. He just couldn't bring himself to leave her all alone, unprotected. Plus, she got so upset when he left. He hated it.

"I need you to be honest with me," she pressed. "Is this about my safety or about my bad behavior when you used to leave me to go fight?"

Dimitri studied Alex. She wasn't going to let this drop. "Both," he finally said in defeat. "It kills me to leave you home alone knowing I'm too far away to help you if something happens."

"Are you kidding me?" she said a little annoyed. "Do you seriously think I can't take care of myself?"

"Nobody can take care of themselves all the time. Look at how protective Luke was of your mother. You know how capable Marlena was and Radek still got to her. Radek is dangerous. We all know his primary goal is to kill you and take your kingdom. I won't leave you alone. If I do, if I let you talk me into hunting again and something happens to you, it will kill me," he admitted. "It's not a risk I'm willing to take."

Alex was studying Dimitri. She would not let him give up something he loved because she had whined about him leaving. "You said both. So I assume you want to protect me, but you also gave it up because I used to worry so much while you were gone, right?"

"That played into the decision, but not much. Sure, I want to make you happy and I could see how it much it upset you when I left to hunt. Especially when Thomas was also hunting that night. I just decided staying home resolved both issues. That's all," Dimitri admitted.

Alex pushed away, walked a several steps then walked back. She repeated the process a few more times then stopped in front of Dimitri. "Okay. Here is what we are going to do," she began. "Right now Thomas can't hunt. The reporters are hounding him constantly. I also believe they are watching us, not as closely because we announced our engagement. It's going to get worse the closer we get to the wedding. Everyone is going to want to get an exclusive picture of my elaborate dress, the venue and my shoes, whatever. The point is, because you are marrying a Deveraux, we are always going to be in the spotlight. So far you have dealt with that very well. I'm not sure I thank you for that enough," she smiled at him. "Anyway, I'll let you take a break from hunting for now. I don't like it, but I have to agree that I am Radek's primary target. If he can get to me, he will. I'm smart enough to know that means if he knew I was home alone he would send a few hundred vamps to our house to attack. He might do that anyway and I'll be grateful to have you there with me."

"Always," he said smiling.

"But once things settle down a little, you are going to go back out there. You will go fight with your men. They need their leader out there, fighting by their side. I'm always going to worry about you. I love you. But you worried about me when this first started. I remember you telling me you didn't want me out there, but you knew the community had to see me, they had to get to know me. They had to know I was capable of fighting. The same is true for you. The warriors need to have you with them, at least occasionally."

"Once Luke married Marlena he rarely joined us in a fight. It was only after her death that he got involved again. And that was only because he wanted revenge," Dimitri argued.

"Well, Luke was...what was it? Nine hundred twenty six when he died, I believe. You're only four hundred and sixty three. That means you have another four hundred years or so before you can start thinking about retirement." She pushed up on her tiptoes and kissed Dimitri, softly at first then more intimately with just a touch of longing.

Dimitri brushed back her hair and rested both palms on the side of her face. "We'll work something out. I understand what you are saying and you're right. When we get back and things calm down, we'll work something out. I promise." He kissed her again. "You're getting cold. Let's get back to the house. There's something I need to talk to you about. But first, I think I need to strip off those wet clothes and get you warm." He smiled mischievously and helped her onto her horse.

Alex watched as Dimitri swung up and gracefully balanced himself on the back of the majestic Arabian stallion. "Is there anything you can't do?" she asked a little annoyed. She loved him dearly, but the man seemed to be adept at everything under the sun.

"Do you have any idea how frequently I've ridden a horse, my dear?" he grinned. "You do remember it was my only mode of transportation for quite some time. I practically lived on the back of one of these."

"Yeah, I remember." She told him as she gave her horse a gentle kick to get him moving and galloped back to the castle.

* * * *

Lilith slipped into the cave and settled in the far corner, positioning herself away from the opening. It had been a long night. The fort was empty and deserted again, but the forest was full of potential targets. She'd actually had fun in the beginning. She found a gray fox right away and turned it immediately. That one had been tricky. It turned on her and she'd barely escaped. As she continued through the forest she encountered raccoons, muskrats, beavers and another fox. She turned them all. Then an idea struck her. She saw a flock of ducks and enjoyed the idea of flying targets. Once she finished with the ducks, she went in search of some other birds. As soon as she saw the sandpipers she had to have some of them. It had taken her most of the evening but she'd finally come across a large group feeding. She was able to turn a few, but they were too quick. Most of them scattered as soon as she reached them. She had some more time before daylight, so she went to work turning woodchucks and a few more raccoons then headed for the cave. Now she'd just sit back and wait. Her only concern right now was her own protection. She wasn't going to sleep tonight. She couldn't risk it. Some of those animals could wander into this cave. If she wasn't alert, they were capable of killing her.

Chaos

Kylee woke and immediately went to the fridge for another lime drink. She needed her IV changed out, but they hadn't left a new bag in the room. She unhooked the line and capped it then wandered outside the apartment in search of Breena. It was still pretty early. She quickly realized nobody else was up. She felt a lot better. She was still weak, but she was slowly getting her stamina back. Well, she'd just go down to the lab and fix a new bag herself. Breena said it was saline and sodium. She didn't know the right portions but she could wing it. If she got it wrong, it wouldn't hurt her.

Kylee exited the building and turned toward the lab then stopped. That smell. She inhaled deeply and started to panic. She knew that smell. It was the same thing that drew her from the building days ago. The deer had that same smell. Kylee glanced around frantically, there had to be another animal in the area. She took another tentative step toward the lab, then paused. The smell was getting stronger. Kylee took quick look around then darted for the door.

Bastian was sitting in the lab when he heard the large door slam shut. He immediately stood and rushed out of the room into the open foyer. Kylee was huddled on the floor breathing hard and looking a little panicked. "What are you doing?" he barked. He moved to her side, leaned down and lifted her into his arms.

"Put me down," she screamed. "You need to get help and find the animal. Hurry, before the kids get up."

Bastian set her on the large bench. "What animal?" he asked scowling.

"Like the deer," she wheezed.

Bastian's gaze shot to the door. "What is it?" he asked. "What kind of animal this time? Did it bite you?" Bastian began running his hands over Kylee searching for a wound.

Kylee shoved his hands away. "Bastian, stop it. I didn't get bit. And I don't know what the animal is. I can smell it. It's just like the deer. That's what drew me out of the lab the other day. It's the same distinctive smell. You have to go find it. The kids will be leaving their bunkers soon. We have to protect them."

"You have to sit right there and catch your breath. Do not try to come outside. Once it's safe, someone will come and help you back to your room. Until then don't move," he ordered. He checked his belt for his dagger, then walked to the door. Bastian slowly pushed it open enough to slide outside then pulled it firmly shut behind him. He took a deep breath, but didn't smell anything. What was Kylee talking about? Maybe it was a shifter thing.

He circled the building and saw it. A raccoon was lying in wait. He knew it was a vampiric raccoon, he could see the teeth. Bastian just hoped he could take care of the thing on his own, technically he wasn't supposed be out here alone. At least none of the kids were up yet, so he still had time. They all knew they weren't allowed out of their rooms until eight and then they were supposed to pair up if they went out onto the field.

Bastian took a tentative step forward, watching the animal, waiting to see how it would react. He didn't see the second one until it was too late. He lunged, stabbed the first raccoon through the heart then pivoted and swiped at the second one, knocking it off his arm. The raccoon hit the ground with a thud, then scrambled back on its feet and disappeared into the thick brush. He turned back to the first one and slammed his dagger through its heart again. He couldn't take any chances. Once he was positive the raccoon was dead he went on the hunt for the second assailant.

* * * *

Orin needed fresh air. These days he spent most of his time indoors caring for Breena. He didn't mind, he wanted to be there for her. They had been given such a special gift, he wasn't going to complain about it. But while she was sleeping, he wanted to enjoy the brisk morning air for a change. He stepped from the building and looked casually around the vast expanse of the fort. It was chilly outside and the grassy field was still covered in dew. Orin was about to wander over to Marta's bakery when he spotted Bastian out of the corner of his eye. The warrior was fighting a raccoon. Orin didn't hesitate, he took off at a dead run knowing the raccoon had to be vampiric and dangerous. The animal was wounded and clearly angry about it. Orin slipped out his dagger and approached from behind. "Bastian, don't attack me. I'm here to help," he called out then lunged at the animal slicing through its side.

Bastian immediately kicked the thing on its back and shoved his dagger through its heart. "Orin, take care of this one. There's another dead one back there. We need to burn them, then search the fort to see if there are any others." He didn't wait, he knew Orin would take care of the body.

Bastian returned to the original raccoon and set it on fire. The blood began to pop and sizzle as the flames got higher. He looked up as Dusty and Nebi approached. "Is it eight already?" he asked.

"Yeah," Dusty told him. "I knew there would be more, but I kept trying to convince myself we'd taken care of all of them."

Bastian remembered what Kylee had said. "Can you smell these things? I mean from a distance. Can you smell them before they're close enough to see them?"

Dusty looked at Nebi. "I can smell them if they're close enough," he said hesitantly. He took a deep breath. "It's hard to tell with the burnt smell surrounding the area, but I don't think I can smell any more. What about you Nebi?"

"No," she shook her head. "I smell the fire and I can smell warrior, but I don't smell any more of those things."

"Good," Bastian said, relieved. "I need you two to do me a favor. Kylee is in the warehouse, just inside the door on a bench. Can you two get her back to her room and into bed? She needs to get back on her IV. Maybe you could get Breena to take care of that."

"No," Orin said immediately moving in beside Bastian. "She didn't sleep well last night. I'll take care of it. We have a couple bags already prepared at the apartment. I'll head over and grab them so we can change them out with the old ones. I've taken care of the other raccoon," he said to Bastian. "Come on you two. If you can get Kylee back to her room, I'll be waiting for you with a new IV." He turned, taking longs strides toward the large building.

Dusty and Nebi opened the door and immediately saw Kylee. She was lying on the bench with her hands over her eyes. "Kylee," Dusty called. "We're here to help you back to your room. Orin is waiting to hook you up to a new IV."

Kylee swung her legs over the side of the bench and tried to stand but failed. When she woke this morning, she thought she was finally better but running to the building had left her tired and weak

Chaos

again. She immediately sat back down and tried to regain her equilibrium.

Dusty moved to the bench, crouched then picked Kylee up. He cradled her in his arms and looked at Nebi. "I've got this. Will you get the door, babe?" he asked quietly.

Once outside Kylee put her hand over her nose. "I thought you said it was safe out here," she said annoyed. "You guys shouldn't be running around with dangerous animals still on the loose."

Nebi looked at Dusty confused. "Uh… Kylee, Bastian and Orin killed the raccoons. It's safe out here now."

"No it's not," Kylee insisted. "You can't smell that?" she asked. "It's getting stronger. That means it's getting closer."

Bastian came around the corner and frowned. "What are you still doing out here?" he asked. "She needs to rest and she's been off the IV too long. Jackie said she needed it constantly for four days."

"She says she can smell another animal," Nebi told him. "But we can't see or smell anything."

Bastian studied Kylee. "Can you still smell it?"

"Yes," she said defiantly. "I know what I'm talking about. It's getting closer. These kids need to get to safety. I don't want either of them injured again."

Bastian smiled. That was just like Kylee. "Actually, all three of you need to get inside. I don't want any of you injured. Which direction? Can you tell?" he asked her.

Kylee tried to move her head around but was limited because of Dusty's grip. "Put me down a minute," she ordered. She became even more annoyed when Dusty looked to Bastian and waited for his nod before he set her on the ground. Kylee took a deep breath. The rapid influx in oxygen helped settle her nerves but she was still annoyed; it also helped her scent the air. She pointed toward the apartments. "That way," she said confidently.

"Okay," Bastian said. "Wait here. I'll see what I can find."

"Sir?" Dusty called. "I think we should leave Nebi here to protect Kylee and I should go with you. What if you find more than one? You're going to need help."

Bastian hesitated but nodded once. He turned to Nebi. "Can you handle this?"

"Yes sir," she told him immediately. "Nothing will happen to Kylee, I promise."

"Make sure nothing happens to you either," Bastian ordered. He and Dusty slowly moved toward the apartments scanning the area for animals as they went. So far, they couldn't see anything. Out of nowhere a sandpiper dive bombed above them. Bastian saw it just in time and tackled Dusty. The bird barely missed the kid's head. Bastian looked around for more of the birds and saw an arrow soar past his head. It hit the bird mid center. The sandpiper fell to the ground with a thud. Bastian slammed his dagger across the small body, slicing the bird in half. "Get the women inside and tell Orin what happened. He needs to call the house and alert the others. Then we need to gather up the rest of the kids and get them inside the gym. There's no way to tell how many more of those things are out here. We need a plan. Hurry, go get Kylee and Nebi."

Chaos

Nebi settled down next to Kylee. She looked up just in time to see a large bird dive from above and head straight for the men. She jumped up and let out a scream, then saw Bastian tackle Dusty. Both men remained on the ground, were they injured? She was considering her options, trying to figure out how to help Dusty and protect Kylee when Gerty shot an arrow from the roof of the warehouse and struck the bird. "Good job, Gert!" Nebi called as she turned to face Kylee.

Kylee smelled the bird before she saw it. Nebi was hovering over her, completely oblivious to the danger. Kylee frantically searched the skyline for the animal. She finally spotted it when the bird pivoted and began its decent. It was headed straight for them, obviously preparing for an attack. Kylee reacted without conscious thought, kicking Nebi's legs out from under her and pulling them both beneath the wooden bench. She exhaled in relief when the bird dropped to the ground with a thud; an arrow protruding from each side of its body. Nebi pushed away and used her dagger to slice the bird in two.

Bastian saw the bird coming in for an attack and knew they couldn't reach the girls in time. One of the women was going to get hurt. He watched in amazement as Kylee knocked Nebi to the ground then pulled both of their bodies under the bench. Gerty flung another arrow and took out the threat with one shot. Sam had been right about that girl. She was a life saver today. Bastian took off at a dead run, passing up Dusty as he darted for the bench. Dusty quickly caught up and the two of them reached the women at the same time. Bastian effortlessly reached under the bench and lifted Kylee into his arms. Dusty took Nebi's hand and pulled her to her feet then the small group ran for the apartments.

Nebi planted her feet and came to an abrupt stop almost causing the two of them to fall to the ground.

Dusty jerked around impatiently. "Come on," he ordered.

Nebi shook her head then looked back at Gerty.

"Oh yeah," Dusty realized the problem. "Hey, Gert!" he called as loud as he could. "Get inside. We'll meet you in the gymnasium in a few minutes." Then he jerked Nebi's hand and darted for the open door.

Bastian stalked into the apartment they were using for Kylee and placed her on the bed. He was scowling and furious. "Orin, I need your phone. Do you mind?" He turned around and spotted Breena for the first time. He nodded in greeting as he tried to calm down. Kylee could have been injured today. She wasn't even supposed to be out of bed.

"No, go ahead. It's open," he began studying the kids for injuries.

Breena was less subtle. She immediately went to Dusty and began running her hands up and down his arms. "Are you hurt again?" she asked anxiously. "Did any of you get injured?"

Dusty grinned and placed his hands on Breena's shoulders pushing her away gently. "I didn't get hurt this time. I'm fine, I promise."

Breena turned to Nebi.

Nebi backed away. "I'm good," she said cheerfully holding up her hands to stave off Breena's advance. "No contact at all. Kylee's okay, too. I already made sure she didn't come in contact with those things or their toxic venom."

Breena spun around to Bastian "And you?" she demanded.

Chaos

"I'm fine until I make a few phone calls." he said as he headed for the door.

Breena was in front of him in an instant. She was looking up and down, trying to find his injury. When she spotted it, she reached out her hand and pulled the sleeve on his shirt up. "You're not going anywhere. I need to see to this."

"I am going to your apartment to call the house," Bastian said calmly. "Thomas and Victor need to be warned. They need to know what's going on out here. I don't want them walking into danger the way I did. Jake and Marta also need to know. Orin, where is Morrigan?" Bastian pulled his arm from Breena and turned to leave the room.

"I am so sick of you macho warriors," Breena said in disgust. "Victor thought his assignment was more important than his health, too. I guess you forgot where that got him," she challenged.

Bastian turned around and smiled warmly at Breena. "I appreciate your concern Breena, but I'm fine. The cut isn't that serious. Anyway, Victor ignored his wounds for over twenty four hours. I only intend to ignore mine for about ten minutes. When I get back you can play nurse." He grinned at Orin. "Just don't let your husband knock me out over it." Then he turned and left the room.

"Orin," Nebi said anxiously.

"What's wrong?" he asked the girl in surprise. She sounded upset.

"Can Dusty and I go to the gymnasium?" she asked anxiously.

"I don't think so. It's not a good idea for anyone to leave the building just yet," Orin decided.

"But Gerty's all alone. What if she's hurt? She was up on the roof when the birds started attacking. She saved us, but what if one of them got to her before she got inside. She's going to be in pain and I can't just leave her there all alone like that when she risked herself to protect us," Nebi argued.

Orin looked at Breena then back to Nebi. "You're right. Someone needs to check on her. I'll get Morrigan and the two of us will head to the warehouse to check on Gerty." He rushed out of the room and darted for the stairs.

Orin planned to leave the apartment building and rush to the bunkers to notify Morrigan. He'd only be out alone for a minute. It was dangerous but he had to risk it. He had just reached the top of the stairs when Bastian appeared in the hallway.

"What are you doing?" Bastian demanded. "We agreed, nobody goes outside alone."

"We're worried about Gerty. She was up on the roof all by herself. If she got hurt by one of those birds, she needs Breena's attention right away. The injury is going to be very painful. If she was attacked by more than one, she could be in trouble," Orin said as he continued down the stairs. "I'm going to get Morrigan. The two of us can check on Gerty and usher any kids that have left their bunkers into the gym."

Bastian took the stairs two at a time until he caught up with Orin. "I forgot about her," he said a little ashamed. "We need to make sure she's okay. I'll go with you."

Chaos

Orin looked at Bastian's arm then back to his face. "You really do need to have that cared for," he sighed.

Tony stood at the top of the stairs. He cleared his throat to get their attention. "Uh, what's going on here?" he asked.

"Tony! I'm glad you're up," Orin said relieved. "We had another attack. Several of those animals were on the base this morning. Some of them were birds that attacked from above. We need to get Morrigan, then he and I need to go check on Gerty. She climbed on the roof to help during the attack but she should be down in the gym by now and she's alone. We also need to gather up the kids and make sure everyone is accounted for and safe. It's too dangerous to go out alone but if Bastian accompanies me to get Morrigan, he'll have to walk back to the apartment by himself. He's already injured and needs to be seen by Breena as soon as possible. We're kind of in a bind here. If you're willing to go with us, you just solved our problem. We'll head out to meet up with Morrigan, then you can escort Bastian back here to Breena to get his arm doctored and bandaged. I'd like to say I trust him, but he is a warrior."

Bastian grunted in disgust. He didn't need a babysitter.

Tony put an arm on Bastian's shoulder. "Come on old man, let's take care of this. The sooner you get that medication, the sooner you can get back to being in charge," he grinned widely. "It's hell having people that care for you, I know."

"Funny," Bastian grumbled. "Hurry up. We need to gather up the kids. They're going to be out wandering around by now. It's after eight."

"Where's Thomas and Victor?" Tony asked.

"I called the house. They're headed our way. I'm grateful we have so many adults out here right now. It's going to help us protect the kids," Bastian mused. They needed a plan. It was impossible to know how many animals were out there just waiting for a target. They needed to get a handle on the situation. Maybe the warriors should resume their nightly hunting schedule here at the fort. It was obvious they had company and their enemy was out there each night taking advantage of their unencumbered access to the forest. At the very least they needed to start patrolling whenever the kids were outside. There were four of them. Once things got settled, he'd sit down and try to work out a schedule. At the very least he was going to find someone to work with him tonight and see what they could find. He had no doubt Tony would help too, and probably Orin.

Chapter Seven

Thomas and Abby entered the large gymnasium. The kids were milling around everywhere, waiting to find out what the next move would be. "I'm going to find Victor and see if we can start formulating a plan," Thomas told Abby. "Don't leave until I get back."

"I promise," she assured him. "I'm going to see if I can find Morrigan."

The two split up and Abby began searching for her brother. She finally spotted him sitting alone on a wooden bench. As Abby approached, she realized Morrigan was upset. He was watching Dusty, Nebi and Gerty. The three kids were talking and joking with each other. So why was Morrigan so upset, she wondered? None of them had been injured today. Abby silently slid onto the bench next to her brother. "Why the long face, bro?" she asked lightly.

Morrigan pulled his attention away from the kids and noticed Abby for the first time. He immediately pulled her into a hug. "I'm glad you made it out," he said sincerely. "I've missed you. It's strange, but I realized our family really hasn't been apart much until recently. It's nice to have you here."

"Morrigan, what's wrong?" She asked as she glanced at the kids again. "None of the students got hurt today so what has you so worried?"

Morrigan studied Abby. It really was good to have her back. It was lonely out here at times, he needed someone to talk to. "I love teaching the kids and at first I thought I was good at it, but seeing all my failures standing together like that has me wondering," he admitted.

"Failures?" Abby asked, surprised. "What do you mean by that? Dusty and Nebi are the most talented kids here. They've come a long way since they first arrived and that has a lot to do with your instruction. Sure they would have figured things out on their own eventually, but their progress has been fast-tracked because of you. And Gerty's not a failure. In fact, from what I hear she saved the day."

"If I had my way, Gerty wouldn't even be here," he said quietly. "I lobbied pretty hard for Ty to send her home after that last attack. She couldn't fight and she had zero confidence. Look what Sam has done for her in just over a week. I failed Gerty and if Ty had listened to me, who knows how many people may have gotten injured today."

"Morrigan," Abby scolded. "You're looking at this all wrong. You absolutely needed to wash Gerty out of the fighting program. I saw her myself. If she tried to fight in the state she was in, she would have gotten herself killed. Who knows how many others would have gotten injured trying to protect her. That's how Nebi got hurt in the last battle. That doesn't mean you failed. It just means Gerty isn't cut out for combat. That's the sign of a good teacher. You made the hard decision. You recognized her lack of ability and cut her from the program. This academy is still a work in progress, but things worked out the way they should here. You washed her and Sam picked her up and focused on Gert's strengths. I have faith that you and the rest of the instructors will continue to make those adjustments as additional kids arrive. All the kids won't be Dusty's or Nebi's but that's not the point of this. We are just trying to make sure those who attend the academy have skills when they return home. They need to be prepared for the new dangers we face. That's the reason we're here. Nobody is asking you to accomplish the impossible. Turning Gerty into a combat fighter is impossible, Morrigan."

Morrigan smiled. "That's an understatement," he laughed. "But I am proud of Gerty. Look at her, she has more confidence and self-assurance right now than she's ever had. And as bad as she is at fighting, she's at least that good at archery. I have to admit, I'm not worried about her anymore."

"Then what's bothering you, other than Gerty?" Abby asked.

"Dusty and Nebi," Morrigan admitted. "Those two are amazing. Other than you maybe, I've never seen that much talent in a kid."

"But?" she pressed.

"But...Dusty does okay shifting into other forms when things are casual. No problem. Get him under pressure and he instantly transforms into that tiger. No matter what I try, he can't overcome that instinct. How are we supposed to send him out into New York knowing he's going to make a spectacle of himself if he gets into trouble? Once he's seen, and you know as well as I do he'll be spotted immediately, he's doomed. Then there's Nebi. I understand her position, but she's a shifter not a panther. Sure, she's lived with her aunt in a panther pack most of her life, but she's so stubborn about it. She won't even try to change into anything else. She says the panther form is good enough for her entire community, its good enough for her. I can't argue with that. I just feel like I'm failing both of them. They are capable of so much more," Morrigan finished, depressed.

"I agree," Abby told him. "And I also think you already know the answer."

"You agree I'm failing them?" he asked.

"No," Abby rolled her eyes at him. "I agree they are capable of a lot more. They're stuck in their comfort zone and refuse to leave it. If anyone can force them out, you can."

"You're not listening," he said annoyed. "I've tried. They won't budge."

"That's because you're not thinking, Morrigan. You keep doubting your ability instead of using that energy to find a solution. That's not like you. You're creative. You helped me. You can help them if you put your mind to it." She watched as another young girl approached the threesome and immediately began to flirt with Dusty. Abby smiled at the irritated look on Nebi's face.

"You were easy to help, all I had to do was come up with a game," Morrigan said.

"Who is that girl?" Abby asked. "The one talking to Dusty."

Chaos

Morrigan was surprised at the change in subject but looked up to see who Abby was referring to. "Tiffany Richards," he said absently. "Why?"

"Because she's the answer to all your problems," Abby said confidently.

"How's that?" Morrigan asked, confused.

"You are such a guy," Abby told her brother, sighing.

"True," Morrigan admitted. "But I still don't get it. Where are you going with this?" he asked watching the four shifters, trying to figure out what Abby was talking about. Nothing came to him.

"Come on," Abby said, standing. "How is Tiffany doing in class? Can she hold her own or is she struggling?"

"Where are we going?" Morrigan asked.

"We're going to talk to Nebi of course," Abby grinned.

"Why?" Morrigan asked hesitantly.

"Because I think it's time Nebi and Dusty learn to play our favorite shifting game," Abby said waiting for her brother to stand.

Morrigan slowly pushed himself to his feet. "They won't play," he protested. "I told you, Nebi won't shift into anything except a panther. I already considered the game weeks ago but I rejected it. There's not much point when one of the players always shifts into the same form."

"She will if the alternative is for Dusty to work with Tiffany," Abby assured him. "Just leave this to me. I'll handle it. Tell me about Tiffany. Is she talented?"

"She's good," Morrigan said. "After Dusty and Nebi she's the most promising of the group."

"Perfect," Abby said smiling, then made a beeline for the kids.

Morrigan followed Abby to the group, studying the kids as he approached. Was Abby seeing something he didn't? Was Tiffany interested in Dusty? How had Abby figured that out so quickly?

"Hey guys," Abby said enthusiastically. She focused on Gerty for a minute. "I thought I'd come over and congratulate the hero. You were great today, Gerty."

"She was awesome!" Dusty grinned as he bumped shoulders with the younger girl.

"Yeah," Nebi chimed in. She was grateful for the distraction. Maybe Tiffany would go away. "She saved my butt for sure."

"I'm gonna go check on Jordan," Tiffany said to no one in particular. "I just wanted to come over and tell Gert what a great job she did today. I'll see you guys later."

Abby watched Nebi closely. If she hadn't been so focused, she might have missed it completely. Nebi was relieved that Tiffany was leaving. This was going to work, she knew it. "See you," Abby told Tiffany as she walked away.

"Morrigan?" Gerty said quietly. "I just wanted to thank you for letting me leave your class. I know I'm a terrible fighter, but I love archery and I'm actually good at it. I'm sure you were getting ready to send me home. In fact, after that battle I called mom and told her I needed dad to come get me. They refused. They said I needed to stick it out. After a long talk, mom gave me the courage I needed to stay, but we all knew I'd never be able to fight. My goal was just to get through this unscathed. I can't wait to call them and tell them what happened today. They're going to be so proud. Anyway, I just wanted to thank you for your patience. I don't think anyone else would have been so kind to me after I messed up so badly and got Nebi hurt."

"You didn't get me hurt," Nebi scolded. "Stop saying that."

"I did, but maybe I redeemed myself today. I'm willing to put that in the past now," Gerty conceded.

"There's a phone in the office over there," Morrigan offered. "Why don't you go call your parents now?"

"Really? You don't mind? It's going to be long distance," she admitted hesitantly.

"Not at all," Morrigan assured her. "I should have offered that to you an hour ago."

"Thank you," Gerty said hugging Morrigan then rushing off to make the call.

"That was nice of you," Nebi told him. "I'm glad she was there to help us. Sure we could have managed without her, but this is so good for her. She's a great kid, she just needed something to boost her confidence. She got that today."

"I agree," Morrigan said feeling a little better about the whole Gerty situation.

"I'm glad we got the two of you alone for a minute," Abby said casually. "There's something I wanted to talk to you about."

"What's that?" Dusty asked curiously.

"Well, it's about you," she told him. "Morrigan tells me you still can't shift into anything other than a tiger under pressure."

"Oh...that," Dusty said, embarrassed. "I really am working on it, but when I panic it just happens."

"Well that's why I wanted to speak to both of you," Abby said cheerfully. "Morrigan and I have come up with a solution."

"You have?" Dusty asked.

"Yes," Abby said. "When we were young, I had trouble shifting. Morrigan made up a game to help me. I think you were outside when we were playing it here a few weeks back."

"Yeah, I saw it," Dusty said skeptically. "It's a cool game, but who would I play it with? It seemed kind of dangerous."

"It's not dangerous," Morrigan corrected. "Not if you take precautions. You won't be able to shift as many times as we did. Abby and I have years of practice. But we started out a lot more basic. You just need to eat something high in protein right before and right after you play."

"But I still don't have a partner," Dusty argued.

Abby looked at Nebi. "Why can't Nebi help you?" she asked innocently.

"I..." Nebi was shaking her head.

"That won't work," Dusty said immediately. "Nebi only takes the form of a panther."

"Sure. But that's by choice," Abby corrected. "Wouldn't you be willing to take other forms if it helped Dusty overcome his

Chaos

problem? I mean you have to realize the danger Dusty will be in if he changes into a tiger in the middle of Central Park or Times Square? Every human in the area will want to hunt him down, either for sport or because they fear for their safety. He has to overcome his tendency to become a tiger and this will help him do that."

"I don't think I can," Nebi said reluctant to try.

"Are you sure?" Abby asked. "You two seemed so close, I thought you'd be the perfect partner, but if you're sure you can't do it we'll get someone else. I don't want to push you if it's too difficult."

"Who?" Nebi asked, worried. The next best shifter was Tiffany. And it wasn't too difficult, she just didn't shift into anything else. She didn't see the point.

"Oh. I don't know," Abby said casually turning to Morrigan. "Who's the next best in the class? It has to be someone who is already accomplished."

"I think that would be Tiffany," he responded slowly, pretending to ponder before answering.

"Wasn't that the girl that just left?" Abby asked still trying to sound innocent. "Maybe she's still close by. We could talk to her now," Abby pretended to look around the room.

"Wait," Nebi said abruptly. "Maybe I could help. What would I have to do?" There was no way she would let Tiffany spend time with Dusty every day. She trusted Dusty, but if they had just the slightest fight, Tiffany would pounce and take advantage of the situation. She wasn't willing to take that chance.

Morrigan was surprised. Abby was brilliant. If they worked this right, maybe both kids would expand their abilities. "I think the best way to handle this would be for the two of you to spend at least an hour together each day. There's an office over there that I will make available to you. The warriors are working on a plan to keep the student's safe. There's a good chance we could encounter more animals. I expect you to follow all the rules we implement. Each day you will select a different animal to study. The computer in the office has the internet. I want you to know everything there is to know about it. The animals must be indigenous to the New York area. That means you will have seven new animals a week to choose from. We have class three times a week. The two of you will report on one of the animals at the beginning of every class. So, out of the seven, pick your favorite three. I want you to be able to answer any questions that come up about that animal. This is going to be a learning experience for the entire class. Whatever animal you choose will be that days focus. After your presentation everyone will practice shifting into that animal. The first fifteen to twenty minutes of every class will be yours before we transition into the combat training. You can start playing the game after you've researched for two weeks. That will give you fourteen animals to start with. When you play the game, you can only shift into those fourteen animals."

"What if we change into something different?" Dusty asked.

"You lose the game," Morrigan said flatly. "I'll let you two decide what the winner gets."

"Is this assignment optional?" Nebi asked.

"It is for you," Abby told her. "But you have to decide now. It's important that Dusty has a partner that can follow this through, all the way. If you can't do it tell us now. We won't think any less

Chaos

of you. We both know you were raised by panthers and you have chosen to restrict yourself to that form. There's nothing wrong with that. Panthers have survived in this region for centuries just as we have. But for this project, Dusty needs someone willing to take various forms. It's the only way he's going to overcome his tendency to default to the tiger. If you don't want the job or you don't think you can stick it out to the end, I'll talk to Tiffany. Once you commit, it's no longer optional. Do you understand?"

Nebi studied Abby. She wondered if this was a trick to get her to change into other forms or if they were just trying to help Dusty. They couldn't know about Tiffany though. She knew Morrigan was worried about Dusty, she was too. He did great in class. As long as there was no urgency he could shift into anything, but put on a little pressure and out came the tiger. "I want to do this," she said with finality. "I want to help Dusty myself."

"Are you sure?" Dusty asked her. He knew she was uncomfortable shifting into anything other than a panther. "I don't want you to do something you don't want to do. I can just work with Tiffany."

"Positive," Nebi said more confidently. "It will be good for both of us," she decided. "Can we start now? The office is empty, can we use the internet while we're waiting for you guys to tell us about the new rules?"

"Sure," Morrigan said. "Let me know if the office is locked and I'll let you in. I'll get you a key later. I'm trusting you two, don't let me down. If you break the rules, computer access will be taken away but the assignment is going to continue," he warned.

"We won't break the rules," Dusty promised. He took Nebi's hand and pulled her toward the empty office.

Abby watched as the two kids walked away. They immediately began discussing the new project. She was sure Dusty was quizzing Nebi. He cared about her and wouldn't want her to do anything that made her uncomfortable.

"Maybe you should be the teacher," Morrigan said still amazed that his sister had solved his problem in a matter of minutes.

"Don't be silly," Abby said turning to him. "I'm a terrible teacher. It never would have worked if I hadn't seen the interaction between Tiffany and Nebi," she admitted.

"So, you think Tiffany is after Dusty?" Morrigan asked. He hadn't seen any indication of that, not even today. "What tipped you off?"

Abby smiled. "Men are so clueless when it comes to women," she said shaking her head. "It's really quite pathetic. I don't think Tiffany is actively trying to steal Dusty away. She's just silently present. Casually complimentary. I saw her praising Dusty for his actions today. That's what tipped me off. She was just giving him a little friendly compliment but she's also manipulating him. She's hoping one day Dusty and Nebi will break up, or just have a fight. That's when she'll make her move. She'll step in, pretend to be the consoling friend, then when the time is right she'll push it a little. If Dusty reacts, she'll act on it. She's hoping it will be enough to win her man."

Morrigan shook his head. "Women are scary, you know that? No wonder I'm still single. The more you tell me, the more terrified I am of the creatures. I assume Nebi knows what Tiffany is up to, since you figured it out in about five seconds?" he asked.

Chaos

"Sure she does," Abby smiled. "Why do you think she was so inflexible when it came to Dusty spending an hour a day with the competition?"

"Of course," Morrigan said, still baffled by what had transpired. The how and why of it didn't matter. The important thing for him was that Dusty and Nebi were on their way to overcoming their personal barriers. Maybe he couldn't manipulate them as well as Abby had, but he could teach them. Abby was right, he needed to stop doubting himself and start being creative again.

* * * *

Kylee sat on the large couch that seemed to be the centerpiece of the stylish apartment. It was frustrating to be locked up inside while everyone else rounded up the kids and made safety plans. She wanted to be involved. She smiled a little. How many times had she ordered patients to stay off their leg, or take a couple days off work to remain in bed? She hadn't listened to their objections and nobody here was going to listen to hers. She glanced back at the notepad from George. It was the third one she'd thumbed through so far and she still hadn't learned a thing. She turned the page in frustration and pondered. There was that symbol again. George's experiments were interesting, but she didn't think studying his activities would help them with Melissa. Patricia had altered the formulas too drastically.

Some of the ingredients George had used, Kylee had never even heard of. Because of that, it was impossible to determine if he was on the right track or not. But each time an experiment failed he noted the results then drew that symbol. It had to have relevance. Kylee turned on the laptop and waited for it to warm up. Maybe she could find that symbol on the internet. It was going to be difficult to track down though. It kind of looked like a coat-of-arms. Was it the Dillinger family crest? She wasn't sure how to go about researching that, but she definitely had the time so she might as well see what she could find.

* * * *

McBride sat on the porch of the small cabin feeling content and relaxed for the first time in his life. Austin was going on about shifter customs and traditions. For some reason it wasn't boring when Austin did it. This was different than hanging out and drinking a beer with his friends in the city. Well, that was a bit of a stretch. Before he came to the shifter camp he never really had a true friend. Sure, he had guys at work that he socialized with and trusted on the job, but Austin was his first true friend.

So much had changed over the past few months. Drinking a beer and relaxing with Austin was so out of character for the old McBride. The old McBride would be sitting home, alone, unable to sleep, anxious for the next day to begin. He understood now why his life had been chaotic and unbalanced for so long. It was his parents fault. He smiled a little, wasn't that what everyone said? Dr. Phil would have a heyday. But for him it was actually true. His mind drifted back to the first time he shifted. He had been so young, almost five years old. He had been playing in his room alone. He always loved to read and his father had brought him a new stack of books the day before.

Rand sat on the floor, trying to make out the words in his new Winnie the Pooh book. He loved those stories. His favorite character was Tigger. He was maybe halfway through the book when he began to fantasize about being a tiger like Tigger. He remembered sitting there on the floor, visualizing a tiger and wishing he could experience such freedom. That's when it happened, all of a sudden he changed. It was almost instantaneous. One minute he was a small child reading a fictional story, the next he was the fantasy. He panicked a little and whirled around to look in the large closet mirror. That's when his tiger tail struck the lamp and knocked it to the floor.

The loud thud made his mother come running. McBride knew he was going to get caught. He became almost frantic, sitting on the floor chanting over and over in his mind. *I need to be a boy again, please let me turn back into a boy before mamma comes in.* He almost made it. When his mother entered the room, McBride was mostly boy with just a little tiger left. The tail and ears were still poking through and his nails were long and deadly.

His mother had panicked. She immediately began screaming hysterically, slammed the door and ran down the stairs. Rand climbed onto his bed and crawled to the corner, terrified of what he had done. He was worried about his mother. He'd never seen her that upset before. Rand sat there, scared and worried for twenty minutes before his mother finally came back. She sat on the bed and asked him what had happened. That's when she had that talk with him. The one about evil demons trying to take over his soul. She'd been so sure of herself, so convincing in her explanation. She'd ordered him to fight the demons in the future and never let that happen again. For almost forty years he'd spent his life fighting. The battle that raged inside him was exhausting. He never truly relaxed for fear the evil that lived inside him would escape again. *It was cruel*, he thought. How could a mother do such a thing to her child?

He smiled at Austin. "I'm glad I came here," he said casually. "It's nice to finally understand my heritage and what I truly am." He took a deep breath. "It feels good to just sit with a friend and relax after a long day."

They both looked up as a car pulled down the short drive. Austin shot a glance at Rand then stood. "I'd say that's my cue. I told Sherrie I wouldn't be long. I don't want to keep my baby waiting or I'll pay for it later." He gave McBride a silent solute then paused. "Hey. I'm glad you're here too," he sobered. "I'm also sorry we didn't find you sooner. I know it had to be hard fighting with yourself all this time."

"Thanks," McBride smiled again. "Now go find your woman before she's mad at me. I can't afford to lose visitation rights. You're the only friend I've got."

Austin smiled back. "Wait until Morrigan gets back. You two are going to hit it off big time. I miss him, but don't tell him that. We've both lived here with the pack all our lives. When Sherrie and I got married, I worried things might change for me and Morrigan but they didn't. Thank goodness. Life with Sherrie is great, but guys need friends too... just to hang with. And don't think because you're single, you and Morrigan can ditch me. I'll find out and come after you," Austin continued up the drive, passing Cornelia on his way out.

McBride watched as Cornelia made her way to the porch. "I didn't mean to run him off," she said pleasantly.

"You didn't," McBride assured her. "He needed to get home anyway. What did you find?"

Cornelia slowly slid into a chair and handed McBride a file. "It might upset you. They have a past," she said soberly.

Chaos

Rand stared at the file for a long time then turned to Cornelia. "Why don't you give me the highlights and I'll read through the details later," he suggested.

Cornelia understood. It was never easy to get bad news about your parents. She knew that better than anyone. At least these two weren't his biological parents. They were just the people who had raised him. She hoped once she tracked down his real parents, the news would be better. "Okay," she conceded. "Bastian had two of his men go out to your parents' house posing as the CDC. They convinced your parents they were in the area because of the increase in West Nile virus cases. Your parents allowed them to take a blood sample. The men assured your parents their systems were clean of the disease and they were given a bag of sample products to help prevent infection. They distributed the bags to a few neighbors to solidify the ruse," she paused. "So, I guess the good news is that your parents are healthy and the bad news is that they've been living under a fake name since you were around three years old." She waited to see if he had questions or some kind of reaction to that. He didn't.

"While they were there, Bastian's men were also able to collect finger prints from both your parents. With the prints and the DNA it was pretty easy to follow their trail." Rand still hadn't said anything. She didn't know how to read his lack of reaction. "Hey, you okay or do you just want to take that file inside and read it when you are alone and able to digest things a little better?"

"No," Rand said immediately. "Continue. I will read the file, but I'd like a verbal explanation from you first. I'm fine, go ahead."

"Okay," Cornelia agreed. "Just keep in mind there are holes in my research. Jane and Robert McBride's history can be traced back, like I said, until you are three. Before that, nothing. The two didn't exist. That's where the prints and their DNA came in. Here is what I've discovered so far. Forty years ago, Jane and Robert McBride arrived in Kentucky with a young son, Randall McBride. Your birth certificate says you were born in Utah. However, in contacting the authorities there, the certificate is a fake. All of their paperwork from that time forward is fake."

"So you don't know where I was born?" he asked.

"Not yet," she said. "That is still one of the holes I haven't been able to fill."

"Okay," he let out a long breath. "Keep going."

"I suspect you were born somewhere in California or Oregon," Cornelia admitted. "I haven't confirmed that yet, but that's the direction I'm leaning."

"Why?" Rand asked.

"Because your parents at the time were Jane and Robert Taylor. I've been able to trace both of them back a couple generations. McBride was your great grandmother's maiden name, on Jane's side. The Taylor's are from California. They lived there for many years prior to the move to Kentucky. Jane and Robert owned and operated a very successful shipping company for several years. Unfortunately, the success of the company came from their smuggling operation rather than their legal endeavors."

McBride's mind was racing. "No wonder they panicked when I announced I was moving to New York to be a cop." At least that made sense to him now. His parents had freaked when he broke the news to them. *Well, that's just wonderful.* His parents were criminals.

Chaos

"They probably worried you'd discover the same thing I did. Having their prints helped, but I would have found this anyway. It just would have taken me longer. If it helps, they were never violent people. There is one arrest for assault that involved another man, but the assault was very minor and the reporting officer actually thought it was a mutual combat situation. Neither party wanted to cooperate, so the charges were dropped."

"Is that supposed to make me feel better?" he snapped. "Knowing that my parents are criminals, just not violent criminals? I hardly think that matters."

"It will," Cornelia said confidently. "Once you get used to the fact that they were smugglers you'll be grateful to know they weren't violent. Anyway, eventually they got caught. Both of them went to prison because they wouldn't divulge the names of any of their associates. Jane was sentenced to ten years but only served four of them. Robert was sentenced to fifteen, but he only served five. They were both model prisoners and were paroled early for good behavior. When Jane got out, she went to work as a waitress at a small café and waited for her husband to be released. Robert got out about a year later. Jane was no longer restricted, but Robert was. They moved to Redding and purchased a small farm. Again, Robert was a model citizen. He was only monitored for six months after his release. A short time after his probation was up, they moved to Kentucky under a new name and mysteriously had a child."

"So where did they get me?" Rand asked.

"I'd say that's the million dollar question," Cornelia told him. "I'm not finding any answers. They covered their tracks pretty well and whoever made the fake ID was a pro. I suspect it was one of those acquaintances they refused to name. Anyway, that's where we're at. I'd like to schedule a time you and I can go out and talk to your parents. You need to read that file first. Between the two of us, we'll catch them if they lie. You have a lot to digest, McBride. I'll call you in the morning and we'll set a date and time to vacation in Kentucky." Cornelia stood and slowly left the porch.

Rand watched as the woman slid into her car and silently backed out of the drive. He had tried to avoid guessing or speculating on his origins, but finding out his parents were really felony smugglers that had served time in prison came as a shock. His mother, the timid, quiet, religious fanatic, was a criminal? Maybe he should have guessed, nobody is that devoted to God. He pushed himself up from the chair and entered the small cabin. Once inside he placed the folder on the kitchen table and grabbed another beer. He would need a little buzz to get through this. Rand moved back to the table and settled into the large chair. After only a slight moment of hesitation he flipped open the folder and began to read. He couldn't procrastinate forever.

* * * *

Bastian sat in the lab scribbling notes. Kylee's documentation on warrior blood had given him an idea. He still had to overcome the coagulation problem but he had a couple thoughts on that as well. Maybe Kylee wasn't researching the warriors for a good reason, but he was going to. He'd been thinking about this for days. If he could find a way to preserve warrior blood it would do so much to assist his people.

They had learned a valuable lesson during Sam's transition. Sam's body was injured, so it drained Ty's system of the blood he needed to survive. When they reintroduced Sam's blood into Ty, he recovered. If Bastian could find a way to somehow preserve warrior blood, they could use it to reduce the impact when a warrior was trying to turn his mate. Sure that rarely happened, but when it did, having extra warrior blood on hand would be invaluable. Bastian saw further benefits though. Warriors got seriously injured all the time. For centuries he'd watched warriors die from injuries that were too severe for the warrior blood to heal. He strongly believed if Luke had stored some of his own blood, blood that his body didn't have to work to change, he might still be alive today. That was the practical implication of what he was trying to do here. He wanted to save lives... warrior lives. If he could just find a way to store warrior blood, the breakthrough would be monumental.

* * * *

Kylee finished her coffee and walked back to the couch. So far she hadn't been able to find anything on that symbol. She knew it had importance. It was somehow significant, but why? She'd never figure it out here in the apartment. She needed to get back to the lab. Okay. She was supposed to stay down for another day, but she just couldn't do it. She had to get out of this room. Breena told her there had been another animal attack yesterday afternoon. A flock of ducks had landed in the fort and went after a couple kids. Luckily, the warriors were on patrol and immediately took care of the threat so nobody got hurt.

Kylee sighed. Things were happening all around her and she was stuck in this stupid apartment. Well, she wasn't staying here any longer. She had things to do. She could admit her strength hadn't returned, not completely, but she was strong enough to move to the lab and work there. It would be easy to hook up the IV while she worked. One day wouldn't matter as long as she continued her treatment. She pulled on a jacket, slipped on her boots and headed to the lab.

Kylee pulled the large door open and slipped inside. Once there, she froze. Bastian was working on something. Why hadn't she thought of that? This was going to be uncomfortable. Over the past two days she'd been going over things in her mind, she didn't have anything else to do. Now that she knew she was a shifter, Bastian's refusal to turn her into a warrior didn't matter. All the obstacles, the barriers keeping them apart, were no longer there. Except one. Kylee knew she could never be with someone that didn't include her in decision making. That was really the crux of it. Bastian had single handedly decided their fate for both of them. He never even discussed the situation with her. He didn't care how she felt about things, he just decided and moved forward with his own plan. That might seem like a small thing, but to her it was huge. She had held out all her life for a partner, not a dictator. She couldn't settle, especially now that she knew how long she was going to live.

Kylee remembered the way her mother used to talk about her father. She never met her dad because he died when she was just a baby. But she was certain of one thing; her mother and father had loved each other very much. Mom loved him so much, she never gave another man a fighting chance. One time, when Kylee was about ten, she'd come home from her first day of school and told her mom about her new teacher. It was a man, a handsome, sweet, gentle man. But most importantly, he was a single man. Kylee had encouraged her mother to not only meet the handsome instructor, but to ask him out on a date. The complex look that crossed her mother's features was instantly burned into Kylee's memory forever. After a few seconds, mom sat on the couch and motioned for Kylee to join her. The two of them sat for hours discussing Kylee's father. Mom told her about their relationship, their partnership and encouraged Kylee to hold out for a man that would love her the way Kylee's father had loved her mother.

Chaos

Kylee had. That's why she was over forty and never had a real relationship. Not until Bastian anyway. She had honestly believed what they were starting, was something special. Then Bastian broke her heart. No, she couldn't live that way. She deserved more. Kylee took a deep breath and approached Bastian. They needed to find a way to work together again. The project with Melissa wasn't over and she had questions Bastian might be able to answer. The one currently on her mind was that crest. Bastian might know what it was, or what it meant.

When Kylee reached Bastian's work station, she casually glanced over his shoulder to see what he was working on and froze. Anger pulsed through her. *How dare he take her private notes! What right did he have to rummage through her personal space and confiscate something she had been working on?* She slammed George's notebook on the counter and glared at Bastian. She was trying to remain calm, but was losing the fight. "How dare you?" she demanded. "What makes you think you have the right to steal my research, my notes and my project?" she began.

Bastian was surprised at Kylee's reaction. He hadn't stolen anything, they were supposed to be working together. He turned his chair to face her, hoping they could talk this out in a rational manner. All hope was lost when he saw her face. He blinked, a little perplexed at her reaction. Why was she so upset?

Bastian's calm demeanor infuriated Kylee even more. He acted as if he hadn't done anything wrong. He should be ashamed, not proud of the intrusion. A clear testament that she was right about him. He was pompous, arrogant and pushy. Just because he was the Great Bastian Carrigan didn't mean he could waltz in and take whatever he wanted. She reached down and grabbed her notebook, bringing it close to her chest. It wouldn't surprise her if Bastian tried to take it back, forcefully if necessary. "This is my project. It has nothing to do with you. You might get away with this behavior in your own lab, but you are not my boss and I don't have to tolerate this kind of intrusion." She was breathing hard, sucking air through her nose trying to calm herself.

Bastian raised one eyebrow. He should be angry, but Kylee's passion was endearing. That sobered him. He was such an idiot and he was doomed. This was pathetic. He was actually turned on by Kylee's outburst. The woman was on the verge of hysterics and all he wanted to do was pull her onto his lap and kiss away her fury. "I beg your pardon," he said, narrowing his eyes at her. "I'd have to disagree with you, as you have somehow covertly obtained a sample of my blood and proceeded to study and dissect it. That little betrayal has everything to do with me. In addition, you are studying my people, which threatens every warrior on the planet. So, as much as you dislike it, I not only had a right to study your material but an obligation to do so."

"If you don't want people studying your blood, you shouldn't leave it lying around. I needed your blood for my project and you conveniently discarded it haphazardly in the trash. Legally, I'd say the blood no longer belonged to you. You abandoned it," Kylee brushed off his accusations and continued to glare at him. "You had no right to invade my privacy. That workstation is mine. That area surrounding the workstation is mine. You had no right to enter my space or remove my property," she accused.

"I see you believe there is a double standard here. Why is that Kylee? Why do you think you have more rights in this lab than I do? Why do you think we should all hold you in awe and respect your privacy when you don't respect the privacy of anyone else?" Kylee blinked, but continued to stare defiantly. "I see you're not going to respond to that. I don't blame you, what could you say without proving my point. You routinely enter my space. If you

Chaos

want evidence of your intrusions, just look in that notebook. You already admitted that you removed a sample of blood from my trash can. A trash can that happens to be in my space, space you invaded to find the discarded flask in the first place. But apparently that's different because you're Dr. Kylee Quintana extraordinaire. You can do whatever you want in this lab and nobody is supposed to question it. I'm not sure what the word partner means to you, but clearly it's drastically different from my definition." Bastian was finished with this. He was tired of the emotions Kylee always brought out in him. He needed a break. He couldn't leave the fort, but he could leave the lab. He stood and retrieved his coat in one fluid motion then stalked out of the room.

Bastian strolled into the barn, trying to relax. He hated fighting with Kylee and it seemed that's all they did anymore. He noticed the horses and decided to go for a ride. He was leading his favorite mare out of the barn when he ran into Morrigan.

"Going riding?" Morrigan asked.

"Yeah," Bastian admitted. "I need to get away for a while."

"I'll go with you," Morrigan said immediately. "Don't argue. We all agreed nobody goes anywhere alone. You go find someone in the house and tell them we're leaving for a while and I'll saddle another horse."

Bastian considered arguing, but Morrigan was right. Just because he was pissed off at Kylee didn't mean he should be reckless. They had all agreed nobody would go out alone. He would honor that promise. "Alright," Bastian said handing Morrigan the reigns. "I'll be right back."

The two men mounted their horses and walked towards the west entrance. "Thanks for joining me Morrigan," Bastian finally said. "I needed a little break."

"No problem. I'm actually looking forward to the ride myself," Morrigan said lightly.

"I've been meaning to compliment you on the work you're doing with the kids," Bastian said. "They've come a long way and it's all because of you. We knew it was important to have you here to help us with the shifter contingent, but all the kids have benefitted from your knowledge and experience. We're lucky to have you," Bastian said sincerely.

Morrigan was surprised. He'd been feeling so down lately. That whole thing with Gerty and then Dusty and Nebi. He was doubting his choice to stick around and teach for the next year. Bastian's compliment meant a lot. "Thanks," he finally said. "I've been feeling like I'm failing lately. It means a lot to me that you think I'm doing a good job."

Bastian was surprised by that. "Do you want to talk about it?" he asked. "I'm curious why you would think you are failing. The kids have come so far under your guidance."

The two men rode into the country, talking about the kids and the teaching. Morrigan began to relay the story of Dusty and Nebi and how Abby helped him get the kids headed in the right direction.

* * * *

Kylee prepared the sodium solution and changed out her IV. She was so frustrated and confused she could barely think. Bastian

Chaos

had left, clearly as angry as she was. This was getting worse, not better. How could they ever work together again when they couldn't be in the same room for more than five seconds without arguing? She always felt so much turmoil when she was around him. She couldn't think straight and maybe she was a little irrational. Bastian was right, she had invaded his space as much as he had invaded hers. She brushed away a tear and stood. This wasn't helping. Kylee realized she was hungry. She knew there wasn't anything to eat in the apartment so she headed for the farmhouse.

By the time Kylee reached the kitchen she was fuming. She'd been thinking about the argument with Bastian all the way to the house. It only took a minute to realize Bastian had tried to turn things on her and make her out to be the bad guy. Just another indication he was the wrong man for her. The guy was selfish and pushy and manipulative. So she'd taken his blood out of the trash. That didn't mean she was invading his space. And of course she felt possessive about the lab, she was there far more often than he was. She was the victim here. Bastian was the overbearing, pushy, condescending man. "Partners my butt," she said slamming the door shut on the refrigerator. She turned to set the food on the table and stared, wide eyed at Abby and Marta.

The two women were watching her. What had they heard? Kylee knew she had a tendency to mumble when she was angry. How much had she revealed?

"Bad day at the office?" Abby asked casually.

"Uh..." Kylee didn't know what to say. "Sorry. I thought I was alone."

Marta stood and took some of the food from Kylee's arms. "Let me help you with this. You're going to drop something and I don't want it to be the IV bag." She set the food on the table and pulled out a chair for Kylee. Then Marta returned to her seat.

"You must be starving," Abby commented. "I know anytime I'm sick and don't eat properly, I binge as soon as I'm feeling better. I guess it's a shifter thing. Our bodies use calories to help us heal so we require a lot of proteins once we recoup."

"I am starving," Kylee said. "I have to admit I still have a hard time thinking of myself as a shifter. I really don't know anything about you guys. Plus, how can I be one if I've never shifted?"

"Simple," Abby told her. "You haven't shifted because you never knew you could. I know it's all new and maybe a little hard to understand, but you are definitely a shifter. You do believe that, don't you?"

"I saw the scientific evidence, so I can't deny I am physically a part of that species. Emotionally, that's another thing completely. Knowing my biological makeup is that of a shifter doesn't mean I have the ability to actually shift," Kylee tried to explain. She was still confused and she felt substandard. How could she be a shifter and not be able to take the form of another animal?

"First of all, the fact that you haven't shifted doesn't mean you can't, or that you won't," Abby began. "Our females are different than the males. The guys take to this more naturally than us girls. Let's use Rand as an example. He shifted when he was around four or five. His parents didn't know what was going on, so they brainwashed him into believing that side of him was abnormal and evil. But all his life his body, his animal side, struggled with his mind. He's lived in constant battle with himself because he refused to shift.

Chaos

Females on the other hand would never have that conflict. We have female members of our society that can shift, but never do. Some of them haven't since they were children. The women don't have that battle within themselves. Not the same as the men do anyway. That's why you are a shifter, but it's never caused you conflict. You probably had other symptoms that you didn't recognize. Does that make sense?" Abby asked.

"Sorry, but none of this really makes sense," Kylee told her. She was starting to calm down from the rant she'd been in, but she wasn't relaxing. This topic was just as confusing and frustrating as dealing with Bastian.

"We're animals Kylee," Abby said bluntly. "It's really that simple. I'd say that's why you were so angry when you walked into the kitchen. You had a disagreement with Bastian I assume, and you're animal side kicked in. I know what that's like. You got annoyed, then you lashed out and you were so furious you wanted to pounce, right?" she asked smiling.

That's exactly what had happened. Kylee couldn't explain it, but she had wanted to lash out physically at Bastian. She thought it was her feelings for him that made her so volatile, but Abby believed it was the shifter.

"Don't worry about it," Abby said. "Eventually you'll get a handle on your emotions. The one thing you need to know is what you're going through is natural. We're all animals," Abby smiled again. "It might feel like a curse right now, but it's also a blessing. At least Thomas thinks so," Abby was beaming now.

Abby and Marta laughed. Kylee was stunned. Was Abby talking about sex?

"Oh, don't look so shocked Kylee," Abby told her. "It's okay to let loose every once in a while. You just need to make sure you're evenly matched. Once you get to know our people you'll find that we typically mate with each other out of necessity. I hooked up with Thomas and he's man enough to handle the wild animalistic side of me, but humans are more fragile." Abby paused. "If you and Bastian work things out, that's not something you'll have to worry about. A warrior can handle mating with a shifter, no problem." Abby looked at Marta, "In fact, I happen to think it's a perfect solution. Warriors have a few...uh...secrets of their own. Right, Marta?" Abby laughed. She didn't know if it was possible to mend the problems between Kylee and Bastian, but she knew Kylee would be very happy if they did.

Marta smiled. "I think you're embarrassing the girl Abby," she scolded. "I take it you're a little uncomfortable talking about intimacy with a man?" she asked Kylee.

"I guess that's pretty obvious," Kylee admitted. "I really don't know anything about it."

"You've never...?" Abby asked, amazed. "Wow."

"Abby," Marta scolded again. "Not everyone indulges themselves as freely as you're people. Some choose to wait for the right person to come along."

"You make me sound like I'm some sleazy hooker or something. I've always been selective and discrete about my activities. It's not like there's been hundreds of men in my life, just a select few," Abby said defensively.

"That's not what I was saying at all," Marta patted Abby's arm. "All I'm saying is that Kylee was raised as a human. Some human's firmly believe a woman should wait until after marriage to indulge

Chaos

in certain activities. It's okay if that's what you believe Kylee," Marta assured her.

"I have no idea how this turned into a moral discussion, but I do have strong beliefs about that particular topic. Mom was very persuasive. She taught me to wait to be with a man until I knew for sure he loved me and was going to treat me the way I deserve to be treated. I guess she convinced me not to settle. We did okay on our own without my father and I've always been fine without a companion. I'd rather be alone than settle for the wrong man," Kylee explained.

"Sensible," Abby said a little amused. "So where does Bastian fit into those plans?"

"He doesn't," Kylee said abruptly. She quickly lifted a chicken leg and took a bite.

"We couldn't help but hear the unflattering things you were mumbling over by the fridge," Marta told her. "I'm a little confused. You don't really think Bastian is selfish and pompous do you? That was just the anger talking, right?"

"Actually I do," Kylee said. "I know he's a friend of yours, and I don't want to offend you but I meant every word. Bastian is not the man I once thought he was. The last couple weeks have shown me that he is selfish, overbearing, pushy, controlling and condescending. I'm glad I discovered this now, I could never be with a man that didn't respect me."

Abby sobered. She didn't know Bastian well, but she knew him enough to know he was none of the things Kylee had just accused him of. "Kylee, Bastian is a warrior. It's impossible for him to be selfish. I don't know what happened between you two, but whatever it was I think you've misread the situation."

"Just because Thomas isn't selfish doesn't mean I'm wrong," Kylee argued. "Bastian isn't the same as the other warriors. You have to know that."

"No. He isn't," Marta admitted. "He's different in some ways, but exactly the same in others. I have to agree with Abby. Bastian doesn't have a selfish bone in his body," Marta paused. "Before you get angry let me tell you about my relationship with Bastian. I believe he is a very special man. In fact, I've never met a more caring, selfless honorable man in my life. I love my dear Jake more than anything in the world, but even he is not as selfless as Bastian. Of all the warriors, Bastian and Victor are the two that always think of others before themselves."

"Apparently Bastian is different with you than he is with me," Kylee objected. "With me, he's demanding and pushy. He constantly gives me orders and expects me to just follow them. The other day, when we were outside with those animals, I told Dusty to put me down and he wouldn't. Not until Bastian gave him the okay. Bastian is not my keeper or my ruler. It is so aggravating."

Abby laughed. "You're pissed at Bastian for something Dusty did? How is it Bastian's fault that Dusty didn't follow your orders without the approval of Bastian?"

"Because Bastian didn't correct him. He just gave a little nod then continued to give orders. That might seem like a small thing, but it's not just that one instance, it's everything combined." Kylee could see the women thought she was foolish.

"Kylee, of course Bastian took charge in the face of danger. That's what warriors do," Marta explained. "Warriors are fierce and protective. They are born leaders. It's what they were made for. If you expect Bastian to just sit back and let others make crucial decisions when there's a threat, you're right, you don't belong with a warrior. You don't deserve one."

"That's not fair," Kylee said narrowing her eyes at Marta.

"Actually she's right," Abby said bringing Kylee's attention back to her. "Warriors protect the ones they love. I very strongly believe I can take care of myself. Having the ability to shift gives me a lot of power and a lot of freedom. Sometimes it even gives me an advantage. Even with all that, Thomas is extremely protective and cautious about my safety. Sometimes to the point of annoyance. He's a warrior, he can't help it. You were here a few weeks ago when we arrived. Didn't you see how angry Thomas got when I played that game with Morrigan? He was furious because he thought I was being reckless with my health."

"Look at Victor and Ariel," Abby continued. "With Ariel's gift, she's the most capable of any of us. She can take out numerous vampires before they come within ten feet of her. But still, Victor hovers when they fight. He watches over her and protects her and is always pushing her to improve her skills. No matter how good Ariel gets, Victor will always be by her side in a battle protecting her. The same goes for Dimitri and Alex. I know you've seen how protective he is over Alex. Sometimes he makes her so angry I worry she's going to punch him."

"That's different," Kylee disagreed. "Alex is the queen. Dimitri has to be that protective of her, he loves her... sure, but he's also responsible for her safety."

Marta smiled. "Kylee, Dimitri doesn't protect Alex out of some sense of duty. He does it because he loves her. He does it because he is so deeply in love with her, the thought of anything happening to her drives him insane. Jake is the same with me, Thomas is the same with Abby, Victor is the same with Ariel and

Ty is the same with Sam. In a warriors eyes, their mate, the woman they love is more than their queen, she's their life. When a warrior falls in love, it's forever dear. They are the most loyal, dedicated men on earth. If you don't understand that, you don't understand Bastian at all."

"Maybe that's true, but Bastian doesn't love me," Kylee said wondering if that was the problem all along. Maybe she'd fallen in love with him, but the feeling wasn't mutual. "I've seen every one of you with your partner's. It's a real partnership. The men love you, but you love them just as deeply. You make decisions as a couple. You talk about important things and decide together. That's not the way things are with me and Bastian. Maybe Bastian is all that you say he is, but not with me. Which is just one more indication that we were never meant to be together."

"Why did the two of you stop seeing each other?" Marta asked. "What happened to make you decide your relationship wasn't working?" she already knew the answer. Jake had told her Kylee refused to see Bastian if he wouldn't turn her into a warrior. Jake was convinced Kylee only wanted to use Bastian, but Marta wasn't so sure.

"I don't see why that matters," Kylee said. "The point is that we aren't seeing each other anymore. In fact, we can't be in a room with each other for more than five seconds without biting each other's heads off."

"I think it does matter," Marta pressed. "I think whatever happened is what convinced you Bastian doesn't love you. It's what has you believing that he's a dictator not a partner."

"Fine," Kylee gave in. "Bastian declared, in no uncertain terms that he would never turn anyone into a warrior. He said there was never any excuse for such a risk. He made it perfectly clear no amount of discussion was going to change his mind. I realize now that I'm not human and that decision saved my life, but it's the fact that he made the decision on his own that matters. If I were human and Bastian and I planned to be together forever, that is the single most important decision we could have made as a couple. But we didn't make the decision together, Bastian made the decision for both of us without a second thought. Without a word to me. Without knowing how I felt about the situation. That's not a partnership. If I overlook that monumental betrayal, I'll have to overlook it for my entire life. I can't live that way," she was crying now. "I just can't."

Abby didn't know what to say. She had to admit Kylee was right, Bastian had a valid point, but that decision was something they should have made together. It impacted Kylee far more than it would impact Bastian.

"Well, I understand where the misunderstanding came from now," Marta said calmly.

"I keep telling you it's not a misunderstanding," Kylee practically yelled. "Bastian didn't love me enough to want to be with me forever. The fact that I'm a shifter doesn't change that. He doesn't respect me or my opinion enough to talk about the important issues. There's no misunderstanding."

"Actually there is," Marta said narrowing her eyes at Kylee. "Please tell me you didn't make those accusations to Bastian. Did you tell him if he didn't turn you that meant he didn't love you enough to be with you forever?" Marta asked anxiously.

Kylee was surprised at the woman's discomfort. She thought back to the day they ended their relationship. She couldn't remember the exact conversation. "I don't think so. After I realized

Bastian had left me out of something so important, I didn't really want to talk about it anymore. I can't be sure, but I don't think so."

Marta was relieved. "Good," she said, letting out the breath she hadn't realized she'd been holding.

"Why does that matter?" Kylee asked.

"It matters a great deal," Marta said evasively. "But before I go into that, I think you should know that Bastian didn't make a decision on this, Kylee. You're upset because you think he left you out of the decision making process. For Bastian there was never any decision to be made. Turning you into a warrior was never on the table. It was never a possibility."

"But doesn't that just prove my point," Kylee asked. "He's too selfish to consider it. He didn't care enough about me to discuss my feelings on the matter."

"No," Marta said. "I know this will offend you, but I think you are the one being selfish."

Kylee was pissed. Marta would never understand. She was too close to Bastian to be objective about this. "I'm sorry you feel that way. I think it's time I went back to the lab."

Marta smiled. "I knew that was going to upset you but I had to say it anyway. I'm not oblivious to Bastian's faults like you think. I just understand him. If you want to understand him too, you'll let me explain," she waited. The ball was in Kylee's court now.

Chapter Eight

Kylee didn't want to take the bait. She knew that was what Marta was doing, baiting her so she could defend Bastian's actions. She kept telling herself to get up and leave, but what if Marta knew something Kylee didn't. What if Marta had a good explanation for Bastian's behavior? She knew everything they had been telling her up to this point was true. She'd seen the other warriors with their partners. Anyone could see how protective they were of the women they loved. If that's what Bastian was doing, Kylee could live with that. But from where she sat, it seemed different. She wasn't even sure Bastian loved her anymore.

Abby was watching Kylee, she was debating with herself. She wanted to stay and find out what Marta knew, but she didn't want them to know how much it meant to her. "I'm curious," Abby finally told Marta. "Maybe you could tell me. Maybe you could help me understand why Bastian didn't have a choice. I kind of agree with Kylee, that was a big decision and they should have made it together. Would you be willing to help me understand? If Kylee wants to listen she can. If she doesn't, she can leave."

"Sorry Abby," Marta told her. "I understand what you are doing, but this is too important. Kylee needs to decide for herself if she cares enough about Bastian to stay and listen, or if she's going to walk away."

She knew it was stupid. She shouldn't let Marta manipulate her this way, but she was too curious to leave. "I'll stay," she said hesitantly.

Marta studied Kylee for a long time before she spoke. "Kylee, do you love Bastian? Do you really care about him, or was this just a casual relationship for you?" What she was about to do might upset Bastian. She wasn't willing to risk that if Kylee didn't love him.

"I don't see why that matters," Kylee objected.

"It matters a great deal," Marta interrupted. "Bastian is a very private man and this is personal. I'm about to discuss something delicate with you. If what you had with Bastian was just a passing fling, I believe we should be finished here."

Kylee didn't speak. Did she want to know what Marta had to say bad enough to admit she was in love with Bastian? That seemed like a big sacrifice to make, in return all she'd be getting was Marta's opinion. Telling this woman how she felt was going to leave her vulnerable. What if Marta said something to Bastian? The room remained quiet for a very long time. Kylee finally gave in. "Yes, I love him."

"I know you won't believe me, but for what it's worth, Bastian is in love with you too," Marta began. "I know it seems like

Chaos

I just keep asking you question after question without giving you information, but did Bastian tell you anything about his parents?"

"Yes, I know his parents have both passed away," Kylee admitted. "His father was killed by vampires during a battle. His mother died when he was fourteen."

"I see," Marta sighed. "He told you how his father died, but skipped over the details of his mother's death. Is that correct?"

"Sort of," Kylee answered hesitantly. She was on shaky ground here. Bastian had confided in her. She promised him she wouldn't tell anyone about his doubts.

Marta smiled. "Before we go into that, I think there is something else you should know. My husband Jake was also in the battle that killed Bastian's father. They were very good friends and they were partners that night."

Kylee's head shot up. Marta's husband Jake was the guy Bastian didn't want to talk to?

"So, he told you about that," Marta smiled inwardly. Bastian must really love this woman to open up to her so freely after such a short amount of time. "Then you might be interested to learn that Jake and Bastian had a very long, very informative conversation about Adrian's death. Bastian no longer has any questions about that particular situation. Jake explained everything to Bastian and the fears he had about that evening are now laid to rest."

Was Marta telling her what Kylee thought she was saying? Had Bastian's fears all been for nothing? She suspected that was the case, but with Abby here she couldn't talk about this freely. "Thank you," Kylee finally said. "I think I understand."

"Good," Marta said. "I've known Bastian for many years. We've talked about a lot of things. You should know, that was never one of them. Bastian trusted you with something he hasn't trusted with the other people in his life. Others that are very close to him. I wish you understood how huge that is. I wish you could understand exactly what that says about his feelings for you," Marta said regretfully. "But I can't fix everything in one day. So I think I'll just move on."

Kylee was watching Marta. The woman seemed genuinely upset and maybe a little sad. Was she trying to tell Kylee that Bastian did trust her with things that were important? She'd put that one on the back burner for now. She was sure once this conversation was over she was going to have a lot to think about.

"So, Bastian's father was a valiant warrior who died in battle," Marta continued. "His mother on the other hand was human."

"What?" Kylee said astonished. "Bastian never mentioned that."

"I'm not surprised," Marta said. "I never met her, obviously she lived a very long time before I was born. Jake knew her, though. He said she was a delightful person and a wonderful mother. From what I know of the family, they were all very close. That's why Bastian took it so hard when his mother died. Adrian was crushed. Warriors are bound to their mates so tightly, it's hard for them to go on when they lose that bind. Which made things all the worse. Bastian lost his mother to death and for the first few years, he basically lost his father to grief. Adrian slowly came out of it though. He had to bounce back for his son's sake. By the time Adrian died, he was coping very well from what Luke and Jake told me. Adrian was so proud of Bastian and always looked forward to the nights they could fight together. Bastian had become an active warrior by then so the two were able to spend even more time together. Anyway, Bastian never really recovered from the death of his mother."

"How did she die?" Kylee asked. She understood how difficult it was to lose someone you loved. That was one reason she stopped performing surgery and moved to the ER. Her mother hadn't caught the cancer soon enough to fight it. Kylee was determined to do something to prevent that in others if she could. She now realized it was because she was a shifter that she could smell cancer on a patient. More than once, she smelled the disease before her patient's knew they were even that sick. She hadn't saved her mother, but it felt like redemption every time she saved someone else.

"Well, like I said, Charlotte was human. Almost from the beginning she tried to convince Adrian to turn her. Of course, Adrian refused. Most warriors do. You saw how dangerous it was when Ty turned Sam. Now days we have modern medicine to help, but three hundred years ago they had very little."

Kylee inhaled sharply. Was Marta about to tell her Bastian's mother had died while his father was attempting to change her into a warrior? "I think I can guess the rest," she said softly.

"Yes, Charlotte died in a failed attempt to change her into a warrior. Adrian came close to dying himself. He was desperate to save her and almost lost his own life in the process. Jake told me that Charlotte wanted it from the beginning. She was enthralled with the new world she had found herself a part of. She loved the idea of living forever. She fantasized about the life their family could have. It bothered her more than most to think her husband and son would live hundreds of years after she was gone. She couldn't stand the thought. Adrian frequently confided in Luke and

Jake. He was beside himself and didn't know what to do. He hated denying her something she wanted so desperately, but he was afraid to risk her life that way.

For some reason a few months after Bastian's fourteenth birthday, Adrian finally gave in. He made all the arrangements and took all the precautions, but things went wrong almost immediately. Charlotte's body reacted badly to the new blood. Tianna was there, she tried everything she could think of but they lost Charlotte. Adrian, in a desperate attempt to save his wife, opened the valve and tried to force more blood into her. He almost bled to death. He was sick for weeks and then afterwards, he was heartbroken.

At fourteen, Bastian was left to cope with the tragedy alone. You know what an impressionable age that is. Luke tried to take him under his wing and once he became the warrior leader, it was easier for him to watch out for Bastian. They became quite close over the years. Then Luke was killed by vampires, the same way his father was. Bastian has always tried to keep people out of his life, he never lets them get too close. I think he's afraid to love. Everyone he has opened up to, everyone he has allowed himself to love, has died. Then, out of the blue you entered his world. Bastian's never had a real relationship with a woman before. He avoids it. You have no idea how amazing it is that he not only opened up to you and allowed himself to love and trust you, but he did it when he believed you were human. Now you have left him, too.

I don't usually get involved in other people's personal lives Kylee, but this is different. You are judging Bastian when he didn't have a choice. Maybe I am biased, but I very strongly feel that you are being unfair. After a lifetime of sorrow over a botched transformation, do you honestly believe he could even consider taking that risk with you? That's why I say he never had a decision to make. It was already made for him long before you entered the picture. The idea of changing you was never on the table, especially so soon after my own transformation and then Sam's. We were both very real reminders of what he lost. Watching Sam and Ty had to be so difficult for him. We all thought one or both of them was going to be lost forever.

I don't know if you knew this, but Bastian didn't talk to me or Jake for months after my transformation. He was that upset over what could have happened. I don't know if telling you this changes anything. I guess that's for you to decide. I just strongly believed you should know that you are reading Bastian's motives all wrong. He respects you and he loves you. The question is this; can you respect him? Can you accept the whole package, not just the part you want to love but the damaged part as well?" Marta stood. "I've taken enough of your time. I won't pry any longer. For what it's worth, I'm glad you turned out to be a shifter. It can make things so much easier if you let it," she turned and left the room.

Kylee and Abby sat in silence. Neither one of them knew what to say. Finally Kylee stood. "Excuse me please, I need some time alone." She turned to leave the room when Abby stopped her.

"I understand your need for some time but remember the rules, nobody wanders around alone. It's too dangerous with the animals," Abby reminded her.

"I'm just going out on the back porch," Kylee said a little annoyed. She didn't hesitate as she walked through the back door.

* * * *

Lilith stood at the mouth of the cave, waiting for darkness to fall. She was tired of this assignment. She would spend the night turning animals, then the warriors spent the day killing them. They weren't getting anywhere. Radek was happy. He was keeping the warriors preoccupied so they weren't in the city killing his vamps. As usual, he was exaggerating his success. Lilith knew a few of the warriors were left in New York and knowing Radek, he didn't have a solution to that problem yet. She was tired of the isolation but Radek expected her to continue the game until he decided she could stop. Unfortunately, the warriors were now coming out at night, too. They were hunting her in an attempt to stop the animal attacks. Things were getting more dangerous with each passing day. She had a close call last night and was barely able to stay in front of the two large men tracking her. She was good in a fight, but she couldn't take on two warriors at a time, nobody could. Lilith let out a frustrated growl. She'd do this one more night, but then she was leaving. She just needed to decide where to go. Maybe Canada. She'd never lived there before. It was definitely time to try a new scene and get a new man... or two... or three. She smiled and slipped into the darkness in search of more animals.

* * * *

Rand McBride stepped onto the porch and spotted Kylee. Abby was right, she was upset. He quietly walked to the bench and sat down next to his old friend.

Chaos

Kylee looked up wondering who was bothering her and grinned. "Rand!" she exclaimed, excited to see him. "When did you get here?"

"About ten minutes ago." He put an arm around her and pulled her against him as he pressed a quick kiss to the top of her head. "It's good to see you too," he said taking a Kleenex out of his pocket and handing it to her as he sat back and studied her intently. "Why so blue?"

"I'm fine," she didn't want to dump on him the moment he arrived. She hadn't seen him for weeks.

"You're right. I'm sure you're fine," Rand said calmly. "Why wouldn't you be fine? You just found out that rather than a normal human, you are a shifter. Your mother was fully aware of your unique biological makeup, but hid your identity from you for almost forty years. She didn't even warn you or explain things to you when she knew she was dying. Why wouldn't you be fine, Kylee?" He glanced up and saw Bastian and Morrigan lead a couple horses into the barn. "Then on top of all that, there's the guy."

"Rand, there's no guy," Kylee said spotting Bastian. "It's over. And I don't blame mom for this." Kylee was trying very hard not to be angry with her mother for leaving her in the dark.

Rand was watching Kylee. "I loved your mom. She was a very special woman. You two were close and clearly loved one another very much. But we both know she should have told you about this. She should have prepared you, Kylee. If I'm annoyed at her, I know you are. It's okay. It would help to know what she was thinking. To know why she thought she needed to leave you in the dark, but even if she thought she had a good reason she should have told you."

"Fine, I agree. Mom should have told me," Kylee conceded. "I thought we were close. I thought we shared everything. It's tough to find out she lied to me about the most important part of my life. I just keep telling myself she must have had a reason. She must have strongly believed it was the right thing to do."

"I'm sorry, Kylee. I know how hard it is to think you're approaching middle age and instantly find out you're not even a toddler. I think you should spend some time around the shifters. Abby and Morrigan are here at the fort, maybe you could try to get to know them better. The time I've spent with Austin, Mason and even Monroe has helped me cope. It's such a drastic change, you need someone you can talk to," Rand pressed.

"How about you?" she said bumping his shoulder.

"You can always talk to me, but I can't stay long. I need to get back to New York. Kahn's trial is about to start. The prelim is in a couple weeks," he said regretfully.

"Oh," she whispered deflated. "So why are you here anyway?"

Rand smiled. "Cornelia and I took a trip to Kentucky to see my parents. Once we were finished, she flew out to California. She's going to hook up with Ty and Sam and see if they can help her track down any leads on my biological parents. I thought I'd take a detour and come to see you."

"Tell me about your trip," Kylee urged.

Rand studied her. Maybe he should help take her mind off her own problems for a while. "Sure," he finally said and began telling Kylee about the visit he had with his parents, that weren't really his parents.

Chaos

Bastian stood in the shadows watching Kylee and McBride. It broke his heart to see her with another man. His stomach clenched and he could barely breathe. *So, this is what jealousy feels like.* He realized that particular emotion was something he had never felt before and he didn't really want to experience it again. He kept telling himself the two of them had known each other for a long time. If they were going to get involved, they would have done it a long time ago. They just had a lot in common, especially now. As Bastian stood there, considering all the things the two shifters did have in common, a thought struck him. Maybe there was a reason for that. Bastian turned and entered the barn. "Morrigan?" he called.

"Yeah," Morrigan answered back. "I'm over here. Just securing the stable before we call it a night."

"About that. I know I've monopolized your time most of the day, but could I get you to do me one more favor?" Bastian asked.

"What's that?" Morrigan inquired as he walked towards the open door.

"I need to go to the lab. Since we promised not to wander around alone I need someone to come with me. It won't take long, I promise. I wouldn't ask if it wasn't important," he pressed, hoping to persuade his new friend.

Morrigan paused momentarily. It was late, he was tired and it was already dark. He studied Bastian and realized this must be important. "Okay, but only for a minute. I'm tired and hungry. It's been awhile since I rode a horse and I'm already paying for that long excursion we took today."

"Thank you," Bastian said relieved. He needed to know if he was right.

Morrigan stood just inside the lab watching Bastian. He knew the man was comparing charts, but he didn't know whose. He was also starting to think whatever Bastian was doing was important and maybe bad news. "Bastian, I realize my mom's in the medical field and if she were the one here with you, she'd be in the loop without asking questions. I on the other hand, know nothing about medicine and science," he shrugged. "Just not my thing. So, can I impose on you to tell me what you are doing and why it was so important that you do this tonight?"

"I'll explain everything, but could I get you to call Jackie again? I need a second opinion," Bastian asked seriously.

Morrigan sighed and pulled out his phone. "Hey, mom. Before we start the small talk, Bastian needs to chat with you."

Jackie cautiously waited for Bastian to take the phone. "Hello, Bastian. I'm afraid to ask what's going on this time."

"Sorry," he said sincerely. "I'll try to stop calling you this way. I apologize for the time."

"Don't sweat it. I'm starting to get used to your late night calls," Jackie teased.

"I only need a minute. I want to send you some documents. If I email you some information will you compare the charts to Rand McBride information and tell me if you think the two people are related?" Bastian asked. "You do still have McBride's charts available, right?"

"Yeah, I have them. Do you think you found a relative?" Jackie asked enthusiastically.

Chaos

"I don't want to say anything until you have a look and tell me what you think. I want an untainted professional opinion," Bastian said evasively.

"Of course. Send me the file and I'll call you right back," Jackie ordered.

Bastian hung up and immediately emailed the information to Jackie Cooper. Once he was done he began pacing the room. How was he going to handle this? He glanced at Morrigan and relaxed. It wasn't his place to explain the situation, it was Morrigan's. "If I'm right, I'm afraid you might be in for a long night my friend," Bastian said softly.

"How's that?" Morrigan asked reluctantly. He glanced down when his phone chimed. "Hey, mom. That was fast."

"I need Bastian," she said anxiously.

Morrigan set the phone on the counter then pressed speaker. "I'm getting tired of being left in the dark. Mom, you're on speaker. Go ahead."

"Bastian, whose information did you just send me?" she asked cautiously.

"I'm not going to hide anything from you, but please tell me what your findings are before I reveal the source," Bastian requested.

"Easy, the documents you just sent me belong to Rand's sister, but you already knew that. So don't be cruel, who is she?" Jackie asked. "Whose DNA was I just looking at?"

"Kylee's," Bastian said softly.

Morrigan's head jerked up and he stared at Bastian in disbelief. "Kylee?" he asked wide eyed.

The room was quiet while everyone tried to digest the new information.

"Well, it makes sense. I can't believe we didn't put it together before," Jackie finally said. "I mean there are so many similarities. We're still stumped why those two don't have a scent, but that's not the only similarity. Kylee knew her mother, but both of those kids' parents are a mystery. Then there's the immediate connection between the two. They didn't know why, but they were instantly drawn together into a strong friendship. That's normal for shifters, it's a pack thing. It all makes more sense now. We still have a mystery on our hands, but I think this might help shed some light on Rand's history as well."

"Both of you seem pretty sure of this. There's no way you made a mistake?" Morrigan asked.

"Not a chance," Jackie said. "That's why Bastian wanted a blind, untainted second opinion. I've double checked and I have no doubt. I'm sure Bastian tripled checked before he sent it my way. No Morrigan, there's no doubt about this. Those two are siblings."

"Then I guess I need to go have a meeting with Kylee and Rand," Morrigan said resigned. "Mom, you need to break the news to dad while I go meet with the new family."

"I agree it should be you that tells them, but I want you to include Abby," Jackie said immediately. "It's not that I don't trust you, but Kylee is so new to our world and this is going to be another blow. She needs a woman there just in case. You focus on Rand. If he needs to talk, be there for him. We need to make sure those two make it through this okay. It's going to be one more revelation

Chaos

in a long line of surprises. I'm counting on you and your sister to handle this for the pack. You'll know what to do. Now go, talk to them before it gets too late. I need to go break the news to Mason," Jackie paused. "I love you, son."

"I love you too, mom. I'll call you tomorrow," Morrigan said disconnecting the call.

"I guess you dodged the bullet on that one. With Kylee and Rand being shifters, this is our problem not yours," Morrigan joked.

"You might want to leave me out of this as much as possible," Bastian warned. "Kylee is a little sensitive about me invading her privacy. I can't think of a bigger intrusion than studying her DNA. She might not like my involvement in this."

Morrigan studied Bastian. "I don't know what happened between you two, but Kylee's a doctor. She might want to see the results herself. If I tell her you and mom already studied them and came to the same conclusion, she'll believe me. I can't leave you out of this. Your conclusion is going to give my news credibility."

"Do whatever you have to. I just wanted to let you know she might not like the fact that I was the one to discover this," Bastian said. "Good luck and I'm sorry. I know you're tired and just wanted to head to the house and relax."

"Come on," Morrigan motioned to the door. "I have work to do and we have that new rule about wandering around alone."

"Oh yeah," Bastian said. He'd forgotten about that for a minute. He reached into his desk and pulled out his notepad. He had work to do since he probably wouldn't be sleeping much tonight. He would just focus on his warrior blood studies. He had a new idea, but he needed to work on some calculations before he proceeded. He turned towards the door and placed a hand on Morrigan's shoulder. "Let's go."

Morrigan stepped onto the back porch and slowly approached the two shifters. "Hey you two, I was wondering if Abby and I could talk to you in the study for a minute."

Rand was watching Morrigan. He was nervous and apprehensive about something. He glanced at Kylee then back to Morrigan. "What's up?" he asked.

"What I need to talk to you about is important, but I'd really rather do it inside," he glanced into the darkness, watching for a threat.

"Okay," Kylee said standing. "It's getting a little cool out here anyway." She motioned for Rand to join her then immediately strolled through the house into the study. The first thing she noticed was Abby. This must be important if both Abby and Morrigan wanted to talk to them. What could it be? She could think of several things if they just wanted to talk to her, or if they were only looking for Rand, but why both of them?

"Hello you two," Abby stood to greet them cheerfully. "I'm sorry about this, Rand. I'm sure you're tired from your trip. We'll try to be quick."

"I'm fine," he said, studying Abby. She too looked a little nervous. He smiled. This sibling he knew well enough to read. He'd dealt with her often over the past few months while he was investigating Thomas. The Coopers knew something they were uncomfortable sharing. What could it be? Rand put a hand on Kylee's back to guide her to the couch. He casually sat on the large sofa and glanced around. He narrowed his eyes when Morrigan silently closed the door, then locked it. "Locking us in, Cooper?"

Chaos

he asked. "As I recall, you also locked me up the last time I visited the fort. I didn't really care for the outcome of that discussion, I certainly hope this isn't a repeat. Otherwise I may never visit this compound again."

Morrigan laughed. "We are sorry about that, but you left us little choice at the time." He glanced back at the door. "This time I'm locking everyone else out, not locking you in." He smiled warmly at Kylee. "You can leave any time you want."

"Good to know," Rand relaxed a little.

Morrigan moved to a lounge chair beside Abby and took a seat. He studied Kylee and Rand. There were subtle similarities if you were actually looking for them. "We asked you here because Bastian has made a discovery," he began.

Kylee sobered. If Bastian made some kind of discovery, why wasn't he explaining it to them?

"I'm not sure what triggered the idea," Morrigan continued. "Maybe it was seeing the two of you together on the back porch."

"I don't understand," Kylee finally said. "If Bastian found something worthy of discussion, why isn't he here to explain it to us?"

Morrigan paused. "He thought you would be more comfortable this way," he told Kylee. "In fact, he wanted me to minimize his involvement because he thought you would be more upset knowing it was him that made the discovery. He thinks you are going to see this as another violation of your privacy. I'm not willing to keep him out of it, though. I'm relying on your objectivity as a doctor. If you can be objective, his involvement gives the results added credibility. When it comes to running tests, DNA comparisons, there is no one better than Bastian Carrigan."

"Are you saying Kylee and I are related?" Rand asked. "I can't see any other reason a DNA comparison would come into play."

"You are," Abby said softly.

Rand directed his attention to Abby. "That's good news," he finally said. "Maybe it will help find my parents. How are we related? Distant cousin's maybe?"

"No," Abby said. "It's much closer than that."

Kylee was floored. She was related to Rand? She'd come to think of him as family but to learn he actually was, seemed unbelievable.

"I don't really know how to soften the impact of this one, so I'm just going to say it," Morrigan interjected. "The two of you are siblings. Brother and sister," he said soberly.

"That's impossible," Kylee objected. "I'd know if I had a brother. Actually, I did have a brother. He died with my father. Rand can't be my brother. You've made a mistake."

Rand's mind was racing. This actually made sense. His human parents found him in a cave. They said they thought he'd been there for days. What if he was with his father, Kylee's father, and they crashed the car. Maybe their father hadn't died instantly. What if he found a cave to hide him in to protect him before he died? Then later, his human parents found him. It all fit.

Chaos

Morrigan handed Kylee the documentation. "Bastian is confident you are siblings. He also sent it to mom for a second opinion. She's also confident you're siblings. Here you go, see for yourself. If you can't read them, you can take them and get a third opinion. We'll need to know who you show them to, though. Shifter DNA is very different than human DNA. If you take it to someone outside our...world, you will be putting all of us at risk."

Kylee hesitantly took the file. She didn't need to show them to anyone else. She'd be able to read them, but did she want to?

"Kylee will not show them to anyone," Rand said with confidence. "We will not risk that kind of exposure. Will you Kylee?" he pressed.

Kylee studied Rand for a minute. "No," she finally said softly. "I'll read them myself." She stared at the folder for a long time. How was this possible? A tear slowly rolled down her cheek. Her mother would have loved knowing Rand was her son. They had an instant connection. By the time she died, mom was so close to Rand. And Rand had grown to love her mother... his mother. She looked up at him. "Are you ready for this?" she asked.

"Go ahead. I don't need to see the paperwork. It's not going to mean anything to me anyway. I wouldn't understand it. I trust Bastian. If he says we're siblings, we're siblings. Do what you have to do in order to accept this," Rand told her.

Kylee looked down at the file on her lap again. It was really that easy for Rand. He didn't need more proof. He trusted Bastian completely. Why couldn't she? If it was anyone else, she'd trust Bastian's conclusions. So why couldn't she trust him with her information? She closed her eyes and thought of the man she loved. She did trust him. He wouldn't have said anything unless he was absolutely positive. Knowing Bastian made this discovery, but thought he couldn't bring it to her himself, made her sad. She'd behaved so badly. It was no wonder he felt that way. She'd thrown such a childish tantrum when she discovered him with her notebook. Apparently he had taken her words to heart when she accused him of invading her privacy. The gulf between them just kept getting bigger and bigger. She realized she had no one to blame for that but herself. She was the one pushing him away. She was the one that kept judging him unfairly.

She handed the file back to Morrigan. "I don't need it either. If I want to look at it later, I'll talk to Bastian about it. I know him. He wouldn't have brought this up unless he was absolutely sure."

Rand put his hand over Kylee's. "I know this is a blow. For me it seems a little surreal to find out my best friend is actually my sister." He smiled at her. "You're my family, Kylee. You've felt like family for years but now its official and an honor. I couldn't ask for a better sister."

Kylee threw her arms around Rand, hugging him tightly. "I can't believe I have a brother," she said enthusiastically. "When mom died I felt so alone. I felt like my family was gone. You have no idea how good it feels to know I do have family left," she sobered. "I wish mom was still alive. I grew up watching her grieve over the loss of the man she loved and her oldest child. She never really got over that. It would have made her so happy to learn her son was really alive. She missed you so much."

"I loved your mother," Rand said quietly. "She was always so loving and caring. It's disappointing to finally learn the identity of my real mother, only to know she's already dead. I'm just grateful I had the opportunity to get to know her the way I did," he smiled. "My mother was a good, caring woman. That's comforting and it makes the time I spent with Amanda even more special."

Chaos

"I'm glad you had the chance to get to know her," Kylee said sincerely.

Rand smiled, "So, I guess I'm really a Quintana."

Kylee sobered. "Actually, that's not true." She nervously glanced around the room. "Quintana was my mother's maiden name. When we moved to New Jersey to stay with Aunt Hazel, mom legally changed our name to Quintana."

"Really?" Morrigan asked. "Do you know why she did that?"

"Not really," Kylee admitted. "Mom wouldn't talk about specifics when it came to dad, his family, where they lived, anything like that. She was always very evasive when I asked about our past."

"Are you two up to talking about this?" Abby asked. "I think it would be helpful if both of you shared everything you know."

"I'll tell you what I know but it's not a lot," Kylee agreed. "I guess I should start at the beginning. I know mom and dad loved each other very much. She said they met and instantly fell hard for each other. They got married almost immediately. A few years later they had Scottie, my older brother," she glanced at Rand. "I was born three years later. From what mom said we were a very happy family. For some reason when my older brother turned three, my father insisted he needed to take Scottie to meet his parents. That's where they were headed when dad crashed the car and died."

"That makes sense," Morrigan said unexpectedly. Abby nodded in agreement. "It's a tradition of ours," Morrigan supplied. "We have a sort of ceremony when our male children are young. The age varies, but it's typically anywhere between two and five. A shifter knows when their son is ready for the ceremony. Its sole purpose is to help the child accept their destiny and teach them how to shift. Some of them already know, but the ceremony helps the child understand shifting is natural, not scary. I'm a little surprised you were ready at such a young age. Normally a shifter that has one human parent isn't ready until later. Sometimes not until their teenage years. We already know you were ready because you figured out how to shift on your own about a year later."

"But if my father was taking my brother to some special ceremony, why wouldn't my mother have accompanied him?" Kylee asked.

"Women can't participate," Abby answered. "Before you get the wrong impression, it's not some sexist rule or anything. It's just that girls don't shift as early as boys do. Most girls can't shift until they are around thirteen or fourteen. Some a little earlier, some a little later. Our people want both genders to see our biological makeup as a gift. Morrigan would be able to explain it better than me because he's attended hundreds of these ceremonies and I haven't attended any. But from what I hear, the ceremony encourages these little boys to shift. They watch as their fathers, brothers, uncles and friends shift. If the girls attended, then couldn't shift, some of them would leave thinking there was something wrong with them. We have our own ceremony when a girl is ready to shift. It works for us," Abby shrugged.

"I understand," Kylee said, wondering what the female ceremony was. She'd probably never find out. She was over forty and had never shifted. The odds that she would shift now was astronomically against her as far as she was concerned.

"I don't know what the time frame is, but if you were a newborn or if your mother had a difficult pregnancy or if her labor was problematic, your father would have left the two of you home." She glanced at Morrigan then continued. "Especially if your pack was warring with another local pack, or if there were two enemy packs living in close proximity."

"She's right," Morrigan picked up. "If there was danger, there is no way your father would have risked it. It's one thing to try to sneak a three year old boy on the verge of shifting across enemy lines. It's completely different to take a human wife and two small children into danger. No shifter would risk that. The other explanation could be vampires. If they had a long way to go, they'd be traveling at night. One shifter with a vulnerable family wouldn't stand a chance against a pack of vamps."

Abby was watching both Rand and Kylee. She almost missed it, but something flashed in Kylee's eyes. Some spark of understanding. "What did you remember Kylee?" she asked gently.

Kylee was surprised that Abby saw through her. She shouldn't be. Abby was very astute. "It's easiest to just continue my story," she began. "Mom said my father was taking my brother to meet his grandparents. Probably for this shifter ceremony you're talking about. Whatever the reason, my father was driving through a mountainous region. I tried to pin mom down to a location, but she refused to tell me. Anytime I asked her where we lived before we moved to New Jersey, she just said out west. Anyway, supposedly dad was driving through the mountains when he crashed. I do remember overhearing her tell my Aunt that there were skid marks. She said the police thought dad was avoiding a reckless or drunk driver, or something. They said that's why he swerved and lost control of the car, then went over the edge."

"If we could figure out where he was, I could probably get a copy of the report. It's so old the file is probably minimal, but cops share information all the time. If I could track down a police department, I could probably get the file on that crash." Rand considered, not really aware he was voicing his thoughts to the group.

"I doubt it would help," Kylee said. "Unless mom was keeping something a secret for some reason. I know she kept a lot of secrets, but I don't see what the point would be regarding dad." She tried to remember everything her mother had told her. "Anyway, my father crashed and went over the edge. The cops found the car and the skid marks, but they didn't find any bodies. They tracked mom down through the registration on the car and that's when they learned there were two people in the car. They searched the area for two days, but didn't find any bodies." She glanced at McBride. "My mom wouldn't talk about it so I asked my aunt one time. She said the police told mom there were animal tracks around the car. The cops believed my father was injured severely in the crash. They said he would have been bleeding severely. They thought the blood attracted the local wildlife to the car and that's what happened to both the bodies. When I asked mom about it, she got really upset. She told me to forget that. I wasn't supposed to ever mention that again."

"What kind of animals?" Morrigan asked.

"I have no idea. Like I said, mom wouldn't talk about it. Aunt Hazel just said there were animal tracks. She said they were in the mountains so whatever it was, probably drug the bodies into the forest and that's why the cops couldn't find my father or my brother."

Rand stood and began to pace. He was thinking through the mystery. His mind had shifted into investigator mode and he was sifting through the possibilities. "Okay, let's walk through everything we know."

Abby pulled out a piece of paper to take notes. "Good idea."

Chaos

"So," Rand began. "My father loads me in the car and heads off to his parents place for this shifter ceremony. He's taking me to his pack, right?"

"I'd have to agree," Morrigan said.

"Then he gets run off the road. We don't know if the cops were right and he was avoiding a drunk driver, or if someone intentionally forced him over the side," Rand continued.

"Why would someone do that?" Kylee exclaimed.

"I'm just guessing," Rand said. "Hear me out. This is what I do for a living. Please, don't interrupt?"

Kylee nodded silently.

"Okay, so the car goes over the side of the mountain and our father is injured. He's somehow able to drag himself from the car and hide me in a cave near Shasta Lake. That means he was traveling through the Klammath Mountain range. I realize that doesn't narrow things down much, but it's a start." He continued to pace the room, obviously deep in thought.

"The new information about the animal tracks could point to a rival pack in the area," Morrigan observed. "Being discovered by a random animal might make sense to the humans, but we are all shifters. I think it's more likely those tracks were made by our kind, not natural predators attracted by the scent of blood. They could just as easily be shifters from his own pack when he didn't arrive for the ceremony, though."

"I don't think so," Rand disagreed. "The cops found those tracks early on. They had to. They continued the search for two days just to be sure, but they had to find the tracks the day of the crash or within a couple of days. I'd bet on it. Word wouldn't have gotten to the pack that there was trouble soon enough for those tracks to be friendly. I suspect our father was run off the road on purpose. We may never know why. But once his car comes to a stop, he takes me and hides me in a cave. I'd guess he was planning on returning for me later. He probably returned to the car, or went searching for the shifters that attacked him. At that point he's killed and the shifters dispose of the body. Isn't that what you guys do? You make sure humans can't find the remains of anything supernatural?"

"It's a plausible theory," Morrigan admitted. "But right now, it's just a theory. Part of it is factual though. Your histories mesh and knowing where you were found will help track down your original pack."

"What's the point?" Rand asked sadly. "I already know my mother died five years ago from cancer and my father is also dead. Neither Kylee nor I will ever know him. The trail is a dead end."

"Not exactly," Morrigan disagreed. "Cornelia is already in California. If we knew his name, she could enlist Sam and Ty to help her track down your father's pack. Maybe you still have relatives out there. So your parents are gone, what about everyone else? You know at the time your father died his parents were still alive."

Kylee debated. Her mother had been so adamant she never reveal her real identity no matter what. Was that because she thought they were in danger? She could trust these guys to help her, she was sure of that. Even if mom was in trouble somehow, that couldn't transfer to her children could it? "Can I ask you something?" she said tentatively.

"Anything," Abby encouraged.

Chaos

"Could there ever be a crime that is so severe the punishment would be transferred from the parents to their offspring?" Kylee was anxious about the answer to this. She wished she knew the rules of her people a little better.

"No," Morrigan and Abby said at once. "If your parents were in trouble for something I promise you, our pack will fight for your safety," Morrigan assured her. "We don't ever punish children for their parent's transgressions. If another pack tried, we would protect you. I promise," Morrigan said confidently. "What are you thinking?"

"I think my mom was hiding. I think she believed we were in danger," Kylee told them. "Why else would she pack me up and move me to New Jersey, then immediately change our names. Once I was old enough she started paying a trainer, someone to teach me how to fight. In the beginning she joined us in the training, but once I surpassed her abilities, she kept paying for me to continue. That's why I could fight off the vampires during that last battle. Working with the droid was just a refresher. I already knew how to fight, I've known almost all my life."

"There's something else," Rand pressed, seeing the stress in Kylee's eyes.

"I told you when I asked mom about the animal tracks she got upset, but it was more. She almost seemed afraid that I knew. I guess it could have been her need to hide my link to the shifters, but I don't think so. When I was about fifteen I found a box. It had things in it that belonged to my father. When I asked mom about it, she panicked. I wouldn't allow her to blow me off like she usually did. I insisted I had a right to know who my father was. She told me his name was Caleb Turner. She used to be Amanda Turner and I was originally Kylee Turner. She explained how she changed our names immediately when we moved to New Jersey. She also made me promise I would never tell anyone our true identity. She said it could be dangerous for us if I mentioned it to anyone."

"Nobody is going to hurt you Kylee. I won't let anything ever happen to you," Rand said protectively.

"Spoken like a true older brother," Abby smiled. "You sound like Morrigan." She sobered and looked at Kylee. "Unfortunately, Rand's good intentions may not be enough. As protective as Morrigan is of me, I was still kidnapped by vampires and held captive for over a week. We will all do our best to keep you safe but you have to do your part, too. We are already under threat by vampires. We are constantly being attacked by those animals. Until we can determine if there is yet another threat to you and Rand..." She paused looking at Rand, "Yes, if Kylee is somehow in danger, so are you."

"I figured that one out already, but I'm a cop. I can take care of myself," he insisted.

"Maybe. But until we understand what the situation is, you two need to be extra careful," Abby argued. "I know you have to go back to New York for the Kahn trial, but you can never be alone. You and Austin have hit it off pretty well. He'll be there for you."

"I'll call him in the morning," Morrigan said immediately. "You can trust Austin."

"I know I can trust Austin and believe it or not, I also trust the two of you." He smiled at the surprised look on their faces. "I will be careful, but I'm not going to panic over this. You shouldn't either. Even if someone has a grudge against us, they don't know who we are. I'll call Cornelia in the morning and give her an update. She was already going to start looking in the Shasta Lake area

Chaos

because that's where the Taylor's, now McBride's, found me. I'll fill her in on the new information and make sure she's aware there could be danger. We should be worried about Cornelia, Ty and Sam, not me and Kylee. If we're stirring up a hornet's nest, those three are the ones in danger of walking into it."

"For now I agree," Morrigan told him. "As long as they know what they're walking into, I think they'll be fine."

"It's been a long day and I have a lot to think about," Rand told the group. "I'm going to turn in for the night." He stood and paused to give Kylee another heartfelt hug. "I'm proud to have you as a sister. We'll explore what that means later." He kissed the top of her head. "Goodnight, sis." He smiled and left the room.

"You okay?" Abby asked Kylee. Morrigan had followed Rand out of the room, claiming he was also tired and wanted something to eat before he went to bed.

"It seems so strange," Kylee admitted. "Rand has accepted everything so easily. For me, it's all so foreign. I keep telling myself somehow we have to be wrong. My father and my brother were killed. I never knew either one of them. But the facts don't lie. There's too much evidence. In my heart I want to be happy that I have my brother back. I guess it's just going to take me a little more time than Rand to accept it all."

"You're also lucky," Abby told her. "You already know Rand. You two are so close. That's another indication we're on the right track. You and Rand hit it off immediately. I think that's because you are from the same pack, and the same family. You have to remember we are animals, Kylee. You don't have the shifter scent, but somehow I think the two of you recognized each other and were drawn together." She put a hand on Kylee's arm. "Get some sleep. I know you have so much to think about, but it can be worked out later. If you need anything or have any questions, you know where to find me. I don't know if anyone has told you, but we are thrilled to welcome you into our community. You've been such an asset as a human, just think what you can accomplish as a shifter."

"Apparently not that much, I can't even shift," Kylee said under her breath. "Goodnight, Abby. Thank you for everything," she stood to leave.

"Kylee, I understand how frustrating it is not to shift when you think you should be able to. Don't get too discouraged over that. You just learned you're a shifter. Like I said before, it's different for women than men. For guys it's instinctual. That's why they do it at such a young age. For us women, it's basically learned. It takes a while to figure it out. I personally think you will shift eventually. You just haven't learned how, yet. Give it time, and if you want, I'll help you. But first, let's figure out the rest. Let's solve the mystery and then we can worry about changing into other forms."

"Do you really believe that?" Kylee asked. "Do you honestly believe I might be able to learn to shift? I mean I'm forty one years old. Wouldn't I have shifted already if I was going to?"

"Not necessarily," Abby told her, leading Kylee out the door. "Give it time. We'll figure it out." The two women walked up the stairs and headed for bed.

* * * *

Lilith paused by a large rock to rest. She'd been stupid and inattentive tonight. Her lack of concentration had almost gotten her

Chaos

killed. If she didn't find that shelter soon, it still might. She took a deep breath and forced herself to stand. She was pissed and disappointed in herself. She'd been injured more times in the past few months than the rest of her life combined. And that was saying something, she'd lived a very long time. Radek was to blame for all of it. The idiot was reckless with her life and her safety. He was so determined to get what he wanted, he didn't care who got killed in the process. Well, as of right now she was finished. She would not risk her life again for that idiot king.

Lilith struggled to slide into the thin opening of a small cave. She'd discovered the hide out earlier this evening, thank goodness. It was much better than the place she'd been staying since she'd arrived. If she moved a rock or two in front of the opening, none of the vampiric animals could get in. The discovery was a stroke of good luck, in her condition there was no way she could fight off another attack. She struggled to push the final rock in front of the opening then settled back, pressing her shoulder blades against the wall of the cave. She was in so much pain. She should have seen this coming.

Lilith closed her eyes and tried not to pass out. It was going to come eventually, the wound was getting worse. Plus, she didn't have any way to clean it out here. She knew this was going to be painful, but eventually her body would heal itself. It had to. The process would take longer than it would have back in New York. If she were in the city, Sammael would be there to help her. She had to admit the annoying wimp had skills when it came to healing. She just hoped her body could repair the wounds without medication. She was even more thankful she'd decided to go hunting first thing tonight. She had debated the issue with herself for several hours before nightfall, vacillating between options the entire time. She'd finally given in to the hunger and set out at dusk. When she realized just how far she had to travel to find the humans, she'd immediately questioned her decision. Now she was grateful she'd fed. That would help with the healing.

She thought back over the night. After a satisfying meal, she immediately went looking for more animals to turn. That's when the trouble began. Almost the instant she entered the forest, she felt the presence of the warriors… at least two of them. That had been a close call, but just when she was about to give up, she found a large log to hide behind. Initially she believed luck was on her side. The small ravine behind the log was perfect for hiding out and observing her enemy. She'd been wrong. Mere seconds after settling into place, she was attacked by a family of woodchuck's that she had turned the night before. Apparently the log and ravine was their home. It was impossible to fight off the animals and go undetected by the warriors. By the time the men left the area, her leg was a mangled mess. Then as she tried to make her way to the cave, the fox she'd turned the first night attacked her again. Her body was mangled and burning from the toxin. Lilith sighed and gave in to the pain. She couldn't hold herself up any longer. As her lifeless form slid to the ground, blackness consumed her as she finally passed out.

* * * *

Martinez froze when he saw the man enter the clearing and head for Typhon's cave. He slipped further into the shadows and watched. Was he a friend of the king? Maybe Typhon thought so, but Martinez knew better. Zaphrey was right, the vampire was a ratfink traitor. Martinez had no doubt, this man's loyalty lied with El Torro. So what was he doing here? Martinez remained hidden in the dark crevasse until the man finally left. He nearly gave in and went after his enemy, but at the last minute decided he didn't want

Chaos

to burn bridges. Typhon had warned him if he wanted to stay, he had to live in peace with his people. He'd need the king's blessing before he killed the traitor. Martinez slipped from the shadows and approached the cave.

He had almost reached the large opening where the king spent most of his time, but stopped when he heard Typhon talking to Athtar and Trumak. They were talking about him. Now what? He didn't want to eavesdrop, but he needed to talk to Typhon.

"So, what do you think?" Typhon asked. "We've been watching him for over a week now. Do you think we can trust him?"

"Well I did," Trumak said. "But since he's standing outside the door spying, I'm no longer sure."

Typhon's head shot to the cave entrance. "Martinez?" he bellowed.

Martinez moved into the opening. Once again he was in trouble and it wasn't his fault. "I'm not spying," he said immediately.

"Then what would you call it?" Typhon asked.

"I needed to talk to you about something important. As I approached, I realized I was interrupting. I was just waiting for you to finish with these two before I came any further," Martinez explained.

"What did you need to talk to me about?" Typhon asked skeptically.

"The man that just left," Martinez said immediately.

"Asmir? What about him?" Typhon demanded.

"I need to know if he's a friend of yours," Martinez inquired.

"Not exactly. How do you know him?" Typhon asked.

"I don't," Martinez admitted. "But I plan to kill him and I need to know if that's going to cause problems between us."

"I see," Typhon said, amazed at this guy's confidence. "Asmir's a pretty good fighter. What makes you think you can kill him?"

"Maybe I can't, but I'm willing to die trying," Martinez said without hesitation.

"I assume there's a reason for this sudden need to kill one of my vampires," Typhon said.

"So Asmir is one of yours?" Martinez frowned.

"He is," Typhon said calmly.

"And if I kill him, will I be banished from your kingdom?" Martinez asked. "Do I need to move on after I take care of that traitor?"

Typhon raised his eyebrows at this. "Traitor?"

"That man, Asmir, is the guy responsible for the loss of both Zaphrey and Gomez. Zaphrey believed he was a traitor. I'm inclined to believe him. He's a murderer and I won't just sit by and let him get away with killing good people. I will avenge both of my friends, but I have to admit I would do it for Gomez alone," Martinez explained.

Typhon was seething. If Asmir had anything to do with Zaphrey's death he would pay dearly for that betrayal. "How can

Chaos

you be sure it was the same man? How do you know the man that planned Zaphrey's death was Asmir?"

"I got a good look at him that night. I also got a good look at his tattoo. El Torro's men all have similar tattoos, but each one is unique. The man might be able to change his appearance or disguise his identity, but not that tattoo. I'm sure. All I need to know now is my status here in your kingdom once I'm finished."

Typhon's mind was racing. Asmir was the traitor. It actually made sense. He had access to the hidden passageways. He also knew exactly where Kenta was the night he was murdered. If he had the key and hooked up with Radek, his people were in danger. "I can understand your desire to avenge your brother's death. However, I need to ask a favor of you."

"What?" Martinez asked skeptically.

"For some reason I'm inclined to believe you. A few things just fell into place with that revelation. Asmir is a traitor to our people, to me... his king. His death is bigger than vengeance for Gomez. I'm asking you to let me kill him. There are a few things I need to know before he dies. Can you give me that?"

Martinez hesitated. He needed to make sure this Asmir guy paid for killing Gomez. But dead is dead, right? It wouldn't be as satisfying if he let Typhon kill the guy, but maybe it would prove his loyalty. The sycophant would still be dead and Martinez could remain in the amazon. "I'll agree on one condition, well actually two," he finally said.

Typhon smiled. He really did like this guy. He had guts. "What would that be?" he answered, amused.

"First, I want to watch. Not because I don't trust you to do it. I want to watch because I need to see him die. I want to see him suffer," he shrugged. "As a traitor, I assume he will suffer?"

"And?" Typhon pressed.

"And before he actually dies I would like you to inform him he is dying, he was caught, because he chose to kill Gomez and Zaphrey. I want him to know he's not only dying for his treasonous acts but for the murder of my friends," Martinez demanded.

"Agreed," Typhon said immediately. "And yes, he will suffer greatly. Nobody betrays me and gets off easy. I won't forget this, Martinez. I know how important it is to you that you avenge your brother. Zaphrey would be surprised that you insisted his death be avenged as well. I'm not surprised, Zaphrey was one of a kind but he would be. Asmir is scheduled to return tomorrow night. I'm afraid if you want to participate in this, you will have to stay in one of my guest rooms. If he sees you, he might run. I want him to walk into this unaware. I plan to take him by surprise."

"No problem," Martinez said. "I can do that."

* * * *

Bastian sat at his workstation in the lab studying his notes. He glanced at Melissa, they'd almost forgotten her the past few days. He felt bad, but her condition wasn't getting worse so she wasn't in any danger. She was actually stable for now. He refocused his attention on the current project and withdrew a vile of blood then began his experiment. Bastian glanced up when he heard a noise. He was surprised to see Kylee standing in the doorway. "If you can give me a few more minutes I'll leave and you can have the lab to yourself," he said flatly. "Maybe we can agree on a schedule for the future."

"I was wondering if we could talk," she said anxiously. She was so nervous. What if he just threw her out, or refused to ever speak to her again?

Bastian continued to focus on his work. "I don't want to fight anymore, Kylee. For some reason we can't be in the same room without you getting angry at me. I don't know what I've done to make you hate me so badly, but I can't do this anymore." He finished working with the blood and turned to face Kylee. He'd actually had a small breakthrough. Nothing monumental, but a place to start.

"I don't hate you Bastian," Kylee said inhaling through her nose and gritting her teeth. She just hoped she could get through this without crying. She'd been crying most of the night. "And I don't want to fight anymore either." She pulled up a chair and sat down. "I know I've been difficult to be around lately and I'm sorry. There are so many things that I got all wrong. I'm not asking you to forgive me. But we still need to resolve the issue with Melissa and I can't do that without you. Do you think we could try to work together again?"

Bastian sighed. "I don't know," he answered honestly. "I really don't know if I can do that. Kylee I loved you, I was planning on spending my life with you. I was going to give up everything for you. In return, you hurt me… you used me. Our relationship was just a means to an end for you. I don't know if I can work with you after everything that's happened, everything I've learned."

"Well… about that," she hurried on. "I think I need to clarify a few things. I was upset when you just declared you would never change me without the slightest discussion. But I've since realized we didn't have a discussion because you wanted to talk and I shut you out. I'll never know what you would have told me if I hadn't refused to listen. That's something I'm going to regret forever."

"It doesn't matter now," Bastian said.

"It does to me, because you told me some other things that day. Things that were completely wrong. I just left and let you believe they were true. Like when you said I was just using you to become a warrior. That hurt me, a lot. I couldn't believe you actually thought I would do something like that. After all the time we spent together, I don't understand how you could think I didn't care about you. How did you not know how I really felt? Then you dropped the bomb about your idea to change yourself into a human. I was shocked, the very idea was stupid and misguided. But after I thought about it, I decided it was also kind of romantic and selfless."

Bastian raised an eyebrow at her. He wasn't sure where she was going with this.

"But monumentally stupid," she reiterated. "I think we both made mistakes and misjudged each other that day. I admit it, I hoped one day you would turn me into a warrior. Not because I was so enthralled with this world that I wanted to be part of it forever, but because I loved you and I wanted to be with *you* forever. It seemed like the perfect solution to me. The only solution. You obviously understood the limitations and problems we faced as a human and a warrior. Otherwise you wouldn't have been trying to turn yourself into a human."

"Of course I did," Bastian agreed. "Maybe it was stupid, but it was the only solution I could think of to give us the life I wanted to have with you." Bastian still wasn't sure what Kylee was leading up to, but obviously her being human wasn't their only problem. If it had been, once she discovered she was a shifter they could have worked things out.

Kylee wasn't sure how to explain the rest. She'd have to tell him she knew about his mother. "I understand that now. At the time I didn't. I thought you were just being stubborn. I thought your refusal to change me was a betrayal. I thought you didn't respect me enough to discuss our possibilities and our future, to come up with a plan together. When you just decided something that was so important, I thought that meant you weren't serious about us. That you didn't respect me."

Bastian realized his inability to talk about his mother had caused some of this. If Kylee had known how his mother died, she might have understood why he couldn't try that procedure on her. Why it was never a possibility for them. "I guess I owe you an explanation," he began.

"No. You don't," Kylee stopped him. "I already know about your mother. I know you couldn't try to change me after that. I mistakenly believed you were making all the decisions for us. You told me I didn't understand what partnership meant. I thought to you a partnership meant you made all the decisions, a relationship where you were in charge. I felt like my feelings didn't matter to you. I ended things because I can't live that way."

"Kylee..." he paused, closing his eyes and taking a deep breath. "I'm sorry. I should have told you about mom myself." He opened his eyes and studied the woman he loved. Who had done it for him? There were several people living here at the fort that new his family history.

"I knew you and still, I decided all those things just because you said you would never change anyone. I judged you and left you even though deep down, I knew better. I'm the one that needs to apologize for this. I'm the one that was being selfish. Marta helped me to understand that. It made me mad at the time, but she was right. I was being selfish when I got mad at you for refusing to change me. I was selfish when I refused to talk about it. I was selfish..."

"Kylee, you're not selfish," Bastian interrupted. "I understand. You were counting on my changing you to fix our obstacle as much as I was counting on changing myself into a human. We were both after the same thing, we were just counting on different solutions. I assume it was Marta that told you about mom?" he asked.

"It was," Kylee admitted. "I hope you're not mad at her. She was only trying to help," Kylee smiled. "She's glad you're speaking to her again. She said you didn't for months after Jake turned her. If I make you mad at her again, I'll never forgive myself."

"I'm not mad at Marta," Bastian assured her. "I'm mad at myself. I should have explained everything to you. I should have told you how my mother died. And how her death has impacted my life. I wasn't making decisions for us. Well, not on purpose anyway. I didn't consider my refusal to change you a decision. I never considered that option, so there was no choice to make."

Kylee was crying now, the tears were running down her face and she didn't care. "Bastian I'm so sorry about everything," she inhaled. "I know that doesn't change anything, but I am so sorry." How was she going to live without this man? Just her luck, she was going to live for hundreds of years but she had to do it without the man she loved. Maybe it was poetic justice. She'd behaved so badly, maybe fate was going to make her pay.

Bastian couldn't stand to see Kylee so upset. He reached for her hand, tentatively waiting to see how she would respond.

Chaos

Kylee felt Bastian's hand and instantly clung to him. She longed for the contact. She wanted him to hold her, but she wouldn't press it. She was just grateful he was still talking to her.

Bastian hesitated. Could he try again? Did he have the strength to try again with Kylee? Their biggest obstacle had been eliminated and he really didn't have the strength to walk away if there was even the slightest chance they could work this out. He stood and crouched in front of her. Then he lifted his hand to her face and wiped away the tears. "Don't cry," he soothed.

Kylee didn't think about it. She pressed her head against his shoulder and savored the contact.

Bastian pulled her into his arms and held her gently.

"Bastian, I love you," Kylee finally said. "No matter what you decide, even if you can't forgive me, I want you to know I'm in love with you. I think I always will be." She didn't have anything to lose. If she had to be alone, at least she'd know she laid everything out on the table and he'd left anyway.

Bastian stood, lifted Kylee into his arms then placed her on his lap as he sat back on her chair. "I love you, too." He kissed the top of her head. "I should have told you that before. Maybe if I had, you never would have doubted me. I know I should have told you about mom. I tried, but it is just so hard for me to talk about my parents. Especially how they died. I realize I told you about dad and my fears, which I was wrong about by the way."

"When I talked to Marta she kind of cryptically told me that," Kylee admitted. "Abby was in the room, so we couldn't talk freely, but I got that impression. I'm so glad. I didn't think it was possible, but you had to figure that out for yourself," she paused. "I understand why you don't talk about your mom. I rarely talk about mine, either. By the way, thank you for running those tests and doing that comparison on Rand and me. I wish you had told me yourself, but I understand why you didn't."

"I just didn't want to upset you again," he pressed his head to hers. "We've both made mistakes and messed this up so badly. Would you be willing to start over?" he asked hoping she wanted the same thing he did.

Kylee smiled. "Do we have to start at the beginning?" she asked. "I'd like to skip all the intro stuff."

Bastian leaned in and kissed her.

Kylee deepened the kiss, pulling Bastian close.

After a couple minutes, Bastian pulled back. "Can I ask you something, Kylee?"

"Okay," she said a little annoyed. She wasn't finished.

"Why do you push me away? That's part of what confused me. Part of the reason it was so easy to believe you were using me. I've wanted to make love to you for so long, but when I try to move to the next step, you push me away. Can you tell me why? If you really love me, why don't you want to be with me?" Bastian asked.

"I'm sorry," she said hesitantly. Well, if they were going to start over and talk about things, she needed to be honest with him about this too. "Uh, I...well, I've never been with a man before." Kylee admitted, biting her lower lip.

Bastian was shocked. "Never?" he asked.

Chaos

Kylee shook her head a little embarrassed. She shouldn't be. It was okay to have morals, but Bastian was over three hundred years old. Would he understand?

"I see," he said. What could he say? "Is that because you've never met anyone you wanted to be intimate with, or because of a religious commitment?" he finally asked.

Kylee studied him. He wasn't really reacting to the news. She didn't know how he felt about it. "Both, I guess. Actually, not really a religious commitment. Okay, I know this is going to sound pathetic, but it's my mother's fault. She talked about dad all the time. She drilled into me over and over again, the importance of saving myself for the right man. She didn't want me to settle for less than she had. In addition to that, she very strongly believed a girl shouldn't share that kind of intimacy until after the wedding."

"I see," Bastian said, a little distressed by the news. "So I can't make love to you until I marry you?" he asked.

"I don't know," Kylee told him. "That was mom's standard. I'm not sure mine's quite that uncompromising."

"I'm not following you," he said, still confused where they stood.

"I've held out this long, so I'm not willing to make love to someone unless I know I'm going to marry him. However, I don't know if I really need the ceremony before we take that step," she paused. "Sorry let me rephrase that, I'm not assuming you want to marry me."

Bastian smiled. "I would be honored to marry you, Kylee."

Kylee narrowed her eyes at him. "Are you just trying to get lucky?"

Bastian laughed. "Of course, but I'm also telling you the truth." He gave her a quick kiss then decided to be honest with her. She already knew he was in love with her, she might as well know just how much. "I'm old Kylee. You know I've been around for over three hundred years. Once I got to know you, I instantly knew I wanted to spend my life with you. I wouldn't have been working so hard on a formula to make me human, if I didn't intend to be with you for the rest of my life. I thought you were human, but I still couldn't stay away from you. That should tell you something," he smiled and played with the charm in his pocket. "I bought you something," he admitted. "When I saw it, I knew it was perfect for you. We hadn't even started seeing each other yet, but I couldn't stop myself. I had to buy it."

"What is it?" she asked curiously. *Could this be real?* So many things had happened over the last few days. *Was it possible that Bastian really loved her enough to marry her? Did he really want to spend his life with her?* She knew that's what she wanted. She'd been so depressed this morning, believing she'd lost Bastian forever. After a night of contemplation, she'd come to the conclusion that she'd thrown away her chance at happiness. Now, here they were talking about marriage.

Bastian removed his hand from his pocket and held out the broach. He'd started carrying it around after Kylee dumped him. It somchow still helped him to feel close to her. He opened his hand to let her see the delicate butterfly resting in his palm.

Kylee gasped. That had to cost a fortune. She reached out and touched the elegant jewel. "Bastian, it's beautiful." She locked eyes with him and hesitated.

Chaos

Bastian took her hand and set the broach on her palm. "It's perfect for you," he said softly. "I especially like the center, the body portion. I think it was originally made for another doctor."

Kylee studied the large broach. It was perfect. She loved it, but he had spent so much money. She knew it had to be expensive with all those diamonds and rubies. "Bastian, it's too much."

"I realize it's not a ring, so I can't call it a promise ring," he smiled at her unease. "But why don't you just consider it my promise to love you forever."

"I don't know what to say," Kylee whispered, stunned.

"You could say thank you," Bastian suggested.

"Thank you," she said, emotion in her voice. "Do you really want to be with me forever?" she asked.

"I do," he murmured softly.

Kylee beamed. "Good, because I want the same thing. And, now that I've discovered I have the biological makeup of a shifter, that means I'm going to live a very, very long time. I have to warn you though. If you agree to a life with me, it's forever. I don't believe in divorce."

"Well, that's convenient," Bastian told her. "Warriors, fae, even shifters don't get divorced. We mate forever. That's why I've waited so long to find you." He gave her another kiss. "I love you, Kylee Quintana. I love you with all my heart. That's never going to change."

"Good," she said happily. "Because I happen to love you, too. You have no idea how much it hurt to be away from you. Losing you broke my heart. I hated it. I hated not being able to talk to you or work with you. I really hated fighting with you."

"Me too," Bastian pulled her closer. "Me too, baby."

The two of them sat there in silence for a very long time. Neither willing to break the spell. They were both savoring the closeness, grateful to have something back they believed they'd lost forever.

Kylee turned and noticed Melissa. She reluctantly decided to bring up work and the problem they still faced in curing their patient. "Bastian?" she asked softly.

"Hum?" he said not wanting the moment to end.

"I hate to bring up work, but there is something I can't figure out. It has to do with Melissa. Could we work for a little while? This has really been bothering me. I honestly think it's important," she sat up and studied him.

"If we have to," he said reluctantly.

"We do," she stood and retrieved the notebook. "But I promise we can pick up where we left off once we're finished with this. Maybe we could relax tonight and watch a movie or something," she suggested.

"I'd like that," he said watching her open one of George's notebooks. "Is that the same book you slammed on my desk the other day? The day you got upset because I was studying your work with the warriors?"

Kylee cringed. "It is. I wanted to ask you that day, but then I had that psychotic episode and ruined it. I am so embarrassed

Chaos

about the way I've been acting lately. Abby said it's the shifter in me, but I don't think it's fair to blame my mood swings on my lineage."

"She might be right," Bastian said taking the notebook from Kylee. "Animals are territorial. That might explain your uh...anger the other day."

Kylee pressed up against Bastian's back, wrapping her arms around his neck. "You can call it what it was. I was completely nuts and I don't even know why. You were right, we were supposed to be partners. I can't explain why I got so angry that day. I just always felt so emotional when I was near you. It was difficult being around you, but being so distant."

"I know," he said leaning back to pull her head down so he could kiss her again. He reached around and pulled her back onto his lap. "I think I like you here better," he said picking up the book. "Now, let's get to work. What did you want to show me? You said you had a question."

"I do," Kylee said flipping the page again. "I've been reading these books. I don't think his formulas help us, but every time he decided he failed, he drew this symbol. I've searched the internet thinking it might be a family crest or something, but I can't find it. I've tried to find the shield without success. Then I tried to figure out what it means to use those daggers for supports but I can't find anything. I know the open helmet at the helm means royalty and I don't know what Ionracas means, or even what language that is. Have you ever seen that before?"

"Yeah," he said glancing at the crest. "It's the symbol Marlena's ancestors designed to depict the warriors. George's drawing is pretty rough, but I'm sure that's what he was aiming for. Ionracas is Irish and it means integrity."

"The warriors?" Kylee asked. "Why would he do that?" George hated the warriors, everyone knew that. *Why would he draw the warrior symbol in his official notepad?* She turned the pages until she came to the next drawing. "Look, every time he fails, he draws that symbol." She continued to flip through the pages, stopping every time George drew the crest.

Bastian considered Kylee's question. Something from his conversation with Jake came to mind. Giving warrior blood to humans was a common practice for centuries. Could it really be that simple? Could the answer to their problem be warrior blood? "I saw those symbols and initially thought he drew them because the warriors were his enemy. I thought he was reminding himself why he was working to perfect his formula. Now I'm not so sure. I never put it together," he confessed. "I didn't even notice the pattern, that those symbols show up every time George failed. I think warrior blood might be our answer."

"What do you mean?" she asked. "Please don't tell me you want to change Melissa into a warrior to save her," she glared at him. "Because I've seen the connection sharing your blood creates. I've spent a lot of time with Sam and Ty, you know. There is no way I could overlook that kind of bond with another woman."

Bastian laughed out loud. "Kylee, I wouldn't consider that for the woman I love. Do you honestly believe I would ever do that for a stranger?"

"No," Kylee admitted. "You wouldn't. So, explain yourself."

"My conversation with Jake was pretty productive. More than I realized. He reminded me of something. Something I knew but I had honestly forgotten. I'm not the only warrior that is hesitant when it comes to attempting the transition from human to warrior. It's extremely dangerous and even without my history, warriors are wary about the process. There is a practice that has been adopted by those who fall in love, but can't bring themselves to risk the change. They've been doing it for centuries. It's a way to ensure their spouse remains healthy and has the longest life possible. They introduce warrior blood into their mate. Just a small amount. The measurements have to be exact, but those women live a very long, healthy life. Most of them live to be over a hundred and rarely have any health issues during their lifespan."

"And you're thinking if we did that for Melissa, maybe it would cure her?" Kylee asked intrigued. "Do you know how much to use?"

"I do, but I have another idea. I'm wondering if George drew that symbol because warrior blood was the cure for his serum. An antidote so to speak," Bastian told her. "If so, it might work with Patricia's formula as well. Melissa's problem seems to be with brain activity. I'm thinking we should use warrior blood, but convert it to a mist. Like a flu shot the humans administer. They can either give the actual shot, or use a mist that is introduced through the patient's nose."

"Could we do that?" she asked excited. "I mean warrior blood begins to coagulate almost immediately. It's an obstacle I could never overcome."

"I think I have a solution," he told her. "I just figured it out today. If you mix it with a sodium and saline solution, you can work with it a little longer. We'd have to mix the blood with something anyway to turn it into a mist. I think we can figure out the right dosage and create a mist that can be introduced to her system through her nose. We might have to give her two doses, but I believe this will work. As long as she gets the subsequent dose within minutes of the first, it's going to be fine."

"Is there any chance we can mess this up?" Kylee asked concerned. "Is there any possibility that by doing this, we are going to turn her into a vegetable for the rest of her life? Or worse, kill her?"

"No," Bastian answered confidently. "I promise, this can't hurt her. It can only help. I know the exact amount she needs."

"Do we need to run it by anyone or can we just get started?" Kylee asked.

"I'll talk to Jake and confirm my calculations are accurate but then I think we can begin. Let's take a break for tonight and start preparing our formula first thing tomorrow morning," he took her hand in his. "Tonight, you promised me a movie." He lifted her palm to his mouth and kissed it gently.

"I did," she agreed. "Plus, I'd like to talk to you about the things I discovered last night. Between myself and Rand I think we've painted a pretty good picture of our past."

"I'd like that," he answered as he set her on the ground then stood to take her delicate hand in his. "Let's go."

"Bastian, does just a small amount of your blood give the other person a connection to you?" Kylee asked hesitantly as they strolled back to the farmhouse. "I don't think I would like that. If Melissa and you had even a slight connection, it would bother me."

"I don't think so," Bastian told her. "Don't worry about that, I'll figure something out." He didn't really know the answer to her question. He had never heard of a warrior sharing his blood with anyone other than his spouse before. He'd need to talk to Jake about that as well.

Chaos

The car pulled up the overgrown drive and came to a stop. Cornelia immediately exited the vehicle. She watched as Ty and Sam stepped out of the car behind her. The three of them walked to the door and paused. This was the end of the road. They'd visited every shifter pack they could find in the area. Every one of them suggested they talk to the hermit. The man lived in the wilderness portion near Shasta Lake. The area was a national forest now, but this man lived on one of the small pockets of private property grandfathered in. Cornelia took a deep breath and knocked on the weathered door.

Almost instantly a man appeared, scowling. "Are you blind?" he asked angrily. "I know you couldn't have missed the dozen 'No trespassing" and 'No solicitor' signs posted along the way. Whatever you're selling, I'm not buying." He started to slam the door but Ty pushed forward and caught it.

"Maybe you could just give us a few minutes of your time," he began. "We're not selling anything, we just need information."

"Then call 411," he said again trying to pull the door shut.

"Are you Caleb Turner?" Ty asked starting to get annoyed with the man.

"Yeah, so what?" he asked.

"So, we've traveled a long way to talk to you. The least you could do is give us a few minutes," Ty said, narrowing his eyes at the man.

"No, the least I could do is shut the door and ignore you," the hermit said. "I don't like visitors. Thus, the 'No trespassing' signs. The least you could do is take the hint."

"Sir," Sam finally spoke. "I understand you've made a home for yourself here. A home where you can be alone and enjoy your privacy. I don't blame you. The scenery here is amazing. We're only asking for a few minutes of your time. I think you'll be glad you gave it to us when we've finished. We have something very important to speak to you about. I promise if you ask us to leave, we will. But not until we've told you what we came here to talk to you about. So don't ask now, it doesn't count until you give us a chance."

Caleb studied the girl. It was easier being rude to the man. He knew these three were supernatural. He couldn't put a finger on the couple, but the other woman was fae and something else. After a long moment he stood aside and pushed open the door, allowing them entry. "I'm letting you in because my parents taught me to respect women. Don't think that means I'll tolerate anything fishy. I might be old, but I can still take that guy over there. I won't hit a woman but I will throw you out, forcefully if necessary."

Sam laughed. She liked the old coot. Well, old in spirit not appearance. The guy didn't look a day over thirty five. "Violence won't be necessary. But don't underestimate Ty, he can hold his own. I told you, once we explain why we're here, we'll leave if you want us to. We've come a long way and I think you're going to want to hear what we have to tell you."

Caleb settled into his rocking chair with a sigh. "Two of you have now indicated what a long way you've come to talk to me. Where exactly are you from?"

"New York," Ty said flatly.

Chaos

Caleb didn't blink, but he was surprised. Why would someone come all the way from New York to talk to him?

"We're going to let Cornelia explain this to you. She's a private investigator," Sam continued. "She's working for a client named Rand McBride. We are trying to find some answers to his past. My name is Sam and this is my husband, Ty." She motioned casually in Ty's direction. "Do you mind if we have a seat?"

"Go ahead," Caleb said flatly.

"Thank you," Sam said, trying to sound sincere. The guy was grumpy but not as crotchety as he wanted everyone to think. "Cornelia, go ahead."

The three of them took a seat then Cornelia began. "Like Sam said, I'm a private investigator. My client goes by the name of Rand McBride now, but he's looking for his biological family."

"I fail to see what this all has to do with me. I don't know any Rand McBride, I don't know any McBride's period."

"How about an Amanda Quintana Turner?" Cornelia asked. "Are you the Caleb Turner that was married to Amanda?"

Caleb took in a sharp breath. He hadn't heard that name for years. The memory was still way too painful. This was the reason he never accepted company. He didn't want to talk about his past. "I believe this conversation is over. I'd like you to leave," he finally told the group.

"Caleb," Sam began. "I know it's painful to talk about family members who have passed on. My family was killed by vampires when I was very young. My mother, father and brother were all killed at the same time. I was the only survivor. For years I never talked about my mother, I barely let myself think of her. The memories hurt too much. It's only recently that I've accepted my past and I'm working hard to cope and move on. If Amanda was your late wife, we really need to know. Please just tell us that much."

Caleb studied the girl. He liked her in spite of himself. She was down to earth and direct. He knew she was being gentle with him, and he was pretty sure that wasn't her typical style. "Amanda was my wife, yes," he finally told her. "But she died a long time ago."

Cornelia knew she needed to handle this with care. The man believed his wife and children were dead. He wasn't going to take the news well. "We understand that you had two children, a boy and a girl?" Cornelia questioned.

"For a couple of strangers, you seem to know an awful lot about my personal life," Caleb said annoyed.

"That's what we're here to talk to you about," Sam put in. "Your family. But it's kind of a long, complicated story. If you will be patient with us, Cornelia will explain everything," she pressed.

"My patience is running thin," he told her. "So I can't promise anything but go ahead, tell me why you're here. I know the locals call me the hermit and that's fine with me. I live alone because I choose to, though. Not because I'm mentally deficient or fragile. Stop trying to soften this. Tell me why you're here."

Okay, Cornelia thought. They would take the direct approach. Then she could answer any questions the man had, if he didn't throw them out first. "We are here because my client, Rand McBride and his sister Kylee are looking for information on their biological father. A father they believe has been deceased for about forty

Chaos

years. If you are the husband of Amanda Quintana, I believe you are also the father of my client and his sister." She waited, wondering if she'd been too direct.

"Kylee?" Caleb said so softly the group could barely hear it. He was stunned. *Was it possible? Could his children actually be alive? But how was that possible? No, it wasn't possible*. Scottie had been killed by the Fraunz pack. He had finally accepted his beautiful, gentle Amanda and their infant daughter Kylee was also killed by that monster. He began shaking his head. "What kind of game are you playing here?" he challenged angrily. "My family is dead. I want no part of this cruel game, or whatever scam you are trying to pull. We're finished here."

"Mr. Turner," Ty said with authority. "I assure you, we are not here to scam you. Rand McBride and Kylee Quintana are very good friends of ours. We are here because they deserve the truth. Once we heard about the hermit that lived in the mountains, the mountains near Shasta Lake, we had to investigate. We came here hoping to find an aunt or an uncle. We never imagined their father, Caleb Turner, may still be alive. Rand McBride was found at the age of three in a cave near Shasta Lake. A human couple took him in and raised him as their own. It was only recently that Rand came to know us. He is still trying to accept his lineage and the fact that he is a shifter, not a human. Kylee is a doctor and always believed she was human as well. She has only known her real identity for about a week. If you are their father, they need you right now. They need to know how all this happened, why it happened, and they need the support of a loving father to help them understand the strange world they have entered. We are simply here to determine the truth. No scam, no game. We just need to know if you are willing to help us find the truth or if you are so set in your ways that you're going to throw us out and continue to live alone and unhappy for the rest of your life."

Caleb was studying Ty. The guy was annoyed and impatient, but Caleb was starting to like him as well. Was it really possible his children were alive? How could that be? But Kylee Quintana? And a three year old found in a cave near Shasta Lake? That couldn't be a coincidence. These strangers couldn't know that, unless there was some truth to what they were saying. "What do I need to do?" he asked. "You say you are here to find out the truth. What exactly are you asking me to do?"

"For now, all we need is a sample of your blood," Cornelia assured him. "We want to run a DNA test. That's how Rand and Kylee discovered they are siblings. We already have their charts on file. We can test your blood and determine if you are actually their father."

Caleb watched the group skeptically. Others had tried to gather the blood of Fritz's pack before. They wanted to know how they had masked their scent. Is that what these three were up to? A trick to get a sample of his plasma? Would someone stoop that low just for his blood? "No," he finally said.

Sam was watching Caleb. Something had triggered distrust. "Does this have to do with your lack of a scent?" Sam asked immediately. "Are you afraid we'll discover some secret you're trying to hide?"

"Is that why you are here?" Caleb challenged. "Because using my dead family to trick me into giving you my blood is pretty low."

Ty was trying to think. *How could they resolve this?* Clearly someone had been after this man's blood before. They could take him with them if he would go. Bastian could run the tests at the fort. Kylee would be there and maybe she could tell him something about her mother that would convince him they were being honest. *But would the man leave his home?* That was the million dollar question. If not, he supposed they could bring Rand and Kylee to him. Sam had to get back to New York. Something about an urgent meeting with Tom, the Deveraux lawyer, that couldn't wait. "There is another way," Ty suggested. "But I doubt you'll agree."

"A way for what?" Caleb asked.

"A way to handle this," Ty said casually. "We don't want or need your blood. I already told you, Kylee and Rand have supplied plenty. If we were trying to figure out your secret, we'd already know it. They don't have the normal scent either. This is about determining the truth. So, you don't trust us. I don't blame you. Under the circumstances I probably wouldn't either. I suggest you return to New York with us. Come meet Rand and Kylee. Talk to Kylee about her mother, Amanda Quintana. Decide for yourself what is going on here and if you are in fact the father of our friends. If you decide we're all wrong, I'll have my pilot fly you back here immediately."

"Your pilot?" Caleb asked. He took a closer look at Ty. It was subtle, but now that he was looking for it, it was obvious the guy had money.

"Yes, Lillie will bring you back any time you want. The trip is on us. Think of it as an all-expense paid vacation. Kylee is staying on an old military base, Seneca Army Depot. They will have accommodations for you. All you have to do is show up."

"And be dissected by the military? I don't think so," Caleb rejected. "I didn't just fall off the turnip truck."

"I'm sorry you feel that way," Ty said standing. "I believe we are finished here. Cornelia will report her findings to Rand and you will never see us again. I can't guarantee you won't see him, though. I think we forgot to mention Rand McBride is a hotshot detective with the NYPD. I doubt he's going to let this drop as easily as we are." He took Sam's hand and headed for the door.

"That's it?" Caleb asked. "No threats? No argument, you're just leaving?"

"We are," Ty said glancing at Cornelia to make sure she was headed out, too. "My plane is at the Sacramento Airport. We will be leaving tomorrow afternoon at three. If you change your mind, just give my card to the front desk and they will direct you. Otherwise, it was interesting meeting you Caleb Turner. I'm sorry you didn't have the guts to meet your children." With that, he pulled Sam out the door and walked to the car. He never looked back. Ty opened the door to let Sam in then climbed in beside her.

Cornelia didn't know what to do. Was Ty up to something or were they just leaving? She glanced at Ty then back at Caleb then shrugged. "Goodbye, Mr. Turner. It was nice to meet you."

Once they were off Caleb's property Cornelia turned to Ty. "Was that some kind of strategy? Because I have to tell you, I feel like I failed."

Ty smiled. "He'll be at the airport, probably before we are," he assured her. "Trust me. He won't be able to resist."

"I hope you're right. It's going to be difficult to explain this to Kylee and Rand if you're wrong," Cornelia sighed.

"I'm not," Ty said pulling Sam into his arms. His gaze moved to the window and Cornelia knew the conversation was over. She drove back to the hotel in silence, considering her options if Caleb was a no show.

Chapter Nine

Martinez was satisfied. Typhon allowed him to remain in the room the entire time he questioned Asmir. He was actually surprised Typhon hadn't kicked him out when Asmir was being questioned about a possible connection between Martinez, Gomez and El Torro. There wasn't one. Not really. Asmir didn't know how important Martinez was to El Torro until he had killed Gomez. Apparently El Torro had been furious. Martinez would explain the connection to Typhon eventually. He glanced again at the spot where Asmir had been killed. So, that's what would happen to him once he died. He'd just vanish into a puff of dust. When Gomez and Zaphrey died there had been such chaos he hadn't actually seen the aftermath of their death. Once things calmed down he'd moved to the spot where he believed they had died but there was no sign of the bodies. Then, Tyrone had frantically ushered them away before he could investigate further.

"Athtar?" Typhon called, startling Martinez and shattering the memory. "I need you and Trumak to hold down the fort here. Martinez and I are going to take a little trip."

Athtar glanced at Martinez. "Are you sure that's a good idea?" he asked hesitantly. "We barely know him."

"Athtar, I need you and Trumak here in case Radek decides to attack before I return. You know our tactics. You can handle things until I get back, my people will follow you. I don't trust anyone else with this. We had a traitor in our midst. I can't be sure we don't have more. You know our weaknesses now. Keep what we learned today in mind if we are attacked and use that knowledge to your advantage."

"But he is so young, are you sure he can be trusted?" Athtar pressed.

"No. But I'm going to give him a chance," Typhon answered. "I don't believe he will kill me in my sleep. I may not fight any more, but I'm not helpless either. I can handle this young one. You take care of things here. I have some questions for my good friend, Ammit. Questions about his spy. I need to know why we were unaware of Asmir's activities and Radek's alliance with this human El Torro. We will leave at twilight," he turned to Martinez. "You will be ready?"

"Of course," Martinez told him. "I'd also like to share some information with you on El Torro that may be of interest."

Chaos

* * * *

Bastian and Kylee entered the farmhouse intending to relax in the study. As they walked through the door, they realized the study was occupied. The entire group was lounging and visiting. Bastian turned to Kylee in question.

Kylee shook her head, she didn't want to visit with the group right now. Tonight, she wanted Bastian to herself. They'd been through so much and she needed some alone time with him.

Bastian turned and, gripping her hand, pulled her up the stairs. He didn't hesitate, he just guided her to his room and shut the door behind them.

Kylee realized she'd never been inside Bastian's room before. As she surveyed the space she noticed a large television sitting on the dresser. She was a little nervous about this. What would she do if Bastian tried to make a move?

Bastian locked the door behind them then took Kylee's hand and pulled her toward the bed. "I don't have any movies up here, but we can see what's on TV. Sorry, I could have tried to kick everyone out of the study, but I don't think they would have gone for it." He glanced at her and smiled. "Is this okay or do you want to go outside on the back porch?"

"Uh… no," Kylee said, still nervous. "This is fine."

Bastian moved in next to Kylee and pulled her into his arms. "Relax," he whispered in her ear. "I won't attack you. I have a TV and you wanted to relax. I promise, I'll behave. Mostly," he added with a mischievous smile.

Kylee knew Bastian was teasing her. He was enjoying her discomfort. Well, she wasn't going to humor him. She was fine with this. She took a step back and sat on the bed. "Comfortable," she said bouncing a little. Then she swung her legs onto the bed and relaxed against the pillows. "Are you going to join me?" she asked casually.

Bastian laughed. Then walked to the fridge and pulled out a couple of Cokes. "Is this okay or would you rather have a beer?" he asked holding up the cans. "I think I also have a little wine left."

"Coke is fine," she said. There was no way she was going to consume alcohol tonight. Who knew what she'd end up doing with alcohol in her system... while she was lying on Bastian's bed. She knew such a small dose of the stuff wouldn't have an effect on Bastian, but it would her.

"Here you go," he handed her the can then laid on the bed, pulling her close. Bastian picked up the remote and flipped on the television. He smiled then handed the small device to Kylee. "Don't get used to this. My room, my remote, my TV. I'm making an exception for tonight. You choose."

Kylee ran through the channels until she found a movie about to start. She'd already seen it, but it was good. She wasn't going to pay attention to the movie anyway. Lying on Bastian's bed, snuggled against him was distracting enough. But, Bastian was playing with her hair and running his fingers down the length of her arm. She couldn't resist. She turned and pushed her weight up on one arm then leaned down and kissed him.

Bastian was a little surprised. He thought Kylee would be nervous and withdrawn all night. Not so, she was kissing him. He wrapped his hands around her waist and pulled her on top of him, slowly sliding his hands up and down the side of her body. He was a little shocked at the intensity of his feelings for her. He knew he loved her, but he'd never felt this way before. Not about anyone. He wanted her more than anything, but he had promised to be good. He was going to keep that promise.

Kylee wasn't thinking. She was just enjoying the feel of Bastian against her. She loved his touch, it was electrifying. She never wanted him to stop. For the second time tonight, she was annoyed when Bastian pulled away from her. He maneuvered her body so it was tucked securely beside him instead of on top of him. Then he took the remote from her hand and turned up the volume. Kylee narrowed her eyes at him. Why had he stopped?

"You did want to watch a movie, didn't you?" he asked casually. "I think I've seen this one, but I liked it."

"You're cruel," she said settling in to enjoy the show.

Bastian turned and kissed the top of her head. "No, I'm not. I'm just trying to keep my promise. So behave. I only have so much control and you're testing it."

The couple cuddled on the bed, each of them trying to stay awake. Neither one had slept in days. Their fight and the agony over their separation had kept them awake most of the night, for several nights. Kylee fell asleep first. Bastian smiled, climbed off the bed and changed into a pair of pajama pants. He hesitated a minute, then pulled off Kylee's jeans and guided her under the blankets. He didn't know what Kylee typically slept in, but trying to sleep in jeans was extremely uncomfortable. Once she was situated Bastian climbed in next to her and pulled her close. Either Kylee was extremely tired or a very deep sleeper. She didn't wake once. Bastian flipped off the television and immediately followed her into a deep, dreamless sleep.

Kylee woke, disoriented and confused. Where was she? She slowly sat up and realized she was in Bastian's bed. And she wasn't wearing any pants. She still had her t-shirt on and her bra, *how had she slept in that thing?* But no pants. Had Bastian removed them? He must have. She glanced down to watch him sleep. He looked so peaceful. He had removed his shirt before climbing into bed. The covers were low enough for her to see he was wearing pajama bottoms. Had he done that for her? She didn't know Bastian's sleeping habits well enough to answer that. Kylee slowly slid off the bed and headed for the bathroom. She needed to pee and hoped she'd find some toothpaste, gum or a breath mint somewhere. If nothing else, she'd rinse her mouth with the left over soda from last night.

Moments later, Kylee quietly pushed open the door and was surprised to see Bastian sitting upright on the bed. She inhaled at the sight of his half naked body. She knew she was torturing both of them, but when was the right time to give in and make love to him? She wasn't sure. Memories of the previous night flooded her mind. If Bastian hadn't stopped, would she have? She couldn't be sure and if that was the case, what was she waiting for? Kylee walked to the bed and climbed back in, pulling the covers over her to hide her bare legs. She felt shy and exposed without her pants.

Bastian reached over and pulled Kylee to him. He'd slept astonishingly well last night. That surprised him. He was usually uncomfortable sharing his bed with a woman and tried to avoid it, but Kylee was different. He wanted her by his side. He had felt relaxed and content holding her close as he drifted off to sleep. He doubted she'd agree to share his room permanently, but one day she would. Someday he would convince her to marry him, move in with him and spend the rest of her life with him.

Chaos

Bastian kissed the top of Kylee's head, then slowly moved down to her ear, her neck, and then back to her ear. He loved the smell of her, it was somehow intoxicating. When he raised his head to kiss her lips, Kylee jerked away. Bastian froze. Was she upset again? "What's wrong?" he asked gently.

"You can't kiss me. I have morning breath," she said alarmed as she raised her hand to cover her mouth. "I assume as a warrior you don't have that problem, but there is no way I'm going to let you kiss me. You'd be disgusted. I tried to find toothpaste in the bathroom, then realized you're a warrior. You probably don't even need to brush your teeth. Lucky for you, but unfortunately I'm a shifter and I do."

Bastian smiled and turned to pull open the night stand drawer. "Here you go," he said handing her a bag of chocolate mints. "You're right, I don't brush, but I enjoy those and I plan to kiss you good morning. So, take what you need then come back here. I wasn't finished."

"I just have to tell you how completely unfair that is. Warriors never get sick, warriors don't have to brush their teeth and warriors never have bad breath." She paused to take a bite of the chocolate mint then closed her eyes and savored the moment; they were amazing and they were probably expensive. She grabbed one more then handed the bag back to Bastian. "I guess these cost about $10.00 a mint?" she asked slowly as she enjoyed her second chocolate piece of heaven.

"I don't know," he said amused. "And I don't care. I like them." He placed the bag back on the night stand. "And I think I'll like tasting them on you." He hovered over her and kissed her softly on the corner of her mouth. "Yep," he said, taking her mouth more forcefully with his. "I like it a lot." Bastian gently rubbed his hands down her body then stopped when he reached her bare leg. He moaned then sat up. "I think we better go find breakfast," he added regretfully as he climbed from the bed. "Otherwise I'm going to reach a point of no return."

Kylee studied Bastian. She was conflicted. They'd talked about being together forever and she believed Bastian when he said that's what he wanted, so why couldn't she just give in? Because she was a novice and he had probably been with hundreds of women. He was three hundred and ninety six. If he had one woman a year; that was almost four hundred women.

"Why are you looking at me like that?" he asked her as he pulled on a clean shirt. "You look...I don't know what. What are you thinking about? Maybe that will help me decide."

Kylee tried to smile to hide her fear. "I don't know what you're talking about," she tried to sound casual. Had it worked?

Bastian returned to the bed and pulled her into his arms. "Tell me," he encouraged. "I want you to talk to me about everything. That's what got us into trouble before. I plan to be honest with you from now on. I want you to know you can trust me. You can always be honest with me. About anything, no matter what it is."

"This is embarrassing," she told him. "I am so out of my league here. I don't know what to do. I can't decide what I want to do. When we're close like that, I don't want you to stop. When you stop and I regain my senses I'm conflicted. I told you I don't need a ceremony, just a commitment and you gave me that last night. So, what am I waiting for? I think I'm just scared," she admitted.

"Scared of me?" he asked concerned. "I won't do anything you don't want, Kylee. I'll never hurt you."

Chaos

"No. Just scared," she said knowing she wasn't making sense. "Scared of the unknown maybe. I know that's pathetic. I'm forty one years old and I'm afraid to have sex," Kylee looked away. "Scared of my inexperience. Scared I'll be so utterly terrible at it that you'll change your mind and decide you don't want me."

"Kylee," Bastian said a little annoyed at her insecurity. "That's not how it works," he cupped her chin and forced her to look at him. "I am in love with you. I'm a little worried about our first time, too. I want you to be ready and I don't want to hurt you. I have to admit I've never been with a virgin before so I have no idea what to expect either."

"Oh, great!" Kylee said closing her eyes. "That makes it worse."

Bastian smiled and waited for her to look at him again. "Why does that make it worse?"

"Because for three hundred and ninety six years you've only shared that kind of intimacy with experienced women," she screeched.

"Well actually, I didn't start having sex the moment I was born, so it hasn't been quite that long," he teased.

"This isn't funny," she scolded. "I have no idea what to do."

"Honey, that's not a problem," he assured her. "The pressure is on me, not you. I'm a guy, it's always good. So stop worrying. You'll let me know when you're ready to take that step. Until then, I'll behave. I promise," he continued to study her, waiting for a signal that she was okay.

"What if I can't let you know?" she asked. "What if I don't know?"

"You will," he said standing and pulling on her hands. "Let's go get breakfast. I'm starving."

* * * *

Radek paced the room waiting for Sammael. He was getting more and more annoyed at Lilith as each night went by. He hadn't heard from her for days. The last vampire he sent to bring him an update couldn't even find her. At least he did find some vampiric animals. But apparently she'd turned them then moved… or fled. What would he do if he found out she had taken off? He'd have to send someone after her.

Sammael walked into the room, curious about the summons. "Yes sir," he said happily.

"I need someone to go to the fort and check on Lilith and the situation out there. I trust you. I need you to go for me."

"To the fort?" Sammael asked. He was a little surprised. Radek never sent him out on assignment.

"Yes," Radek said a little impatiently. "I need you to find Lilith. If she's still there get an update. The animals were working so well, but with limited access to the area I'm having a hard time getting word on what's going on. I also need to know if Lilith is still there doing her job, or if she deserted."

"Okay," Sammael agreed. "When do you want me to go?"

Chaos

"Leave now," Radek decided. "I know you won't make it to the fort, but Tico can tell you how far to go tonight. He also knows where to hide to get shelter from the day. You should arrive tomorrow night just in time to find a cave. Take refuge until dark then spend the following evening searching for Lilith."

"Do you mind if I eat first?" Sammael asked. "That way I won't need to waste time finding a meal."

"No, go ahead. But hurry. I want you on your way tonight," Radek said in dismissal. Sammael would handle this. He just hoped the guy was smart enough to find Lilith and not get himself killed by the warriors or the animals. He wanted word on the situation. He thought once again of Hector. Sure, the guy was insubordinate but he was also the best strategizer Radek had ever met. Things had moved along so much smoother when Hector was coordinating this war. Now he was stuck with Lilith and Sammael. The woman kept getting injured and now she was missing... and Sammael was a timid wimp. Could things get any worse?

* * * *

Bastian studied Kylee as she sat watching out the window. Before he had a chance to say anything she finally spoke.

"Bastian?" she asked not looking his way. "Would you be willing to work out with me this morning?" she turned to face him. "I haven't practiced for a long time. My partner sort of abandoned me."

"Actually, your partner was fired," he said taking her hand. "Do you feel up to it? You seem better since the injury, but are you sure?"

"Oh, that." Kylee had forgotten about her wounds. "I am better." She pulled up her shirt to show him where the wound had been. "I guess there was an upside to having warrior blood invade my body. The outside healed so quickly there's no scarring."

"You could have died," Bastian scolded. "You should have told me about the wound on your back."

"I know," Kylee said a little ashamed. "But I was mad at you at the time. Thanks for flying back to fix me."

"It was the least I could do for the woman I love." He lifted her hand to his mouth and kissed her fingers. "If you're sure you're up to a challenge let's do our training outside. It's such a nice day and I don't think we'll have many more of those."

"What about the animals?" she asked. "I know the warriors have been hunting at night, but couldn't there still be more animals out there?"

"There might be, but you'll smell them before we're in danger," he assured her. "I think it will be fine. That comes in handy by the way. You have a special gift. None of the other shifters can do that you know? Only you."

"Well, I should be able to do something. I can't shift," Kylee mumbled discouraged.

"Hey," Bastian said worried about her tone. "What's that all about? You've only known you were a shifter for what, a week? How do you know you can't shift?"

"I never have," Kylee thought that was answer enough.

Chaos

"So?" Bastian countered. "I don't see how that matters. You just need to learn how, that's all. We'll work on the fighting, but I can't help you with the shifting. Maybe you could spend some time with Abby."

"Maybe I will, but right now I just want to work out with you," Kylee insisted. The two of them left the house and casually made their way to the large field.

* * * *

Victor and Thomas sat on the bench outside Marta's bakery. They were watching Kylee and Bastian. "I'm glad they worked things out," Thomas told Victor.

"Me too," Victor admitted. "Do you think this is strange, though?"

"What?" Thomas asked. "That all of us are finding our mates?"

"Yeah," Victor said. "It just seems so unlikely that five of us have found our true mates within a few months of each other after being alone for centuries. Well except you," he grinned. "You are still an infant." He laughed at the annoyed look on Thomas' face then continued. "If I hadn't seen it myself, I'd never have believed it. But anyone that sees Alex and Dimitri can't deny they are truly in love. I know how much I love Ariel and Ty and Sam are inseparable. Then you and Abby and now Bastian and Kylee. The only ones left are Nick and Dante. What are the odds that something like this would happen after all these years?"

"I think it's the war," Thomas said. "Maybe things are happening now because of the war."

"That's what Ariel said," Victor admitted. "She thinks Radek breaking the treaty has put things in motion that would have happened eventually, but maybe not until later."

"Like what?" Thomas asked.

"Here's how Ariel explained it. I think maybe she's right," Victor mused. "Anyway, she thinks that Alex and Dimitri would have gotten together anyway. Alex is the queen and Dimitri is the warrior leader. Once Alex got involved in our world, it was inevitable they would meet and fall in love. They are clearly made for each other."

"I agree," Thomas said. "It was only a matter of time before they met. And time was running out. Even if dad hadn't been killed, I think Alex would have returned soon and she would have met Dimitri. Dad was just waiting for her to come back to talk to her about everything."

"I also think Ariel and I would have met eventually," Victor continued. "I think it would have taken longer for us, though. We didn't really run in the same crowd. But eventually we would have met. Ariel had moved back to New York permanently and she is so close to Dimitri. Plus, she knew Tony. It was only a matter of time. The war brought us together for sure. Radek kidnapping Abby is what pushed us together prematurely."

"True," Thomas agreed. "What about Ty and Sam?"

Victor shrugged. "Who knows how or when they would have met. Sam was out hunting. I met her, Ty may have eventually encountered her too. She was also at the ball the night of the bombings. Sam was slowly entering our world whether we liked it or not. I think it was only a matter of time for them, too."

"What about me and Abby?" Thomas asked. "If it wasn't for the war, I'm not sure we ever would have met."

"I think you would have somehow. Obviously the kidnapping was instrumental in the two of you meeting. That's why she was there to save your butt in the hotel. I don't have an explanation but I'm confident you would have met at some point. But that's the thing, maybe it would have been a hundred years from now. Who knows how or when or where? Clearly the war has brought the two of you together."

"I agree," Thomas conceded. "And I'm glad I found her now rather than later. I guess the same goes for Kylee and Bastian." He glanced again at the couple on the field and smiled. The two were sort of training, but mostly Bastian was playing. "I've never seen him like that before," Thomas said seriously. "He deserves this."

"Me either," Victor admitted. "And I've known Bastian all his life. He used to be carefree and happy like that before his parents died. Since then, Bastian's always been so serious and withdrawn. Kylee's good for him. She obviously makes him happy. I don't know her well enough to gage her feelings, but I hope she's committed to him. I hope this is permanent."

"None of us do, but look at her. She's clearly happy," Thomas countered. "I guess only time will tell."

Kylee was laughing. When she and Bastian had started this, she was serious. She wanted to train. But Bastian was goofing off. He wasn't at all serious. At first that annoyed her, but before long she was having fun, too.

They continued to wrestle, each one trying to get the best of the other. Before Kylee could react, Bastian kicked her legs out from under her and lowered himself on top of her. Now, he was kissing her. First her neck, then her ear, then across her cheekbone and finally her lips.

Kylee was lost in his kisses so it took her a minute to recognize the smell. Once she did, she panicked. She immediately tried to pull away in an attempt to push Bastian off her. She needed to find the animal.

Bastian initially thought Kylee was playing but after a short time he realized she was upset. "What?" he asked. "Honey, what's wrong? Am I hurting you?"

"No," she said anxiously. "Get off me. The animals."

Bastian immediately jumped up and pulled Kylee with him. "Where?" he asked trying to survey the area. "Which direction?"

Thomas and Victor noticed the change in Bastian's body language. They both jumped up at the same time and rushed to the couple. "What's wrong?" Victor asked as they approached at a dead run.

"Animals," Bastian yelled. "Where are they Kylee?" he pressured.

Kylee saw them first. "Up there," she pointed to the sky. About a dozen sandpipers were headed their way. "We're not going to make it," she said anxiously.

Bastian grabbed Kylee's arm. "You can handle this," he pulled a second dagger from his belt. "Take this," he shoved it at

Chaos

her. "You get my back and I'll get yours. Don't worry about Thomas and Victor, they're good together."

Kylee took the dagger and braced for the attack. The smell was getting stronger as the birds closed in. Kylee took a deep breath and planted her feet. She could do this. She knew Bastian would try to protect her and she was going to get his back. If any of those things attacked from behind, she would kill them. Kylee's eyes darted from one bird to another. Would they all attack at once or were they going to spread out? Either scenerio was possible.

Victor pulled out his ninja stars and waited. Once the birds got within a few feet he would act. Two of them dive bombed toward the small group at the same time. Victor reacted. He flung the stars and waited. Both birds fell onto the field. Thomas and Victor dropped to the ground instantly and cut the birds in two.

Kylee was amazed. Thomas and Victor were so accomplished at this. She was captivated as they swept in, sliced the birds in two and almost in the same fluid motion planted their feet and prepared for another attack. Would she ever be that good? Probably not. Fighting was the warrior's specialty. Kylee was so focused on the air, she almost missed the fox charging her way. She wasn't sure she could handle something that big. "Bastian?" she called. "I think I need help."

Bastian whirled around and saw the fox immediately. He grabbed Kylee and shoved her body behind his, determined to shield her from the danger. He barely had enough time to prepare before the fox attacked, but he would not let the thing get past him. He had to protect Kylee. After a short battle, Bastian lunged and struck the fox directly in the heart. He didn't hesitate, he crouched and plunged his knife into the heart again. Once he was satisfied the fox was dead he turned back to Kylee. "Be careful, don't forget that's there. If you fall on it, or even bump up against it, you're going to get injured."

"Don't worry," Kylee told him. "I won't forget." She screamed and swung her knife over Bastian's head just in time to deflect another bird.

Bastian sliced the injured bird in two then stood. "Thanks babe," he told her and refocused on the attack. He was surprised to see an arrow flying through the air. One of the kids had spotted the animals. It had to be Gerty or Vivian. They were both good, so it didn't matter which one was helping them. As additional birds entered the area, the arrows continued to fly. They were coming from two different directions now. Each time a bird dropped, Victor, Thomas or Bastian took care of it. Kylee continued to study the area, watching for another ground attack.

Before long, a small group of woodchucks ran from the forest directly toward her. "Bastian," she called. "There's more," she pointed in their direction.

By now, Orin, Morrigan, Rand and Tony had joined them. Kylee relaxed a little. They needed all the help they could get. The attack seemed to be giving the animal's courage. A flock of ducks joined in the fight and then several beavers, another fox and some raccoons charged the field. The group was busy now that they were being attacked from the air and from the ground. At least they had Gerty and Vivian. The two girls were working frantically to take care of the ducks and the sandpipers. Kylee glanced around the field and spotted Dusty and Nebi, the teens were clearly anxious to join the fight. Kylee became even more determined to do her part. If a couple of kids could fight so valiantly, she could too. She plunged her knife into a raccoon then used the dagger to flip the animal on its back. Once she was sure it was stunned, if not dead, she crouched

Chaos

down and stabbed it again. That kill was all hers and she was proud of herself for the accomplishment. Before long, the field was clear of animals.

Bastian stepped to Kylee's side. "You did good," he whispered in her ear. "Are we clear?" he asked. "You're the only one that can smell them. Are we clear for now?"

Kylee stepped away from the group and the carnage as she walked toward the forest. She'd only taken a few steps when Bastian grabbed her arm. She jerked around annoyed, then softened when she saw who it was.

"Not too close," Bastian told her. "We don't want one of those things jumping out of the trees at us. We need time to react."

Kylee inhaled. Nothing. That must be all of them. She turned to Bastian and shook her head. "I can't smell any more. Why did they all attack at once like that?" she asked, perplexed. They hadn't done that before.

"I don't know," Bastian admitted. "I guess they're unpredictable."

Vivian and Gerty had climbed from the roof and were running their way. Nebi and Dusty reached Gerty first. Dusty picked her up and swung her around. "Thanks kid," he smiled at the girl.

Vivian reached them and Nebi pulled her into a huge hug. "You two saved our butts again." She left her arm around Vivian's shoulder and led her to the adults. At the same time she wrapped her other arm around Gerty. "I'd like to present the heroes of the day... again." Nebi told Morrigan and Victor. "I think they deserve an award of some kind. The ground animals are hell, but I hate those birds."

"We all do," Morrigan smiled. "Thanks you two. We all owe you a debt of gratitude for your quick thinking up there today." He hugged one girl after the other.

Kylee was watching from a distance. She laughed at the look on each girl's face. She had no doubt being hugged by the sexy, single instructor was award enough in their minds. She was so engrossed in watching the kids she didn't notice Bastian at first. He was running his large hands over her arms, then her legs. She reached down and took his hands in hers, pulling him upwards. "I'm not injured," she said rolling her eyes. "How about you?" she grinned. Once he was standing before her, she began running her hands over his body. She was enjoying herself... a little too much. When she finished checking his arms, she knelt before him and wrapped her fingers around his ankles. No injuries there. She glanced up and smiled when her eyes locked with his. He was enjoying this, too. Kylee slid her hands over his shins then gradually made her way to his knees. This felt like a slow, provocative dance to her and she loved it. Somewhere in the back of her mind she knew she was playing with fire, but at the moment she really didn't care.

Bastian was watching Kylee with amusement as her hands moved from his ankles to his knees. She continued upwards, sliding her hands over his thighs, then she slowly worked her way backwards until her hands reached his buttocks. This had gone too far. He needed to stop it immediately, while his brain was still functioning enough to remember why. Bastian quickly reached behind him, gripped her hands securely in his, then clasped them in front of him. He gently tugged upwards, pulling her to her feet. Once she was standing before him, he needed contact. He shifted and moved forward, instantly melding their bodies together like magnets. "You're an evil woman," he whispered. "But behave, there are kids watching."

Chaos

Kylee blushed. She'd completely forgotten about the kids. Her eyes darted to each of the teenagers and she relaxed. None of them seemed to be watching her seductive display. She gave Bastian a half smile then shrugged. "I guess you're not injured," she concluded. "We both got lucky."

"Not yet," Bastian smiled back. "But keep this up and I'm going to break my promise."

Kylee raised up on tiptoes and kissed Bastian. "Thanks for saving me. I never could have handled that fox on my own." She casually wrapped her arms around his neck and leaned against his muscular chest, perfectly content.

"No problem," he said, laughing as he leaned down and pressed his lips to the top of her head. "Anyway, we're even. You took care of that bird before he took a chunk out of my neck."

Victor approached the two. "Bastian, I think everyone else should get inside, but I want the warriors to join me in the forest. It's daytime so we don't have to worry about vampires. Let's walk the area and make sure we got all the animals."

Bastian nodded and took a step backwards. Kylee turned and approached the kids. "Come on, we need to get inside. These guys will handle the rest. I'm pretty sure we got them all, but the warriors are going to check."

"Make that the warriors and McBride," Rand said scowling. "Has that happened before?"

"A few times," Thomas admitted. "And you thought it was boring out here at the fort."

"It is when you're locked in a bunker," he countered. Rand noticed movement next to him and turned to see Morrigan. "I guess you need to make that the warriors and a couple of shifters."

"And two fae," Tony said sliding in next to Victor. "So we going to pair off or what?"

"Yeah," Victor told the group. "Tony you're with me. The rest of you find a partner."

The group instantly paired off. Thomas hooked up with Bastian, Rand with Morrigan and Jake silently joined the group pairing with Orin.

"Okay good," Victor said when he saw everyone had a partner. "We have four groups, so two of us need to start at the south and two groups at the north end. We'll slowly make our way towards the middle. Once we meet up, we'll assume the forest is clear."

"We'll go with you," Thomas told Victor.

"Orin and I will start at the north end, Morrigan and Rand, you come with us," Jake decided.

The group split up and entered the forest to scour the area for additional animals.

* * * *

A while later, Kylee was sitting at her workstation in the lab. She was jotting down ideas on preserving warrior blood to keep her mind preoccupied. Once the men had left for the forest, she quickly ushered the kids to the cafeteria. Then she put Dusty, Nebi, Gerty

Chaos

and Vivian in charge. Dusty and Nebi decided to go after the other kids and round up any stragglers. Vivian and Gerty would stand as lookout for any incoming animals. Kylee was confident they could handle the task and it made the four of them feel important and needed. It was good for them to have a little responsibility. Once she was sure they'd be okay, she came back to the lab. She wanted to check on Melissa and run her vitals before she and Bastian introduced the blood. She really hoped this would work, but she was still apprehensive about the procedure. She knew she was being selfish, but she didn't want Melissa and Bastian to have any kind of bond… no matter how small.

Kylee looked up and saw Bastian and Marta enter the room. "Are you guys finished already?" she stood and slowly walked toward Bastian.

Bastian smiled. "We're finished, but it took longer than I thought it would. I think you've been working and lost track of time again."

"Did everything go okay out there?" she asked, worried about the others.

"It went fine," Bastian told her, he put an arm on Marta's shoulder to guide her into the room. "We found another fox and a raccoon and a few more beavers." He walked to the cabinet and started pulling out supplies. "We took care of the animals and nobody got hurt. There's no guarantee Lilith won't turn more tonight, but until then I'm confident it's safe out there," Bastian pivoted until he was facing Marta. "This will only hurt a little."

"What are you doing?" Kylee asked.

"Marta has volunteered to donate the warrior blood we need for Melissa," he said absently.

Kylee grinned. "Really?" she turned to Marta. "Thank you so much."

Bastian was glad he'd enlisted Marta. Kylee was clearly happy about the change in plans and he'd do anything in his power to make Kylee happy. Now that he had her back, he was determined to keep her. He'd never do anything to lose her again. "I thought you had a good point last night. I don't know if giving just a little blood creates a bond. I've never known this to be done with anyone but partners. In those cases, they already have a close relationship," he paused. "I don't want to be bound to any woman but you Kylee, not in any way. I also realized I could never ask the other warriors to make that sacrifice either. It wouldn't be fair to ask Thomas or Victor to do something I wasn't willing to do. And it wouldn't be fair to Abby or Ariel, either. I decided we needed a female donor. That way any bond that was created would just be a bond of friendship at most. I'm grateful Marta agreed. Otherwise we couldn't have started today. I think Sam will be back tomorrow, but I didn't want to wait that long. Marta came through for us, like she always does." Bastian gave Marta a grateful smile.

"It's really not a big deal," Marta insisted. "Just a little blood and my part is done. If it helps this poor girl, it's the least I can do."

Kylee watched as Bastian carefully took a vile of Marta's blood in the special container he had developed. Then he gently wiped the wound and bandaged it. He walked to the fridge and handed her a small box of orange juice. "You probably won't need this, but all my patients get one."

Marta drank the juice then stood to leave. "I have work to do," she explained. "I hope this works. It would be nice to get that girl back to the city where her loved one's can visit. I'm sure that boyfriend of hers is missing her."

Chaos

Bastian walked Marta to the door, spoke to her softly, hugged her and then gave her a quick kiss on her temple. "Thank you," he said before she walked out the door.

Kylee watched Bastian return to his work space. "She's like a mother to you, isn't she?" She was touched by the gentle way Bastian took care of Marta.

Bastian glanced up and spotted Kylee. "I guess she is," he admitted. "I know that seems strange. Marta is only forty three and I'm almost four hundred. But she's always been protective of me... and caring like a mother. She reminds me a lot of my own mom."

"I'm glad," Kylee said moving to stand next to Bastian. "It's nice to have someone that can help fill that void."

"Marta's like that with all the warriors," Bastian explained. "She's always been like a second mother to Alex and Thomas. She lived in the house and helped raise them most of their lives. Her mother worked for Luke, so Marta grew up with Thomas. She's protective of all the warriors, but I think more so with Victor and me because we don't have mothers of our own. She tries with Dante, but he rarely allows it. She's very attentive and thoughtful that way. Marta's a very special lady. I hope you take the opportunity to get to know her. She likes you." He smiled at the face Kylee was pulling.

"She thinks I'm selfish and foolish," Kylee disagreed.

"No, she doesn't. She likes you," Bastian insisted. "Now, let's do this while the blood is fresh. We'll have to be quick. I want to mix the solution in that container then add the blood. We'll need to cap it off immediately. The less oxygen the blood is exposed to, the better."

The two worked carefully to measure just the right amount of blood with the solution then administered it to their patient. Once they were finished Kylee breathed a sigh of relief. "When do you think we'll know if it worked?"

"We should have some indication by tomorrow I think." Bastian told her as he carefully gathered up the leftover warrior blood and supplies. He moved to the secure garbage can and threw it inside.

Kylee watched Bastian methodically clean the area they had just used. She knew he was doing that for her. He was making sure there was no way she could come in contact with Marta's blood. How had she ever believed this man was selfish? She was such an idiot. Moisture gathered in her eyes and she blinked rapidly to fight back tears. It wasn't just the cleanup that was getting to her. It was everything. After a casual mention of her concerns about sharing his blood with Melissa, he'd found another donor. No questions, no arguments, he just quietly found somebody else. She was so lucky to have him in her life.

Bastian turned to study Kylee, she had gotten very quiet all of a sudden. He immediately dumped the garbage in the bin and moved to her side. "What's wrong, sweetheart? This is a good day. With any luck Melissa will improve by tomorrow and she can be moved back to New York. Please don't start crying. It makes me feel so helpless when you cry."

"Thank you for enlisting Marta to help with this," she swallowed hard. She wasn't crying yet, and she wasn't going to. But it was difficult, she was so touched by Bastian's thoughtfulness. "It means a lot to me. I can't believe you did that."

"I did it for us," he told her softly. "I don't want to be bound to Melissa any more than you want me to. If there was the slightest

Chaos

chance that could happen, I needed to find someone else. I'm just glad Marta was here." He leaned in and took Kylee's mouth with his. "I love you more than anything in this world. I don't want something like sharing my blood, not even with a victim like Melissa, to come between us. It was selfish really."

"Bastian, you don't have a selfish bone in your body. I was a complete idiot to ever think you did. I'm not sure I deserve you. You are so much better than I am. Not the scientific stuff, well you are better at that than I am too, but I mean you are a better person than me. You always think of everyone else first. Marta's right, I am selfish. When you mentioned giving Melissa blood to heal her, my first thought was about me. I didn't want you to do it. Melissa was a distant second. Her wellbeing never crossed my mind. Warrior blood might save her life but all I could think about was me. All I could think of was the connection you might have with her and I desperately needed to prevent that."

"I like that you're selfish when it comes to me," Bastian kissed her softly. "And don't think for one minute I would be any less selfish when it comes to you," he smiled. "Rand is lucky you two are siblings. Otherwise I may have seriously considered killing him. Well, I probably wouldn't have killed him but he would have been critically injured."

"What?" Kylee asked, shocked. "Why?"

"When I saw you two together on the back porch, I was insanely jealous. I couldn't stand to see how close the two of you were. Our estrangement made things even worse. I tried to reason with myself, which is why the thought struck me that you acted more like relatives than a couple. So, I guess running those DNA tests was a little selfish on my part. I wanted to eliminate the competition, so to speak."

Kylee laughed. "Rand and I have never been anything more than friends. It was almost instant. I met him in the ER and we hit it off right away. I'm so glad. I'm grateful I brought him home to meet mom. They became so close during the short time they had together. It was almost as hard on him as it was on me when she died. That time they had together is even more precious now that we know she was his mom, too."

"I'm glad you have him," Bastian said seriously. "Family is important. I'm glad you have a brother," Bastian grinned. "And, I don't have to hurt him."

"Very funny," Kylee laughed again. She should be mad at the threat, but she wasn't. She understood. Her reaction to him giving Melissa blood was a form of jealousy, too. She hadn't realized that before. Since the moment they'd decided to try to cure Melissa with warrior blood, all Kylee could think of was hurting the woman. Her animal instincts were fighting for control and Kylee wasn't sure she would have been able to subdue them. She would forever be indebted to Marta for saving her from that particular fate. She liked Melissa. She didn't want to hate her for an unknown connection to the man she loved. And after all the time she'd spent caring for the girl, she really didn't want to physically harm her.

"We have awhile to wait. Do you want to help me work on your warrior project?" Bastian asked. "I've had a couple ideas with that, too."

"I'd love to," Kylee agreed. She pulled out a stool and smiled. Bastian was back. Their friendship was back. And... their partnership was back. Once again Kylee realized no man would ever replace what she had with Bastian. They had way too much in common. He was her perfect mate and she planned to do everything in her power to keep him, forever.

Chaos

* * * *

Sammael stood in the small cave and studied Lilith. She was in bad shape. He considered his options. If he just left her here, she would probably die within a few days. He had never liked the woman. It was tempting. But on the other hand, if he returned to Radek and informed him Lilith had disappeared, the king would probably send him out to find her. He didn't want to be away from the cave for that long. What to do? Sammael jumped a little when his cell phone buzzed. He wasn't used to carrying the thing. Radek didn't even know he had it. The king was oblivious to technology. He was stuck in the past and probably would be forever. Radek didn't realize it, but that was an occupational hazard. If he ever did engage in war with another vampire community, his inability to keep up with the times would be his downfall.

Sammael glanced at the display then quickly answered the phone. "Yes sir," he said respectfully as he made his way outside. He wasn't sure what he was going to do with Lilith, but if she was at all coherent he didn't want her overhearing this conversation. There's no telling what she might remember.

"Sammael, there has been a development," Ammit said curtly. "I have to admit, I'm concerned."

"Concerned?" Sammael asked. "I don't understand."

"I'm wondering why I didn't receive this information from you," he asked. "Why my man inside hasn't been keeping me in the loop."

Sammael was shocked. Ammit was doubting his loyalty? "I've told you everything as soon as I learned it. It's been more difficult lately. Before Hector died we knew everything. Radek relied on him. He told him everything. Once Hector began sleeping with Lilith he learned even more. It was easy for Hector to pass me information, which I immediately passed on to you. Once Hector died, Radek started to confide in Lilith. Again, it was easy to eavesdrop on them. With her in the room, Radek was always preoccupied. But lately, he's not talking to anyone. He's keeping most of his plans to himself. I don't understand how you could doubt my loyalty, sir. What have you heard that makes you question my motives?"

"What do you know about a man named El Torro?" Ammit demanded.

"Not much," Sammael admitted. "I heard Felix use that name, but Radek immediately excused me. He sent me to fetch him a meal. I tried to linger, but didn't dare push my luck. Radek is very impatient. If he has to wait too long, his crazy comes out. That's the only time the name was mentioned," Sammael paused, trying to recall the conversation. "Felix was being sent to Mexico to help build an army. He was adamant that Radek needed to send him there when he learned he would be leaving. Felix mentioned this El Torro guy and said the man could help Radek's cause. That's when Radek ordered me out of the room. Radek hasn't mentioned him since."

"And what have you heard from this Felix?" Ammit asked. "I assume he is one of Radek's vampires."

"Yes, he belongs to Radek. Although not in a master, submission way as far as I can tell. Anyway, we have not heard a thing since he left. Nothing at all and Radek is beside himself. He was furious with Lilith because she couldn't find him. But he couldn't waste any more time looking because things abruptly fell apart in New York. Lilith enlisted a human named Kahn, some drug lord Lilith had dealings with in the past. This Kahn guy was supposed to make things difficult for Thomas Deveraux. He was killing humans and framing Thomas for the murders. Eventually Radek expected Kahn to eliminate Thomas all together. It was all part of his plan to undermine the queen's security. But Kahn failed and was sent to prison. It was around the same time that Felix went missing. Radek sent Lilith to find him even though things were falling apart with Kahn. She could trace Felix to Mexico but then he vanished. His whole regiment is missing. Radek is still fuming. He doesn't talk about it, but sometimes he paces the room mumbling. Something about Felix being incompetent and he's worried Felix is trying to take over Mexico himself," Sammael explained. "That's all I know. Nothing concrete or noteworthy. Why does this El Torro guy make you doubt my commitment to you?"

"Felix is dead," Ammit explained. He went on to provide Sammael with the information they had received from Asmir. "Is it possible Felix reported back to Radek? Do you think Radek has information on our secrets?"

"No," Sammael said confidently. "Felix disappeared. Radek hasn't received word from him or any of his group since they left for Mexico. If Felix had information, he never got the chance to share it with Radek. I'm positive of that. Lilith is a different story. I can't be sure what she knows. She was hunting Felix alone. She never said how she traced him to Mexico, but she's also never mentioned top secret information on your security or Typhon's. If she knows, she's keeping it to herself."

"Good," Ammit said relieved. "Is there a chance Lilith will confide in Radek? I thought they were lovers."

"I think they've had a falling out," Sammael said. He went on to explain the situation and Radek's intent to blame Lilith for any fallout. "The man thinks he'll have the chance to speak to you again and play you... trick you into killing Lilith for him."

"Radek's a fool," Ammit muttered. "So what would Lilith do with that kind of information if she has it?"

Sammael glanced back at the cave. "She may not have it, but if she does she could be planning on using it herself. She's ruthless and desperate for power. I think she's as crazy as Radek, more so in some ways," Sammael paused. "That might not matter now, though."

"Why is that?" Ammit asked.

"Because Radek sent me to the fort to track down Lilith. His runners haven't been able to find her. I did. She's been attacked by the animals she turned. She's in bad shape. I was just debating whether to take her back to Radek or leave her here to die," Sammael confessed. "What would you like me to do? If she has information that could harm you, this is the perfect solution. But there is a downside. If I don't bring her back with me, Radek will probably send me out on a tracking mission to find her. If I'm tied up on a wild goose chase, I won't be able to gather information. I'll be miles away from the cave. With Hector and Zaphrey gone there wouldn't be anyone to spy on Radek. He trusts me, but he thinks I'm weak. He may never share his plans with me. Letting Lilith die, keeps anything she knows secret. But if I take her back, it shows Radek I'm loyal and more competent than he originally believed."

Ammit thought about the situation for a minute. "Take her back," he finally decided. "We can't have our only spy running around the country chasing ghosts. I need you near Radek. At the very least you will know when and if he decides to strike. The man's an idiot, but he's dangerous. The very idea he could force a shifter to mate with him is preposterous."

"I agree," Sammael said softly. "Sir, I'll do my best to get closer to Radek, but he doesn't seem to be trusting anyone these days. I am loyal to you. I hope you believe that."

"If I didn't trust you, we wouldn't be discussing this new information. Don't let me down Sammael. There are four kingdoms counting on you," Ammit disconnected the phone.

Sammael returned to the cave and studied Lilith. She considered herself above the rest of her kind. So how had the woman allowed herself to be injured this severely? Sammael shook his head and settled in for a long day. He'd need to bandage the wounds and doctor them before they left. Otherwise she would die on the way back to Radek. But first, he was going to take a little nap. He was tired from the long trip and a little worried. His inability to gain information was making his king doubt his loyalty. He would just have to push harder, having Ammit doubt him was unacceptable. He would have to rectify that quickly, but how? Sammael shrugged, he'd think of something. But right now, he needed sleep.

* * * *

Lillie entered the jet and searched for her boss. They'd been delayed. Adding the new arrival had forced her to file a new passenger list with control. For some reason they were suspicious of the change. It had taken her forty minutes to convince them he was merely a client. Tyson Electronics had encountered an unexpected problem while visiting California and needed Caleb Turner to fly back to New York with them. Once she cleared it with the authorities here, she'd really run into a snag with the military. Lillie was making a stop at the base, which remained closed, and the authorities weren't happy about a civilian entering the restricted area. Especially one they knew nothing about.

She had to call Ty on that one. She always arrived at the airport early to deal with any snags or itinerary changes but she was hesitant to disturb her boss at the crack of dawn. The only thing that had persuaded her to do just that was the knowledge that if she waited, Ty and all his traveling companions would be stuck inside the jet waiting for hours before they cleared up this mess. The military was stubborn. Even Ty couldn't persuade them. He eventually called Thomas and had the billionaire mogul work things out with his contact. It was now five o'clock at night but she finally had approval to leave. She spotted Ty and walked toward him to give him the good news. "It shouldn't be long now, just a few minutes to slip us in. Sorry about the delay."

Ty smiled. "Thank you once again for achieving the impossible, Lillie. I appreciate all you do. I know sometimes I ask a lot of you."

"After all this, I think we owe you a vacation," Sam told her. "Maybe a weekend in Mexico or a few days in the Bahamas?"

"Either sounds wonderful but not necessary," Lillie assured her. "I'm just doing my job. I like a challenge," she glanced at Ty. "You definitely challenge me," she smiled and made her way to the cockpit.

"You really should get out more," Ty told Caleb. "With all the terrorist activity these days, people like you seem threatening to the humans."

Chaos

"If you'd left me alone in my cabin, where I've been content to remain for the last forty years, my lack of travel wouldn't be a problem," Caleb retorted. He wasn't exactly surprised by the extravagant plane. He'd figured out the guy had money, but he had to admit he was a little impressed. The flight would be comfortable and maybe even enjoyable. He'd never let them know that, though. He didn't know these people and he still wasn't clear on their motive.

Hours later Lillie touched down at Seneca. She was ready for a break. After arguing with the airport, then the military, and flying this group across the country, she was ready for bed. Actually, she was starving. She needed food, then she was ready for bed. She shut down her systems then exited the plane. Ty had already opened the large door and was leading Sam down the stairs.

"Thank you once again for a lovely flight," Sam hugged Lillie. "You have to be starved." She glanced up to see Thomas and Abby approaching the runway. "I'm sure Abby will find you something to eat and direct you to your room. We'll see you in the morning."

Ty gave Lillie a friendly hug then pushed her towards Abby. He could tell his pilot was nervous around the Deveraux's but he didn't know why. "Go ahead, she won't bite." He laughed when both women shot him a dirty look.

"Come with me, Lillie. You've had a long flight. I'm sure you're starving and you must be exhausted," Abby started toward the house, Lillie by her side.

Caleb Turner exited the plane and studied Thomas. Another one of the unknown men. What exactly were they anyway? He knew this guy couldn't be his son, so where were the two shifters that supposedly belonged to him?

Cornelia silently walked down the stairs and stopped beside Caleb. "This is Thomas Deveraux," she said, watching as Thomas held out a hand to the new arrival. "Thomas, this is Caleb Turner."

"It's a pleasure to meet you," Thomas said immediately. "The woman that just left with Ty's pilot is Abby Cooper."

"Not your wife?" Caleb asked.

"Not yet, but she will be," Thomas assured him.

"Then what are you waiting for?" Caleb asked curiously. "She's a shifter, but I don't know what you are, is that the hang-up?"

Thomas smiled. "It's complicated. As a Deveraux I have to do this right or the media will never stop hounding us. And yes, Abby is a shifter. She's the daughter of the local pack leader. I am a warrior."

Caleb had never heard of warriors. He knew he had grown up sheltered, but he didn't like others knowing that. He always hated feeling ignorant, which is why he rarely left his cabin. Keeping up on current events held no appeal to him these days. Would that change if his children were really still alive? No, he couldn't let himself hope. The disappointment might just be too much for him to take if he did. "Is that an occupation?"

Thomas laughed. "You really do live in the backwoods don't you? You've never heard of Deveraux Industries?"

"No," Caleb said annoyed.

"Come on," Ty said amused. "You'll have to forgive Thomas. He's never had this experience before. He's somewhat of a big shot these days. I'm not surprised you've never heard of warriors. Don't worry, most shifters haven't. Well, the one's that live outside of New York anyway. We're harmless."

"So you're a warrior too, as are you?" he asked looking at Sam.

"I am now," she said proudly. "We'll explain later. Right now, I want you to meet Kylee and Rand. Cornelia, would you mind taking Caleb to the study at the farmhouse? I'll track down Kylee and Ty can track down Rand."

Sam walked into the lab and stopped. She was smiling as she cleared her throat, sorry she'd interrupted. Kylee was sitting on a tall stool, Bastian was standing in front of her. The two were locked in an intimate kiss. "Sorry to interrupt. I guess you two made up," she said amused.

Kylee straightened and tried to push Bastian away. Bastian remained where he was, shifting his head slightly to glance at Sam. "Welcome back," he said casually. "I have to say your timing could be better. Did you have a good trip?"

"Yeah, great, blah, blah blah and all that." She moved her hand in dismissal. "Sorry, I don't have time for small talk. I need Kylee to join us in the study."

Bastian raised an eyebrow. "You found a relative?"

"Uh… yeah," Sam said cautiously. "You could say that."

"And you brought them back with you?" Kylee asked nervously. She looked at Bastian, would he come with her? She felt stupid asking, but she needed him to be there.

Bastian felt Kylee's entire body stiffen. She was worried about this. "It's okay," he soothed. "You can do this." He studied her for another minute. "Why don't you go ask Breena to sit with Melissa and I'll come with you," he offered.

"Thank you," she said softly. She pushed off the stool and left the room.

"Why are you so nervous?" Bastian asked Sam as soon as Kylee was gone.

"You have to promise not to say a word. We need to see how this plays out," Sam warned.

"I won't make that promise if it will hurt Kylee," Bastian told her.

"We don't want to hurt anyone," Sam insisted. "We think we found Kylee's father. He's resisting it, though. He's positive his entire family was murdered by a warring pack. He's also skeptical of us. I'm surprised he agreed to come back. Ty kind of tricked him into it. Anyway, he won't give us blood for a DNA test because he thinks we're after the secret. Apparently others have tried to get blood from his pack to figure out why there's no scent. He's basically decided that's why he's here. Bringing him to a military base hasn't helped his skepticism. Bastian, we're not a hundred percent sure this is her father. It seems to fit, but what if we tell her and then it turns out we were wrong. I don't want to get her hopes up and then dash them that way. We just thought if we could get Kylee and Caleb Turner together, maybe they would both know things about Kylee's mother, Amanda. If there was some kind of information that only family would know, maybe that would be enough for Caleb to let us test him."

Chaos

"I understand," Bastian told her. "But I'm going with her. I'm going to be there for her, so don't try to keep me out of that room."

"Deal," Sam said smiling as she heard the two women approaching.

Kylee and Breena walked through the door. Bastian immediately noticed Breena wasn't as cheerful as usual. "Breena, are you sure you're up to this?" he asked worried.

"I'll be fine," she assured him. She glanced around and spotted the cot. "I'm just going to relax on that cot and read my magazine." Breena immediately walked to the bed and laid down. "Go, meet your guest. I'm fine, I promise. Orin just ran over to Tony and Megan's for a minute. Once he gets my note he'll join me."

Bastian hesitated only a moment then took Kylee's hand and led her out the door. She was shaking. Bastian released her hand and began rubbing her back. "It's okay. You can do this," he told her again. As a shifter, she must be sensing Sam's nervousness and her body was reacting. The group entered the foyer and Bastian spotted Rand, Ty, Cornelia and a stranger in the room. He kept his hand on Kylee's back as they stepped through the door, determined to be there for her if she needed him.

Kylee stepped into the Study and froze. Her body went stiff, but her legs started to buckle beneath her. This wasn't possible. Her father was dead. He loved her mother and never would have left her. But that was her father. She'd recognize that face anywhere. She couldn't breathe. As she tried to suck in air, Bastian moved in front of her, pushing her back against the wall. He was supporting her weight, thank goodness. Otherwise she probably would have fallen to the ground by now.

"Look at me," Bastian said sternly. "Kylee, look into my eyes." Once she locked eyes with him, he placed one of his hands behind her neck and leaned down to whisper in her ear. "Take a deep breath, you can handle this. I know it's a shock, but you are strong enough to face this. You're not alone."

"You knew?" she accused. "You knew my father was here?"

Bastian pulled her close and once again rubbed Kylee's back. "Sam said they thought he might be your father, but they weren't one hundred percent sure. She made me promise not to tell you. We didn't want to get your hopes up then dash them if Sam was wrong."

Kylee still couldn't breathe. She needed air. She needed a minute away from that man.

Bastian felt Kylee struggling to breathe. He casually maneuvered her outside the door and shut it behind him. He continued to run his hands down her arms, trying to sooth her. "You recognized him immediately. How? I thought he disappeared when you were an infant."

"I have a picture," Kylee whispered, finally able to breathe again. "I have a photo of my mother and my father together. They were happy. It was one of the things I found when I was fifteen. Mom eventually gave it to me. She wanted me to know my father as well as possible for a dead man." She glanced at the closed door. "She loved him so much. She grieved every day of her life for him. How is this possible?"

"I don't know," Bastian admitted. "Do you have that photo here? It might help."

"Yes," Kylee nodded. "It's in my room."

Chaos

"Let's go get it," Bastian took her hand and led her up the stairs. The photo might help convince this man Kylee was really his child. But he also thought the short walk would do Kylee good. Once they returned to the closed door he placed his hands on her shoulders. "I know you can do this. You are strong enough to handle anything, no matter what. I'm here for you. Whatever happens in there just remember you are not alone. You have me, and Rand is going through the same thing you are. He just didn't have the benefit of that photo." The instant Kylee showed him the picture he knew it was her father. The guy hadn't changed much. The new arrival was definitely Caleb Turner, Kylee's father. "You ready?" he asked.

Kylee took one more deep breath then nodded. She watched as Bastian slowly turned the knob, opened the door then took her hand and led her back into the room.

Caleb was studying the woman as she entered the room and slowly walked hand in hand with the large man to the couch. When she first walked in, his heart had stopped. She looked so much like his Amanda. Could these people be right? Was it possible that his children had survived? None of this made sense. Amanda would never leave him. They were so in love, so happy together. She would never have taken that away from him. She would never deprive him of his children. But why had the girl reacted that way to his presence? If she was his Kylee, she wouldn't remember him. The last time he saw her she was three weeks old. Maybe she didn't know that and these people were really messing with him. His head shot up at the sound of Sam's voice.

"Kylee are you okay?" Sam asked gently.

Kylee nodded.

"I know how hard this is for everyone involved," she began. "It's a very emotional experience to meet family when you've lived for years believing all your family is gone. I know that better than most."

"Are you Caleb Turner?" Kylee asked, her voice a little shaky.

The man looked at Kylee, it was eerie how much she looked like his late wife. "I am," he finally said. He glanced at the man, Rand McBride. The guy resembled him, too. But he wasn't ready to accept this theory without some sort of explanation.

"How could you leave us?" Kylee demanded. "How could you let mom live all those years loving you, missing you, grieving for you when all this time you were alive. Why didn't you come back?"

"Are you saying Amanda is still alive?" he asked, shocked.

"No. Mom died five years ago," Kylee told him. "She loved you and grieved for you every day until the day she died. I'm glad she's not here to see this. I'm thankful she never had to find out you were alive all this time. It would have killed her to know you didn't want us."

"Kylee," Ty cut her off. "That's enough. You have no right to judge this man until you hear his story. He didn't run off with his secretary to live the high life in Vegas. He has believed for forty years that his family was killed by his enemy. The locals call him the hermit because he's locked himself up in a cabin in the mountains with his memories and his grief. A cabin near Shasta Lake because that's the last place he saw his son."

Rand looked up. "Is that true?" he asked the man.

Chaos

Caleb could feel the emotions in the room. They were running high, and it wasn't just his. He was still skeptical, but he didn't think actors could fake emotions like this. Not the emotions he was sensing, smelling. "I placed my three year old son in a cave for protection forty years ago and never saw him again. So yes, what Ty said is true. I came here thinking this was some kind of trick, but now I'm not so sure." He turned his attention to Kylee. "What I don't understand is how you could recognize me. If you are my daughter, we were separated when you were only three weeks old."

Kylee glanced at Bastian, who gave her a quick nod. "Because I have a picture of you," she told him. "My mother gave me a picture she saved. She wanted me to get to know my father and see how happy they were together. She told me what a wonderful, caring man he was. She talked about you all the time. At night, I would go in my room and pull out that picture and wonder, what would our life have been like if only you had come home. If you hadn't been killed in a freak car accident. I imagined you being a doctor, or a physicist. Mom told me I got my interest in medicine from you. She always wanted you to become a surgeon. Instead, she convinced me to become one instead."

Caleb was shocked. Amanda had urged him to become a surgeon, but he wasn't interested in that kind of medicine. He liked experimenting. Creating cures, not operating on people. "Do you still have the picture?" he asked tentatively.

Kylee handed the photo to Bastian. She knew she didn't have the strength to walk across the room to hand the picture to her father. He was her father, she knew it. She didn't understand it, but she knew. Rand had been standing in the corner. When he learned Kylee had a picture of both their parents he was curious. He moved to Bastian and held out his hand.

Rand studied the photo for several seconds then took a deep breath and handed it to Caleb Turner. The two men were the same. After forty years, the man had changed very little. He had lost weight and his face was different. In the photo he was happy and carefree. Sitting here, years later he was somber and skeptical. But it was definitely the same person. No wonder Kylee had such a strong initial reaction when she first walked into the room.

Caleb took the picture half expecting it to be of someone else. The pain was instant at the sight of Amanda. His beautiful Amanda, gone a mere five years ago. Why had she left him? Why did her Aunt tell him she was dead? None of this made any sense. He was gripping the photo, memories running through his mind. He remembered exactly when this picture had been taken. They had just found out that Amanda was pregnant with Scottie. Katerina had insisted they take a picture to remember the moment. She said it would be one of those memorable times in their lives that they should never forget. Caleb hadn't forgotten it, even without the picture. He closed his eyes to fight the memories and the tears. His family had been taken from him so long ago. He grieved for his dear Amanda every minute of every day. But if these two were his children, he wanted to get to know them. First, he had to know for sure. Caleb turned to Ty. "You said if I gave you some of my blood you have someone here that could run the tests."

"Yes. Bastian can do it," Ty assured him.

"Who is Bastian?" Caleb asked.

"I am," Bastian said calmly. "I own and operate AC Pharmaceuticals. If you're willing to give me a DNA sample I'll run it right now."

"Are you Kylee's husband?" he asked.

Chaos

"No. Not yet," Bastian told him casually.

"Why not?" Caleb asked. "You obviously love her. And I can see she loves and depends on you. Why haven't you married her?"

"Uh..." Kylee began. "You might be my biological father, but you haven't been in my life for forty years. I don't think it's appropriate to come into the room and grill Bastian about his intentions."

"Well, he said not yet. That means he intends to marry you. I'm just wondering why he hasn't done it yet." Caleb asked. "Is your culture so different than ours that marriage isn't important here?"

Ty laughed. "He asked Thomas the same thing. As soon as we arrived, he wanted to know why Abby wasn't his wife."

"You what?" Kylee asked dumbfounded. "Why would you do that?"

"Because where I come from a man marries the woman he loves immediately when he discovers he loves her. What is the point in waiting? Why wouldn't Bastian want to begin his life with you immediately? That's what we did," he mused. "I only knew my sweet Amanda two months before we got married. I'm grateful we did. Our time was too short, if I had waited I would have missed out on so much."

"That's a good point," Rand teased. "Bastian, why haven't you married my sister yet? You two have been together what, at least forty eight hours now. What are you waiting for?"

"I see," Caleb said with understanding. "I guess that is a little soon for a wedding," he turned his attention back to Bastian. "I think I've heard of you." He watched the man Kylee was obviously in love with. "At least your company. They have a good reputation for the most part. I'll let you take my blood to run a DNA test, but I want to participate. I want to watch you run the tests."

"That's fine with me," Bastian assured him. "That way I can't sneak a secret sample of your special blood and have it tested."

"I don't care if you make fun of me," Caleb said unconcerned. "Our pack has kept our secret for decades. I will not be reckless with my blood."

"Wait," Kylee said immediately. "You don't believe us?" she accused. "You don't believe Rand and I are your children? You think Ty and Sam brought you here to sneak a sample of your blood?"

"It crossed my mind," Caleb answered honestly. "I'm beginning to believe you are my children. But I want to be sure before we take this any further. I need answers as much as you do Kylee. I don't understand any of this. I can't imagine how this is possible. Let me be sure."

"Well, they don't want your blood," Kylee said flatly. "I realize mine is defective, but Rand is a shifter and they've already taken his."

"Defective? How?" Caleb asked.

"I can't shift," Kylee told him.

"Nonsense. If you are my daughter, you can shift," Caleb said confidently. "And at least one of your other senses will be exceptional. But, before we discuss this, let's see if you are in fact my daughter." He turned his attention to Bastian. "Shall we?"

Chaos

Kylee stood. "I'm coming with you," she looked at Rand.

Rand shook his head. "Not me." He casually took a seat. "You know that stuff is like a foreign language to me. I'll trust you. We'll just wait here."

Kylee laughed. "You're going to have a long wait. To do a DNA test, a rush test, will take about eight hours."

Caleb smiled. Well, they passed that test. He knew DNA testing usually took about seventy two hours, but that's because the labs process at their own speed. For one man to complete the process alone it would take the correct lab conditions and approximately eight hours.

Rand narrowed his eyes at Turner. "You knew, that didn't you?" he accused.

"I did," Caleb admitted. "Most people don't. I wanted to see if you were going to bluff."

"I'll take you to the lab, take your blood and see if Breena wants to get started processing it. But Kylee's right. We won't have the results for about eight hours." Bastian told him as the three left the house.

"You said you already have the tests on these two?" Caleb asked.

"I do," Bastian said with understanding. The man seemed to know about science. He might already know his own charts. "Would you like to see them?"

"You don't mind?" Caleb asked, surprised. If Bastian was willing to show Caleb the charts before his tests were complete, it would give these people credibility.

"Not at all," Bastian told him affably. The group stepped into the lab and spotted Breena and Orin.

Breena stood. "Hello," she said cheerfully. "I'm Breena and this is my husband Orin." She held out a hand to Caleb.

"It's nice to see someone decided to get married," he glanced at her stomach. "How much longer?"

"About a month," Breena said excited.

"Are you feeling okay?" Caleb asked. "I heard fae have a hard time during pregnancy. Shouldn't you be resting?"

"I do rest most of the time, but I needed to keep an eye on Melissa while Kylee met you." Breena explained, glancing at Melissa. "No change so far," she told Kylee and Bastian.

"What's wrong with her?" Caleb asked as he sat in the chair and held out his arm for Bastian to take blood.

"Mad scientist experiment gone wrong," Kylee said. "We're trying to reverse it."

"I thought you said you were a surgeon," Caleb studied Kylee, had he already caught her in a lie?

"I used to be," she admitted. "And I said that's what mom wanted. So, I humored her. Once she was gone, I quit."

"And now you work for Bastian?" Caleb asked.

Chaos

"No. Now I work for Thomas and Alex Deveraux," Kylee corrected.

"I think I have a lot to learn about your world," Caleb surmised.

Bastian finished taking blood then walked to the desk and pulled out two folders. He handed them to Caleb. "Here you go." The files weren't labeled. Bastian wanted to see how much this Caleb Turner really knew about science.

Caleb glanced at the first file then sighed. So, he was being tested this time. He flipped it open and began to study the documents inside. Once he had gone through everything, he pushed it aside and opened the second file. Moments later he stood and paused as he slowly ran his fingers through his hair. "Okay, I'm convinced. These are my children." He took a long, hard look at Kylee. "You look so much like your mother." Caleb was trying to remain calm, but he was anything but. His kids were alive. He didn't understand it, but he was thankful for it.

"Just like that?" Kylee asked. "Reading my chart then Rand's chart has convinced you of our origin?"

"Yes," Caleb told her. "Now I think we have a lot to talk about. I have questions, and obviously you have questions. Can we return to the study where it's more comfortable?"

"Yes," Bastian said, guiding the two of them out of the room. He glanced back at Breena. "You still okay here?"

"We're fine," she assured him, surprised by this stranger's statement. Could Rand and Kylee's father really be alive?

Chapter Ten

Kylee walked back into the study and saw that Thomas and Abby had joined Rand and Cornelia. Morrigan was also in the room. She turned to the man that was obviously her father. "You've met Thomas and Abby, but I'm not sure you've met Morrigan. He is Abby's older brother. Their father is the local pack leader. Their pack has been wonderful. They've willingly helped Rand and I get through this difficult time. I'd like them to stay while we talk if that's alright with you."

"Rand?" Caleb asked. "Do you feel the same?" He didn't know these people but if his son was a detective, he was a good judge of character. If Rand wanted them here, they could stay.

"I do," Rand said instantly. "I trust them, if that's what you're asking."

"Then they stay," Caleb said sitting in the large comfortable chair. He briefly wondered what Rand's heightened sense had turned out to be. As a child, he seemed to have a sixth sense about the strangest things. Maybe that's why his son had chosen a career in law enforcement. Maybe he could still read people in a way others could not.

Bastian led Kylee to the couch and pulled her down next to him. He'd been thinking about what this man had said. Caleb Turner was right. He loved Kylee and she loved him. What were they waiting for? He wanted to marry her. She seemed to want to marry him. Why not just do it? Once they were finished here, he needed to make a phone call.

"Since we all have questions someone needs to go first. Do you want me to start?" Caleb asked Kylee and Rand.

"I gather you got whatever it was you needed while you were gone?" Rand asked.

"I did," Caleb said watching his son. "I'm convinced you are my son. I don't understand how you are sitting here, but I have no doubt you were my Scottie."

"Well, it's Rand now," he said uncomfortable with the old name. "I'm glad you're satisfied." Rand studied the man for a moment. "I'm afraid it's going to take more than that to satisfy me. I'd like to know how I ended up with human parents that made me feel like my gift was evil and Kylee grew up without a father and a mother who was constantly depressed. If you think you can explain that, then please by all means, you go first."

Caleb smiled. Rand had no idea how much they had in common. "I'm not sure that I can," Caleb admitted. "I too would like to know why I've believed for forty years my wife and kids were killed by my enemy. But I will tell you what I know."

"I guess that's a start," Rand encouraged.

"I'm not sure where to begin," Caleb paused, there was so much these two didn't know. "I guess I'll just start with the events of that day. There was increased vampire activity in the area during that time. To make things worse, we were warring with a neighboring pack. Traveling was extremely dangerous. We'd been planning this trip for months, but had put it off because of Amanda's pregnancy. I wasn't comfortable leaving Amanda alone while she was pregnant. Scottie was three and it was past time to hold the shifting ceremony, so we couldn't wait much longer. We were living in Dunsmuir at the time. The pack was fairly disbursed but we'd arranged to hold the ceremony near Redding where my parents lived. Amanda and I decided she should stay home. She was human and it was going to be hard enough for me to protect Scottie. We didn't want to put her and a three week old infant in that kind of danger.

Scottie and I set off around noon. Everything was going well for about thirty miles or so. That's when I noticed the vehicles. There were two of them. The first one was tailgating me. The terrain was dangerous, and I got a little worried. I planned to pull over at the next turnout and let them pass until I saw the second car. It pulled up beside me and I recognized the passenger. He was a member of our rival pack. I immediately knew they were after me and my son. The highway was a two lane interstate, but traffic was light. I was able to maintain control as we continued to travel down the mountainous terrain. As we approached Shasta Lake, the two cars boxed me in. There was a cliff to the right, a car to my left and another car on my tail. I sped up, trying to give myself an escape route. The other vehicles also sped up. We came around a corner and the car to my left swerved abruptly. I slammed on my breaks and the car behind me clipped my bumper. I was then sideswiped

Chaos

and the two of them pushed my vehicle over the cliff. Once my car came to a stop, I grabbed Scottie and fled into the forest.

I was injured pretty severely but I knew I had to get Scottie out of there. If those pack members knew my son was with me, they wouldn't stop until they killed him," Caleb explained.

Morrigan interrupted. "Is that normal? Is it typical where you live for enemy packs, or warring packs, to kill women and children?"

"There was nothing normal about the war we were fighting, but no. Those are not typical tactics used by our people. However, for this pack leader it was normal. Our enemies were ruthless. The pack leader considered me a traitor, so my family was specifically targeted. I found a cave and hid Scottie inside. I made him promise me he wouldn't leave until I came back. I realize he was only three, but we had a very close bond. I told Scottie how important it was that he didn't move and I promised him I would return as soon as I could. I left confident my son would be there when I returned.

I made my way back to the car and was very careful to cover my tracks. My plan was to lure the shifters in the other direction, away from Scottie. Once I reached the car, I spotted the tracks. The shifters had taken the form of a bear and they were scouring the area in an attempt to find me. I knew my only hope was to track them and take them out one at a time. So, that's what I did. There were five of them. By the time I'd killed the last one, I was in bad shape. I had three broken ribs, internal bleeding, a broken ankle and apparently a concussion. I couldn't walk, but I was trying to crawl back to the cave. The only thing on my mind was getting back to my son. I know I passed out at least a couple times along the way. I also vaguely remember seeing a man on a horse. The next thing I remember is waking up in an unfamiliar home.

Once I realized someone had removed me from the forest, I panicked. I went a little crazy. I had no idea how long I had been out and I didn't know where Scottie was. I went completely nuts. The woman was terrified and sedated me. They kept me under for a little over a week. When I woke the second time, I controlled myself a little better. I forced the man to take me back to the forest. I made him return me to the exact spot where he found me. We wandered around most of the day before we finally found the cave. I knew we had the right place because Scottie's favorite truck was left inside. I went a little nuts again. I thought the guy was going to knock me out.

He took me back to his house, but I snuck away before they could drug me again. I traveled all night and finally made my way to my parents' house. Dad was worried, then furious. He rallied his friends and escorted me back to my place. They knew I would never make it alone in my condition. I agonized the entire way back to Dunsmuir. What was I going to tell Amanda? Our son was missing and it was all my fault. I was so sure my enemies had taken my son and killed him. How could I break that kind of news to my wife?

When we pulled up to the cabin, I instantly knew something was wrong. Everything was pretty much a haze after that. I ran into the house and saw the mess. Our things were thrown all over the place. Personal keepsakes were smashed, quilts were shredded. I remember running through our home, room to room, calling for Amanda. Dad called Fritz and we searched the immediate area. Fritz agreed with me, our home reeked of shifter. My enemies had finally found us and gotten their revenge. I pretty much broke down at that point. I was sure my family was dead. My wife, my son and my newborn daughter. I shut myself away for over two weeks.

That's when Fritz and Kat paid me another visit. I hadn't eaten in two weeks and I was still healing from my wounds.

Chaos

Katerina began to nurse me back to health. Fritz told me he had a plan. We were all close. Losing Amanda was extremely hard on the two of them as well. We'd all been through so much together. Once Fritz laid out his plan, I agreed to help. I wanted revenge. I mistakenly believed killing those responsible would make me feel better. It didn't," Caleb shrugged. "Fritz, myself and several pack members targeted our enemies and killed them. We took out Fraunz and his two top fighters Bradley and David. The rest of the pack immediately surrendered. They worked out an agreement with Fritz and we haven't had many problems since.

I stayed in the house for another week, but Katerina talked me into moving. She knew the constant reminder would make it impossible for me to move on. I knew I'd never really move on, but I also knew I couldn't live in that house alone. Kat also convinced me to write to Amanda's aunt. She told me I had to make sure Amanda hadn't escaped and moved away. That she wasn't in hiding waiting for me to come and get her. Frunz was the pack leader of my enemies. When Fritz captured him, he brought him to me. We quizzed Fraunz extensively, but never did get answers. I needed to know why he killed Amanda and my children instead of just coming after me. Fraunz denied killing them. He never admitted it, even in the end. Kat was convinced that meant something. She was still holding out hope that Amanda had survived. I finally wrote Hazel. Fritz and Kat convinced me that if nothing else, it would give me closure. I guess it did. Hazel wrote me back and told me Amanda and Kylee had been killed while I was away. She chastised me for leaving them alone. Then she explained that the police had contacted her because they found charred and very limited remains of my wife and newborn daughter. There wasn't much, but according to Hazel there was enough left in the ashes to positively identify Amanda. They had also found my car and believed I was dead. The authorities decided Hazel was Amanda's only living relative."

"What?" Kylee jumped to her feet. "Hazel told you we were dead? Why would she do that? We were living down the road from her. We spent every Sunday with her. Why would she lie? Why didn't she tell mom you were still alive?" Kylee was pacing in front of the couch.

Bastian reached up and took her hand. "Sit back down, babe. We'll figure this out."

"That's a good question. It's one I've been asking myself ever since you walked through that door," Caleb told her. "Once I got the letter I gave up. I moved from the cabin and took up residency at my grandfather's old place. It was located near Shasta Lake, the last place I'd seen my son. I figured if someone had found him, I would eventually hear about it. I never did. I stopped going out. I eventually locked myself up in that cabin and never left. Fritz and Katerina still visit, but I think even they have given up on me. I tend to be depressing company."

Rand was considering the man's story. He obviously left a lot out. For instance, why was he considered a traitor and why was his family targeted? He'd get to that later, but for now he'd fill Caleb Turner in on his history. Rand proceeded to explain the story as his adopted parents had relayed it. He described his childhood and his first shifting experience then the situation with Thomas and how he discovered his true nature and the subsequent hiring of Cornelia to look into his lineage.

Caleb sat silently digesting the information he'd just received. He had mixed emotions. He was grateful somebody had found his son, someone that loved and cared for him. However, he was also distressed by the fact that his son had lived almost his entire life believing an evil demon was trying to take over his soul. Another layer of guilt consumed him. For forty years he'd felt guilty his family had been killed because of that one decision so long ago. Now he felt guilty that one decision had damaged his son's life for so long.

"I'm sorry," Caleb told Rand sincerely. "I'm so sorry you had to live that way. I'm sorry I wasn't there for you. I'm sorry I left you alone in that cave." He put his hands over his face and laid his head back against the chair.

"Stop saying you're sorry," Rand ordered. "If your enemies were really that bad, you probably saved my life. Are you sorry about that?"

Caleb's head shot up. "Of course not," he studied McBride.

"Then apology not accepted," Rand told him. "And thank you. I have some additional questions but I want Kylee to talk about Amanda for a minute and what she knows about that time. Then I'll come back to you if that's okay."

Kylee had been thinking about that letter. If her Aunt Hazel hadn't told her father they were dead, would they have gotten back together? "I can't figure out why my aunt lied to you. I keep thinking about that. I do know she didn't like you, at all," she glanced at Caleb.

"I already knew that," Caleb told her. "She never forgave me for taking your mother away from her. But I can't believe she'd hate me enough to make both me and Amanda suffer that way. She loved Amanda. I just don't think she would do that to her."

Kylee shrugged. "I don't know. I loved Aunt Hazel, but she was selfish. I recognized that when I graduated from college and mom moved to New York to be close to me. Aunt Hazel never forgave me for that. She never spoke to me again. Anyway, I guess that's one possibility. Maybe she thought if mom believed you were dead, she'd stay in New Jersey. Which worked, for a while anyway. But I also know mom was afraid. Could Hazel have been trying to protect mom from whatever scared her? You've talked about your enemies and said they were specifically after your family. What would this Fraunz guy do if you were dead, but he knew me and mom were still alive?"

"He would have sent someone after you," Caleb said, sure he was right. "He thought I betrayed him. I guess I did," Caleb shrugged. "There is no way Fraunz would have allowed my daughter to survive. He would have made sure my family line ended with me."

"Sounds like you really pissed this guy off." Rand observed.

"That's an understatement," Caleb affirmed.

"You said you were positive the shifters had been in your house," Kylee continued. "What if something happened? Something that scared mom. She took off, changed our name and went into hiding on the other side of the country, hoping nobody would find her. Then, one day she gets this letter. A letter supposedly from you. There's a problem with that though, mom was one hundred percent sure you were dead. I know that. Mom did not have any doubt about that. She was positive you and Scottie were killed that day. I think mom would have told Aunt Hazel to lie if she believed we were at risk. And Aunt Hazel would have done it. It kept us there, in New Jersey."

"I agree," Caleb said, considering Kylee's explanation. "Why was she so sure I was dead?"

"I don't know for sure," Kylee admitted. "I just know she was. Since I was little, mom told me you were killed in a car accident. Her initial story was that you were run off the road by a drunk driver. She said you died instantly. Aunt Hazel was the one that told me about the tracks. When I asked mom about that, she panicked a little. At the time I thought she was so upset because the possibility you and Scottie were eaten by animals was too morbid. Now that I think about it, she was scared. She was genuinely afraid. That's when mom told me the police theory. She said there were skid marks. The police thought you had swerved to miss another car. They didn't know if it was a drunk driver or a reckless driver or what, just that you had clearly swerved and lost control of your car. The vehicle went over the edge and crashed into a tree. Apparently it took a couple days to find the car and when they got down to the crash site, they spotted animal tracks surrounding the vehicle. In their opinion, the tracks explained the absence of bodies. They believed one or both of you were injured. Apparently there was blood in the car. So, they thought the blood attracted the animals, and they took the bodies. It only took them a few weeks to declare the two of you dead. I still have your death certificates back at the house."

"Seriously?" Rand asked amused. "That's unusual. They typically won't issue a death certificate without a body. I guess this is why."

Kylee looked at her father. "I assure you, mom was certain you were dead. She really had no doubt. I can also tell you she loved you until the day she died. If you are even considering the possibility that mom left you and ran away with your child, forget it. Mom never even went on a date. She talked about you all the time. She told me to hold out for someone like you. She loved you with all her heart."

"Thank you," Caleb said humbly. For about a second he wondered if Amanda had left, but he knew how happy they were.

He knew Amanda loved him that's why none of this made sense to him.

"I can also tell you mom lived her life afraid. I never understood that either. I was very young when she started the training sessions," Kylee turned to her father. "Mom hired a trainer to teach me to fight. She said the city was dangerous and I needed to know self-defense. At first she trained with me, but later she stopped. I continued the lessons for a couple more years, though.

When I was a teenager, I found a box that contained information on you. When I asked her about it, she freaked out. She literally panicked. She didn't talk to me for days. Then, she brought me the box and told me all about you. That's when she gave me that picture. Then she told me it was very important I never, under any circumstance, tell anyone my true identity.

Mom reluctantly told me your name. She said when we moved to New Jersey, she changed our names. She claimed it was because she wanted a fresh start. She would never tell me where we were from. Her standard answer was out west. When I asked her about relatives, she evaded the question. Then I got the lecture again about never doing anything that would identify me as a Turner. I had to keep that secret for the rest of my life. Mom wanted me to know about you, but she insisted everything she told me was a secret."

"So," Caleb studied Kylee. "You knew your mother was afraid of something out west and you promised her you would never reveal your true identity. Is that correct?"

"Yes," Kylee answered.

Chaos

"Then maybe you can tell me why you would send a private investigator to California looking for relatives of Caleb Turner?" he was a little angry.

"Why does that upset you?" Rand asked.

"Because if Fraunz was still alive, Kylee would be dead," Caleb said, fuming. "After everything your mother gave up to keep you safe, you threw all her precautions, all her warnings out the door and divulged all her secrets."

"So, I was in danger?" Kylee asked. "I always thought mom was just paranoid."

"It may look as if Amanda overreacted, but in light of the situation, I'm proud of her. She even fooled me. There's no way Fraunz would have known she was still alive and well. Ty said you've only known you are a shifter for about a week. Is that true? Amanda never explained that part to you?"

"It's true," Kylee told him. "I don't understand how mom could do that to me. How could she die and leave me in the dark that way."

"I don't know," Caleb told her honestly. "I don't understand why she didn't just tell you what you were. She told you about me, she prepared you to defend yourself. So why not help you prepare for your future? I honestly can't understand what Amanda was thinking."

"Maybe she wasn't sure I was a shifter. I told you I'm defective. I can't shift. Maybe she hoped I would take after her and she didn't need to explain," Kylee suggested.

"You are not defective and I'm sure you can shift," Caleb told Kylee confidently.

"Okay, I realize I've only known about the shifter thing for about a week and during most of that time I was sick," Kylee began.

"Why were you sick?" Caleb asked.

"I accidentally came into contact with warrior blood. Apparently it's fatal to shifters if left unattended. It made me pretty sick so I've been recovering from the illness."

Caleb looked at Bastian, "Worse than other blood? Why?" he asked.

"We don't know," Bastian said honestly.

"But you're fine now?" Caleb asked Kylee.

"Yeah, I've recovered completely." She assured him, touched by his obvious concern. "But my point is I have never shifted. Rand shifted when he was four. Then, the rest of his life he battled with himself, forcing his body not to shift. I've never had that problem. I've never even felt the slightest stirring. Maybe mom knew something about me that we don't," she suggested.

Caleb was considering what Kylee was saying. At her age, she should have felt something. Even if it was just subtle signs. Not necessarily the desire to shift, but the rest. "Shifters that don't shift are quick to anger. They fly off the handle at the drop of a hat sometimes."

Bastian choked, then cleared his throat and covered his mouth to hide a grin.

Kylee elbowed Bastian in the ribs. "Knock it off."

Chaos

"I can see you've been experiencing some of that yourself," Caleb smiled.

"Some," Kylee admitted. "Abby told me it was just the shifter in me, but I didn't think it was fair to blame it on my biology."

Caleb studied Kylee. "Is that new, or have you always felt that way?"

"It's new," she told him.

"And your mother died five years ago?" he asked.

"Yes," Kylee narrowed her eyes. What was he getting at?

"Did you develop any habits growing up? A special tea you always drank, a vitamin you always took, anything your mother gave you? Something that continued to be a habit after her death?" Caleb asked.

"Sure," Kylee said. "A couple of them."

"Tell me about them," Caleb ordered.

"Well..." Kylee began. "Mom told me I had a blood disease. She warned me never to let anyone take my blood or study it for any reason."

"I can see you didn't listen to that either. Is there anything your mother taught you that you did listen to?" Caleb asked even more annoyed.

"Look," Kylee glared at him. "You have no right to come here out of the blue and judge me for my actions. I kept those secrets for over forty years. I followed her direction for over forty years. I don't have to explain my reasons for deviating to you."

Caleb smiled. "Tell me about your habits."

Kylee sucked air through her nose then continued. "She told me the disease was not life threatening, but that I needed to take a vitamin to prevent muscle cramps. Mom started giving those to me when I was very young. But I haven't taken them for almost five years."

"You stopped after she died? Why?" Caleb asked. Kylee didn't have a blood disease, but he thought he knew why she never shifted.

"Not on purpose," Kylee told him flatly. "Mom's death was hard on me. I took a month off work and locked myself away from everyone. I didn't eat for days. I got so weak I finally forced myself to start eating again. Eventually I realized I hadn't taken those daily pills for weeks. There was no cramping, no side effects, nothing. That's when I stopped taking the pills altogether. I kept waiting for something to happen, something to change because I was no longer taking the vitamins. It never did, so I've never taken a pill again."

"Anything else?" Caleb asked.

"Anything else I use routinely?" Kylee clarified. "Not daily, but mom had some tea I liked. I haven't had it in months though, I've been out here at the fort."

"Did you drink that weekly?" Caleb asked.

"Uh..." Kylee thought. "Sure, probably. I didn't have a regular routine, but I'm sure I had a glass at least once a week, more in the winter."

"That's why you don't shift, the tea combined with the vitamins. Your mother made sure you never shifted," Caleb told her. "Now that you've stopped drinking the tea and you don't take the vitamins you're starting to experience the side effects of being a shifter. It's going to get worse. Some people can control it, like Rand did. Others eventually erupt, hurting anyone in their path."

Kylee looked at Abby and Morrigan. "Is that true?" she asked.

Morrigan nodded. "I've known that to happen. We have shifters that prefer to live as humans. Shifters that don't shift. Most of them are female and living among humans. There are ways to minimize the effects, but attacks have happened. I've never heard of a pill or tea that prevents those effects, though."

"Are you saying mom was drugging me to make sure I never shifted?" Kylee asked in disbelief. "How did she know what to use? Where did she get those pills and the tea?"

"I believe she was drugging you. Now that you've stopped taking my formula, the shifter is trying to come out," Caleb told her. "You only need that stuff once a week, I don't know why Amanda gave you a daily pill."

"Your formula?" Kylee asked.

"Yes," Caleb grinned. "My formula. I developed it for our people. It made it easier for them to hide among the humans."

"If I only needed the pills once a week, could taking them daily have a stronger impact on me?" Kylee asked.

"What are you getting at Kylee?" Bastian inquired.

"Maybe mom believed she'd changed me. Maybe she didn't tell me I was a shifter because she believed I wasn't anymore. Could regular doses alter me that much?" Kylee asked.

"No," Caleb said immediately. "But it's possible your mother didn't understand that." He was thinking about Amanda and the pills she gave Kylee.

"What are you thinking?" Rand asked. "You're pondering something, working out an explanation."

"Amanda didn't understand science at all," Caleb began. "She could make Kylee vitamins or tea because she'd created that mixture a hundred times before. She knew the recipe, but she didn't understand the concept. She wouldn't have understood it was drastically different than the nectar. It is possible Amanda believed giving extreme amounts of the tea would permanently alter Kylee's biological makeup. That would explain why she died and left Kylee unprepared," Caleb said absently. He was still considering.

"What nectar?" Morrigan asked.

"What?" Caleb asked. "Oh, the nectar. It was a formula I created to eliminate our scent. We were being tracked by shifters. It was very difficult to hide from them. My father and I developed a nectar that we drank daily to mask the scent. It enabled us to hide from Fraunz and his followers. I later discovered that drinking it every day actually changed us genetically. Once our pack began having children, their offspring were born without the shifter scent all together." He turned to Abby and Morrigan. "You had to notice they don't give off the usual scent."

"We did," Morrigan agreed. "That's why it took so long to discover they were shifters."

Chaos

"I guess that probably baffled you," Caleb told them a little amused.

"A little," Abby admitted.

"You have mentioned your enemies numerous times," Rand told Caleb. "You've also said you were considered a traitor. That you betrayed this Fraunz guy and he was specifically after your family. Now that we have the basics, are you going to fill in the rest?"

Caleb studied his son. "It's a long story," he began. "I'll try to give you the basics but even that is going to take a while." Caleb paused waiting for someone to object. Nobody did so he continued. "My father and a man named Fernando were very good friends since childhood. My grandfather was the pack leader while the two grew up. My father had other interests, chemistry. He didn't want to replace my grandfather as the leader of the pack when he passed away. So, dad and Fernando came up with a plan. In our society the pack is always turned over to the oldest son of the current pack leader. There is only one exception. If, during the crowning ceremony, another pack member challenges the new leader to a dual and wins, that member becomes leader. My father convinced Fernando to challenge him. Then he threw the fight. Fernando became leader and my father was free to explore other options.

This made both of them happy. They actually led the pack together. Nobody knew that but me. Anytime there was a problem or decision to be made, Fernando came to dad and the two discussed their options and made a decision together. It worked well. Fernando was a great leader. He had charisma and great social skills. Everyone loved him. Dad was less social and more comfortable remaining in the background. This went on for years. Finally, the two married and began a family. I was born first, then a few months later Fernando had twins. Fritz was the oldest by a few minutes, then Fraunz."

"Are you serious?" Rand asked. "This was all about two brothers fighting over power? Our family was ruined over a couple control freaks?"

"You are only half right," Caleb said soberly. "Fritz and Fraunz were my best friends. We were inseparable as children. It didn't take long for me to see how competitive they were. Every time we got together one of them would challenge the other to some off-the-wall game or stunt. At first I joined in. It was fun when we were little. I was in my mid-teens when I realized Fraunz wasn't playing anymore. I came to believe he actually hated Fritz. There was something dark and sinister about the way he interacted with his brother. The stunts became more and more dangerous and I worried one of them was going to get killed. Eventually I talked to Fritz about it, but Fritz loved Fraunz. He wouldn't even consider the possibility that Fraunz might have less than honorable intentions. Fraunz masked his feelings pretty well. Fritz admitted their competitive nature sometimes got the best of them, but refused to believe Fraunz was trying to hurt him.

Things continued for a few more years. The three of us had graduated from High School when a new family moved into the area. A couple with one daughter, Katerina. They were immediately welcomed into the pack. Fritz and Fraunz both fell for Katerina. I think they were both instantly and legitimately attracted to her, but when each of them found out the other wanted to pursue her, the competition was on."

"Of course," Morrigan sighed. "There's always a woman involved."

Chaos

Caleb grinned. "Fraunz made the first move. He took Kat out a few times and convinced himself they were destined to be together. Unfortunately, Kat saw the sinister side of Fraunz and was put off by it. Amanda and I were already married by then. Katerina and Amanda bonded almost immediately, so Kat felt comfortable talking to me about the situation. It only took a few dates before Kat was scared off by Fraunz. She told me she thought he had a dark soul. I warned her the break up would be ugly. Fraunz was planning their future. He claimed she was his true mate. After the first date he decided they would be married and stay together forever."

"Where was Fritz during all this?" Abby asked.

"Fritz loved his brother. At first, he planned to pursue a relationship with Katerina and turn it into another competition. The best man wins and all that. But after Fraunz had his first date, Fritz backed off. He could see how much Kat meant to his brother. No matter how much he wanted to get to know Katerina, he wouldn't hurt his twin that way. While Fraunz dated Katerina, Fritz avoided her. That was difficult for me, because Amanda and Kat spent a lot of time together. For that reason, during this time, Fritz also avoided me. Eventually, Katerina broke things off with Fraunz. He was livid. Initially he blamed Fritz. He was sure his brother had been pursuing Kat behind his back. After a while Fraunz had to admit he'd been wrong. Fritz continued to avoid Katerina to prove his loyalty to Fraunz."

A few months later the two met accidentally. Kat was instantly drawn to Fritz and she pursued him. Fritz continued to avoid her. Well, he tried to anyway. It didn't last long. The two were made for each other. They ultimately began to date and have been inseparable ever since."

"Did that start the war?" Kylee asked.

"Not exactly, but I think it was the beginning of the end," Caleb told them. "At first Fraunz told himself Kat would dump Fritz just like she dumped him. But that didn't happen. The longer they dated, the more upset Fraunz got. He looked at it as a lost competition. Eventually, Fritz and Katerina announced their engagement. They were going to have a simple ceremony the following week. The night before the wedding Fraunz called me upset and insisted I come over. It was late and I didn't want to go, but Amanda talked me into it. She thought Fraunz needed me. By this time, I was tired of the competition and didn't want to listen to Fraunz complain. He was obviously drunk and he sounded desperate. Once I got to his place, I realized he was completely smashed. He was also dangerously furious. He insisted I had to choose sides. I had to pick. He told me Fritz got the girl, so it was only fair he got me. I refused to choose. I told Fraunz the three of us had been through too much to pick sides.

That's when Fraunz confessed his plan. He was going to ambush Fritz when he left Katerina's house that night and kill him. He planned to destroy the body, kidnap Katerina and force her to marry him. The ceremony was already planned and he was sure nobody would know he wasn't Fritz. He insisted it was time for me to choose, which brother was I loyal to? He thought it was only fair that I not only choose him, but that I assist him with his plan. Of course I refused. I wasn't going to kill my best friend. He insisted and wouldn't let me leave. Finally, I told him I would help, but that Amanda wasn't feeling well and I needed to get home to check on her first.

I rushed home and briefly told Amanda what was going on. I left her to pack up our stuff while I went to warn Fritz and Katerina. Kat believed me immediately. Fritz took a lot of persuading. He

Chaos

truly loved his brother and couldn't believe the feeling wasn't mutual. He wouldn't consider the possibility Fraunz might be planning to kill him. Kat finally convinced him to pack up and leave for the night. She told him if I was wrong, no harm done. They'd just come home and get married the following day as planned. No one would ever know of my accusations. But if I was right, it would save his life. Fritz reluctantly agreed. The four of us took off and fled to the forest. Once we found a cave to secure the women, Fritz and I returned to Kat's home. A short time later Fraunz approached Katerina's house and hid behind the trees. Fraunz's friends, Brad and David, were with him. Fritz had to admit he'd misjudged his brother. We both knew we could never return to the pack again.

Fritz and I made our way back to the cave and the women. We both panicked a little when we saw Jim's dead body outside the cave. Inside, Amanda was trying to remain calm but failing miserably. She was in the process of bandaging Katerina's arm. Apparently Jim had tracked us to the cave. Fritz and I left before he arrived. Kat smelled him coming and was able to attack from behind before he realized she was there. Kat was injured pretty severely, but Jim was dead. That made things even worse. Jim and David were brothers and the best trackers in the pack. We knew we needed to get out of there. Once David realized his brother had been killed, he wouldn't rest until he tracked us down and got revenge. The four of us headed deeper into the forest. We did our best to confuse the scent and hoped it would be enough for the night.

I got a few hours' sleep, but woke early the next morning. We needed to let dad and Fernando know what was going on. I volunteered to go and Fritz stayed to protect Amanda and Kat. We thought Fraunz might be watching Fernando's house, expecting Fritz to report in. Dad of course was beside himself. He couldn't believe Fraunz had gone so far. He understood our need to remain hidden and agreed to speak to Fernando. I told him we were going to have the wedding ceremony tonight anyway. I could oversee it and Fritz didn't want to risk waiting.

I spent over an hour with dad brainstorming options to mask our scent. Dad had a few brilliant ideas for me to try. After I left the house, I stopped at the supermarket for supplies. That was my first mistake. Brad spotted me and followed me into the forest. Luckily I sensed him and was able to throw him off pretty quickly. When I reached the cave we decided to relocate. We had the wedding ceremony that night and then I started working on a way to eliminate our scent. The following morning Kat and Amanda went hunting for berries. Instead, they found my parents. Dad was barely alive, mom was almost as bad. She was struggling to pull dad through the forest in a wagon. Dad was barely conscious. The women got my parents back to the cave and I doctored their wounds.

Mom said Fraunz, Brad and David paid them a visit late the previous night. They were angry at Fritz for escaping. Fraunz was furious at me for betraying him and at Katerina for dumping him and choosing Fritz. The men told my parents that Fernando was dead. They claimed he had a heart attack earlier that day. None of us believed it. Fraunz killed his father. I have no doubt about that. He wanted the pack to be loyal to him. Fernando told dad he was going to disown Fraunz at the same time he announced to the pack there wouldn't be a wedding. Fraunz couldn't allow that, so he killed his father. Fraunz then demanded my parents tell disclose our location. He was desperate to know where we were hiding. Mom and dad didn't know, so the three of them beat my parents and left them for dead. That's when mom and dad joined our little pack out of necessity.

Over the next few weeks dad and I perfected the nectar. The six of us began drinking it nightly. In a very short amount of time, it seemed to work. None of us could detect a scent, shifter or otherwise on each other. Once we no longer worried about Fraunz and his thugs detecting us, we could move around more freely. Living in the forest gradually got easier, which was a good thing because our group was slowly growing. A few others were abused by Fraunz and his group, but the majority of our new members just didn't approve of the way Fraunz was running the pack. Eventually we developed a community or pack of our own."

"And you say this nectar changed you genetically?" Bastian asked.

"It did. My people didn't need it after Fritz and I killed Fraunz, Brad and David but it had a permanent impact on our community. All of our offspring were born without a scent," Caleb explained.

"Do you want a job?" Bastian asked seriously.

"I've heard your company is top notch, but no thanks," Caleb said evasively.

"What do you plan to do now?" Rand asked. "Will you be returning to California?"

"I haven't decided yet," Caleb said honestly. "I'd like to stick around for a while and get to know my kids. I've missed out on so much of your lives. I'd like to learn as much as I can. Maybe I'll stay. There's not much left for me in California."

"I think I'd like that," Kylee told him. "I feel like I know you better than anyone here because mom talked about you all the time, but I'd like to really get to know you. I'd like to see for myself what kind of person you are. Maybe you could work here with me at the fort. We're hoping Melissa will be cured, but if not maybe a fresh perspective will help."

"We'll see," Caleb said, he wasn't sure he wanted to work here with Bastian.

"You still sound skeptical," Morrigan observed. "Why? Do you think we're not trust worthy? Maybe we're still trying to steal your blood?"

"I gave my blood to Bastian," Caleb reminded him. "I'm trusting him with that secret. If I'm wrong, my enemies will already have what they want."

Bastian narrowed his eyes at the visitor. "What do you mean by that? You think I'm going to give your blood to your enemies? That's highly unlikely since I don't even know them."

"At least one of them works for you," Caleb told him casually.

"What?" Bastian asked surprised. "Who?"

"One of Fraunz's followers works at your Sacramento plant. In fact, a few months ago he kidnapped one of our females and was on his way to the lab to conduct tests when we rescued her."

Bastian was going through his employees. If the guy tried to take a kidnapped victim to the lab, he had to be in management. It had to be Rick Woodside. "Was this guy one of my managers?"

"Yes. He is," Caleb told him.

"I'll take care of it in the morning. Rick is going to find himself unemployed and unable to find a new job," Bastian said angrily.

"If you fire him for kidnapping one of my pack members you're going to cause contention between our packs again. I'd

Chaos

appreciate it if you didn't do that. We're tolerating each other, but things are still a little tense," Caleb told him.

"Was Rick loyal to Fraunz?" Bastian asked.

"Yes," Caleb admitted. "They were close, but not as close as Brad and David. Rick surrendered and promised not to cause more trouble so we let him live among us," Caleb explained.

"Kidnapping isn't considered trouble?" Morrigan asked.

"Of course," Caleb sighed. "Look, things are pretty good for us now. We even have members that openly live among the humans. Our pack doesn't have to hide anymore. We don't want to change that. Sure, Rick and his brother cause problems here and there, but we handle them," Caleb shrugged. "Pack members like my mother for instance, weren't happy hiding in the forest. They need modern conveniences. This works for us. When Rick and Ronald get out of line, we handle it."

"Who is the pack leader now that Fraunz and his father have died?" Abby asked. She wondered if her father could help somehow.

"Our pack leader is Fritz. Since Fraunz died that pack has had several leaders. Fernando's brother, Rodriguez took over for a while. He couldn't control them and was eventually ousted by another one of Fraunz's friends, Tony. Rodriguez moved away within days of the takeover. He feared for his family. So, he packed up and left without a backwards glance. Ronald couldn't stand Tony being in charge so he challenged him to a fight and won. Last I heard Ronald is still basically in charge, however I think their pack is mostly living their own lives. They need a good leader, but no one is willing to handle the mess Fraunz and the subsequent leaders have created," Caleb shrugged. "Maybe someday a shifter will move in and fix things, but for now we make do with what we have."

"It's late," Cornelia said standing. "I'm tired. I think I'll call it a night." She slowly made her way out the door and up to her room.

Kylee turned to Caleb. "I know it's late and you probably want to go to bed, too. I was just wondering if you would tell me about my relatives. You said your mother lives in the city. What about your father?"

"Dad never truly recovered from that beating Fraunz gave him. I guess that's one reason I don't feel bad about killing him, even though I've learned he didn't kill you two and your mother. He did so many other horrible things, I still believe justice was served. Anyway, dad was frequently ill, mostly pneumonia. He passed away a little over two years ago."

"Oh," Kylee said disappointed. "I'm not naive enough to think we are all just going to jump in and immediately be one big happy family. I know it will take time, but do you think I could meet her someday? Your mother I mean. I spent the last five years thinking I was all alone. I believed I didn't have any family left. Now, in a matter of days, I've discovered I have a brother, a father and a grandmother. It's a little surreal, but exciting for me." She glanced at Rand a little worried about her request. She wasn't sure how he felt about all this. He still had parents, granted he was upset with them at the moment, but he had them.

Rand smiled at Kylee. He understood where she was coming from. But for him the whole situation was bizarre. He had so many emotions jumping around in his head right now. The last few weeks felt like information overload and he was having a difficult time computing everything. "Me too," he finally told her.

Chaos

"I'd like that," Caleb told Kylee. "And I know mom would love to meet you," he turned to Rand. "You too. I also want the two of you to meet Fritz and Kat. I know they aren't really family, but to me they are. We've been through so much together, especially the last few years. I'd like them to meet my kids and I want you two to meet them. I think you'll instantly see why we are so close. Now, I need to make a couple phone calls then I'd like to go to bed. We can continue this in the morning," Caleb paused. He wasn't sure how to proceed. He wanted more than anything to pull his children into his arms and hug them, to never let them go. But Rand was so distant and he wasn't sure how Kylee felt about all this.

Kylee stood and walked toward her father. "Goodnight," she said softly, leaning in to give him a hug. "I think this is easier for me than Rand," she said stepping back. "I know you already. At least part of you. I had mom to relay stories and feelings about you. I know how happy you made her and how much she loved you. Rand didn't have that. I feel like I just got a miracle, I know that sounds corny, but I don't know how else to describe what I'm feeling."

Caleb leaned in and gave Kylee a gentle kiss on her forehead. "I feel the same," he said softly. "Goodnight, sweetheart." He turned to Rand and studied him for a minute. "Goodnight Rand."

Rand almost let him leave that way. He already had a father. Did he really need another one? But Robert McBride, or Taylor or whatever, wasn't really his father. And he had lied to Rand his entire life. Plus, Robert was human, this man wasn't. Rand knew he couldn't ignore his heritage for hundreds of years. Once Robert died, Rand would seek out Caleb Turner anyway. He might as well get to know him now. Rand crossed the room and stood before the stranger. He slowly held out his hand and waited.

Caleb knew this was a big step for his son. Rand was just like Caleb in so many ways. Even at three, Caleb had understood that. He took Rand's hand and held it for a moment. Would Rand ever allow himself to be close to his father the way Scottie had been? Caleb hoped so, but only time would answer that question. Caleb's relationship with his own father had been unique. He knew that. He knew all sons didn't have that kind of bond with their dad. Losing Scottie was hard, but knowing he would never have that kind of bond with his son made it so much worse. Now that he had a chance, he would not ruin it. He would be there for Rand, but he would let Rand set the terms. Otherwise, he'd lose his son all over again and there was no way he would ever allow that to happen. "Goodnight son," he finally said dropping Rand's hand and leaving the room.

Kylee turned and wrapped her arms around Rand. "Goodnight," she said stepping back. "I love you, and I'm so glad you turned out to be my brother."

Rand kissed Kylee's cheek and smiled. "You are pretty lucky to have me," he laughed jokingly then turned and headed for the door.

Kylee laughed too, then turned to see Bastian standing behind her. "Goodnight everyone," she took Bastian's hand and pulled him from the room. "I know I'm asking a lot Bastian, but would you mind terribly if I stayed with you again tonight? I'd rather not be alone right now. Everything Caleb told us is running around in my head. I slept so well last night, I just wondered if..."

"Of course," Bastian told her, pulling her toward his room once they reached the top of the stairs. "I like having you in my arms. For some reason, I find it relaxing."

Kylee smiled. "Me too," she pushed herself up on tip toes and kissed Bastian gently as he closed the bedroom door.

Chaos

* * * *

Kylee stretched as she opened her eyes. At first she didn't remember where she was, but she needed to pee. As she swung her legs over the side of the bed she remembered the night before. She'd slept with Bastian, just slept. He hadn't even tried anything. She still wasn't sure how she felt about that. Kylee took a deep breath and stood. Before heading to the bathroom she glanced around the room and spotted him. Bastian was relaxing in the large lounge chair watching her. She gave him a brief smile before she stepped into the adjourning bath and closed the door behind her.

Bastian watched as Kylee woke, stretched lazily then headed for the bathroom. He wondered what she would think about him stocking toiletries for her this morning. She'd been so self-conscious about bad breath yesterday. Abby was a lifesaver. He had no idea what a shifter female would need in the morning. The small bag Abby provided had things inside he'd never heard of. He'd set it out on the counter, leaving the unknowns inside the bag but laying out the toothbrush, toothpaste and mouthwash to make sure Kylee spotted them immediately.

Bastian smiled. He liked waking up next to Kylee. He liked holding her all night, too. That surprised him. It was something he'd never experience before. Sure, he'd been with other women, he was several hundred years old. But they were different. He'd never actually spent the night with any of them. He never took women to his place, that way he could silently slip away once they fell asleep.

Kylee exited the bathroom and walked to Bastian. He was surprised to see she was still in the oversized t-shirt and shorts she'd slept in. He figured she would take the time to shower and freshen

446

up while she was in there. Kylee slowly walked to Bastian and picked up his coffee mug. She studied him as she lifted the steaming liquid to her lips. Bastian wondered if she knew just how enticing she was like this. Before he realized what she was doing, Kylee placed the mug on the table and sat in his lap. He was treading in dangerous waters here.

"Thanks," Kylee said sincerely, stretching a little to give him a quick, gentle kiss.

"You're welcome," he said, placing his hand on the small of her back and pulling her close. He pressed his lips back to hers and kissed her more forcefully. A moment later Bastian pulled away and kissed Kylee's forehead. "You gonna shower before we start the day?"

"Huh?" Kylee asked, surprised by the abrupt shift in gears.

"I want to head down to the lab and check on Melissa," he said casually. "I was wondering if you needed to shower or if you plan to go down like that," he asked with a grin.

"I know we need to check on Melissa," Kylee admitted. "I just thought we could maybe...." she didn't know what to say.

"Kylee," Bastian said pushing her hair away from her face. "Don't take this the wrong way or think it's a rejection, but I don't think the time is right for that."

"How can I not take that as a rejection?" she asked, hurt.

"Because I want you more than you know," he assured her. "But you have been through so much the last few days. You're emotions are all over the place. You're not ready for this. If I took you to bed right now, I'd always wonder if you regretted it. I won't take advantage of the situation. You have standards, I won't let you change those for me," he said giving her another quick kiss then placing her on the floor and standing. "Go get dressed, sweetheart. We need to check on Melissa."

Kylee took a deep breath then returned to the bathroom. After a quick shower she wondered what she was going to wear. She was just about to slip back into yesterday's outfit when she saw the pile of clean clothes sitting on the counter. When had Bastian put those there? Had he come in during her shower? She immediately felt self-conscious but pushed it aside. She planned to make love to the man, had tried to instigate something less than an hour ago. Who cared if he saw her in the shower? It was only a matter of time before they would be together. She was certain of that. Bastian was the only man for her. Somehow she felt safe and secure around him. She'd saved herself for the perfect man and Bastian was the perfect man. She had to admit, staying true to her values all these years was the right thing to do. There had been times in her past when she'd wondered if she was being silly. Not anymore. It made her relationship with Bastian even more special somehow. Knowing he was the only man she would ever be with made her even more grateful to her mother for instilling those morals. She pulled her hair into a ponytail and exited the bathroom, ready to start the day.

Bastian stood and the two of them left the room hand in hand, headed for the lab and Melissa.

* * * *

The sleek jet landed smoothly on the runway at Seneca. It had been a long flight and Lillie was anxious for some down time. Ty had kept her busy the last few days. She glanced around absently, the sun would be setting soon. She smiled when she lowered the stairs and Alex and Dimitri appeared. They were followed by Atticus and Tala. Lillie was finally starting to get used to being around Alex and Thomas Deveraux. Conditioning she supposed. She forced a smile and greeted her passengers.

"Thanks for another great flight," Alex told her. "You look a little tired. I'll make sure to mention that to Ty. He needs to give you more down time I think." She turned to leave but stopped when she saw Bastian and Kylee approaching.

"Any word yet?" Alex asked anxiously. "Has Melissa responded to the uh...new procedure?" She finished cryptically. She'd gotten so used to Lillie being around she'd almost slipped.

Kylee couldn't help it, she was so excited she was ready to burst. "It's working," she said, enthusiastically. "It's actually working."

"Really?" Alex asked relieved. "Really working or just kind of working?"

"Really working," Bastian assured her. "I'd say in a day or two she'll be completely coherent. She's probably going to need Mason Cooper to get through this, but it looks promising."

Alex turned to Tala. "Uh..." she stopped. She knew Tala would be tired.

"I'll take care of it," Tala assured her. "It will only take a minute then Atticus and I are going to settle in for the night. We'll see you all in the morning." Tala and Atticus walked toward the lab hand in hand.

Chaos

Lillie paused then took advantage of the silence. "I'm beat," she finally said. "I'm gonna turn in myself. I assume I can use my regular room?"

"Of course," Alex told her warmly. "Go on in. There's no need for you to wait out here for us. I'll make sure the door is shut and everything is closed up tight for the night. Thanks again for everything."

"My pleasure," Lillie said flinging her bag over her shoulder and heading for the apartments.

"I assume Tala's going to take care of Melissa's memory tonight," Bastian commented.

Dimitri nodded. "We can't take any chances with this."

"Are you sure that's wise?" Kylee asked. "I mean her brain is still healing and now Tala's going to go in and change things. Do you think it's safe?"

"Tala won't harm her," Alex said with confidence. "We need Melissa's story to match the one we set up. She can't say a word about Lawson or Patricia. When she talks to the police she has to tell them one man did this, and she has to identify Kahn as that man. Tala believes the sooner the memories are taken care of, the better. I'm going to trust her with this. She understands her gift and how this stuff works better than we do."

"I guess," Kylee said not convinced. The group walked in silence, making their way across the fort. "Bastian and I have been talking and we think Melissa should be moved back to New York immediately. It would do her good to have her boyfriend close. I'm sure it will help him as well. Plus, it gets her out of here and away from the danger. Do you think we could move her in the next couple days?"

"I don't think that will be a problem," Alex said thinking. "I'll call the Coopers tonight. I'm sure Jackie will take over her care and Mason has already agreed to take her on as a patient as soon as she's ready. Hopefully he can help her overcome any emotional obstacles she encounters because of this."

"Dimitri, can I talk to you for a minute?" Bastian asked. "There's something I need to appraise you of tonight."

Kylee and Alex both looked at Bastian, then Dimitri.

"You two go ahead," Dimitri told the women. "We'll be right behind you."

Alex put an arm through Kylee's and started for the house.

"What's up?" Dimitri asked Bastian as soon as the women were out of sight.

"I knew you were on your way and didn't want to bother you, so I took care of things by myself. I hope you're okay with it," Bastian paused.

"Well, if you tell me what it is, I'll be in a better position to answer that," Dimitri joked.

"I want to marry Kylee," Bastian told Dimitri. "I asked Nick to go to my house and get the ring my father left me. My mother's ring. He and Dante are supposed to be bringing it out tonight. One of my pilots agreed to fly them here in the chopper. Pete and Greg agreed to watch things in New York while Nick and Dante are gone.

Chaos

I know they're retired and haven't been warriors for years, but things are pretty slow in New York so I hope you are okay with it."

Dimitri thought about the situation for a minute. It was pretty quiet in New York lately. He didn't exactly like having all the active warriors in one place, but under the circumstances it was probably okay. He, Alex, Tala and Atticus had talked a lot about the current war on their way back from Dublin. They needed to go on the offensive soon. He was tired of always being on the defensive with Radek. Something had to change. The four of them brain stormed for hours but hadn't come up with a concrete plan. He needed to have a meeting with his warriors anyway, he wanted their input and expertise. Maybe he could do that tomorrow since they'd all be at the fort. "It's fine," he finally told Bastian. "But why did you bring both Nick and Dante here just to deliver the ring?"

"I want to marry Kylee right away," he shrugged. "It seemed like a good idea. It's difficult to get everyone in the same place these days. Right now, everyone I would want at my wedding is here. With Kylee's father and Rand still on base, it seems to me like a perfect opportunity. Sam agreed to marry Ty without a lot of fanfare and planning. I'm hoping Kylee will do the same. If so, we're ready," Bastian smiled. "If not, everyone can disburse as planned."

"Has your pilot left already?" Dimitri asked.

Bastian checked his watch. "No, he's scheduled for takeoff in about twenty minutes. Why?"

"Tom, the attorney for Deveraux Industries has called Alex about a million times. He's desperate to meet with Alex, Thomas and Sam for some reason. If you don't mind, I'll have him hitch a ride with Nick and Dante. It's a good opportunity to handle the problem in person."

"Sure, let me call him. I'll tell him not to take off until he hears from me and to prepare for another passenger. I'll also let him know he'll be taking Melissa back to the hospital when he leaves." The two men walked through the front door of the old farmhouse and proceeded to the study in search of Alex and Kylee.

A few hours later, Lillie stood at the large window watching the passengers exit the chopper. She'd never flown a helicopter before. She'd never had an interest in anything but airplanes. A man she'd never seen before climbed out of the small door first, then came the two hotties. The ones she'd seen at the airport when she took Alex and company to Dublin. Lillie continued to watch the men walk from the helicopter to the farmhouse. All three of them were good looking and confident. Her focus remained on the two younger men. They were built like Greek Gods, any woman would die for a few seconds of their attention. She smiled at herself. She'd always had a weakness for hot guys and those two were definitely hot. They both had sexy brown hair, her personal weakness. The shorter one with the darker hair looked like trouble. The taller one with copper streaks seemed more sensible and controlled. She laughed out loud. As if she had any business trying to judge a man's character. She'd not only fallen in love and married Brad, but she'd been floored when she discovered he was cheating on her. Lillie dropped the curtains and climbed into bed. She wasn't interested in men anymore. She was better off alone. She would just keep telling herself that until she actually believed it. Eventually her brain would accept her new reality and she wouldn't feel so lonely and depressed all the time.

Chaos

Tom walked purposefully into the farmhouse and was directed to the study by Abby Cooper. Thomas, Alex, Dimitri, Ty and Sam were already inside. He knew this wasn't going to be a private meeting with three people. It would be a meeting with the three people involved and their significant others. It was probably better that way. Once he entered the large room he decided to get straight to business, they didn't have a minute to waste. Time was quickly running out. Tom sat on the couch and pulled a file from his briefcase. He flipped open the folder and was about to begin when Alex interrupted.

"I trust the flight was comfortable?" Alex asked.

"Fine thanks," Tom answered without emotion. "I think we should get started here. There may be a lot of questions and it's late."

"Sure," Alex agreed. "Would you like something to drink first?"

Tom glanced at the tray Abby had set on the small table in the center of the sitting area. "I'll take a Coke. Thanks," Tom said removing a glass of ice and the can from the tray. Once he'd poured the liquid into his glass, he took a sip then reached for his file again. "I'm sure you are all wondering why this meeting was so important."

"You might say that," Thomas agreed.

"It's about a trust your parents set up," Tom told them passing out copies of the trust to Alex, Thomas and Sam. He paused as he studied Samantha Reed. "I realize you know by now that Marlena was your aunt. What you might not know is that Marlena and Luke knew about you. They knew you were their niece."

"I've kind of figured that out myself. I mean the mysterious Scholarship America that doesn't really exist. I know it's fictitious and that account covered my college tuition and more. Then there's the instant job at the best company around once I graduated," Sam told Tom. "So what's this?" she glanced at the papers he'd handed her.

"That's a copy of the terms of the trust," Tom told her. "An account was set up for you, Samantha. Initially it was the scholarship fund, but the Deveraux's continued to use the same account under the name of Scholarship America to contribute regular funds into a trust. The sole beneficiary of that account is Samantha Reed," he told no one in particular. "The urgent part is the clause about you getting married," he said, looking back toward Sam.

Sam looked at Ty then back to Thomas and Alex in confusion. "What about me getting married?" she finally asked.

"Well, if you look at the balance of the trust you will see you're a pretty wealthy lady," Tom explained.

Sam began skimming the paperwork then froze when she saw the figure on the second page. Her head shot up and she stared at Tom, wide eyed. "Is this right?"

"It was at the first of the month. You own stock in D-Tech and your income is directly impacted by how well the company performs. It changes almost daily. Luke was brilliant at investing, so a portion of the funds are tied up in stocks. Don't worry, even if the company went bankrupt you wouldn't lose everything. You will always get a monthly stipend. I guess that's the best word for it. You just get extra if D-Tech does well. It's a built-in incentive for you to do your best work."

Sam was floored. Her mind was racing. She was rich, extremely rich. "Okay, so I'm a millionaire. What does that have to do with me getting married recently?" Sam asked.

"There's a clause in the trust regarding what happens when you get married. The trust was set up so you would receive the funds when you turned thirty five. I should have talked to you sooner, but things have been so hectic lately. Every time I set up a meeting, somebody cancelled. It became urgent after your wedding."

Alex looked up from reading her packet. "Rather than having us all thumb through this and try to find that clause, would you just explain the basics Tom?"

"Of course," Tom agreed. "Luke and Marlena worried about someone taking advantage of Sam. They wanted to make sure nobody could marry her for the money." He glanced at Ty. "Please don't kill the messenger. I know you are wealthy and didn't marry Samantha for her bank account. But at the time this was set up, there was no way to know who Samantha would choose for a husband."

"I understand," Ty said cordially. "Don't worry about offending me. Just explain the trust."

"Thank you," Tom said looking back at Sam. "They just wanted to protect you. They weren't trying to cause problems."

"We all understand that Tom," Thomas said a little annoyed. "Please, get to the point."

"Basically the four of you have paperwork that needs to be signed immediately. We are getting down to the wire here. If the paperwork isn't signed by the end of the month, the trust will be frozen. That's only three days away. That means Samantha won't have access to any of the funds. It will technically still be hers but as long as she is married to Ty, she can't access it. If they were to divorce, the trust would be opened again. Otherwise, it will be transferred to their children upon Sam's death."

"I see," Alex mused. "So explain to us what we are signing." She already had a general idea from the little she'd read but she wanted to hear it from Tom.

"Well, Sam has to sign the actual trust acknowledging she understands and agrees to its terms and conditions. Her signature basically activates the trust. Thomas, you and Alex need to sign the trust as well. Your signature binds the contract and signifies your agreement to all the terms contained within. Once the two of you sign, you can't stop the monthly deposits. You basically are agreeing Sam has a valid property right and the money continues until her death. Ty has his own contract that must be signed. Basically he is signing away any rights state law grants him as Samantha's husband. It's a binding agreement relinquishing his monetary rights. If he divorces Samantha, he receives nothing. He can't touch the trust. His signature is his promise not to try. It's iron clad, he would lose any attempt to fight it anyway."

"That's not fair," Sam exclaimed. "Ty didn't make me sign a prenup and that's basically what this is. If we get divorced, I'm entitled to a portion of his wealth but he doesn't get any of mine? No way. How could Luke and Marlena do this?" Sam was mortified. She couldn't let Ty sign that contract. It was unfair and insulting.

Chaos

"Tom?" Alex asked. "Would you mind giving us a minute alone?"

Tom studied Alex momentarily, then he nodded once, stood and walked out the door shutting it behind him.

"Sam," Ty said soothingly.

"No," Sam cut him off. "This isn't fair to you. I won't let you sign something like that. It's insulting, why aren't you angry about this?"

Ty smiled. "Because I knew Luke and Marlena very well. They didn't do this to hurt you or the man you married. They did it to protect you. You have to remember at the time this was prepared, you were human. I'm sure they assumed you would marry a human. Think about your life when they were alive. They did this because they loved you. If they had lived long enough to know I would be your husband, they never would have required my signature on that paper." Ty took Sam's face between his hands. "Honey, I love you. That money is yours, you should have it. I don't mind signing that contract. No matter how many times I keep telling you the money doesn't matter, I know it matters to you. I think this will help us."

Sam closed her eyes. She wanted to cry. She wanted to scream. This was so unfair. How could she make this choice?

"Sam?" Alex asked. "What are you struggling with?"

Sam glanced at Ty then decided to try to explain. "I know the money doesn't mean anything to Ty, but it's uncomfortable for me. I hate that Ty had to buy the house himself. I hate that he pays the bills and I'm not contributing to the household, not really. My first thought when I saw that huge figure was relief. I could do my part in this marriage. I could finally contribute. I instantly felt like Ty's partner instead of baggage."

"Sam," Ty scolded. He was going to continue but stopped when he saw the look Alex was giving him.

"Maybe it's stupid, but that's how I feel," Sam continued. "It ruins everything if Ty has to sign that contract for me to get the money. Even with that bank account, Ty is so much richer than I am. I know, without a doubt, that Ty never once considered making me sign a prenup to protect his assets. This feels wrong and unfair. So, I have to choose between insulting my husband and being an equal partner. If Luke and Marlena loved me, how could they do this to me?" A tear escaped and Sam impatiently brushed it away.

"You may not believe me, but I don't think they did this to hurt you," Alex began. "Like Ty said, they were protecting you from other humans. Luke knew and understood humans. He dealt with a lot of greedy, manipulative, unscrupulous men and women over the years. He also watched several men enter my life for the sole purpose of getting my money. I very strongly believe they thought they were helping. They were trying to protect you. Think of it from the opposite side. You can see Ty doesn't have any problem signing that contract. That's because he loves you and has no intention of leaving you or trying to get your money. But if you were marrying someone that only wanted your money, that man would have a problem with this contract. It was actually a pretty good idea, when you were human anyway."

"But I'm not human anymore," Sam argued. "And we are at war. If something happens to me, I want Ty to have all my assets. Of course he doesn't need them, but he should have them. That's what he would want if something happened to him. I wouldn't

Chaos

know what to do with Ty's company but I have no doubt he's leaving it to me anyway." She turned to look at Ty. "Aren't you?"

"Of course," Ty said understanding where she was coming from. "You're my wife. As far as I'm concerned it's yours already."

"Exactly," Sam said glaring at Thomas and Alex. "Do either of you have that clause in your trust? Will Dimitri have to sign a contract saying he gets nothing if you die or leave him Alex?" She looked at Thomas. "Does Abby have to sign one agreeing not to ask for anything if the two of you split or if you die, Thomas? Because I don't see anything in here that says Ty gets everything if I die."

"Actually, there is a slightly different clause in our trusts," Thomas answered. "And I think Alex and I can fix this."

"How?" Sam asked. "And what do you mean slightly different?"

"Well, we are supernatural," Thomas answered. "I'm the son of a warrior. Alex is the daughter of the Fae Queen. Our trusts and the included stipulations had to be worded very carefully. The simple answer to your questions is no. Dimitri and Abby will not be required to sign anything when we get married. Our trust is different because fae, warriors and even shifters mate for life. It's different than humans. Sam, you know that fifty percent of human marriages fail. That's where my parents were coming from. Our marriages very rarely fail. Sure it happens every so often, but it is very, very rare. Because of that, Alex and I have a different clause in our trust. One I think we could add to yours. Tom won't know the difference but all of us will."

"I agree," Alex told the room. "I was reading the paperwork Tom gave me. It gives Thomas and me the authority to make changes, albeit very slight ones. That's why we both have to sign the trust with you, Sam. Both Thomas and I have a trust. Ours stipulates the restrictions are eliminated after ninety nine years. To a human, they see that as a lifetime. For us, it's merely a season. Tom thinks he has protected us, the same as that trust protects you. He's comfortable with the wording. To us, it's basically irrelevant."

"You mean I won't get any of your money until I put up with you for ninety nine years?" Dimitri said feigning shock. "That's it, the weddings off."

Alex smiled a little and winked at Dimitri. "Thomas and I can insist the language be changed to match the language in our trust. Tom will go for that. He won't understand the difference, but he'll do it."

"But I don't see how that helps," Sam argued. "We are in a war. As much as I hate to think about it, there is a chance either Ty or I could be killed in the very near future. If that happens, I want to know Ty gets all my possessions. As my husband, he has a right to them. I need to know he will get my money and my stock."

"Well now you're just being greedy," Thomas teased. "Ty's not successful enough for you? He has to have stock in my company as well as his own?"

"My stock," Sam said, not amused. She felt like the only one in the room that was taking this seriously.

"I believe we can do something with that as well," Alex continued. "I think Tom would go for the change if we had a clause in there that said upon your untimely death Ty receives everything unless Thomas or I object."

Chaos

"No offense, but why do you have the authority to deny Ty something that is rightfully his?" Sam asked.

"I'm fine with that," Ty assured her. "Sam, this is about fooling the humans. The whole thing is mute anyway. I'm never going to leave you and you won't leave me. We're in this forever. If Tom needs this to believe he's following Luke and Marlena's wishes, just give it to him." Ty didn't like talking about Sam's possible death. He just wanted to sign the stupid contract and move on.

"Do you think we would deny Ty what's rightfully his?" Alex asked Sam a little hurt.

"No. I guess not," Sam admitted. "I'm just insulted by this whole thing and I don't know why Ty's not."

"Because I love you and the money doesn't matter to me," Ty told her.

"Sam, if you can trust me and Thomas, we can fix this," Alex assured her. "Tom will be satisfied with what I have in mind. The whole point of that clause is to make sure nobody marries you for your money, then murders you and walks away with millions. We all know that's never going to happen. Trust us to fix this. I wish I could guarantee both you and Ty will make it through this war intact, but I've learned a hard lesson from mom's death and then Luke's. Sometimes things happen that we don't anticipate and can't avoid. During war, danger can't be prevented. Having said that, I for one choose to be optimistic and believe we are all going to get through this alive. The only acceptable fatalities are vampires. So, let's fix this so you can start spending a little money on your wardrobe, already." Alex smiled as she looked at Sam's worn jeans and sweatshirt.

Sam studied Alex for a long moment. She was considering her options. "Only if I sign a similar contract," Sam finally agreed. "Go ahead and redo my contract, but write one up for me to sign as well. Anything Ty has to agree to regarding my money, I have to agree to regarding his."

"No," Ty said immediately.

"Ty," Alex sighed. "Like you said the whole thing is mute anyway. When we are finished you will have a contract that says if the two of you get divorced neither of you get anything that belonged to the other party prior to marriage. It will also stipulate that if one of you dies prematurely, Thomas and I are the only ones that can object to the other party receiving everything. The only way any of this will matter is if either of you get killed in this war. So, just make sure that doesn't happen," she studied Ty. "You know we would never prevent Sam from receiving what's rightfully hers in the event of your death, the same as we wouldn't prevent you from getting everything she owns in the event of Sam's death. If you're uncomfortable with me or Thomas having control, put your brother's name on it."

"I don't need to do that. I do trust you, I just don't like this," Ty said with a little less conviction.

"Ty," Thomas put in. "I don't think you understand where Sam is coming from when she says she doesn't feel like she's on equal footing. I don't completely understand that either. We both come from money. Wealth doesn't mean anything to us, it never has. But Marlena struggled with the same thing Sam's struggling with for years. I think Alex suffers a little as well." He smiled at his sister. "She doesn't think she deserves an equal portion of dad's property. She's wrong, but she struggles sometimes. That's why she keeps trying to sign everything back over to me."

Chaos

"I didn't think you knew. I didn't think you would understand," Alex told Thomas.

"I do," Thomas assured her. "But like I said, you're wrong. So you can stop trying to give dad's stuff back. I'm a busy man and constantly having to thwart your efforts is exhausting. From the moment you entered dad's life, you were his. As far as he was concerned you are his daughter. I agree, you're my sister in every way that matters. Once dad married Marlena they were equal partners. But your mom had a hard time with that for years." Thomas turned and locked eyes with Abby. "My future wife also struggles with this a little bit."

Abby nodded and loved Thomas even more for understanding her reluctance.

"I understand where Luke and Marlena were coming from," Ty admitted. "But it just feels like signing those contracts makes our partnership less somehow." Ty studied Sam for a long moment. "I guess this way it's equally unfair and insulting. And, like you said, it's really mute anyway. We're not getting divorced. If you can talk Tom into making the changes, I'll do it. I won't like it, but I'll do it." He never took his eyes off Sam. If she needed this from him he'd do it for her, for their relationship. He wanted her to have that trust. They didn't need the money, but Sam needed this. It was important to Ty that always had everything she wanted or needed. She was intimidated by his wealth. This money would help make things a little more level, or equal in her eyes. Maybe they would finally be partners in every way.

"Bring Tom back in and see what you can do," Sam told Thomas. "Make your changes and we'll sign the paperwork. I do trust you. I know you'll take care of Ty if something happens to me and I know you'll take care of me if anything happens to him. Since we're never splitting up the rest really doesn't matter."

"I agree," Ty said pulling Sam against him and kissing her with more emotion than he intended. He could feel Sam's worries melting away. They were in this together. And he had to admit, if she signed the same contract he did, that would help Sam feel like they had equal standing. If the tables were turned, he'd have done the same thing.

Thomas instructed Tom to make the necessary changes. Tom agreed to all of them. He didn't understand, they weren't really changing anything. But if that's what they wanted, he'd make the changes and they could sign the paperwork in the morning. Within minutes, Tom was headed for his room to work on the new contracts. The rest of the group said goodnight and headed for bed.

* * * *

Shortly after the helicopter arrived with Nick and Dante, Bastian and Kylee stepped into Bastian's room. Bastian closed the door softly behind them. Tonight was the night. He was going to ask Kylee to marry him. Nick brought the ring as requested but before Bastian could get it from his fellow warrior, he had to listen to Dante ramble on about an epidemic and warriors dropping like flies. Bastian was a little amused. Dante was sort of right. It was strange that so many warriors had found their mates in such a short period of time, but he agreed with Victor. He never would have met Kylee if it wasn't for this war. They were both in the same profession, chances were good they eventually would have run into each other somehow. But he truly believed it would have been years down the road. Now that he knew Kylee, he didn't want to wait another day.

Chaos

"Do you want to watch a little TV before we call it a night?" Kylee asked walking toward the television.

"No," Bastian said immediately. He walked to the bed and casually sat down, pushing himself backwards until he was leaning against the headboard. "Can I talk to you about something?"

"Sure," Kylee immediately agreed. She walked to the bed and sat next to Bastian, curious about his change in mood.

Bastian pulled Kylee against him. He was feeling a little nervous. He thought they were ready for this but what if Kylee said no?

Kylee rested her head against Bastian's chest. She liked it when he held her close like this. She really liked it when he ran his fingers through her hair. She casually reached up and pulled the elastic from her ponytail. Her long silky strands instantly fell to her shoulders. Kylee absently lifted her hand to her head. She was about to comb her fingers through her hair to settle the mess when Bastian stopped her.

"Let me," he said running one hand over Kylee's head.

Kylee relaxed again, resting her head on Bastian's chest. They sat there for a long time quietly enjoying the feel of each other. "I thought you wanted to talk to me," Kylee finally said.

"I do," Bastian said softly. He took a deep breath. "Kylee, I love you."

Kylee sat up and studied Bastian. She knew he had something on his mind but was it something good or something bad? "I love you, too." She assured him, leaning in to kiss him gently.

Bastian gave her half a smile. "I'm glad," he paused. "I want you to know I've never felt this way about any other woman in my life. I truly believe you are my soulmate. I feel like we were meant for each other. I want to be with you forever, Kylee."

Kylee didn't move. She couldn't breathe. What was Bastian leading up to? "I want to be with you, too."

"Will you marry me, Kylee?" Bastian asked.

Kylee's eyes began to water. "Are you serious?" she asked. "I mean, is this a hypothetical someday question, or are you really proposing?"

Bastian pulled the ring from his pocket. "I'm really proposing," he told her holding it out for her to see. "I want to marry you Kylee. I want to marry you right away. Will you make me the happiest man alive and agree to be my wife?"

Kylee touched the ring. It was so beautiful.

Bastian took Kylee's left hand and held it gently, waiting for an answer. "I need a yes or no," he finally told her.

"Yes," Kylee whispered. She watched as Bastian slid the ring onto her finger. "Bastian it's so beautiful. I've never seen anything like it before."

"It was my mother's," he told her. "I hope that's okay. Dad gave it to me a few years after she died. Mom would have liked knowing my wife would wear her ring forever, but if that bothers you I'll buy you something else."

"No," Kylee closed her hand so Bastian couldn't take it. "I love it. I loved it the moment I saw it. Knowing it was your mother's makes me love it even more." She flung her arms around Bastian's neck and kissed him long and hard. "I love you, Bastian. I would be honored to be your wife."

"I'm glad, because it would be an honor to be your husband." He was so happy. He knew with this woman by his side all his dreams would finally become reality. He stood and wrapped his arms around Kylee's waist, pulling her gently but securely against his chest. "You have just made me the happiest man in the world," he whispered softly before placing a soft kiss to the side of her neck. "I want to celebrate our future, right now, with you. How about champagne? Maybe I can find some downstairs."

"How about this?" Kylee leapt upwards, wrapping her legs around Bastian's waist as she kissed him passionately. Bastian caught her easily and moved one hand to her thigh to support her weight.

Moments later Bastian pivoted to the side and set Kylee back on the bed. "That works too," he laughed as Kylee reached up and pulled him on top of her.

Bastian pushed himself up on one elbow. "I wanted to talk to you about when," he told her hesitantly.

"When?" she asked. "When we are going to get married?"

"Yes," Bastian said studying her. The next part was going to be just as difficult as the first. "I don't want to wait," he paused. "But I know some women have specific dreams about how their wedding will be. I'd like to get married right away, but if that ruins plans you've always had I guess we can wait a little while."

Kylee thought about it. She knew some girls started making wedding plans when they were teens. She hadn't. She didn't really have any plans or dreams to consider. "To be honest, I never really thought about my wedding. I'm not sure I ever really believed I would have one." She smiled at Bastian. "Not waiting sounds good to me. What exactly did you have in mind?"

"Are you busy tomorrow?" he asked hopefully.

Kylee laughed. "Are you serious?" she paused, watching Bastian. "Of course you are." She considered what he was saying. Rand was still here, and so was her father. She didn't really have any other friends besides her new supernatural ones and they were all here at the fort. "Everyone that I care about is here. But what about you. Is there anyone missing that you want to invite to your wedding?"

"Not really," Bastian told her. It was mostly true.

"Who?" Kylee asked. "There's someone missing, who is it?"

"The warriors are like my brothers," he began. "They are the most important ones, and Marta and Jake of course."

"Right. But they're all here. Who do you want at the wedding that's missing?" Kylee asked.

"Oberon. Ariel's father," Bastian paused. "He's always been very good to me. I never actually thought I'd get married. It seemed so unlikely that I'd ever open up to anyone this way. After a few hundred years you kind of give up on love coming your way. Anyway it never seemed like a real possibility, but I always thought if somehow I ever did find a mate, it would be Oberon that married me."

"Oh," Kylee processed that. She didn't really care who married them. Maybe Oberon could get here in time to be involved.

Chaos

"Could he fly out? Do you think he could get here in the next day or two? We could wait."

"I think shifters have more specific ceremonies than warriors do. We don't really have our own customs. We just use the fae's. It seemed...convenient I guess and warriors usually marry fae anyway," Bastian paused. "But shifters do have ceremonies and customs to consider. I realize you are new to that world, but it's what you are Kylee. We should talk to Morrigan and Abby and if you're comfortable, your father. They could tell us what we need to know. Then we can go from there. I think there are requirements on who performs the ceremony."

"I'd like to talk to my father," Kylee decided. "Ceremonies might be different when you come from different packs. He's my father. If I'm going to accept that, I also need to accept his ways and customs. The ceremony should be performed in accordance with his traditions."

Bastian kissed Kylee again. "I think that's a good way to think about it." He was proud of Kylee. She was dealing with all of this so well.

"We've had several of those video meetings. Could Oberon attend the wedding by video?" Kylee asked hopefully.

"Maybe," Bastian said considering the possibility. "He has one of those setups in his home. Alex installed them in each of the council member's houses just in case they needed to meet. It's too dangerous to have all the council members in one place right now. Unfortunately, the study's not big enough to hold all the guests and a wedding. Don't worry about it. My brothers are here, that's all that really matters."

"I bet Sam could fix that problem. I'll talk to her tomorrow and see if she can move the system to a more appropriate setting. Then, you can talk to Oberon and make sure he's available to attend." Kylee was considering their conversation. Were they really planning a wedding? "Are you sure you're serious about wanting to marry me tomorrow?"

"I am," Bastian studied her. "How do you feel about that, honestly?"

"I think it's doable. It will have to be in the early evening. I need time to get a dress and set things up, but we don't want to be out after dark. There's not a lot I need to do though, so I think we can actually make this happen. It's kind of Déjà vu. I never thought I'd follow in Sam and Ty's footsteps. Their wedding was so beautiful. I doubt I can pull off that kind of event in such a short amount of time, but I'm okay with that if you are."

"Our wedding will be beautiful and memorable. I promise," Bastian said laying back and pulling Kylee in close. "I'm so glad you're okay with this. I want to marry you right away," he told her, emotion coming through in his voice. "I love you more than anything in the world. I can't wait for you to be my wife." He sat up and studied Kylee. "I can't wait to make love to you."

Kylee smiled. "Why wait?" she asked playfully.

"Nope," Bastian shook his head. "We're going to do this right. In honor of your mother and the values she taught you. We're going to wait until tomorrow night. I won't be with you until you are my wife."

Kylee was touched. Once again she wondered how she had ever thought Bastian was selfish. She had been so monumentally stupid. She'd almost lost this special, wonderful man because she

Chaos

was too stubborn to listen to him. Well, she'd never do that again. "I guess I should thank you for that, but right now I'm not sure I'm happy about your chivalry."

"Of course you are," he smiled at her. "You ready for bed?"

Kylee nodded, then moved to the bathroom to change. She walked back to the bed and climbed in next to Bastian. "I think I like your bedroom better than mine," she observed. "It's bigger. That hardly seems fair. I mean, I've been here longer and more often than you. Why did you get the bigger room?"

Bastian laughed. "Necessity," he finally told her. "This room was...outfitted for a warrior. We have special needs."

"Oh, the hidden fridge in the closet?" Kylee guessed.

"Exactly, among other things," Bastian said pulling Kylee against his body. "Now go to sleep. We have a busy day tomorrow." He gave her a gentle and loving kiss. "Goodnight baby." He still couldn't believe that by this time tomorrow night Kylee would be his wife.

Kylee flung her leg over Bastian's and moved closer. She traced her finger over his lips then moved in for a kiss.

Moments later Bastian pushed her away. "I want to do the right thing here, but I only have so much resolve. Go to sleep. We've waited this long, we can hold off until tomorrow night." He kissed her gently on the temple then forced her to roll over and held her against him, spoon style.

Kylee was so excited she didn't think she'd get any sleep. Surprisingly after only a few minutes her eyes grew heavy and she silently drifted into a deep, restful slumber.

Bastian lay awake for over an hour watching Kylee sleep. He was happier than he'd ever been and grateful he'd met Kylee during this time in his life. He was also a little sad. He wished his parents were alive. He wished they could be at the wedding. Mostly, he wished they had the opportunity to meet the woman he loved. The wedding would be special, he'd make sure of it. But he also knew his parent's absence would leave a hole. No matter what arrangements he made, his wedding day could never be perfect without them. He assumed Kylee felt the same way. Her father would be there, but she had to be just as sad as he was that her mother couldn't attend such an important event. He'd just have to work harder to make the day special. He could never fill the void, but he would make sure Kylee knew how much she was loved.

Chapter Eleven

Kylee woke before Bastian. That was unusual. He was always such an early riser. She studied him, lying there so peacefully. It was hard to believe such a hot, sexy man was going to be hers for all of eternity. Her gaze fell to his masculine chest. She wanted to reach out and touch it, but she was afraid that would wake him up and he probably needed the rest.

"I can feel you staring," Bastian mumbled groggily, still not opening his eyes. "It's impossible to sleep with you gawking so loudly."

Kylee's heartbeat practically jumped from her chest when Bastian smiled that sexy grin of his just before his eyes slowly slid open. "Not funny," she mumbled as she threw off the covers and swung her legs around in an attempt to climb from the bed.

"Not so fast missy," Bastian replied as he snaked his arms around her waist. Before her mind registered his intent, Bastian lifted her small frame back to the center of the bed. Seconds later the gorgeous warrior hovered above her, elbows on either side of her head to support his weight. His taught body was pressed seductively against hers, locking her in place. She should feel trapped, but the only thing her mind registered at the moment was desire. "I want a proper good morning before you rush off." Kylee watched as Bastian lowered his head and lovingly kissed her temple, then her cheek and her jawline, then down her throat and finally her collarbone.

Kylee willingly accepted that her mind had turned to mush. If this was how her mornings would begin for the rest of her life, she was definitely game. But wait! A niggling thought grew into a full-blown panic as she remembered where she was. Morning breath! Kylee braced her feet against the bed and her hands against Bastian's masculine chest in a futile attempt to push him away. She had to escape, but Bastian was not cooperating. He continued pressing tiny kisses along her neck, her jawline, her cheekbone. Kylee wiggled her body and began to panic even more. She needed to get away and fast. "I have to go to the bathroom before I can give you a proper good morning. So don't even try to kiss me until I take care of a few things," she growled, annoyed that Bastian was completely unaffected by her protests.

Bastian had no intention of letting Kylee get away. She was being ridiculous but he would humor her…this time. He continued to press gentle kisses to Kylee's neck then took her earlobe in his mouth as he reached out with one hand and silently opened the nightstand drawer. A couple seconds later he was holding a peppermint breath strip. "Open up," he teased.

Kylee narrowed her eyes and studied the item in Bastian's hand. Where had that come from? "I guess that will work just this once, but for the record I prefer the chocolate mints." Kylee tried

Chaos

to sound disinterested and aloof. "If I'm going to be your wife, I expect to be pampered. You know, my husband should spare no expense to give me what I want and all that. You do want me to be happy don't you?" Kylee grinned as she fluttered her eyelashes. She was surprised when Bastian placed the strip on her tongue and waited patiently for it to dissolve.

Bastian waited a few seconds then responded. "You think your being coy, but you have no idea my dear. I like buying things for you. I enjoy taking care of you." Bastian shifted to the side then softly ran a hand down one arm. When he reached her hand, he pressed their palms together then gently entwined their fingers, never taking his eyes off hers. The act was the most romantic thing Kylee had ever experienced. The man took her breath away with the smallest of gestures. Seconds later, Bastian wrapped his other arm around her waist and pulled her body against his. "As soon as you are my wife, I am going to spoil you rotten," he knew the strip would be dissolved by then so he pressed his mouth to hers and savored the moment. The kiss was passionate and filled with so much emotion Kylee never wanted it to end. Finally, Bastian lifted his head and smiled at her again. "I agree, I like the chocolate better." He kissed Kylee's forehead then climbed off the bed holding a hand out to help her up. "You want the first shower?" Bastian asked casually as he walked to the sitting area and began to make coffee.

Kylee blinked in surprise then sobered as reality set in. They would need to get started if they wanted to pull off a wedding this evening. "You go ahead. I think I'll head to my room and get some fresh clothes." She walked over to Bastian. "I've been thinking about everything we need to do today since I woke up, and to be honest I'm a little overwhelmed."

Bastian pulled her into his arms. "I don't want you to stress about this. We'll just take things one at a time. The first thing we need to do is break the news to everyone. Once we do, we're going to have tons of help. I promise, our wedding will be wonderful."

"Well, one of the things I've been thinking about is breaking the news to everyone." She moved backwards so she could look Bastian in the eyes. "I was wondering if you would mind terribly if we talked to my father and Rand first. I know that's not fair. The other warriors are as much family to you as my father and my brother are to me. I was just hoping..."

"Shhh," Bastian said softly placing his forefinger over her lips. "I think that's a good idea. We'll both shower then meet back up to look for Caleb and Rand. Once we've talked to them, we'll have a better idea what preparations we need to make today anyway. Hopefully the two of them will join us while we tell everyone else. Caleb can compare ceremonies with Abby and Morrigan and we'll all be on the same page." He smiled at the grateful look she was giving him.

"Why are you amused?" Kylee was already feeling self-conscious, she hated it when Bastian laughed at her.

"Because you thought we were going to argue over that. I don't mind talking to your father first. And if we're going to talk to him, it's only natural to have Rand present as well. The warriors are like family, but those two *are* your family," he paused. "But I do have one request."

"Anything," Kylee said instantly.

"Once we're finished with your family, I'd like to talk to Marta alone. Maybe while I talk to her, you could gather everyone into the study," he requested.

Chaos

"Okay," Kylee said hesitantly. She was a little hurt that Bastian wanted to talk to Marta without her.

"I need this, Kylee. Marta's been like a mother to me. Sometimes she was the only one I could talk to. We just need a moment alone. Then I'll bring her to the study to hear the details with everyone else." Bastian wanted this as much for Kylee as for himself. He was hoping Marta would agree to make Kylee a wedding cake for tonight, but he wanted it to be a surprise.

"Okay," Kylee agreed. Bastian was right. He deserved a private moment with the woman that had stepped in for his mother. A thought hit her unexpectedly. Bastian didn't have any family left. She knew how that felt. After her mother died she'd been so alone. It made her sad every time she thought about her mother not attending the wedding, but she had her brother and her father now. Bastian didn't have anyone. If he needed time with Marta to make up for that, she'd give it to him. "Bastian, I'm sorry you don't have any family that can attend the wedding. I know how it feels to be alone. Finding my father and discovering Rand is my brother was a miracle, but before that I was alone too. I know how hard that can be, particularly on special occasions."

Bastian kissed Kylee's temple. "I know you do. And you're my family now. I have the other warriors and they're like brothers to me, I also have Marta, but you're my real family now," Bastian smiled. "Go shower, we have a busy day ahead of us."

Bastian, Kylee, Caleb and Rand sat on the back porch. It was starting to get chilly. Bastian was sure it would snow in the next few weeks. He was waiting for Kylee to take the lead, but she seemed nervous. "Caleb?" Bastian began. He casually took Kylee's hand to give her confidence. "Kylee and I have decided to get married."

"I see," Caleb said soberly. He'd seen this coming but still wondered what this meeting was all about.

Rand was watching Kylee, she looked happy. He knew she loved Bastian. Not that long ago she'd been so sure things were over for good between them. He'd been sure she was wrong. "When's the big day?" he asked her enthusiastically.

"Today," Kylee answered hesitantly.

Rand laughed. "You never were a procrastinator," he shifted his gaze to Bastian. "Well, you're going to strap on the old ball and chain anyway so I guess there's no reason to wait. You might as well drown immediately."

Bastian lifted Kylee's hand to his lips. "I have a slightly different viewpoint on the matter, but I guess the outcome is the same."

"So why are we sitting out here in the cold?" Caleb asked. "Are you here to ask my permission?"

Bastian studied Caleb Turner. "I suppose," he finally answered. "But mostly we wanted your help. Neither of us know a lot about shifters. We aren't familiar with their traditions and ceremonies. We were hoping you could help us with that."

"As my father," Kylee said quickly, "I also wanted you to be the first to know." She glanced at Rand. "And as my brother I wanted you to be here, too. I know this might seem sudden but..."

"Kylee," Caleb stopped her. "The moment I met the two of you, I could tell you were in love. I told you then, Amanda and I fell in love and got married almost immediately. I wanted as much time with her as I could possibly have. I know it's not the same.

Chaos

With us, she was human and I wasn't. I knew sixty or so years with her would never be enough. Look at what happened. I didn't get my sixty years. If we'd waited, I would have missed out on so much. I'm flattered that you wanted to tell me first and I'd be happy to explain the wedding ritual to you." Caleb settled into his chair and began to describe his people's ceremony in detail. When he was finished he glanced at Rand. "I'd suggest you have Rand perform the ribbon ceremony. You two are close and it should be family."

"What family member typically does that?" Kylee asked.

"Uh, well..." Caleb paused. "Normally it would be the woman's father. If he's not available the next closest relative. But since you barely know me, I think you would be more comfortable with Rand doing that."

Rand studied his father. "What if I'm not comfortable with it?" he asked. Caleb was Kylee's father. He'd missed out on most of her life. He shouldn't miss out on this. Rand knew if Caleb didn't do this, both father and daughter would regret it later on. Eventually these two would develop a strong relationship. They were already developing a bond. He wouldn't let either of them miss out on something so important. He knew they would always be close, Kylee had already accepted Caleb as her father.

Kylee was watching Rand. She wanted her father to do this, but she didn't want to offend Rand. Was he serious or was he just trying to give her a way out?

"I'm not comfortable as the center of attention, you know that Kylee," Rand continued. "Plus, I don't know these customs. I'm certainly not comfortable trying to perform some ceremony I have never even witnessed. I'll participate in any other way, but not with this. You're just going to have to find someone else," Rand said vehemently.

Rand wasn't comfortable with public speaking, Kylee knew that. Maybe he was telling the truth. "I'd really like it if you would perform the ceremony," Kylee told Caleb. "You said it's typically the woman's father that does this. You're my father. I know we're still getting to know each other, but I'd really like you to do this for me. If you're willing."

Caleb couldn't speak. He'd missed out on so many important milestones with his kids. He'd missed Kylee's first steps, her prom, her high school graduation. He just assumed he'd also miss out on this. He blinked several times, trying to hide the moisture forming in his eyes. "Are you sure?" he finally choked out.

"Positive," she said hugging him tightly. "Now you just have to come up with a job for Rand." She smiled at her longtime friend. She was still getting used to the fact that he was really her brother. "I'd like him to be involved too somehow."

"I think I have the perfect job for him." Caleb continued to explain the ceremony and the role other family members usually played. Especially the role Rand would be playing in Kylee's wedding.

An hour later the large group sat in the study wondering what this was all about. Kylee wasn't saying a word. She was silently waiting for Bastian to arrive. The entire group turned their attention to the door when they heard someone come in. It had to be Bastian, Marta and Jake. The trio entered the room laughing, then sobered when the saw they were the focus of attention.

Dimitri was the first to speak. He knew what this was about, but that didn't mean he had to make it easy on his friend. "I'm so glad you finally decided to join us, Bastian."

Chaos

Before Dimitri could ruin his mood Bastian decided to cut him off. "No problem," he said joyfully. "Sorry you guys had to wait, it didn't take as long as I anticipated for Kylee to get you all together." Bastian walked over to Kylee and took her hand, pulling her to her feet then walking to the front of the room. "We've decided to get married," he announced. "And since everyone is here already, we thought we'd do it tonight."

Victor laughed, spraying coke across the floor. He'd been a little surprised at Ty's abrupt wedding, but not that shocked. Ty was pretty spontaneous and at the time Ty's family was here, so were all the warriors. Plus, Ty and Sam had that extra bond. But this was shocking. Bastian was so careful and cautious. Everything he did was detailed and meticulously thought out. He wasn't at all spontaneous. Maybe Kylee was good for him.

Alex stood, walked to Kylee and pulled her into a big bear hug. "Congratulations," she smiled at the couple. "It sounds like we have our work cut out for us. I've been planning my wedding for close to a year now and I still have tons to do," she shrugged. "Sometimes I wish I was just a normal fae. Then I could have a normal wedding instead of this monumental, extravagant event. You have no idea how lucky you are."

Kylee glanced at Bastian. "I think I have a pretty good idea." She looked back at the rest of the group. "I know this seems sudden, but we don't want to wait. I don't need anything big or fancy. I just want to be Bastian's wife." She shifted her attention to Caleb. "Dad would you mind explaining your pack's ceremony to the group. I'd like to hear if it's the same or different than Abby and Morrigan's pack."

A short time later, the group disbursed. Nick and Dante admitted they were prepared for this. Once Bastian asked for the ring, the two of them made the rounds and brought suits for all the men just in case they needed them. However, the women were on their own. There was no way two bachelors were going to try to pick out dresses for the women. That left the guys free to take care of set up and decorating while the women went shopping. Ty offered up Lillie. She was still at the fort and he thought she could fly the group to Hancock Airport near Syracuse so they could have more options. Romulus didn't have that much to choose from. The women instantly agreed, positive they'd be able to get everything they needed in one trip.

The group split up and frantically began working on wedding preparations. They didn't have a lot of time and they all wanted to throw Kylee the wedding of her dreams.

* * * *

Radek was locked in his room, alone. He continued to pace back and forth. Things were falling apart. Why couldn't he find a competent assistant? He had trusted Hector. That had been a mistake. He still didn't know if Hector and Lilith had hooked up behind his back. That alone infuriated him. But at least when Hector was here, things always went their way. Then, Hector went and got himself killed. Radek had to admit his situation had grown increasingly worse since Hector's death. Lilith had tried to fill that void, but the stupid women kept ending up back at the cave on the verge of death. He was tired of her ineptness. He had mistakenly believed once that human was dead things would improve, but they hadn't. Surely, Sammael was tired of nursing her back to health by now, too.

Radek's thoughts shifted to Sammael. He was small and Radek considered the boy a weakling. But, if it wasn't for Sammael

Chaos

Lilith would be dead this time. How had she been so stupid? She knew she had to avoid the animals she was turning. Obviously she hadn't been up to the task. He considered the situation. It was ironic, really. He'd sent Lilith to the fort believing she would get herself killed or cause enough trouble that the three meddling kings would take care of her for him. Yet, he was the one that sent Sammael out for an update. He couldn't be angry with the kid for saving Lilith's life. Sammael was just showing his loyalty. Radek could tell Sammael didn't care for Lilith either, probably because he doubted Lilith's loyalty to Radek. Now he was going to have to find another way to dispose of her. On top of that, he still didn't know what to do about his other problem.

Even with most of the warriors out at the army facility, he was still losing too many vampires. Out of desperation he'd been sending them to the wilderness to hide out in the caves. But they weren't staying out there. Vampires needed food, groups of them kept wandering into the city. With so few targets, the warriors took the inexperienced vampires out almost immediately. He needed to increase his army, not lose them as soon as they arrived back in town. He needed a plan. He needed a brilliant plan, and he needed it fast.

* * * *

Abby was thrilled. She had the perfect dress and shoes to match. The rest of the women were still rifling through the various racks searching for something they liked. Abby spoke briefly to Alex, paid for her items then excused herself to take care of other necessities. She assured the women she'd meet them back at the plane, then hurried off.

Several hours later, Abby approached the tarmac with her arms full. She was just about to climb the flight of stairs when she noticed Lillie standing in the doorway. The pilot didn't look happy.

"What exactly is that?" Lillie asked pointing to the box Abby was carrying.

"Does it matter?" Abby asked.

"It does if that's produce," Lillie told her. "I haven't done the proper paperwork to transport produce."

"Then it's not produce," Abby said coyly. "Now, do you mind moving out of the way? I kind of have my arms full here." Abby raised an eyebrow in challenge.

Lillie studied the woman. She knew they were planning something important, but she wouldn't lose her livelihood for people she barely knew. "This isn't a joke," Lillie said soberly. "I could lose my license if I allow it."

Abby sighed. So, this wasn't going to be easy. "I'm not sure what you think I have in here but your license is not in jeopardy," Abby told her flatly. "For one thing, you're not transporting anything over state lines, we're not leaving New York. For another, we are flying to a very secure military base. Nobody is going to question you about your cargo once you arrive. And finally, you've informed me I'm not allowed to transport produce. I get it. Now, don't you have some kind of preparations to make before we leave? As enjoyable as this little chat has been, this stuff really is heavy and awkward. I'd like to get my things situated before everyone else arrives."

Lillie studied the woman for another moment before she continued down the stairs and pushed past Abby. She understood the message. Abby wouldn't back down. She was going to do what she wanted. Lillie could fight it or she could pretend she didn't know. Since the party tonight was important to Ty and Sam, Lillie was going to turn a blind eye and hope for the best. Abby was right, nobody was going to bother her once they got in the air. And, if she didn't mention there might be produce on the flight, nobody here would know. It was in everyone's best interest to let this be. She walked to the nose of the plane and began her preflight inspection. She was counting on that saying, hoping it was accurate. With any luck, what she didn't know wouldn't hurt her.

* * * *

Kylee stepped into her room and closed the door. It had been a busy day, but fun. She'd really enjoyed shopping with the women. They were all so accepting of her. For the first time in her life, she felt like she belonged somewhere. She finally belonged. Kylee walked to her bed and slowly sat on the edge. Was this really happening? Was she about to get married? She smiled when she thought of Bastian. Not only married, but married to the most wonderful man in the world. And her father was going to be included in the wedding. She jumped at the knock on the door but quickly regained her composure and rushed to open it.

Kylee wasn't sure who might be knocking, but when she opened the door she saw the last person she expected.

Marta smiled at Kylee's obvious surprise. "I've been sent to escort you to the study," she said softly. "We're going to make you the most beautiful bride ever."

"I know I live in a magical world, but as far as I know that kind of magic doesn't exist." Kylee stepped into the hallway then followed Marta down the stairs.

"No magic required," Marta assured her. "Just you and a little TLC." The two women had reached the study. Marta paused, waiting for Kylee to enter first.

Kylee took one step into the room then stopped in shock. Everyone was here. Alex, Ariel, Sam, Abby, Megan and Tala. She looked back at Marta, who gave her a gentle push, then closed the door securely behind them.

"The star of the evening," Alex said walking to Kylee and pulling her to the middle of the room, then pushing her into a chair.

Kylee was too shocked to respond.

"Any special requests before we get started?" Megan asked.

"Uh, I'd like to still look like me when you're done," Kylee managed.

The women laughed. "Of course you will dear," Marta assured her. "This is so exciting. I loved my wedding, don't get me wrong, but there was no fuss. It was just me and Jake in St. Lucia with strangers. I don't regret it for a minute, but I really wish Alex, Thomas and the rest of my family could have been there."

Alex stepped beside Marta and took her hand. "I wish I could have been there, too."

The entire room jumped when a loud knock interrupted their conversation. "I got it," Sam announced pushing herself off the couch. "If it's Bastian, I'll get rid of him. The groom is not allowed

Chaos

to see the bride before the wedding." Sam flung open the door and froze in surprise. "Oh, uh..." she turned back to Kylee.

"Who is it?" Kylee immediately questioned.

"Your father," Sam said hesitantly, "And a couple of strangers."

Kylee stood and turned to face Sam. "Well go ahead and let them in," she said airily. "There's no rule about the father not seeing the bride is there?" Kylee moved into the doorway. Her gaze fell on Caleb, then moved to the three strangers standing beside him. "The fort is becoming awfully crowded for a restricted area." She grinned at her dad, waiting for an explanation.

"Kylee," Caleb said taking her hand and pulling her to his side. "I'd like you to meet your grandmother, Joanne McBride." His gaze remained on his mother momentarily. "And this is Fritz and Katerina," he motioned to the additional guests.

Joanne's hand covered her mouth. "You look so much like your mother," she finally whispered. "I have to admit, at first I was skeptical. Caleb has been locked up in the old cabin for so long. I worried somehow he'd been fooled. But one look at you and there's no doubt. You are my Caleb's daughter. Mostly you are dear Amanda's daughter. There really is no denying it." Tears formed in the woman's eyes.

"Now mother," Caleb scolded. "We talked about this. Today is Kylee's wedding day. It's a day of happiness. Not a day for crying."

"Nonsense, Caleb." Katerina stepped forward and linked an arm through Joanne's. "Everyone knows women always cry at weddings." Katerina held out a hand to Kylee. "She's right. There's no mistaking it. You are definitely Amanda's daughter. It's a pleasure to meet you." Katerina smiled warmly when Kylee took her hand briefly then let it drop.

Fritz was more cautious. He simply held out his hand in greeting. "Fritz Delacruz," he said flatly then dropped Kylee's hand immediately.

"I have to apologize for my husband," Katerina said at once. "He still thinks this is all impossible. He's not convinced you are who you say you are." She smiled sheepishly at Kylee. "I'm afraid the fact that you are marrying Bastian only puts more doubts in his mind. He thinks this is all a conspiracy to get your hands on our blood."

"Why don't you just give them our bank account number and a few signed checks while you're at it?" Fritz grumbled. "My concerns are none of their business, Katerina."

"Keep it up and I'm going to slip them a vile of my blood. It might be interesting to compare it with what they already have," she said annoyed. "Stop being rude, Fritz. This is important to Caleb."

"Maybe after you meet Rand you'll reconsider," Kylee said trying not to be offended. She turned to her father. "Why don't you take Mr. Delacruz to the warehouse? I think Rand is still helping over there. I'm sure the two of them will need hours to scrutinize each other before they form some kind of truce anyway."

Caleb laughed at Kylee's observation. She was right of course. "Shall we leave then?" he asked his mother.

"I'm not going anywhere," Joanne said, still focusing on Kylee. "Would you do an old woman a favor and allow me to participate in your preparations?"

Chaos

Kylee beamed. "I'd love that," she said enthusiastically. "Katerina, you're welcome to stay as well."

"Thank you. I think I'll do just that." She turned again to Fritz. "Behave," she demanded. "Don't ruin this for Caleb."

"I think you should come with us dear," Fritz objected.

"And I think you should take a Valium. I guess we'll both have to be disappointed." Kat turned and walked into the study away from her husband. Joanne and Kylee followed. Sam shut the door firmly behind them, laughter in her eyes. She liked Katerina Delacruz. Fritz, not so much but his wife was wonderful.

Kat began shaking her head. "I am so sorry about that Kylee," she finally said. "He can be painfully bullheaded at times."

Abby moved in to greet the two new arrivals. "Shifter men are like that," she said casually. "Don't worry about it. The men will straighten him out in no time. You think shifters are bad, wait until he comes up against a group of warriors." She looked at the others and laughed. "They are the most overprotective beings I've ever met."

Katerina relaxed. She knew Caleb wouldn't be fooled about this. There was no way he could accept two strangers as his children unless he was absolutely positive. That was enough for her. The women settled back into a casual routine, laughing and joking the entire time. Katerina and Joanne were accepted instantly. It was nice to have a little girl time. Kat missed that. She hadn't really developed a close friendship with anyone since Amanda's death. Well, her disappearance anyway. She studied Kylee, the woman looked so much like Amanda. Regret engulfed her again, why hadn't Amanda trusted her? So much time had been wasted. She shook off her feelings and focused on Kylee. Today was a day for celebration. Before long Kylee's hair and makeup were perfect and her dress and flowers were prepared.

"Now you just need something old," Joanne observed. She reached into her pocket and pulled out a beautiful diamond necklace. "This was my grandmother's," Joanne explained. "She gave it to me on my wedding day. Now, I'd like you to have it."

"Oh, I couldn't," Kylee gasped. "It's too..."

"Please Kylee," Joanne insisted. "I thought my grandchildren were gone forever. You have no idea how devastating that was. We all knew Caleb would never remarry. Now here you are, all grown up and getting married yourself. I need you to accept this small gift from me. It will make me feel like I'm truly a part of your life now. I desperately want to be part of your life. I hope you will allow that. I'll take whatever I can get, big or small. I just want to get to know you and your brother."

Kylee jumped up and hugged her grandmother. "Thank you so much!" she exclaimed. "I would like that very much. I'm not sure how often Bastian and I will get out to California, but I hope you won't mind if we stop by for a visit when we do. I think you should know that mom did talk about you and my grandfather. She was very careful not to tell me your names, but she talked about my father's parents sometimes. She loved you very much and I know she missed you," Kylee turned to Katerina. "She also told me about you. She wouldn't tell me your name either, but she talked about her best friend. I hope I have the chance to get to know you as well."

"Thank you," Katerina said, emotion in her voice. "It's hard knowing Amanda was alive all that time and she never contacted me. I have to admit the knowledge has been hard to accept. It hurt so much to lose my friend to death. I think it hurts more knowing I lost her to fear."

Chaos

"I know," Kylee said with understanding. "The first would have been out of mom's control. The second was her choice."

"Exactly," Kat said trying to compose herself.

"I hope you know, mom didn't see it that way though. I know she didn't look at what she did as a choice. She saw it as a necessity. I understand that now. She never opened up to anyone, not even me. Not really. I know she missed your friendship almost as much as she missed my father."

Sam stepped in. "I know you need to talk about this, but after all that work on Kylee's makeup I'd hate to see her cry." She smiled at her friend. "Come on Doc," Sam said giving her a little tug. "You need to get into your dress and we need to find your father. It's almost time for the ceremony to begin."

"Not so fast," Marta stepped in. "Kylee, you stay here and get dressed. I'll go find your father. We don't want to ruin the surprise. Your wedding will be more special if you and Bastian see each other for the first time when you walk down the aisle."

"Good idea," Katerina said. "I'll help you find Caleb." The two women headed for the door.

The rest of the group began to funnel out of the room as well. Kylee watched Katerina leave. She could see why her mother was so fond of the woman. Kylee barely knew her, but she already liked her.

Joanna stepped up beside Kylee. "She's a very special lady," she said softly, watching Katerina disappear down the hall.

"Huh?" Kylee asked. "Oh, aren't you going to join them?"

"Would you mind terribly if I waited here with you?" Joanne asked. "I could help you with your dress."

"Of course not," Kylee said pulling the dress off the hanger and walking back toward Joanna. "My mother couldn't help but talk about Katerina. Mom never mentioned her name, but she talked about a very special woman. It was obvious mom missed her best friend very much."

"Like I said, Kat is a special lady," Joanne repeated. "She's just as beautiful on the inside as she is on the outside. I refer to it as having a pure soul. My William was like that. I wish he could have met you, Kylee. He would have loved you instantly." Joanne grew silent, lost in her memories for the moment.

"William was my grandfather?" Kylee asked, turning around so her grandmother could secure the back of her dress.

"Yes," Joanne said softly. "And he too was a special man. You couldn't know him and not love him. He would have been so thrilled to learn you and your brother survived that awful war," Joanne paused. "Caleb says there is a war going on here, between the vampires and this group you are part of. Is that true?"

"It is," Kylee said hesitantly. What was her grandmother getting at?

"I don't suppose there's any chance you could just come back to California with us and forget the conflict altogether, could you?" Joanne asked.

"No," Kylee said honestly. "That's not something I'd consider even if I didn't have Bastian. I wouldn't abandon my friends and run to safety. But Bastian has responsibilities here. He's a warrior. That's what he does. He protects his people. He would never consider going away and I would never consider leaving his side."

"I kind of guessed that's what you would say, but I had to try," Joanne admitted. "It's just that I thought I lost you to war a long time ago. I don't think I could bare losing you again. Is Rand as devoted to the cause as you are?" Joanne asked.

"I think so," Kylee told her. "We haven't actually talked about it, but I think he's in this as much as I am. He's made a lot of friends in the shifter community in a very short amount of time. I really don't think he would abandon them now. He's another kind of warrior, I guess you could say. I think that's why he became a cop. Rand is loyal and protective of those he loves. He has a very strong sense of right and wrong and he won't tolerate wrong in his presence. He's another one of those pure souls you were talking about. I guess he takes after our father and grandfather."

"Maybe you don't realize it but you do too," Joanne assured her. "Caleb hasn't been himself for a very long time, but before all this happened he was fearless and larger than life. I heard how you followed a patient out here because you thought she was being abused by a husband or her boyfriend. Not many people would sacrifice time and money like that just to make sure a patient was safe. But you did. Caleb is like that too," Joanna smiled. "You look like... and in some ways act like your mother, but you also have a lot of my son in you. Please be careful. Don't put yourself at risk unnecessarily."

"I promise," Kylee said soberly, slipping into her shoes.

"Now enough of that," Joanne said casually as she swiped her hand in dismissal. "I want to hear all about this man you are going to marry. Tell me about Bastian Carrigan. Tell me how you two met and why you fell in love."

494

Kylee smiled and began telling her grandmother about the man she was about to marry.

* * * *

Katerina followed the other women to a large building located on the military compound. She knew they had converted their workout gym into a reception hall. Katerina envisioned wooden floors and workout mats. She wondered what kind of wedding this would be in such a masculine setting. But, who was she to talk. Her wedding was a simple ceremony, held in a lonely forest with a couple of friends. Nothing spectacular, no crowd to celebrate, but it was one of the most cherished memories she had.

The women ascended the stairs and entered an enchanted room. That was the only word Katerina could think of to describe it. The area was large and well lit. Half a dozen enormous windows circled the room letting in just the right amount of light. The floor was covered in beige carpet and small trees were systematically distributed around the room. Each tree was adorned with hundreds of sparkling white lights. Flowers were tastefully scattered throughout the area creating an intimate garden feeling. Rows of chairs were set up to accommodate guests. There was a large aisle down the center of the room for the bride to make her dramatic entrance. There was also a white archway covered in vine and delicate flowers centered at the front of the aisle.

Katerina's gaze moved slowly around the room, taking in the magical scene until she spotted her husband. Fritz was sitting in the far corner with Caleb and several other men. The entire group was laughing boisterously and carrying on. Kat sighed. She would never understand men, not completely. Fritz was so rude to Kylee, but here he was now laughing and joking. All signs of anger were

Chaos

gone. Kat continued to watch her husband and sobered. She knew he was angry, but was he acting this way because he still felt guilty? Probably. They were both devastated that day, forty years ago. Thinking about Caleb's panicked call still sent chills running down her spine. Caleb had trusted them. They were responsible for Kylee's safety in Caleb's absence. Believing Amanda and her infant daughter were killed on their watch had been so hard to live with all these years. Fritz never really recovered. The guilt seemed to worsen after the birth of their twins. Then, things got even worse after Caleb's phone call. Discovering Amanda had escaped and gone into hiding with her infant child seemed to push Fritz over the edge. He was so angry these days. Katerina hoped he would eventually get over it. It was unfair to blame Kylee for her mother's actions. Surely Fritz would realize that.

Kat took a step toward Fritz then stopped. She was still angry with him. Maybe a little more time to herself would be better. She took a deep breath then turned and headed in the opposite direction, following Abby and Ariel across the room. She silently approached the two women who had stopped in front of the far wall. Abby was the first to notice her.

"Hey," Abby said in greeting.

"I wondered if you could use my help with anything," Katerina said studying the small table in front of them. "Oh, good. You were able to get the star fruit. That's one thing I missed at my wedding. We had to use wild berries instead. It wasn't the same of course. There's nothing like the sweet but slightly tangy taste of star fruit. I love the way it crunches like an apple but it's sweet like pineapple and kiwi," Katerina smiled. "It's like three fruits all in one."

"For me it has more of a citrus tastes mixed with apples and like you said… tangy," Abby added. "We were lucky. I almost had to leave it at the airport." Abby hesitated only a moment before changing the subject. "It looks like your husband is in better spirits."

Katerina glanced in her husband's direction. "I'm sorry for his bad behavior, he's not usually like that."

"It's not us you need to apologize to," Ariel said flatly. "It's Kylee."

Kat nodded sadly.

"I could understand if Fritz was skeptical," Abby said looking in his direction. "This all happened so fast and from the outside I'm sure it seems unbelievable. But that's not what Fritz was feeling when he met Kylee earlier today. Fritz was angry, I could smell it. Why is your husband mad at Kylee?"

"Strange, isn't it?" Katerina began. "After taking that nectar every day for years, a real biological change occurred in us. Our scent is gone completely. Yet, nothing can mask the aroma of fear, anger or even love." She almost sounded sad by the revelation.

"It sounds like you're trying to avoid the question," Ariel said impatiently. "Why is your husband angry with Kylee?"

Katerina smiled. "It's nice to know Kylee has such loyal friends," she sighed. "I'm not really avoiding your question, maybe just stalling a bit. It's difficult to explain. But honestly, Fritz is not angry with Kylee. He's angry with her mother, Amanda. We both are. Amanda's actions caused so many of us so much pain, including herself. It's more complicated because Kylee looks so much like her mother. It's hard to look at her and not think of Amanda. Anyway, Fritz is angry but mostly he just feels guilty."

"Guilty? Why?" Abby asked.

"Because we were Kylee and Scottie's Padrini," Katerina said solemnly.

"Oh!" Abby exclaimed in understanding. She studied Katerina. "You do know none of this was your responsibility though, right? You know there was nothing you could have done to stop what happened, don't you?"

Katerina shrugged.

"What's a Padrini?" Ariel asked, confused.

"It's sort of like godparents," Abby explained. "But more, I guess. When a shifter accepts the honor of being a child's Padrini, they promise to protect that child forever. Most Padrini's are close relatives, mainly brothers or sisters. But as we all know, you don't have to be tied by blood to have a close relationship with someone. If it was your custom," Abby said turning to Ariel, "Dimitri would be your padrino or godfather. It makes sense that Caleb would ask Fritz and Katerina to be their children's Padrini. From what I hear they were closer than brothers."

"Yes. They are," Katerina answered softly.

"Okay, but nobody can protect a child totally and completely unless they live with them. Unless they are by their side 24/7," Ariel countered thinking of her kidnapping and the impact it had on Bastian. "If you and Fritz have carried that kind of guilt all these years, it's time to put it behind you. I understand feeling that way at first, but eventually you had to realize there was nothing you could have done to save them," Ariel pressed. She wasn't entirely sure Dimitri had forgiven himself for the horror she had experienced as a teen.

"I appreciate your kindness, but we were responsible for Kylee at the time," Kat explained. "We knew Caleb and Scottie were on their way to Redding for the ceremony. We knew Amanda and Kylee were alone and vulnerable. That's why we stayed behind, to protect them. But we failed the entire family. We made a promise and we didn't keep it. It doesn't matter that our enemies didn't kill Amanda and Kylee. What matters is that Caleb trusted us and we didn't uphold our end of the deal. As a result, something happened that scared Amanda. Something so terrifying she fled the area and hid out in New Jersey. That tells volumes. I would never tell Caleb this, but Amanda was not cut out for our world. I don't think we'll ever know what sent her running. I'm sure she panicked. But honestly, I don't understand how she could live with her aunt instead of coming to us for help."

"You say that like there were problems with the aunt," Ariel observed.

"Don't get me wrong, Amanda loved her Aunt Hazel. She just detested her lifestyle. Hazel was your typical spinster. She never married because she couldn't get along with anyone. She hated Caleb, mostly because he took her niece away. The only person that could tolerate Hazel for any length of time was Amanda. But as much as Amanda loved her aunt, she couldn't even take her annoying quirks for long," Kat looked up at the two women. "I just don't understand how she could live for thirty five years without contacting me. She had to know we could protect her. Like I said before, Amanda's fear and inability to cope in our world caused so much pain for so many people." A tear ran down Katerina's face and she slowly wiped it away.

Chaos

"Why do you think Amanda wasn't made for our world?" Abby asked. "Kylee fit in immediately. Even when she thought she was human, she did just fine. In fact, Kylee was amazing in battle. Some of that had to come from her mother."

Katerina smiled. "Kylee fought in a battle? Against who?"

"You sound amused," Abby observed.

"Not amused," Katerina corrected. "Proud."

"Trust me that battle was nothing to joke about," Abby said seriously. "Several hundred vampires attacked the fort. That's when Rand finally accepted his gift and joined us. Kylee paired up with Bastian. She had to be terrified, but she valiantly and fearlessly joined our small group and fought off vampire after vampire, until the threat was neutralized. We were grossly outnumbered, but she never faltered. That kind of courage is unusual."

"I agree," Katerina said softly. "Does Caleb know about this? He's going to be so proud of her. It will demonstrate to him how much his daughter takes after her father."

"Not unless Kylee told him," Ariel said narrowing her eyes. This wasn't the reaction she'd expected.

"Do you mind if I tell him?" Katerina asked, excited. She glanced at the two women and realized they were annoyed at her. Well, she couldn't blame them. She wasn't really answering their questions. "I'm not surprised Kylee was fearless and competent in battle," Katerina told them. "But she gets that from her father, not her mother. Amanda was shaken from the beginning. I realized that immediately. The night the four of us fled to the forest, Amanda and I were attacked. Fraunz sent one of his shifters after us, a tracker. Amanda was near hysterics by the time I took care of the threat. It took me a long time to calm her down. I never did calm her completely. She finally regained her composure, but it took a lot to convince her she needed to be strong for Caleb. She tried hard, she really did, but every day was a struggle for her. She just couldn't deal with the constant fear. I know she never really got used to our life. Even in peaceful times, living with the supernatural can be difficult. I think it takes a certain type of human to manage it. Amanda loved Caleb more than anything, because of that she really did try hard to cope. She just wasn't strong enough to make it in our world, I guess."

The three stood silently cutting star fruit and placing it on a crystal tray. Nobody really knew how to respond to Katerina's revelations. Moments later, Fritz approached the small group. Kat noticed him, but pretended like he wasn't there.

Fritz maneuvered his body to position it behind his wife, wrapping his arms tightly around her waist. He leaned in and gently kissed her neck. "Are you going to forgive me?" he asked quietly.

"Maybe eventually," Kat said coldly.

"You know, this is supposed to be a celebration," Fritz pointed out. "Neither one of us will be able to celebrate properly if you're angry with me."

"I guess you should have thought of that before you embarrassed us in front of Kylee's friends." Katerina closed her eyes. She couldn't look at Fritz or she'd give in to his charm.

"Well, since they're strangers..." he began then stopped. That was the wrong approach to take with Kat. "I'm sorry," he finally said. "I was wrong."

Chaos

Katerina smiled as she turned to her husband. "Caleb already took care of this himself," she observed, smiling a little. She studied Fritz for a moment then nodded in approval. "Good, he's better at it than I am."

"Better at what?" Abby asked. She was trying not to eavesdrop but they were standing right next to her.

"Better at putting my stubborn husband in his place," Katerina admitted. "I always give in too quickly. I just can't stay mad at him and he knows it." She glanced at Fritz. "I'd be careful though if I were you," she looked at Abby then Ariel and back to Fritz. "Kylee has some pretty loyal friends here. I don't think they'll tolerate anyone insulting her again."

"She's right," Ariel said stepping forward. "I've heard you and Caleb are close."

"Very," Fritz said soberly, he knew he was about to be bullied. He hated being bullied by women.

"So are we," Ariel shrugged. "And there's more of us," she casually flicked her fingers and the two large candles decorating the table burst into flames. Ariel turned, winked at Katerina then casually wandered off. Abby joined her.

"I guess I'm supposed to be intimidated now? Was that your doing?" Fritz asked, studying his wife.

"No," Katerina said casually. "But I did enjoy it. This is a very tight group. I don't think we want to offend them," she smiled. "They told me Kylee's already participated in a battle." Katerina beamed with excitement. "She thought she was human, but she still went out on the battlefield and fought hundreds of vampires with the rest of them."

"Really?" Fritz considered, impressed. "I guess I have underestimated that girl." He pulled Katerina in close. "I really am sorry. I didn't mean to embarrass you. It just took me off guard when I saw the girl. She looks so much like Amanda. I guess I was a little shocked and didn't handle that meeting as well as I should have."

"I'd say that's an understatement, but I understand. She took me by surprise, too." Katerina took her husband's hand and led him toward the sitting area. "I think we're about to start. The girls were looking for Caleb so he could escort Kylee over from the farmhouse."

Just as Katerina and Fritz began to sit down, Morrigan and Abby approached. "Um, I'm afraid you can't sit there," Morrigan said flatly.

"Why?" Fritz asked in challenge, glaring at Abby. He still wasn't sure how he felt about her and the gorgeous blonde's antics earlier.

"Because we take our traditions and ceremonies very seriously here," Abby said returning the glare. "I realize Kylee is officially a member of your pack, but we also consider her ours. And since you're in our territory, we expect you to honor our traditions."

"Padrini's sit on the front row, next to the rest of the family," Morrigan told them. "Joanne should be here any minute. We'll make sure she joins you."

Fritz looked at Katerina in shock. She must have told them, but why?

Chaos

"Abby, I didn't share that with you to get special consideration here. It was the only way to help you understand," Katerina objected.

"I know," Abby assured her. "But this will be Kylee's only wedding. I think it's important that we do this right. When she looks back on this day, I want her to remember it as perfect. She won't know the difference today, but one day she will. How will you explain it a hundred years from now if you sit back here, like a casual member of the audience, instead of front and center like you're supposed to? How will her father explain it?"

Fritz nodded in agreement, then took his wife's hand and made his way to the front row.

Abby glanced up and saw Sam and Ty enter the room. "I was beginning to wonder where those two disappeared to," she told her brother. "Sam needs to get the video conference up and running." Without another word she was gone.

Sam and Ty approached Bastian. "You ready to get this show on the road?" Ty asked joyfully.

"I'm so glad you could make it," Bastian said sarcastically. "I hope I'm not tearing you away from something important."

"We decided to meet with Lillie before we came over," Sam provided. "We thought it might be a good idea to find out if she planned to join us for the big event."

"I guess that's wise," Bastian said, thinking about the upcoming ceremony. They all agreed it was best to keep Lillie in the dark. She was already more involved than she should be. Radek was unpredictable and humans were too vulnerable. "So what's the verdict? Did she plan to attend the wedding?"

"She begged off," Ty said. "She said to give you her apologies, but she just didn't feel like she knew you and Kylee well enough to attend. We talked her into coming over later to have dinner, though."

"Good," Bastian said, relieved. "Things would have been complicated if she planned to be here, but I wouldn't feel right about excluding her. It makes me feel better that she agreed to join us later."

"Us too," Sam concurred. "Now, I think I need to take care of the electronics before the bride arrives. Ty, I might need you." She gave him a little push and the two of them walked to the side of the room where the enormous TV was positioned.

Caleb stepped into the large foyer and headed for the study. The door was closed, so he knocked before entering. His mother opened the door and stood aside to let her son enter.

Kylee took a deep breath and stood. "Are we ready?" she asked anxiously.

Caleb inhaled sharply. His daughter was beautiful. Sure, she looked a lot like Amanda but Kylee had a special beauty that was all her own. He was so proud of the woman his baby had become. As he stepped in beside her, he felt so much love. He also felt a twinge of regret for all the special occasions he had missed out on.

Kylee looked up at her father and froze. He looked so proud. She knew they'd made the right decision. Having her father involved in her wedding was going to make this day even more special. "Thank you," she said as emotion swamped her. "I'm so glad you agreed to participate today. I know we really just met, but I feel like I've known you most of my life. I owe that to mom." Kylee took a deep breath and fought back tears. "I wish she could be here today. I wish she could have met Bastian. She would have loved him." She slipped an arm through her father's.

"I think she is here," Caleb told his daughter. "In spirit anyway. I believe she's watching over us today. I'm sure she would like to be here in person, but I know she's proud of you." Caleb kissed the top of Kylee's head. "I'm proud of you. And I'm grateful you're marrying Bastian. I don't know him well, but I can already tell he loves you very much. I also know he'll take good care of you and treat you with respect. It's a good start."

Kylee paused to look into her father's eyes. "He is all of that and so much more. I hope you'll stick around long enough to get to know us both. I mean really get to know us, Rand too. I understand if you need to get back to California, but please stay as long as you can."

"I promise," Caleb said relieved. He wanted to stay, but didn't know how the kids would feel about it. "Now, let's get you to the gymnasium. I remember my wedding day and Bastian is going to be anxiously awaiting your arrival." He paused long enough to take his mother's hand and escorted the two women out the door. As he walked down the long drive, headed for the military base, he realized there were only three women that held importance in his life these days, and two of them were by his side. The third was waiting for them in the large building that had been turned into a reception hall. Today was a very good day. He hadn't been able to say that for a long time. Caleb let himself get lost in the moment. Pictures of his own wedding flashed through his mind. He'd been so in love and so completely naive. Loving Amanda was the best and worst thing he'd ever done. His world scared her. It was dangerous and because he'd underestimated the power of her fear, he'd lost everything for a while. If he was careful maybe he could get at least a part of it back, starting with today. This special day with his daughter. He knew somehow he would cherish every second of this day for the rest of his life.

Rand was waiting outside the double doors as the small group arrived. "Joanne, if you will come with me we're about ready to start. I'll escort you to your seat." He held out an arm and waited for her to accept it.

"Joanne is fine for now," she said softly. "But one day, I really hope you will acknowledge the fact that I'm your grandmother."

"I can do that," Rand said stopping at the front of the room. "Did you need help into your chair granny? Or do you think you can manage it yourself?"

Joanne narrowed her eyes at Rand McBride. The boy was so much like his father. "Better," she said with a smile. "We're making progress." Joanne casually sat down next to Katerina. She turned her attention to the familiar couple and patted Kat's leg, ignoring her grandson's scowl. "The two of you are making progress too," she said nonchalantly. "I'm glad you realized you belong with the family."

Fritz was about to respond when he heard the music begin. Everyone's attention turned to the back of the room, anticipating Kylee's entrance. Fritz turned his attention in the opposite direction. He wanted to see the groom's face the instant he saw his bride. That would tell him all he needed to know.

Rand opened the door and stepped outside. "You ready for this?" he asked Kylee. "You still have time to bolt," he offered. "If you want, I'll steal a car and we can escape to Mexico. I hear they have some pretty good beaches."

Chaos

"Not a chance," Kylee said taking a deep breath. "I'm the luckiest woman in the world." She glanced at the door.

"But...?" Rand asked sensing Kylee's nervousness.

"But you know how much I hate being in the spotlight." She cringed a little at the thought of walking all the way to the front of the room. She'd worked out in there almost daily with Bastian. She knew what a huge room it was. The walk down the aisle was going to be excruciating. "Promise me you won't let me trip and fall on my face," she said turning her attention back to her father. "If I do, it's going to embarrass the entire family," she warned.

"Trust me," he said confidently. "The family's reputation is going to be fine."

"Okay. Here we go then," Rand said opening the door. He stood back and watched as his new father walked his new sister down the aisle. He couldn't help it. He was proud of Kylee. He knew she was going to be happy with Bastian. They were good for each other. He glanced up and saw the look on Bastian's face. There was so much love in his eyes. Rand took a deep breath and followed his family up the aisle. It hit him instantly. The smell of love was strong in this room. He glanced around and realized the aroma wasn't just coming from Kylee and Bastian. There were a lot of couples attending this wedding. He'd never considered marriage for himself. His career was too demanding and dangerous. But right now, in a room full of love and happiness, Rand hoped he would find a partner for himself someday. He was a little surprised at the sense of longing he was feeling, but he supposed it was only natural. He'd learned so much about himself over the past few weeks. His entire life changed the moment he embraced his destiny. Rand knew from personal experience that one significant change always brought subsequent changes in a person's life.

He reached the front of the room and slipped in next to Joanna. The woman was a pro, he thought. She didn't even blink when he referred to her as granny. In fact, she'd been amused by it. Rand found that endearing. He'd never had grandparents before. One of the consequences of being raised by fake parents with a fake life, he supposed. That particular change might be interesting. He jumped a little when Joanna reached over and took his hand in hers.

Caleb reached the front of the room and positioned Kylee across from Bastian. The couple hadn't taken their eyes off each other since he and Kylee walked into the room. He spotted the ribbon and carefully wrapped it around his forearm. As he faced the small crowd and began to speak. Caleb began with the usual explanation of their heritage and their people. When he got to the portion of the ceremony that pertained to Kylee's heritage he got a little choked up. It was difficult to talk about Kylee's mother and his father now that they were gone. As he spoke, he gently wrapped the white ribbon around Kylee's arm then handed her one end.

Caleb faced the room and explained that the ribbon represented family bonds. He casually wrapped the ribbon once around Bastian's wrist and handed that end to the groom. Once Caleb was confident the couple would hold the ribbon securely in place, he began to explain Bastian's new role. Bastian and Kylee met and began to form a new bond. That bond gradually grew over time, tying him to the family as well. Caleb flicked his wrist and the ribbon slipped from his arm and transferred to Bastian's. Only one small strand remained loosely around Caleb's arm. "With this ceremony, Kylee and Bastian have become their own family unit. Kylee is still bound to her original family, but mostly she's bound to Bastian. Today is the beginning of a new life with her mate," Caleb turned to the large screen. "Oberon?" he called.

Oberon began to speak. He too talked of family and tradition.

Chaos

Bastian was surprised. This had to be Kylee's doing. He loved her a little more for that. She wanted this day to be special for him, too.

Oberon continued to talk about Bastian's heritage, his parents and his life as a warrior. Finally, he recited the wedding ceremony of their people. Once the ceremony was over Oberon smiled. "Caleb, I believe there is one final tradition before we let the groom kiss his bride."

"Just a short one," Caleb agreed. "Rand?"

Rand stood and walked to a round table. He retrieved a small plate and stood before the wedding couple.

"Kylee, you are a shifter. But, up until recently you've lived your life as a human." Caleb motioned to Rand, who cut the single cherry in two, placed the two pieces onto a spoon and handed it to Caleb. "This signifies your life as a human." Caleb said placing one piece of the cherry between Kylee's lips. He then handed the spoon to Kylee, who offered the remaining half to Bastian.

Bastian casually slid the spoon between his lips, never taking his eyes off Kylee.

Caleb continued. "This cherry is a symbol of that life. It's sweet and juicy and satisfying," Caleb paused. "The fruit is good. For some, it's enough," Caleb motioned to Rand.

Once again Rand sliced two pieces from the star shaped fruit placed prominently on the plate. He slowly handed it to Caleb then stepped back. Out of the corner of his eye he saw Abby and Morrigan stand. Then he saw Katerina and Fritz stand and make their way to the table where Abby, Morrigan and the fruit was. After a short exchange Abby and Morrigan returned to their seats. Kat and Fritz began distributing plates. Caleb smiled. He was touched and relieved that his two friends had accepted their role in this wedding.

"Star fruit on the other hand is unique and exotic." Caleb took a slice of the star fruit and another half slice of cherry and placed it on Kylee's tongue. "A simple cherry combined with the sweet taste of star fruit makes the treat complete. Embracing your shifter does the same in life. Living life as a human can be satisfying and good. But, living life as a shifter makes you unique. It completes you and makes life more satisfying. I can only assume the same is true for Bastian. Once he embraced his destiny as a warrior, his life was more complete. I know you think you can't shift but I know you will eventually. As the two of you begin your life together I encourage you to embrace your true identities. You may have different traditions. You may have different opinions or goals. But as long as you hold on to who and what you are, everything else will work itself out."

Kylee looked out at the audience and realized they all had their own slice of star fruit. She glanced at the large screen where Oberon, Mara, Mason and Jackie Cooper, Travis Monroe and his wife Katherine, and Austin and his wife Sherrie were in attendance. They too were holding a small plate with a single slice of star fruit.

Caleb spoke again. "As a community we will now partake of the star fruit ourselves. We do this in honor of your union and in honor of two individual, unique people coming together to form a special bond. A bond that if cherished and protected, will last an eternity." Caleb pulled unexpectedly on the ribbon, yanking it out of Kylee's hand. Bastian continued to hold his end, so the strand created a single line that fell to the ground. "But if either of you neglect the other, or your commitment to the other, the bond may be broken. The same as this symbolic bond was just broken," Caleb

Chaos

paused. "Your people are at war and your future is uncertain. That makes it even more important for you to rely on each other. Hold firm to the bonds that have brought you here today. We all wish you luck, health and a very long and happy life together." Caleb raised the fruit to his mouth, waiting for the audience to do the same. Once everyone had taken a bite of their fruit, Caleb smiled at his daughter then turned to his new son-in-law. "Now, kiss your bride so we can get this party started."

Bastian didn't hesitate. He pulled Kylee into his arms and kissed her gently. He was filled with emotion as he stepped back and smiled at his beautiful wife. Right now, he was happier than he had ever been in his life. He had a good childhood, but this moment topped even that. He promised himself he would do everything in his power to make Kylee the happiest woman in the world.

Kylee slipped her hand in Bastian's as the crowd began to move forward to congratulate them. She barely noticed as the warriors pushed aside chairs and set up tables in preparation for the evening meal.

Marta slipped from the room and walked to the small office that contained the wedding cake. Jake moved in behind his wife and wrapped his arms around her waist. "That was a nice reminder of the promises I made to you just a few months ago."

Marta turned around, wrapping her arms around her husband. "It was a wonderful ceremony," Marta agreed. "I'm happy for them. It's about time Bastian found a little bit of happiness." She gave Jake a quick kiss then pushed him backwards. "Now, help me get this cake into that room. Our work has just begun here."

Jake laughed then moved in and took over. They had placed the large concoction on a rolling table to make it easier to move around.

Marta slid her arm through Jake's and the two of them casually moved toward the reception that was just getting under way.

* * * *

Victor gently took Ariel's hand and led her out of the room. He grinned at the curious look she shot his way. He was grateful she didn't resist as he silently closed the door behind them.

"What's up?" she finally asked once they were in the empty corridor.

"I wanted a moment alone with you," Victor tried to act casual but his heart was racing and he was questioning his timing.

Ariel furrowed her brows. Something was up. She sensed Victor's apprehension and tensed.

The two reached the end of the hallway and stopped. Victor gently pressed Ariel's back against the wall next to a large window. He took a deep breath as he placed his hands on the chair railing to either side of Ariel, trapping her between his arms. "I've been wanting to do this for a while, but the timing just never seemed right." He took a deep breath and locked eyes with the woman he loved. "I'm not sure this is the right time either. I guess that ceremony touched a chord," he shrugged. "It reminded me of our life and our love."

"Me too," Ariel whispered. She wasn't sure what this was all about. But so far it sounded like something good.

Chaos

Victor pulled his hand from his coat pocket. "I've been carrying this around for months," he admitted. "Once you agreed to marry me and I recovered from my injuries, my first stop was Tiffany's." Victor smiled at the shocked look on Ariel's face. He opened his hand to display a large, diamond ring.

"Victor!" she finally exclaimed.

"You already agreed to marry me," he smiled at her. "But I think it's time we make it official."

Ariel flung her arms around Victor. The ceremony tonight had touched her heart too. She was feeling a little emotional and vulnerable right now. Sitting there, listening to the ceremony, she realized she didn't want to wait an entire year before she married Victor. She wasn't ready to get married immediately the way Ty and Bastian had, but she also didn't want to wait until summer. She took a step back and smiled at Victor. "Well, what are you waiting for? Put that gorgeous thing on my finger already."

Victor laughed and slipped the ring on Ariel's left hand. "I'm glad you haven't changed your mind," he said only half joking. "I'm looking forward to the day you will be my wife."

Ariel stared at the ring in shock. It was huge and obviously expensive.

"Is it okay?" he asked nervously. He thought he knew what Ariel liked, but this was important.

"I love it!" she assured him. "It had to cost you a fortune," she paused and grinned mischievously. "But I'm worth it."

"I think so," he said relieved. "I love you and I hope we have the kind of partnership Caleb and Oberon talked about tonight. I swear I will never take you for granted. If I do, promise me you'll tell me. I never want to neglect you in any way."

"Oh, don't worry," Ariel assured him. "I intend to remind you how much you love me every day for the rest of our lives. And anyway, a girl can always use more diamonds." She teased, then sobered. "Can I ask you a serious question?"

Victor studied Ariel, "Of course," he said as he started to play with her hair.

"Do you still want to wait until summer before we get married?" She was trying to make it sound like she didn't care either way but she wasn't sure she'd pulled it off.

Victor froze. Did Ariel want to move the wedding up, or back? He knew he didn't want to wait any longer, but was he ready to move it forward? He watched Ariel closely and considered his response. "Have you changed your mind?" he asked.

"I think I have," she finally said. "But if you're not comfortable changing the date I understand."

"Changing the date to when?" he asked cautiously. The more he thought about it, the more he thought sooner was better than later.

"I don't know. I just don't think I want to wait until next summer." She watched Victor for a reaction. She thought he looked relieved. Maybe he wanted to get married soon, too. "This is the second wedding we've thrown together in less than a day. Well, I guess we had a little longer for Ty and Sam's but still..." she trailed off. "Anyway, I think both weddings turned out wonderful in their own way. I realize Alex has to plan something extravagant and larger than life, but we don't." Ariel stopped, watching Victor. He

Chaos

still hadn't responded. "Will you please say something? I'm kind of stressing out over here."

Victor smiled at Ariel's distress. "I love you more than life itself. You are the most special woman I've ever met. I'm comfortable marrying you any time you want. In fact, if you want, we can go inside right now and ask your father to perform the ceremony tonight."

"Sorry, that's not going to work for me," Ariel said, relieved. "I want my parents to be physically present when we get married. I also expect Atticus and Tala to be in the same room, which is why I know it may be a few months before we can pull this off. I just know I don't want to wait until July or August. We've already started our life together. I know we're devoted to each other. I guess I'm just anxious for it to be official," she smiled. "And I want to buy an expensive, beautiful extravagant dress," she laughed. "I think I want a long, silky white outfit that I will never wear again."

Victor pulled Ariel close. He lowered his head so their lips were almost touching. "Then that's what you will have," he whispered softly. Then, he closed the distance and pulled her even closer as their lips met in a gentle, loving kiss. Moments later he pulled back slowly. "I guess we should get back inside before someone misses us. I'm sure your parents would like to see you before they shut down that digital connection in there."

"Okay," Ariel agreed sliding her hand into Victors and taking a step toward the noisy room. "I can't wait to show mom my new ring," she smiled as she began to play with the large diamond. She turned to Victor, "I know I should keep it to myself and let this day be all about Kylee, but I can't. I'm too excited. Do you think she'll forgive me?"

"Of course, it's Kylee. She's going to be so excited for you, she won't even care you flashed your bling on her wedding day."

Ariel slapped Victor's chest and laughed as they walked through the door and disappeared into the crowd.

* * * *

Kylee turned to Bastian in surprise when Marta and Jake walked through the doors. "That's why you wanted to talk to Marta alone?" She was touched once again by Bastian's thoughtfulness. He was always thinking of her and doing things for her. Special, selfless, thoughtful things. She really didn't feel like she deserved such a wonderful husband. Moisture began to form in her eyes so she quickly blinked it back. She didn't want to cry today. Not even happy tears.

Bastian moved back to Kylee's side. "I wanted you to have the perfect wedding and Marta agreed to help make that happen. She's amazing don't you think?"

"That's an understatement," Kylee agreed astonished by the large, intricate wedding cake moving her way. "Marta's a miracle worker." She stood in stunned silence as Jake and Marta moved the rolling table in front of the couple. Once they stopped Kylee moved forward and pulled Marta into a tight hug. "Thank you so much. This cake is the final touch that makes my wedding perfect."

"I'm glad you like it," Marta said humbly. "I truly enjoyed making it. Jake, why don't you get everyone's attention so we can cut the cake then get started on dinner. All these men have to be starving."

Chaos

Bastian watched as each member of the crowd redirected their attention to the front of the room. Everyone he loved was here, either in person or digitally. He'd told Kylee it would be okay if Oberon wasn't present, but it just wouldn't have been the same without him. He was touched that Kylee had arranged for Oberon to take part in the ceremony. He was lucky to have such a thoughtful wife.

Bastian glanced at Caleb, Rand, then once again he scanned the crowd. Finally, he turned his attention back to Kylee. Their wedding was perfect. Bastian knew their union would be perfect too. Sure, they'd have struggles and disagreements. Everyone did. But he also knew he was finally going to be happy again. He hadn't believed that was possible. Bastian lovingly fed Kylee a bite of cake, then kissed her softly. As they locked eyes, he could see Kylee was genuinely happy, too. He realized he saw the same intense love he was feeling mirrored in Kylee's eyes. At that moment he knew, without a doubt, his life would be changed forever. He would never be alone again.

Bastian casually parted his lips to accept the small sample of cake Kylee was holding out for him. As his friends and loved ones cheered loudly, Bastian pulled Kylee into his arms. He knew the months ahead would be dangerous and uncertain. But as long as he had Kylee, nothing else mattered. Their love was strong enough to guide them through anything. He smiled at his new family. Finally, his life was complete. He lowered his head and pressed his lips to Kylee's, then deepened the kiss. From this moment, on he would cherish every minute for the rest of their lives.

THE END